*Home
for the
Holidays*

ALSO BY HEATHER VOGEL FREDERICK

The Mother-Daughter Book Club

Much Ado About Anne

Dear Pen Pal

Pies & Prejudice

Spy Mice: The Black Paw

Spy Mice: For Your Paws Only

Spy Mice: Goldwhiskers

The Voyage of Patience Goodspeed

The Education of Patience Goodspeed

Hide-and-Squeak

THE MOTHER-DAUGHTER BOOK CLUB

Home
for the
Holidays

Heather Vogel Frederick

Simon & Schuster Books for Young Readers

New York London Toronto Sydney New Delhi

For Patty, who is the Tacy to my Betsy

SIMON & SCHUSTER BOOKS FOR YOUNG READERS
An imprint of Simon & Schuster Children's Publishing Division
1230 Avenue of the Americas, New York, New York 10020
This book is a work of fiction. Any references to historical events, real people,
or real locales are used fictitiously. Other names, characters, places, and incidents are
products of the author's imagination, and any resemblance to actual events
or locales or persons, living or dead, is entirely coincidental.
Copyright © 2011 by Heather Vogel Frederick
All rights reserved, including the right of reproduction in whole or in part in any form.
SIMON & SCHUSTER BOOKS FOR YOUNG READERS is a trademark of Simon & Schuster, Inc.
For information about special discounts for bulk purchases, please contact Simon & Schuster
Special Sales at 1-866-506-1949 or business@simonandschuster.com.
The Simon & Schuster Speakers Bureau can bring authors to your live event. For more
information or to book an event, contact the Simon & Schuster Speakers Bureau
at 1-866-248-3049 or visit our website at www.simonspeakers.com.
Also available in a Simon & Schuster Books for Young Readers hardcover edition
Book design by Lucy Ruth Cummins
The text for this book is set in Chapparral Pro.
Manufactured in the United States of America
0812 OFF
First Simon & Schuster Books for Young Readers paperback edition October 2012
2 4 6 8 10 9 7 5 3 1
Library of Congress Control Number: 2011275301
ISBN 978-1-4424-0685-8 (hc)
ISBN 978-1-4424-0686-5 (pbk)
ISBN 978-1-4424-0688-9 (eBook)

THANKSGIVING

"The holidays struck Deep Valley like a snow-ball, exploding with soft glitter in all directions."

—Maud Hart Lovelace, *Betsy Was a Junior*

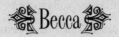

Becca

> *"When there are boys you have to worry about how you look, and whether they like you, and why they like another girl better, and whether they're going to ask you to something or other. It's a strain."*

—*Betsy in Spite of Herself*

"D-E-F-E-N-S-E! DEFENSE, CONCORD, DEFENSE!"

I finish off the cheer with a star jump and a high kick, then fling my maroon-and-white pom-poms skyward, catching them neatly on the way down. As the pep band strikes up "We Will Rock You," I look up in the stands to see if Zach Norton is watching.

He's not.

He's too busy talking to Cassidy Sloane.

Third sees me, though, and waves his trombone from where he's sitting with the rest of the brass section. I wave feebly back.

My friend Ashley swats me with a pom-pom, her dark eyes flashing with mischief. "I didn't know you liked Third," she teases.

Third is actually Cranfield Bartlett III, but nobody ever calls him that, not even his parents.

"Shut up! I do not," I reply, through teeth clenched in a big smile. Ms. O'Donnell, our cheerleading coach, is a stickler for big smiles.

"Eyes on the field, girls," she calls to us.

Ashley and I turn around just in time to see Darcy Hawthorne intercept a pass. There's a roar from the stands behind us—it's almost the end of the fourth quarter, and Concord is down by six. We desperately need another touchdown. Along with everybody else on our side of the field, I scream my head off as Darcy runs the ball back down toward our end zone. He makes it almost as far as the center line before Acton manages to tackle him. Music explodes from the pep band, and Coach O'Donnell gives us the signal to launch into another cheer.

"First and ten, do it again! GO, Concord, GO!" we holler, whipping the crowd into a frenzy.

Turkey Day game is always a big deal for Alcott High. Thanksgiving is when we play our archrivals, and across the field, the visitor stands are a mass of blue and gold. For a split second I find myself wishing I was wearing one of Acton High's cheerleading uniforms. I look so much better in blue than I do in maroon.

On the other hand, we get to wear yoga pants instead of the miniskirts the Acton cheerleaders stupidly chose. Not that I have anything against miniskirts, but it's *freezing* out here. At least they should have opted for fleece leggings under their skirts. Their legs are practically as blue as their uniforms.

I cast a worried glance up at the sky. No sign of snow yet. I really, really hope the weather forecast is wrong. My grandparents are in

Heather Vogel Frederick

town from Cleveland for the holiday weekend, and Gram and Gigi, my best friend Megan Wong's grandmother, have promised to take the two of us shopping tomorrow. I don't want to miss out because of some dumb snowstorm.

Up in the stands, Megan reaches a purple-gloved hand from underneath the blanket she's sharing with Gigi and Gram and waves at me. I wave back at her, and at my grandfather and my brother Stewart and his girlfriend, Emma Hawthorne.

As much as it grosses me out to admit this, Stewart and Emma are kind of cute together. Well, as cute as two total dorks can be, I guess.

My dad blows me a kiss. I blow him one in return, and he stands up and pretends to catch it and tuck it into his pocket. It's silly and kind of embarrassing, but I don't really mind. For one thing, I'm used to it—we've had this little ritual since I was a kid—and for another, my dad needs all the love he can get these days. He lost his job a few weeks ago.

The insurance agency he worked for in Boston has been struggling for a while, and they finally had to lay off some employees. My dad was one of them. He's really sad about it because he worked there a long time, and he liked his job. He's worried, too, I can tell. He and my mother haven't said much to my brother and me, aside from asking us not to say anything about it to our friends for now, but we're not stupid. Stewart's a senior in high school, and I'll be getting my driver's license in a few months. We're practically adults.

As for keeping it quiet, how long is it going to take people to figure out what's going on when they spot my dad driving around town with the

PIRATE PETE'S PIZZA sign on the roof of our SUV? Or when they open the door and there he is with their half-pepperoni, half-veggie combo, wearing an eye patch and a Pirate Pete's skull-and-crossbones baseball cap?

I know he took the job to help out our family and everything, but couldn't he have found something less embarrassing? He says it's perfect because it lets him keep his days free for job hunting, but still. Stewart doesn't care, of course—he's oblivious anyway—but I know my mother finds it just as mortifying as I do. Even she couldn't talk him out of it, though.

"Money is money, Calliope," my father told her. "I'm not in a position to be picky right now."

Last night, after we met my grandparents at the airport, I overheard my mother and Gram talking in the kitchen. Mom told her that the layoff couldn't have come at a worse time, what with her finishing up her master's degree in landscape design, and Stewart knee-deep in college applications. If my dad doesn't find a new job soon—something a heck of a lot better than delivering pizzas—she doesn't know how they're going to manage.

Everybody seems to forget that it's scary for me, too, not to mention inconvenient. I'd really been hoping for a car of my own when I get my license, but fat chance of that happening now.

There's another roar from our fans, and I snap out of my sulk and automatically slap a smile on my face. Out on the field, Darcy dodges a pair of Acton linemen and sprints toward our goalposts. The linemen grab at his jersey, but he wrenches away and surges forward, crossing

Heather Vogel Frederick

into the end zone and slamming the ball onto the ground.

Touchdown!

With less than a minute to go in the game, we're tied with Acton! The crowd hardly needs any encouragement from us, but we do our best anyway as both teams get into position for the goal kick.

> Everybody do the Concord rumble,
> Everybody do the Concord rumble,
> Everyyybodyyy rrruuumbbble!

As Darcy's best friend Kyle Anderson, our kicker, takes his spot on the field, you can practically hear all of Concord hold its breath. The ref's whistle blows and Kyle moves forward, keeping his eye on the goalposts. Then he slams his foot against the ball, sending it flying up toward the gray clouds overhead. Up it soars, up and up and—through!

It's a win for Concord!

"Take it home, girls," shouts Coach O'Donnell as our side of the field explodes with excitement. There's nothing forced about the smile on my face now. We treat Acton to the traditional Turkey Day gloat, the very same cheer they fired off at us last year when they won:

> You might be good at baseball,
> You might be good at track,
> But when it comes to football,
> You might as well step back!

GOBBLE-GOBBLE-GOBBLE-GOBBLE

Goooooooooooooo, CONCORD!

Fans come pouring down out of the stands, pushing and jostling. Among them I spot Darcy's girlfriend, Jess Delaney. Stuck to her like a tall, skinny barnacle is Kevin Mullins. Kevin just doesn't take a hint. He's had a crush on Jess since we were all at Walden Middle School, and she's just too nice to give him the boot. That's the difference between Jess and me. I don't put up with stuff like that the way she does.

Kevin used to be the smallest kid in the entire school, which was due to the fact that he skipped a bunch of grades. Cassidy calls him the Boy Genius. He shot up this past summer, and now he towers over Jess, who is petite. They probably weigh the same, though. My dad says if Kevin turned sideways and stuck out his tongue, he could pass as a zipper.

"Great job, Becca," Jess tells me. She's wearing a white cable-knit beanie, and only the tail of her thick blond braid is visible. I would kill for hair like Jess's. Mine is blond, too, but it's not thick and wavy like hers.

"Thanks."

She cranes her neck over my shoulder, looking for Darcy. Jess is lucky. Not only is Darcy Hawthorne a great athlete, he's also popular, smart, and a really nice guy. Plus, he still has a trace of the English accent that he and Emma both brought back with them from their year in England. There's nothing more appealing than a cute guy with an accent.

Heather Vogel Frederick

"Gotta go," Jess says, spotting him. "See you tonight!"

"See you!" I reply. She melts into the crowd, with Kevin trailing behind.

"What's tonight?" asks Ashley.

I make a face. "Book club." Not that I don't like book club, but it is Thanksgiving, after all. I was kind of thinking jammies, leftovers, a nap, maybe snuggling up with some holiday classic on TV. My grandmother really, really wanted to attend one of our meetings, though, and tonight was the only night everybody could get together. Cassidy Sloane is in my book club too, and she plays for an elite girls' hockey team. They have some big tournament down in Rhode Island this weekend, and for a while it didn't look like she'd be able to make it to our meeting at all. Which was fine by me, because the less time I spend around Miss Zach-Stealer Sloane these days, the better. But in the end, it turned out she doesn't have to be there until tomorrow morning.

"Wow, what a fabulous game!" says my father, squeezing through the crowd to reach us. The rest of my family is right behind him.

"No kidding," says Gram, draping a blanket around my shoulders. She gives me a hug. "That was a great halftime dance, sweetie."

"Thanks."

"You girls look half-frozen," says Megan's grandmother. "I think there's still some hot chocolate left in my thermos if you'd like some."

"Thanks, Mrs. Chen," Ashley replies, "but I promised I'd get right home to help my mom." *Call me later*, she mouths to me as she turns to go, pretending to hold a cell phone up to her ear. I nod.

"We should head home and help your mother too," says Gram, linking her arm through mine as we inch our way toward the parking lot. Ahead of us, my brother is acting all mushy-gushy over Emma Hawthorne. He has his arm around her and keeps leaning down to kiss the top of her head. Gak! So gross! I hate PDA when it involves my brother.

I glance over at Megan and scrunch up my nose. She smothers a laugh. Megan knows exactly how I feel about this stuff. That's the good thing about best friends. Most of the time you don't have to say a word, and they still totally understand you.

It's not that I don't like Emma—she's okay. It's just, knowing that she's my brother's girlfriend makes things a little weird sometimes. Plus, we probably never would have been friends if it weren't for the book club. Megan's the only one in it I'm really close to. I have almost nothing in common with the others, and I'm still surprised I like them as much as I do.

Which isn't always all that much. For instance, I'm not wild about Cassidy Sloane these days. Ever since school started this year, she's been hanging out with Zach Norton again.

I look over to where the two of them are standing on the sidelines. Cassidy has her camera out and she's taking his picture. Zach is clowning around and laughing his head off over something she's saying. Watching them, it's easy to see that he likes her. You can just tell when a guy is interested in a girl, you know? And it's written all over Zach's face that he likes Cassidy.

Last spring, after he asked me to the Spring Formal, I really, really thought maybe he liked me. After all, I didn't have to pester him or drop hints or anything. He picked up the phone all by himself and called. Would he have done that if he didn't like me?

But now he can't take his eyes off Cassidy Sloane, the red-haired giantess from my Mother-Daughter Book Club.

I just don't get it. Back in eighth grade, when Zach surprised Cassidy with a kiss, she was so disgusted she slugged him with her baseball mitt. After that they didn't talk for a whole summer, so I figured that was that and maybe I'd finally have a chance. Even when they patched things up I was still hopeful, mostly because Cassidy made it very clear they were just friends. Plus, she spent most of last year practically glued to Tristan Berkeley, the snotty but incredibly good-looking English guy whose family did the house-swap with the Hawthornes. Tristan needed an ice-dancing partner, and Cassidy fit the bill.

I swear she has all the luck. These days the only guy who's interested in me is Third. Who is fine and everything, but he's, well, Third. Kind of a moose, dorky smile, even dorkier sense of humor. He's not exactly Prince Charming.

My mother says I spend way too much time thinking about boys, but I can't help it. Boys are the most interesting thing on the planet.

Most boys, that is. Spotting Third lumbering in our direction with his trombone case, I tug my grandmother through an opening in the crowd. "I can't wait to get home," I tell her. "I'm starving."

"I don't know which I'm looking forward to more," she says, trotting along beside me. "Thanksgiving dinner or the meeting tonight."

Gram was ecstatic when my mother told her she'd get to come to book club. She's hardly stopped talking about it since she got here. My grandmother is the whole reason we're reading what we're reading this fall.

We held our first meeting of the year back in August at Kimball's Farm. Usually, we wait until the end of each year's kick-off meeting to go out for ice cream—it's one of our little rituals—but this year we decided to meet there to celebrate the Hawthornes being home from England. We were just sitting down at a picnic table with our ice cream cones when Jess's mom asked whose turn it was to pick something for us to read.

"I think it's yours," Mrs. Hawthorne told her. Emma's mother is a librarian and super organized, and she's been in charge of the club since the beginning.

"No, Phoebe, I think it's Becca and Calliope's turn," Mrs. Wong said, taking the teeniest lick ever of her strawberry ice cream cone. Megan's mother treats sugar like it's the enemy.

My mother pounced on this the way I pounce on Motor Mouth lip gloss whenever it goes on sale. "That's right! It is. And we've got just the thing."

I looked at her blankly. This was news to me. "We do?"

"Uh-huh," she said, nodding.

"Well?" asked Mrs. Hawthorne.

"The Betsy-Tacy books!"

I let out a groan. This was my mother's idea of "just the thing"? Those books Gram was always going on about? My grandmother gave me the entire set practically the day I was born, and they've been sitting on the bookshelf in my room forever. They were her absolute favorite when she was growing up, which tells you how old they are.

What happened next, though, was probably the high point of my entire three years with the book club.

"What are the Betsy-Tacy books?" asked Emma.

Stunned silence fell over the picnic table. Megan and Jess and Cassidy and I stared at her, our mouths literally dropping open. Emma Hawthorne has read every book in the universe.

"You don't know them?" asked my mother, flicking a glance at Mrs. Hawthorne. "That surprises me, Emma. They're classics, after all."

"Really?" Emma frowned.

"Absolutely. They're about a group of girls growing up in a little town in Minnesota called Deep Valley."

"How many books are there in the series?"

"Ten."

I'll never forget the look on Emma's face as long as I live.

"TEN?" she screeched, whirling around to her mother. "How come you never told me about them?"

"Well," said Mrs. Hawthorne, "it's not that I didn't know about them"—she flicked a glance back at my mother, and I sensed a little tug-of-war going on—"or about the author, Maud Hart Lovelace. I just never got around to reading them."

I could tell that my mother was trying very hard not to gloat. It's almost impossible to one-up Mrs. Hawthorne.

I decided to rub it in. "I've read them," I said, which wasn't exactly true. My mother read the first few aloud to me when I was little, but I never finished the series. Emma didn't need to know that, though. "Ages ago."

From the expression on Emma's face, you'd have thought I just announced that I was growing a tail. "You *did?* How come you never mentioned them?"

"You never asked," I replied, trying not to look too smug.

Cassidy's mother frowned at me. "Are you sure you want to read them again?"

Across the picnic table, my mother gave me Winona eyes. Gram made up that expression. Winona Root is a character in the books, and this one time Betsy and Tacy and their friend Tib try to hypnotize her into taking them to the theater. It doesn't work, of course, but it's pretty funny the way they all stare at her, trying.

Winona eyes or no Winona eyes, I knew that if I said no, my mother would never let me hear the end of it. There's just no dealing with my mother. "Sure," I replied. "Why not?"

My mother swiftly closed the deal. "Becca's grandmother has offered to buy a complete set for each of you, if you all agree to read them."

"That's very generous of her," said Mrs. Hawthorne. "She must really love these books."

Heather Vogel Frederick

"She loves Maud Hart Lovelace the way you love Jane Austen, Phoebe," my mother told her. "Mother was born in Minnesota, and she grew up reading the Betsy-Tacy series. She made sure I did too. It's kind of a family tradition."

I shot her a look. Talk about stretching the truth! A family tradition? For her and Gram, maybe, but not for me.

"Can you tell us a bit about the books?" asked Mrs. Delaney. "I'm afraid I'm not familiar with them either."

"Absolutely," my mother replied. "Deep Valley is a small town, very much like Concord, only in the Midwest. The stories follow Betsy Ray and her family and friends as they grow up in the late nineteenth and early twentieth centuries—"

Cassidy let out a groan when she heard this, but my mother was ready for her.

"I know, I know, more musty, dusty old books, right? These are different from all the other ones we've read so far, though. They have a very modern sensibility." My mother fished around in her tote bag and pulled out *Betsy-Tacy*. "This is the first book, and it starts when Betsy Ray and Tacy Kelly are five years old—"

"Whoa, dude—I mean, Mrs. Chadwick—are you seriously expecting us to read about a couple of *five-year-olds*?" Cassidy protested. "We're sophomores!"

"Wait, wait, let me finish," my mother hurried to explain. "The books follow the girls all the way through high school and into college and beyond. See?" She dumped the rest of the books in her tote bag onto the table and held one of them up, waving it triumphantly. "The last one is called *Betsy's Wedding*."

The picnic table grew quiet as my friends chewed on that.

"You girls are going to feel right at home in Deep Valley, I promise," my mother continued. "Betsy and her friends are fun-loving, and they like pranks and mischief, and above all"— she paused dramatically and lowered her voice—"they like boys."

Cassidy snorted. "That clinches it for me," said her mother, elbowing her sharply. "Count me in."

Emma sighed happily. "Ten whole books I haven't read!"

"I don't have time to read ten books," grumbled Cassidy, who looked like she wanted to pop somebody with her ice cream cone. Or better yet, her hockey stick.

"Nonsense," said Mrs. Sloane-Kinkaid. "What about all that time you're spending in the car these days?" She reached over and plucked a handful of books from the table. "One hockey tournament in Connecticut and you'd knock these right off."

"On top of all my homework? Mom, get real! I'm already a week behind on *The Grapes of Wrath*." Cassidy crossed her arms and scowled.

"I thought we were going to get to pick the books this year for a change," said Jess softly, looking disappointed. She'd been pushing for some story about a racehorse. Jess still had that stupid horse crush of hers. I got over mine back in fourth grade.

"I thought so too," said Emma. "I want us all to read *Jane Eyre*."

"How about a compromise?" suggested Mrs. Wong. "What if we

Heather Vogel Frederick

split the year up this time, and spend the first half—between now and the end of December, say—reading the Betsy-Tacy books, then move on to something else after that?"

"That sounds good," said Mrs. Delaney, and we all nodded.

Cassidy still didn't look convinced. "You mean we're going to read all ten books between now and January?"

Mrs. Hawthorne, who'd been scanning the information on the jacket flaps, pursed her lips. "We could just read the four high school books, I suppose."

"But you have to start at the beginning!" my mother protested. "You'll miss too much!"

"You have a point," said Mrs. Hawthorne. "And Clementine is right, the first four are pretty slim. What if we breeze through them for September's meeting, then dive into *Heaven to Betsy* and *Betsy in Spite of Herself* for October and November? That will take us up through their sophomore year, the same age as you girls."

"But Mom, we can't just ignore half of an author's body of work!" said Emma.

I crossed my eyes at Megan, who squelched a smile. Only Emma Hawthorne would use a term like "body of work."

"Nothing's stopping you or anyone else from reading the rest of them," said her mother. "But this might be a more realistic goal as a group."

And that was that, and now here we are three months later. I look over at Gram, who's smiling at me expectantly.

I smile back at her. "Yeah, Gram, I'm looking forward to tonight too," I tell her, and surprisingly, this isn't a complete lie.

I'd been so sure I wouldn't like the books, but my mother was right—they really are pretty modern. Especially once the girls get into high school. Sure, the slang they use is ridiculous—nobody says stuff like "Hully gee!" these days—but there are crushes and dances and parties, and they're always on the phone to each other, and on top of that, Betsy totally feels the same way I do about school, plus she and her friends love to shop, and they love clothes.

Megan has been flipping out at all the descriptions of the outfits. We both adore vintage styles, and she's started calling her shirts "shirtwaists," like they do in the books, which is a little over-the-top if you ask me, but that's the way Megan is when it comes to fashion.

My stomach growls as we get into the car. Gram laughs. "Time to unbend and really eat, right?"

"Yup," I reply, scaring myself a little. Mom and Gram do this all the time—quote from the Betsy-Tacy books to each other—but it's not really my thing, and this is the first time a reference hasn't gone completely over my head. I hope it doesn't mean I'm getting old.

Thanksgiving is just about my favorite meal of the year, and I only had a tiny breakfast this morning so I'd be really hungry for it. My mother and Gram spent all day yesterday cooking, and as we come trooping into the house we're greeted by such wonderful smells that I want to tear into the turkey right then and there. But cheerleading is a real workout, and I don't smell so wonderful myself, so I run upstairs to take a quick shower and change.

Mom likes us to dress up for Thanksgiving dinner, so I put on a skirt and a black cashmere turtleneck I found at Sweet Repeats, my favorite consignment store on Newbury Street in Boston. It's from some swanky shop in London, and Gigi nearly fainted when she saw the label. "The bargain of the century," she told me, when she heard what I paid for it. "Good work, Becca."

With any luck, Megan and I will get a chance to hunt for more bargains there when we go to Boston tomorrow.

As my mother and Gram and I enter the dining room with a parade of platters, and my father starts to carve the turkey, Grampie rubs his hands together. "All of my favorites!"

"Especially the sweet potato casserole with mini marshmallows," says my brother happily, dishing himself up a huge serving.

"Pig," I whisper to him.

He plops an equally huge serving onto my plate. "Pig yourself," he whispers back. "It's your favorite too."

He's right; it is. And Gram is right too. If there's ever a time to unbend and really eat, it's Thanksgiving. The second we finish saying grace, I plow into the food on my plate like it's my last meal on earth.

Afterward, we all pitch in to clear the table and do the dishes, then Dad and Grampie and Stewart wander into the family room to watch a little football.

"I'm going to take a nap so I'll be fresh for the meeting tonight," says Gram, yawning.

"Me too," says my mother. "How about you, honey?"

"Maybe," I tell her. "I think I'll watch a movie up in my room first, though."

I fall asleep halfway through *Miss Congeniality*—one of my all-time favorites—and the next thing I know, I hear my mother bellowing at me from downstairs.

"Rebecca Louise Chadwick! What are you doing up there? We're going to be late!"

"Coming, Mom!" I call back. I try to keep the irritation out of my voice, but it's hard. My mother can be really aggravating.

I leave the turtleneck on but change out of my skirt into jeans, then pull on a pair of black suede ankle boots. Dashing into the bathroom to brush my teeth, I glance in the mirror and decide to give my hair one last run-through. As long as I'm doing that, I figure I might as well fiddle with my mascara and eyeshadow, too. Megan and I agree that it's always best to put a little effort into how you look, because you never know who you might run into. Finishing up with a fresh coat of gloss on my lips, I grab my purse and head downstairs.

"Really, Becca," scolds my mother, who is waiting with Gram in the front hall. "You need to learn to be more punctual."

I give her a rueful smile and nod earnestly. I've learned that the best way to deal with my mother is not to argue, but just to agree with everything she says. She's not really mad at me, anyway. She's mad because November was our month to host book club, but everybody voted to have it at Cassidy's.

Heather Vogel Frederick

We won't be meeting again until January—we decided to skip the holidays since our schedules are all really hectic—so we're choosing Secret Santas tonight, and everybody thought it would be more festive to do that at the Sloane-Kinkaids'. The minute the Thanksgiving turkey's cleared off the table, and sometimes even before, Cassidy's mother whips out the Christmas decorations. She has her own TV show—*Cooking with Clementine*—and since their house is the set, they're on a different schedule from the rest of the world.

My mother's been simmering about this for weeks.

"It's like she has a bunch of elves hidden in the garage or something," I heard her grumble to my father a couple of nights ago. "It's not humanly possible to decorate that fast."

My father, who like me finds it easier just to go along with my mother, didn't even look up from the paper. "Yes, dear," he murmured. "Elves, dear."

"Oh, for heaven's sake, Henry," my mother snapped back. "There are no such thing as elves!"

You just can't win when it comes to my mother.

"Hey, Becca, would you give this to Emma for me?" asks my brother, galumphing down the stairs.

I make a face when I see the title. *The Poems of Emily Dickinson.* Who reads this stuff? Besides my brother and Emma, I mean?

Stewart grins and lopes off across the hall to the living room. He knows I think he's a dork. The annoying thing is, he doesn't care.

My mother hands me my jacket impatiently, then pokes her head into the living room after him. "I hope you two boys manage to have fun without us."

"Don't worry, we're well fortified," my grandfather replies, scooting a plate of turkey sandwiches to the center of the coffee table, well out of Yo-Yo's reach. Yo-Yo is our Labradoodle. He's pretending to snooze by the fireplace, but one eyelid is cracked open and one large furry ear is cocked toward the table, and I can tell that those sandwiches are on his radar screen. "Plus, we have some fun of our own planned," Grampie continues, nodding at the Scrabble board that he and Stewart are busy setting up.

I smirk at my brother, and this time his face flushes. Rearranging letters to make words—are you kidding me? This is supposed to be fun? Besides, who wants to play a BORED game when there are perfectly good TV shows to watch?

My father sneaks up behind us. "Arrggh!" he growls, tickling my mother in the ribs.

She shrieks and jumps. "Henry!"

He grins. Slipping on his eye patch and cap, he asks, "Can an old sea dog offer three lovely wenches a ride?"

"No way," I tell him. That's all I need—to be seen driving around Concord in the Pirate Petemobile.

"Such a shame you have to work tonight," says my grandmother.

My father shrugs. "I guess some people prefer pizza to turkey, and besides, it pays double time and a half plus tips." He gives my mother a kiss on the cheek. "Have fun, dear."

Heather Vogel Frederick

He heads down the hall to the garage, and Gram and I follow my mother out the front door.

"Concord is so pretty at night," says my grandmother with a sigh, tucking her arm through mine. "Especially this time of year."

She's right. The tree won't be up in Monument Square for another week or two—there's always a holiday parade in early December, along with a big tree-lighting ceremony—but a lot of the shop windows on Main Street are already decorated for Christmas. A few even have wreaths on the doors. Not Pies & Prejudice, though, the tea shop that Megan's grandmother opened last month. Megan's mom made sure of that. She hates the commercialism of the holidays, and Megan said she made Gigi promise she wouldn't get sucked into it too early.

The plan is to meet at Pies & Prejudice for breakfast tomorrow before we head out on our shopping trip. Afterward, my mom and Mrs. Wong are going to hold down the fort while Gigi hits the sales with Gram and Megan and me.

Just thinking about tomorrow makes me want to dance down the street. I love to shop, and the day after Thanksgiving is like the Kentucky Derby or something for people like me. I'm still smiling as we turn down Hubbard Street to Cassidy's.

"What a beautiful old house!" says Gram, pausing at the entrance to the brick walkway that leads to the Sloane-Kinkaids' Victorian. It really is a cool house—it even has a turret. And last year Cassidy's mother had it restored to its original color for an episode on her TV show.

"If you like houses that are painted dog-tongue pink," says my mother with a disdainful sniff.

I saw the paint cans in the garage, and the official color is actually Sonoma Sunrise, not dog-tongue pink. There are two shades for the trim, too: Lemon Meringue and Wedding White. I think it looks great.

Mrs. Sloane-Kinkaid calls their house a "painted lady." That's the term for Victorian homes that are painted more than one color, she told us.

"All that gaudy gingerbread!" scoffs my mother, casting a baleful glance at the fancy woodwork under the eaves and along the porch railing. Mrs. Sloane-Kinkaid explained all about gingerbread, too—she says it's kind of like jewelry, the perfect accessory for a painted lady. I totally agree. I'd love it if our house had gingerbread on it, but fat chance of that. Everything about our house screams "traditional!" Boring is more like it.

"I prefer the simplicity of Colonial architecture to Victorian frou-frou," my mother says loftily. "It's much more in keeping with our historic town."

"I don't find it gaudy, Calliope," says Gram. "I think it's perfect."

Me too, but I know better than to say so. My grandmother is about the only person on earth who can contradict my mother and get away with it.

My mother surveys the front porch, noting the pumpkins and wheat sheaves piled by the front door and the turkey flag hanging

Heather Vogel Frederick

from the rafters. There's not a Christmas ornament in sight. "There's no reason we couldn't have had book club at our house," she sputters. "Clementine didn't find time to decorate after all."

The door flies open before we can knock. "Ho-ho-ho," says Mrs. Sloane-Kinkaid as we step inside.

"Wow," I reply. The front hall looks like Santaland at Macy's.

My mother blinks, then scowls. "Elves," she mutters.

"Lovely," says Gram, looking around. "Just lovely."

A garland of fresh cedar greens embedded with twinkle lights is twined around the entire length of the banister leading upstairs, and a matching one outlines the arched entry to the living room. Red velvet ribbon is wrapped around the coat tree, around the legs of the hall table, and around the staircase balusters. More ribbon is tied in bows on the chandelier overhead. Cassidy's least favorite of her mother's decorations, what she calls the weird mannequins, stand on either side of the door leading to the dining room. The boy mannequin is dressed as Santa, of course, and the girl as Mrs. Santa. They're holding signs that read: WELCOME MOTHER-DAUGHTER BOOK CLUB! As a final touch, there's a clear glass bowl filled with red and green ornaments—and more twinkle lights—on top of the hall table, and two large red-leaved poinsettia plants flank the base of the stairs.

"It's so nice to see you again, Grace," says Mrs. Sloane-Kinkaid, taking my grandmother's coat. "We're just tickled that you could join us."

My grandmother smiles. "Wild horses couldn't keep me away from Sunday Night Lunch."

In the Betsy-Tacy books, the Ray family eats their main meal at noon on Sundays, so they always have sandwiches for supper. Mrs. Sloane-Kinkaid thought my grandmother would get a kick out of it if we used their term for the meal for our book club meeting tonight. She was right, because Gram is beaming.

"Except it's Thursday night, and nobody's hungry," mumbles my mother, obviously not willing to let the whole Christmas decoration thing go.

"Who's not hungry?" asks Cassidy, jogging down the hall from the kitchen. Murphy, her family's scruff-muffin of a dog, is right at her heels, and her little sister Chloe is perched on her shoulders. "I'm starving. What took you guys so long?"

"Cassidy," her mother chides. "Don't be rude."

"I'm not being rude, just honest." She grins at us.

Cassidy Sloane is always hungry. She eats like a horse and never gains an ounce. It's totally not fair. I know it's because of all the time she spends at the rink, but still, I'd kill for her figure. She's built like her mother, tall and lean. Mrs. Sloane-Kinkaid used to be a model, a famous one, and Cassidy and her older sister Courtney obviously got her genes. As my eyes slide over to my mother, I can't help hoping that in my case maybe the family genes will skip a generation.

"BECCA!" Chloe squeals. She's eighteen months old, and does a lot of squealing.

"Chloe!" I squeal back, reaching up for her. I'm one of Chloe's regular babysitters now that Cassidy is so busy with her hockey team, the

Heather Vogel Frederick

Lady Shawmuts, and with Chicks with Sticks, the girls' hockey club she coaches.

I give her a kiss, and Chloe pats my turtleneck. "Ooo," she says, and gives it a kiss. Everybody laughs.

"See if you can teach her to say 'cashmere,'" calls Gigi from the living room, where she's sitting with the rest of the book club. "The girl's got good taste."

"Mother!" protests Mrs. Wong.

Gigi winks at me.

"I like your outfit, too," I tell Chloe, running my finger over the brown velvet headband that's nestled in her blond curls.

"*Oui, mademoiselle,* you look *très chic,*" adds Megan. She switched to French this year at school, leaving me without a study partner in Spanish class. Gigi put her up to it. She loves everything French.

Chloe grins at us. She's still dressed in her Thanksgiving outfit: brown velvet leggings and a matching dress with a pattern of autumn leaves on it. She looks adorable. But then, Chloe always looks adorable. She's the cutest little kid I know.

I carry her into the living room and pause by the sofa. "Hey, Emma." I pass her the book of poems my brother gave me. "Stewart asked me to give this to you."

"Thanks," she replies, taking it from me.

Chloe spots Jess sitting next to Emma and starts to squirm. Jess babysits for her too, when she has time. She's a lot busier this year at Colonial Academy, the fancy private boarding school here in Concord that she goes to. She's there on a full scholarship, thanks to my mother, who's on the board of trustees and who recommended her for it. My mother always wanted me to go there too, but fat chance of that. Not with my grades. Homework is not on my Top Ten List of Fun Things to Do. Which is fine, because Colonial Academy is a girls' school, and I would rather shave my head than go to a school that didn't have boys in it.

I hand Chloe to Jess and move closer to the fire that's blazing on the hearth.

"Everything looks just beautiful, Clementine," says my grandmother, glancing around at all the greenery and glowing candles.

"It smells good too," I add, taking a deep sniff. I love holiday smells—pine, cinnamon, yummy things baking in the oven. I think if I had to pick one time of year as my favorite, this whole stretch from Thanksgiving to Christmas would be it.

"I'm just sorry we didn't get the tree up in time for you," says Mrs. Sloane-Kinkaid. "The crew wasn't able to squeeze it in before they left yesterday."

My mother shoots my grandmother a knowing look. "Elves," she whispers.

"I'm glad there's no tree yet," says Mrs. Wong. "Thanksgiving is my favorite holiday, and I like to savor it. There's too much rush-rush these days."

"I know, Lily, and I agree with you," Cassidy's mother replies. "If

I didn't have the holiday special to film this weekend, I'd have waited another couple of weeks to decorate."

"I don't mind if Christmas hurries up this year," says Jess.

Of course she doesn't. That's because she gets to spend it with Savannah Sinclair and her family, skiing in Switzerland. She's been talking about nothing else ever since she found out she was going. Savannah is a senator's daughter, and she and Jess roomed together at Colonial their freshman year. Things didn't go so well back then, but they got over it and now they're good friends. This year the two of them are in a quad with Adele and Frankie, Jess's other best friends at Colonial, and all three of them are going with the Sinclairs to Switzerland for the holidays.

We're probably going to be stuck here in boring old Concord. My family was supposed to go on a Christmas cruise with the Wongs, but we had to cancel after my dad lost his job.

"Soup's on, ladies," says Cassidy's stepfather, appearing in the doorway with a tray of mugs.

Cassidy's older sister, Courtney, is right behind him. She's carrying a platter of sandwiches, and so is the guy who's with her. I don't recognize him, but I figure he must be Courtney's boyfriend, because Cassidy's been talking about how her sister was planning to bring him home for Thanksgiving. I size him up. Tall, athletic-looking, sandy hair, brown eyes. Megan looks over at me and lifts an eyebrow in approval. I raise one back in silent agreement: seriously cute.

"Where are my manners?" cries Mrs. Sloane-Kinkaid, springing to her feet. "Book club—meet Grant Bell."

Courtney's boyfriend grins. "Hi."

"Hi," we chorus back.

Courtney tucks her arm in Grant's and smiles up at him as her mother goes around the room making introductions. I can't help feeling a pang of envy. Does everybody in the world have a boyfriend but me?

Stanley clears his throat. "On the menu tonight, we have Clemmie's famous carrot-yogurt soup, plus Mr. Ray's famous turkey-and-stuffing sandwiches—cut bite-size, for delicate appetites." He suppresses a shudder as he points to the second platter. "And these, uh, other sandwiches too."

"The secret to good onion sandwiches," says Mrs. Sloane-Kinkaid, swinging into TV chef mode, "is to use only the best bread, lots of sweet butter, and Bermuda onions that have been sliced paper thin and sprinkled with vinegar—I used an herbed rice vinegar—plus salt and pepper, and allowed to marinate for at least an hour."

In the Betsy-Tacy books, onion sandwiches are a staple at the Ray family's Sunday Night Lunch. They sound totally gross to me, and by the look on his face, it's obvious that Stanley thinks so too.

"Hope somebody brought breath mints," mutters Cassidy.

"And a killer dessert," adds Emma.

"Emma Jane Hawthorne!" says her mother.

Emma smiles sheepishly. "Sorry. I'm sure your sandwiches are really good, Mrs. Sloane-Kinkaid."

　　　　　　　　　　　　　　　　　Heather Vogel Frederick

"Actually, there is a killer dessert," says Cassidy's mother. "I made fudge."

"Oh, good!" says Gram. "It wouldn't be a true Deep Valley party without fudge."

Mrs. Sloane-Kinkaid passes her the platter of onion sandwiches, and she selects one and takes a bite. "Mmm—nice and crisp and light. Just the thing after a big Thanksgiving dinner."

The sandwiches make their way around the room to mixed reviews.

"Sheesh, Mom, these are *awful*," says Cassidy, gagging.

"No kidding," I gasp as my eyes start to water.

"Surprisingly good," says Mrs. Hawthorne, and Megan nods in agreement. "I like them too," she says.

Megan has a cast-iron stomach. You'd have to, to survive her mother's cooking. Anything probably tastes better than the tofu-infested casseroles Mrs. Wong is always dreaming up. I used to dread going to Megan's house after school, because there were never any decent snacks. I mean, kale chips? Who serves kale chips to elementary schoolers? All that changed, of course, when Gigi came over from Hong Kong to live with them. Megan's grandmother is a fabulous cook.

"I guess nobody ever kissed anybody back in Deep Valley, did they?" Cassidy says, leaning over and breathing in Jess's face.

"Cassidy!" Jess fans the air indignantly with her napkin.

I set my onion sandwich aside and concentrate on the mug of

soup, which is delicious. I didn't think I'd have room for dessert, but when Mr. Kinkaid reappears with the fudge, there's no way I can resist. Cassidy's mom's fudge is almost as good as Gram's.

"Shall we get down to business here before we pick our Secret Santas?" asks Mrs. Hawthorne. She always likes to get down to business.

Megan nudges me with her foot under the table. I nudge her back. The two of us have hatched a plot to make sure we choose each other.

"First of all," continues Mrs. Hawthorne, "I'd like to introduce our honored guest. I hope you've all had a chance to meet Becca's grand-mother, Grace Gilman, who is the reason why we're reading the Betsy-Tacy books this fall. Mrs. Gilman, perhaps you'd like to tell us a bit about your relationship with the series."

Gram looks around the room, smiling. "I am so thrilled that the 'Winding Hall of Fate,' as Betsy calls it, led me here to your meeting tonight! I can't remember a time when I didn't know about the Betsy-Tacy books. I guess when you're a girl, and you're from Minnesota, it's pretty hard not to. Maud Hart Lovelace was born and raised in Mankato, which is just a hop and a skip from my hometown of St. Peter."

"Do you have a favorite?" asks Gigi.

Gram doesn't even hesitate. "*Betsy and Tacy Go Downtown*," she replies. "I adore that book. Aspiring writer Betsy getting her uncle Keith's trunk to use for a desk; meeting the fun-loving Mrs. Poppy; and of course the wonderful Christmas shopping trip." Her eyes crinkle

Heather Vogel Frederick

around the edges as she looks over at Megan and me. "My guess is that unlike Betsy and Tacy, though, you girls will be buying more than just ornaments tomorrow, right?"

"Oh yeah," I reply, slapping Megan a high five.

"I loved *Downtown* too," says Mrs. Delaney. "I especially love the way Betsy's parents support her dreams of being a writer, and let her go to the library all by herself, and out to lunch at a restaurant, too."

"Me too," says Emma. "That was my favorite part. Well, that and Mrs. Poppy—I love her! She's so cheerful and ..." Her voice trails off as her gaze wanders over in my mother's direction.

Mrs. Poppy is built kind of like my mother, on the large side. Actually, Mrs. Poppy is a whale. A really nice one, but a whale. She and her husband own a hotel in Deep Valley, and she loves to eat.

Fortunately, my mother is too happy thinking about the book to realize the direction Emma was going in. "And of course we can't forget Winona eyes," she adds.

"What are Winona eyes?" asks Cassidy.

Mrs. Sloane-Kinkaid frowns. "Didn't you read *Betsy and Tacy Go Downtown*?"

"Um," says Cassidy.

"Cassidy! You promised!"

"Mom—I told you, I hardly have time to tie my shoes these days!"

Gram explains to her about how the girls tried to hypnotize Winona into taking them to the theater by staring at her. "Let me demonstrate for you," she says, goggling intensely at Cassidy, who laughs.

"Let's talk about the boys," says Mrs. Delaney. "Who's Team Tony and who's Team Joe?"

In the high school books, there are these two guys that Betsy Ray likes—well, there are more than two, actually, but the main ones are Joe Willard, who's handsome and supersmart and a good writer but kind of standoffish, and Tony Markham, who's handsome and funny and a good dancer but a little on the wild side.

I'm Team Tony, of course, and so is Megan. Jess is Team Joe, like Emma—no big surprise there. Cassidy thinks the whole idea is stupid and refuses to choose.

"I guess I'd have to say I'm Team Tony," says Gram. "How could anyone resist a T.D.S.?"

"What's a T.D.S.?" asks Cassidy, and her mother's mouth drops open.

"Cassidy Ann Sloane!" she exclaims. "You haven't read *Heaven to Betsy*, either?"

Cassidy squirms a little. "I started it."

Mrs. Sloane-Kinkaid closes her eyes and shakes her head. "I apologize for my daughter, Grace. After you bought her the books and everything."

"Cassidy, you've got to read them all!" says Emma. "They're really good."

"Will you all please get off my case?" grumbles Cassidy. "It's not

Heather Vogel Frederick

that I don't want to, it's just that seriously, between hockey and school, I've got my hands full."

My grandmother leans forward and pats her knee. "No need to explain yourself to me, dear. School has to come first. And hockey, too. T.D.S. stands for 'tall, dark stranger'—Tony Markham, the mysterious boy who shows up at Deep Valley High School."

"Kind of like Tristan Berkeley did last year at Alcott High," says Megan, and Cassidy turns bright red. She does not like to be teased about Tristan.

"What I want to know is how the Deep Valley girls all stay so slim," says her mother, taking pity on her and changing the subject. "They're always eating! Muffins, cake, banana splits at Heinz's!"

"Don't forget fudge," says Mrs. Delaney, helping herself to another piece.

"You must remember that it's the early 1900s," says Mrs. Wong, who always takes everything seriously. "There aren't very many cars and the girls walk everywhere. Plus, a *valley* implies that there are hills, so that would give them even more exercise too." Mrs. Wong loves geography.

"Thank you, Lily," says Mrs. Hawthorne, pulling a sheaf of papers out of her tote bag. Among them are maps of Deep Valley, which she distributes to each of us, along with a second handout. "You've just provided me with the perfect introduction to this month's fun facts."

FUN FACTS ABOUT MAUD

1) Maud Hart Lovelace was born on April 26, 1892, in Mankato, Minnesota. "I lived the happiest childhood a child could possibly know," she once said. She drew on those happy childhood memories for the Betsy-Tacy series.

2) She knew very young that she wanted to be an author someday. "I cannot remember back to a year in which I did not consider myself to be a writer," she once recalled. "I remember following my mother around as a tyke, asking her, 'How do you spell "going down the street"'?' See? I was writing a story already."

3) When Maud was ten, her father printed a booklet of her poems, and at eighteen, she sold her first story to a magazine. She grew up to write a number of short stories and historical novels for adults, but today is best known for her books for young readers.

4) *Betsy-Tacy*, the first of the Deep Valley books, was published in 1940. It was an instant success, and was followed by nine others. *Betsy's Wedding,* the final book in the series, was published in 1955. Maud also wrote three additional stories

Heather Vogel Frederick

set in Deep Valley: *Winona's Pony Cart*, *Carney's House Party*, and *Emily of Deep Valley*.

5) Deep Valley is based on a real place—Maud's hometown of Mankato—and the characters are based on people she knew growing up, including her best friend Bick Kenney, who became Tacy Kelly in the book. If you travel to Mankato today, you can tour Maud's and Bick's homes, which are right across the street from each other, just as Betsy's and Tacy's are in the books, and you can sit on a replica of the hillside bench where the real-life Maud and Bick, as well as their fictional counterparts, would often meet.

"It's just like Louisa May Alcott and the Orchard House here in Concord," says Emma. "Louisa based her characters on real people too."

"Maybe you'll end up writing about Concord and all of us someday," Megan tells her.

My mother gets a funny look on her face at this. She's probably thinking about Emma's father and *Spring Reckoning* again. Mr. Hawthorne is a writer, and my mother is convinced that one of the characters in his novel—not a very flattering one—was based on her.

Cassidy reaches over and prods Emma with her toe. "I guess I'd better be nice to you so you don't talk trash about me in all those books you're going to write."

"Maybe we should give you Winona eyes to make sure you don't," I suggest, and we all stare at Emma solemnly until she starts to laugh.

Mrs. Sloane-Kinkaid glances at her watch. "I hate to break up the party, but it's been a long day, and we have to get up at the crack of dawn to drive to Rhode Island."

"Yes, of course!" says Mrs. Hawthorne. "I totally forgot about the hockey tournament. Are you girls ready to choose your Secret Santas?"

We nod, and she pulls a Santa hat out of her tote bag, along with a pile of pens and three-by-five cards. Megan's mom starts passing them around.

"Let me remind you how this works," says Mrs. Hawthorne. "You'll each choose a name, and you will become that person's Secret Santa for a week. Seven days—seven presents. Keep them small, okay? No spending a lot of money."

"I would encourage you all to think about homemade gifts," says Mrs. Wong.

"Fat chance," mutters Cassidy, who hates crafts. I smile at her. My feelings exactly.

"When will we find out who our Secret Santas are?" asks Jess.

"At our next meeting."

"We have to wait until *January*?"

Mrs. Hawthorne nods. "Probably. We moms haven't had a chance to check our calendars and set a date yet."

"I have a snoggestion," says Gram. "Snoggestion" is another of my grandmother's favorite terms, along with "Winona eyes." It's what

Heather Vogel Frederick

Betsy Ray's father calls a really great suggestion. "If you're interested, that is. Some of my friends back in Cleveland are big Betsy-Tacy fans too, and every year we have an ornament exchange. We pick names, just like you're about to do, and then look for ornaments that have something to do with one of the books to give to each other."

"Sounds like fun," says Mrs. Delaney.

"Especially if you made the ornaments," adds Mrs. Wong.

Megan's eyes slide over to mine. Her mother can be like a dog with a bone when she gets going on something.

"We could have them be the final Secret Santa gift, and you girls could give them to each other at our next meeting when we do the Big Reveal," says Mrs. Sloane-Kinkaid.

Mrs. Hawthorne nods. "Good thinking, Clementine." She peers over her glasses at me and my friends. "Girls? Are you in?"

"Wait a minute," says Gigi. "How come they get to have all the fun? I think we grown-ups should give each other ornaments too."

After a quick vote, Megan's mother passes out three-by-five cards to all of them, too.

Megan and I exchange a surreptitious glance as we write down our names on our cards. We made a pact as soon as we heard about the whole Secret Santa idea, mostly because we know each other so well, and this way we'll be able to pick out great presents. The plan is to turn down one of the corners on our card, so that when we reach into the hat we can feel around for it.

But something goes wrong.

Megan picks first, and when she pulls out the card and looks at the name on it, she flicks me a sharp glance and shakes her head, one really quick, almost invisible shake.

Uh-oh, I think. *That can't be good.* Who did she pick, if she didn't pick me? And even more importantly, who am I going to get stuck with?

Not Cassidy, I plead silently as the Santa hat makes its way slowly around our circle. *Please, please, please, don't let me pick Cassidy.*

Besides the fact that I have no idea how to shop for someone who never uses makeup or wears jewelry, and who forgets to use deodorant half the time, and thinks about nothing but hockey, I really, really don't want to be forced to buy presents for my crush's crush. I've liked Zach Norton since kindergarten, and if it weren't for Cassidy, I know he'd like me, too.

I reach into the hat and grope around for a card with one of its corners turned down. But since I'm the last one to pick, there's only one card left.

I pull it out.

I turn it over.

My heart sinks.

CASSIDY.

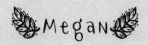
Megan

"Betsy and Tacy went downtown on their Christmas shopping expedition. This was a tradition with them. They went every year, visiting every store in town, and buying, at the end, one Christmas tree ornament."

—*Heaven to Betsy*

My eyes flutter open, and I stare groggily at my bedroom ceiling. Something is clanking noisily outside.

Oh, no! Throwing back the covers, I stumble across the room to the window. My sigh of disappointment fogs up the glass pane as I stare glumly at the snowplow scraping along Strawberry Hill Road. The storm must have started last night after we finally went to sleep.

"Becca!" I whisper. "Becca, wake up!"

She makes a noise somewhere between a snort and a groan and flops the pillow over her head. I cross the room and snatch it away. "Becca! It's *snowing*!"

That gets through. She sits up, rubbing her eyes. "What about our shopping trip?"

This is why I love Becca. We totally think alike.

The two of us stayed up late last night talking. About our shopping strategy for today, of course, but mostly about boys—Zach Norton, who she's still stuck on, and Simon Berkeley, my long-distance boy-friend.

Really long distance.

Simon lives in England. He and his brother Tristan and their parents swapped houses with the Hawthornes last year, and that's how I got to know him. I glance at the framed photograph of the two of us that's on my bedside table. Cassidy took it one day last spring when the three of us were at the Old North Bridge, and she really caught Simon's spirit. I smile every time I look at it. He's so cute, with his curly blond hair and brown eyes. If I close my eyes I can practically hear him laughing. Simon has a great laugh.

The last time I saw him in person was in July, when our book club went to England on a Jane Austen research trip. We've been IMing and e-mailing and video-chatting since then. I really miss him. We were supposed to talk yesterday morning before the football game, but he didn't call, and when I tried him there was no answer, which is weird. He's always super punctual.

"Megan?" Becca repeats groggily, snapping me out of my day-dream. "Do you think we'll have to cancel our trip?"

It's going to be a complete tragedy if we don't get to go shopping because of the stupid weather. "Let's go talk to my parents and find out."

We throw on our robes and slippers and head down the hall to the kitchen, where my parents and Gigi are having their morning coffee. Well, my dad and grandmother are having coffee. My mother's

Heather Vogel Frederick

holding a steaming mug of one of her green tea concoctions.

"Is the shopping trip still on?" I demand.

"Good morning to you, too," replies my mother mildly. "Did you sleep well?"

Becca nods. "Really well, thank you, Mrs. Wong. Can we still go shopping?"

My mother laughs. "Not to be deterred, are you, girls?" She turns to my dad. "Jerry? What's the verdict?"

"No to Boston—the highways are too icy." He holds up a hand as we start to protest. "But yes to downtown Concord, and maybe—just maybe, depending on whether the snow lets up and whether road conditions improve—to the mall."

"I vote you stay in Concord," says my mother, taking a sip of tea. "It's better to shop local anyway."

She's actually happy that this freaky weather sabotaged our plans! Outraged, I open my mouth to retort. Before I can, though, Gigi swoops in.

"Cheer up, girls. No snowstorm is going to spoil our fun." She steers us toward the table, which is decorated with an orange tablecloth, a scattering of gourds, tiny pilgrim salt-and-pepper shakers, and a paper Thanksgiving turkey. My grandmother's doing, of course. Gigi loves holidays, and celebrates all of them with abandon. "I've got hot chocolate and croissants all ready for you. I think real whipped cream is in order on a morning like this."

"Mother!" my mom protests, as Gigi heads for the refrigerator.

"We're going to be having breakfast at the shop in a little while!"

My grandmother flaps a hand dismissively. "The girls need energy if they're going to be walking all over Concord today."

Becca and I slump in our seats. Shopping in Concord is hardly the same as shopping in downtown Boston.

"Eat up girls. I can't wait to get going!" Gigi says brightly, setting a plate of croissants on the table in front of us. "We're going to explore every single store in town. We won't leave a stone unturned. I want to check out Arrivederci, that new shoe shop that just opened, and I saw some fabric at the Whole Nine Yards the other day that I know you'll love, Megan. We'll even hit the five-and-ten! Plus, Josephine's is carrying a new line of bath salts and soaps from France—and who knows, with all the extra time we'll have without the long drive into the city, we might be able to squeeze in some of their special pampering. And if my wonderful son-in-law"—she pinches my dad's cheek, like he's little Chloe or something—"can get us as far as the mall, so much the better. Who needs the hassle of city traffic?"

"Us?" Becca whispers. But she's smiling, and so am I. Suddenly the day doesn't seem like a complete loss.

My grandmother is amazing that way. Somehow she always manages to turn lemons into lemonade. Even I'm starting to think that this will be much more fun than going to Boston.

At least we don't have to spend Black Friday stuck at home.

For the longest time I had no idea why the day after Thanksgiving was called "Black Friday." When I was little, I thought it had something

Heather Vogel Frederick

to do with the color of the clothes the pilgrims wore. Later my mother told me it was because it's a dark day for mankind and a blot on our national psyche. My mother can get like that sometimes, especially when it comes to shopping. She is totally anticonsumerism. If she had her way, we'd all make our own clothes out of old flour sacks, like the pioneers did. Her motto? Reduce, Reuse, Recycle. Mine, on the other hand? Shop, Shop, Shop! I can't help it. I love shopping. I'm not just talking about buying, either. I have just as much fun looking—well, almost as much fun. I love checking out clothes, and shoes, and jewelry and other accessories, and thinking about how things go together, and getting ideas for my own designs. Fashion is my art form, and going shopping gives me inspiration.

Anyway, a couple of years ago my dad finally explained to me that Black Friday is the day most stores in the United States finally start to turn a profit for the year and see their numbers go from debt-red to profitable black. So now, when I come home with too many shopping bags, I just tell my mom I'm doing my part to help the economy.

Forty-five minutes later my mom and dad and Gigi and Becca and I are creeping down Strawberry Hill in my dad's SUV. He was right about the roads, because even with chains on our tires the streets are still really slick and icy. We skid a few times, and almost slide into a snowbank once, and I'm relieved when we finally pull up in front of Pies & Prejudice, my grandmother's tea shop.

Last spring, Eva Bergson, the skating teacher here in town who was part of our Mother-Daughter Book Club, passed away. She was

Gigi's best friend, and she left my grandmother some money for her to start a tea shop. It's been in the works for months and just opened a few weeks ago. It's already really popular. Of course, it didn't hurt that the *Boston Post* did a big write-up on it, thanks to Mr. Hawthorne, who knows the book review editor, who's good friends with the restaurant critic. So far it's only open for lunch and afternoon tea, but Gigi is thinking about expanding to serve breakfast, too.

"You get to be my guinea pigs this morning," she tells us, her dark eyes shining with excitement as she climbs out of the car. My father opens the trunk, and Gigi loads us up with containers full of delicious-smelling things, then herds us inside.

As usual, my grandmother is dressed to the nines. This morning she's decked out in a black wool coat with black boots and red accessories—red cashmere scarf, red purse, and red leather gloves. She looks like she's heading off for a shopping spree in Paris or Manhattan instead of tiny Concord, Massachusetts. But then, that's how Gigi always looks.

I glance over at my mother, who threw on an old down jacket of my dad's and one of those hats—I think they're called balaclavas—that cover everything but your face. Not a good look, especially since it's olive green, which is a terrible color on her. She's smiling, though—I think she's excited that she gets to run the shop today. She and Mrs. Chadwick volunteered to take the reins while we go shopping.

I helped Gigi with the color scheme for Pies & Prejudice, and it still makes me smile every time I walk in the front door. Stepping

Heather Vogel Frederick

into the tea shop is like stepping into summer.

There are lace curtains at the windows, and the walls are painted in wide stripes of cream and yellow. Gigi hired an artist to paint quotes from famous authors along the tops of them: "You must drink tea with us," from Jane Austen's *Sense and Sensibility*, and "You can never get a cup of tea large enough or a book long enough to suit me," by C. S. Lewis, the guy who wrote the Narnia books. Mrs. Hawthorne picked that one out, and it totally sounds like her and Emma.

There's another quote from some guy I've never heard of named Henry James: "There are few hours in life more agreeable than the hour dedicated to the ceremony known as afternoon tea." That one reminds me of last summer when we were in England and had tea at the Pump Room in Bath. The last quote is my favorite, though: "Come, let us have some tea and continue to talk about happy things." That's by Chaim Potok, another writer I'd never heard of, and it makes me think about sitting at the kitchen table with my grandmother every time I read it.

Everything about Pies & Prejudice is sunny and fresh. The white wooden tables, the white wicker chairs with their plump yellow-and-white-striped cushions, the white linen tablecloths and yellow-and-white-striped napkins, and most of all the white vases filled with cheerful yellow roses that are on the center of each table and elsewhere around the room.

From the black-and-white tiles on the floor to the big white wooden hutch along the wall next to the cash register, the shop is crisp and clean and spotless. Gigi found yellow-and-white polka-dotted shelf paper for the hutch's shelves, which are loaded with all sorts of tea-related merchandise: teapots and teacups and tea towels, tea accessories and books about tea, and of course, boxes and tins filled with different kinds of tea. There are gleaming jars of jam from Half Moon Farm, too, and other little goodies as well.

On the other side of the cash register is a glass case filled with yummy things—pies, of course, since the tea shop grew out of the pie business my friends and I ran last year, but also cookies and brownies and muffins and tarts and cakes and scones and stuff. A blackboard behind it lists all the soups and sandwiches and salads that Gigi offers, along with daily specials and tea options. Adults can order a full English cream tea, with sandwiches and sweets served on tiered plates just like they do at the Pump Room, or they can order "Just a Cuppa," as the menu calls it, along with a single scone or other treat. For little kids, there's the Peter Rabbit tea, which includes "Mr. McGregor's Watering Can" (a small teapot filled with hot chocolate or cambric tea, which is mostly warm milk), tiny peanut butter and jelly sandwiches, ants on a log (celery sticks spread with peanut butter and sprinkled with raisins), and a mini cupcake. That's Chloe's favorite.

Gigi is having a blast with all this. She's met half of Concord already, since everybody from the mayor to the postmistress has stopped in, and it didn't take the girls at Colonial Academy long to discover it either. My dad says it's already giving the local coffee shop a run for its money.

One of the best things about Pies & Prejudice is that it's keeping Gigi

Heather Vogel Frederick

out of my mother's hair. She and my mother don't always see eye to eye on everything, and having a project to keep my grandmother occupied has helped make things a lot more peaceful at home. Gigi is here by seven, when my dad drops her off before work (and has his second breakfast, one that doesn't include tofu or spelt), and she doesn't get home most days until nearly dinnertime. I've been helping her out on Saturdays when I can, and my mom drops by to lend a hand, too, when she's not too busy with her boards and charities and fund-raisers. Mom's kind of a wet blanket, though, because she gripes about sugar all the time and keeps wanting to add whole wheat flour and flax-seed to everything.

We carry our boxes and trays and containers into the shop's tiny kitchen, then take our seats at the table Gigi's set for us.

"Jerry, didn't you already eat at home?" says my mother sternly, as my father spreads his napkin in his lap.

His eyes go all wide and innocent. "That tiny little whole wheat bagel? That's not a real breakfast."

My mother looks pointedly at his belt. My dad is sporting a muffin top these days. He's been in hog heaven ever since Gigi came to live with us a couple of years ago and took over most of the cooking, but his waistline has suffered in the process.

The bell above the door jingles, and Mrs. Chadwick and Becca's grandmother breeze in, along with a gust of cold, snowy air. My father springs back up to help them with their coats.

"Your shop is darling!" says Becca's grandmother, looking around in delight.

"Thank you, Grace," says Gigi. "Come and have a seat. I hope you're hungry."

"You wouldn't think so after everything I ate yesterday, but I'm starving!"

She and Mrs. Chadwick join us at the table, and Gigi beckons to me to join her back in the kitchen. She hands me a white ruffled apron and white ruffled cap.

"Let's give them the whole Pies & Prejudice experience, shall we?" she asks. I nod, even though I'm a little embarrassed for Becca to see me dressed in this getup.

Sure enough, as we head toward the table with our trays of food, Becca starts to laugh. I stick out my tongue at her.

"Breakfast is served, ladies and gentleman," Gigi announces.

"Mmm-mmm," says my dad. "What have we here?"

"The Rise and Shine Special—a casserole with eggs, chicken apple sausage, and Half Moon Farm's herbed goat cheese," Gigi replies. "Plus, there's fresh fruit salad and cranberry-oat-almond scones, hot out of the oven. Well, hot out of the oven half an hour ago back home. Usually I bake them here."

After everyone is served, Gigi and I sit down too, and for a few minutes it's quiet as we all dig in.

It's not completely silent, though. My dad is a noisy eater, and Mrs. Chadwick keeps making these happy little grunting noises. Becca kicks me under the table every time she does, and it's all I can do not to crack up.

Heather Vogel Frederick

"You should offer cooking classes," says Becca's grandmother, licking scone crumbs off her fingertips. "People would pay good money to learn to make these scones. *I'd* pay good money to learn to make these scones!"

Gigi's eyes light up. "Grace, you're a genius! That's a wonderful idea! I could offer them one evening a week, maybe." Her face clouds slightly. "Although I'm not sure how I'd fit in one more thing at the moment."

"Perhaps it's time to hire some part-time help," my father suggests.

Gigi nods. "Perhaps." She pours him some more coffee, then turns to my mother. "I don't know whether the storm will keep people away, Lily, but I figure they'll want something hot if they do come in, so I made a double batch of that Thai Butternut Squash soup that's been so popular. There are three quiches in the refrigerator, too, so all you and Calliope need to do is make the sandwiches, okay?"

Becca glances surreptitiously down at her cell phone, which she's holding on her lap. Becca and her cell phone are inseparable. "Ashley says hi," she whispers to me.

"Tell her hi back," I whisper in return. Ashley was supposed to come shopping with us today too, but she ended up going to visit her cousins in Connecticut for the weekend.

"She wants to know if you've heard anything from Simon yet?"

I shake my head. I checked my computer before we left the house, but there still weren't any e-mails or other messages.

Becca gives me a sidelong glance. "I hope everything's okay."

She knows better than to bug me about it, but Becca's like that sometimes. She just can't resist stirring things up. The truth is, I'm kind of worried. He knows this is Thanksgiving weekend, and that I've got a lot going on with my grandparents in town and our shopping day and everything, but still, we were supposed to talk yesterday morning, and he's never missed one of our video-chat dates before. I've decided that if I don't hear from him by tonight—or tomorrow morning at the latest—I'm going to call.

To get back at Becca, I mention a tidbit I overheard at the football game yesterday. "Can you believe that Zach Norton volunteered to be the equipment manager for the Lady Shawmuts?" I tell her. "He's down in Rhode Island this weekend, watching Cassidy play."

Becca's face clouds. She obviously hasn't heard this, but she pretends like she has. She hates it when other people know stuff before she does, even me. "Yeah, what's up with that?"

I feel really mean all of a sudden, because I know how much Becca likes Zach, and it's pretty obvious that even though he asked her to Spring Formal last year, he doesn't like her back. Not the way Simon likes me. Which has been kind of hard for her to swallow.

I've tried telling Becca that Zach is just one small fish in a very big pond called Alcott High, and that there are plenty of other boys out there who would be thrilled if she'd pay them some attention—like Third, for instance, who is the nicest guy in the world, even if he is a little bit of a goofball—but she's totally stuck on Zach Norton. And she's not happy that he's spending so much time this year hanging out with Cassidy.

I'm still not sure where Cassidy fits into all this. By the end of last

Heather Vogel Frederick

school year, we all thought she liked Simon's brother, Tristan. Every time I ask Simon about it, though, he just shrugs and says his brother is "awfully closemouthed about these things."

I don't know when Cassidy would have time to squeeze a boyfriend in anyway. She barely has time to breathe these days, what with elite hockey and Chicks with Sticks. Plus, sophomore classes are hard—a lot harder than freshman classes were. Especially math. Cassidy and I are in the same Algebra II class, and if it wasn't for Becca's brother, Stewart, who tutors us both, we'd be in big trouble.

"So are you enjoying the Betsy-Tacy books so far, Megan?" asks Becca's grandmother, pouring me some more hot chocolate.

I nod. "Thank you so much for getting them all for us, Mrs. Gilman," I reply politely, and my mother gives me an approving smile from across the table. *Two points for me*, I think, feeling an unfamiliar glow of virtue. I don't always remember to be polite.

"You're so welcome," Becca's grandmother replies, giving me a mischievous smile. "It's part of my secret plan to take over the world. I wish I could make everyone read these books—they're so good."

I nod. Surprisingly, I agree with her. Even though I haven't read all of them yet, so far I feel like these are girls I can actually relate to. Not that I couldn't relate to the March sisters in *Little Women*, or Anne Shirley in *Anne of Green Gables*, or Judy Abbott in *Daddy-Long-Legs*, or even the Bennet sisters in *Pride and Prejudice*. But Betsy Ray and her friends seem, I don't know, more real to me somehow. Deep Valley High in 1910 isn't exactly Alcott High in the twenty-first century, but it's not that far off. The characters are always talking about "the Crowd"—all their friends—and it reminds me of the friends Becca and I hang out with. And then there's all the stuff about clothes, which I love, and the way they're always calling one another on the phone, and the fact that they're just as interested in boys as we are.

"Are your shopping lists ready?" asks Gigi.

I review mine quickly in my head. I need to find something for her, of course, and for Mom and Dad. And I want to buy presents for Becca and Ashley. I'm Emma's Secret Santa, so I have to find six little gifts for her, plus an ornament. And then there's Simon.

Simon.

I shove the thought of him away. I don't want any worries to creep in and spoil our fun; I need to focus on the day ahead of me.

After the dishes are washed and put away and Gigi is finished giving my mom and Mrs. Chadwick their final instructions, we all put on our coats. Becca and I kiss our moms good-bye—and in my case, my dad—and head out into the snow.

Shopping with two grandmothers turns out to be a really, really great strategy. Half an hour later, Gigi's already bought me a bracelet and two tops—not for Christmas but "just because," as she puts it— and Mrs. Gilman is at the cash register paying for new boots for Becca.

"Score!" whispers Becca happily, swinging her Arrivederci bag back and forth.

I love it when stores take the time to design a really fabulous shopping bag. Arrivederci's is lime green, with a wide band of black around

Heather Vogel Frederick

the top, black handles, and their name spelled out in this really cool black font. I make a mental note to see if I can track it down, because the lettering would look awesome on the front of a T-shirt.

I glance down at my own two bags, a lavender-and-white-striped one from the Whole Nine Yards and the plain brown one with little black pawprints on it from the Concord Pet Shoppe. I found the cutest present for Pip as one of Emma's Secret Santa gifts. Both bags are nice, but neither one is as splashy as Arrivederci's, and they're certainly not the kind of thing I'd want to hang on my wall, like I did with the one from Bébé Soleil that Gigi brought me back from Paris.

When I was in eighth grade, I designed this baby outfit for the daughter of Jess's housemom at Colonial Academy. I didn't think it was all that special, but my grandmother loved it so much she secretly borrowed it and took it with her on her annual trip to Paris for Fashion Week. She showed it to the buyers at Bébé Soleil, and now they carry a line of my clothing. My dream is to be a fashion designer someday, and even though I wasn't thrilled at first—baby clothes aren't exactly my career goal—now I think it's pretty cool. For one thing, I'm piling up a lot of money in my college fund, which makes my mother insanely happy. Plus, it's fun. And as Gigi points out, it's a foot in the door.

To celebrate signing the contract, Gigi had the Bébé Soleil bag framed for me, and I hung it on the wall over my desk. It's bright orange, with a stylized yellow sun shining on a garden full of flowers that are actually babies. It's adorable and classy at the same time, and so *French*. So "je ne sais quoi," as Gigi puts it. Which now that I'm taking French at school I know means literally "I don't know what"—that indescribable quality that makes something special.

"Where to next?" asks Becca's grandmother.

"Kitchen store," says Gigi. "There's something I want to get for Clementine." She glances at her watch, then at Becca and me. "Somehow I have a feeling you two aren't all that interested in kitchen gadgets."

"Um, yeah, maybe not," I reply.

She smiles. "How about you go on ahead to Josephine's? I called a few minutes ago, and they've had several cancellations due to the weather. They said they'd be happy to squeeze us all in for facials. You girls are booked first, and Grace and I will go after lunch. My treat."

I throw my arms around her. "Thanks, Gigi!" Josephine's facials are legendary. They're also very expensive.

"We'll meet you back at Pies & Prejudice," says Becca's grandmother.

Becca and I scurry away, clutching each other in giddy excitement. I've had facials before, but never one from Josephine's.

The salesroom is decorated in a soothing palette of dove gray and lavender, and equally soothing music drifts in from hidden speakers somewhere. The receptionist checks us in and invites us to browse for a few minutes while the "artistes," as she calls them, prepare our rooms. Becca and I have to stifle our giggles as we look around at the displays of perfumes and luxury soaps and shampoos and bath things and makeup. The price tags are *insane*.

"Guess we won't be buying our Secret Santa stuff here," Becca whispers.

Heather Vogel Frederick

"No kidding. Isn't it all gorgeous, though?"

"Mmm-hmm," says Becca, picking up one of the lotion samples and squeezing a dollop onto her palm. She rubs her hands together and sniffs them, smiling blissfully. "I think I want to live here."

The receptionist returns and beckons to us. We follow her down a marble-floored hallway to a pair of plush, toasty-warm rooms lit by flickering, scented candles.

"See you when I'm beautiful," says Becca, fluttering a newly moisturized hand at me as she disappears into one of them. I go into the other, and before long I'm lying under a towel on a table while a woman in a white coat steams, creams, exfoliates, and massages my face, all the while murmuring soft compliments. My nose is working overtime trying to decipher all the scents, and I take mental notes like crazy, thinking maybe I need to consider adding a line of facial products to my future fashion line. I could even call them "Ray of Sunshine" after Betsy, who is just as crazy about "beauty aids," as she calls them, as Becca and I are.

"Is it my imagination, or is the snow letting up a little?" asks Becca when we emerge a while later, our faces glowing.

"Wishful thinking," I tell her. "And by the way, you look amazing."

"So do you."

It's true. Gigi got us the deluxe facials, which included an expert makeup consultation. I've never seen either of us with makeup this perfect.

"Too bad we can't stop in here every morning on the way to school, huh?" I ask.

"No kidding," says Becca, glancing around hopefully. "Maybe someone will notice us."

But the only ones who do are her grandmother and Gigi.

"Look at these ravishing beauties, Grace!" says Gigi.

"I only hope I'm half as gorgeous when Josephine's is done with me," Becca's grandmother replies.

Becca and I take a seat at their table, feeling pleased with ourselves. A moment later Mrs. Chadwick appears with a menu. "Ladies, may I interest you in a little lunch?"

"Nice look, Mom!" says Becca, grinning broadly at the white ruffled cap and matching apron.

Her mother swats her with the menu. My mother pokes her head out of the kitchen and peers at my face. She frowns.

"Too much around the eyes," she says. My mother hates makeup.

Gigi leans across the table. "Don't listen to her," she's whispers. "It's just right."

"What was that, Mother?" asks my mom.

"Nothing, dear. How has business been today?"

"Brisk. You were right about the soup—it's almost gone."

"I guess we'd better make sure we get some, then. Shall we order?"

After we finish lunch, Becca's grandmother and Gigi head off to their appointments at Josephine's, while my dad drives Becca and me to the West Concord Five & Ten. This is my father's favorite store in town, and he's always happy to find an excuse to go. It's kind of like a cross between a hardware store, a toy shop, and maybe a crafts store. They carry just

Heather Vogel Frederick

about everything a person could think of, from kitchen appliances to school supplies to yarn to oddball stuff like fishing lures and Chinese paper lanterns. Becca and I snap up a couple of Secret Santa gifts while my dad happily roots around in the plumbing supply section.

By midafternoon the snow finally starts to subside. We duck back into the tea shop—for actual tea this time—to plot our strategy for the rest of the day. We decide to skip the mall, since we've been able to find so much stuff right here in town, in favor of finishing up with the rest of the stores in Concord, and possibly a trip into Boston tomorrow. If I can convince my mother that I won't be permanently damaged by a double dose of shopping, that is.

By four o'clock it's getting dark, my feet hurt, and I'm actually feeling shopped out, which almost never happens. I'm more than happy to call it a day. Dad drives everyone home, and I head to my room with my purchases, eager to see if maybe Simon finally left me a message.

I dump my shopping bags on the bed and cross the room to my desk. Flipping open my laptop, I sit down and wait for it to boot up, then hop online. There's still no sign of him—no little icon on the IM or video-chat screens—so I open my e-mail instead. Ha! He sent me a message. It's about time.

I click it open and scan the first line. All of a sudden I can't breathe.

> I don't know how to tell you this, so I'll just say it: I
> think we should cool it for a while.

This can't be what I think it is. It just can't!

> I really, really like you, Megan, but living this far
> away is just too hard, and I think we should both be
> free to date other people.

He's breaking up with me? In an *e-mail*? I can't believe that Simon Berkeley would do something like this.

But he did.

> I'm sorry I didn't call you yesterday, but I didn't want
> to ruin your holiday. I've been thinking about this
> nonstop, and wanted to make sure I was making the
> right decision. You're an amazing girl, Megan.

Not amazing enough, apparently.

Tears trickle down my face as I force myself to read the rest. I'm not stupid—I can read between the lines. When Simon says he thinks *we* should both be free to date other people, he's actually saying that *he* wants to be free to date other people. He probably already has—maybe stupid Annabelle Fairfax or one of her stupid friends. Annabelle is Simon's cousin—well, distant cousin—and she's a real piece of work. Emma nicknamed her "Stinkerbelle." She's pretty, though, and so are the girls she hangs out with. Maybe Simon just couldn't resist.

Heather Vogel Frederick

I'll call or write in a while after you've had a chance to think this all over. I'm sure this is coming as somewhat of a shock, but I do hope you'll understand, and perhaps even see that I'm right. Happy Thanksgiving to you and your family. Love, Simon

My eyes linger on the word "love" before I close my laptop and cross back to my bed. I curl up among my shopping bags and stare at the wall, numb. Tears start again in earnest.

There's a knock at the door. I don't respond.

"Megan!" It's my mother. "We're going to eat dinner soon."

"I'm not hungry."

She pokes her head in. "Aren't you feeling well? A touch of affluenza, perhaps?"

I can't believe my mother is trying to make one of her stupid anti-consumerism jokes! Talk about bad timing. I turn my head away, and she comes over and sits down on the edge of my bed. Seeing the tears on my face, her tone softens. "What is it, sweetheart?"

The tenderness in her voice undoes me. "It's Simon!" I wail. "He just broke up with me. In an *e-mail*!"

"Oh, sweetheart." She reaches over and strokes my hair, which makes me cry even harder. "I know how hard this must be for you."

I shake my head. She couldn't possibly know. No one could.

"Maybe it's for the best," she continues. "You're awfully young to be pairing up."

"Mom! That's a horrible thing to say!"

"What I mean is, it's way too soon for a serious relationship. At your age, you should just be having fun. Getting to know boys as friends, doing things in groups, that sort of thing. You know, being part of a Crowd, like Betsy and Tacy and their friends."

"This is *real life*, Mom, not a book," I tell her bitterly. "And you don't know what it's like, anyway! You probably never had anybody dump you!"

She chuckles softly. "Sure I did."

I'm so surprised to hear this that I stop crying. "Really?" It feels strange having this conversation. My mother and I love each other and everything, but we don't usually have these kinds of heart-to-hearts. Gigi is the one I usually go to for that.

She nods. "Of course. And it felt like my heart would break every single time. Your father and I even broke up for a while before we got married."

"You did?" My voice shoots up in surprise. I sit up and reach for a tissue.

She nods again. "We dated in college, and then after graduation we decided to go our separate ways. I had that internship in Washington, and your dad was working for a computer company here in Boston. We both dated other people, but I found myself comparing everyone else to him. Apparently he felt the same way, because he called me out of the blue one day a couple of years later, and six months after that we were married."

I mulled this over. Maybe it would work the same way for Simon

Heather Vogel Frederick

and me. Maybe we were still right for each other, but just not right now.

"And don't forget what happens to Betsy," my mother added, looking over at the pile of books on my bedside table.

"No spoilers!" I tell her quickly. "I'm just starting *Betsy Was a Junior*."

My mother crosses her heart. "No spoilers, I promise." She leans over and kisses the top of my head. "Would you like to come join us for dinner?"

I shake my head. I really don't want to have to talk about this with Dad and Gigi. Not right now.

"Can I bring you a tray instead?"

I lift a shoulder. "I'm not very hungry."

"Tea and toast, then?"

"Cinnamon toast?"

She doesn't hesitate. "Absolutely. Butter, cinnamon sugar, the whole nine yards."

I muster a smile and point at the lavender-and-white-striped bag I'm sitting on, the one with the Whole Nine Yards logo.

She smiles back. "Try not to worry too much, sweetheart. I know it hurts right now, but life has a way of sorting itself out."

"Really?"

"Really." She gives me another kiss. "I love you, Megs."

"I love you too, Mom."

She goes out and shuts the door behind her. I lie back on my pillow and close my eyes. Life has a way of sorting itself out?

Right now that doesn't seem the least bit likely.

Jess

> *"Long, low, reckless, the bobsleds flew from the top of the Big Hill along a hard-packed frozen track in a thrilling sweep, almost to the slough."*
> —*Betsy and Tacy Go Downtown*

"Thanks for stopping by!" my mother calls to a group of customers as they head for the door. "Drive safely, now."

"Happy Thanksgiving!" Emma and I chorus.

The bells over the farm-stand door jangle as it shuts behind them. My mother leans back against the counter with a sigh, pushing her dark bangs off her forehead. She looks frazzled, which is not surprising. Yesterday was mostly a bust because of the snowstorm, but today has more than made up for it. We've been crazy busy from the minute we opened this morning.

She frowns at one of the shelves behind me. "Jess, honey, could you go out to the barn and bring over more blackberry jam?"

I turn around in surprise. "Are we out already?"

"Yep," says Emma. "I just sold the next-to-the-last jar."

"Whoa. That went fast."

Heather Vogel Frederick

"It's a good problem to have," my mother replies, a smile replacing her frown. Which is true. Our family has come to count on the year-end boost from the Thanksgiving Weekend Harvest Festival sales. Half Moon Farm is a lot more profitable than it was a few years ago—our signature brand of goat cheese has taken off in a big way, and we've had to almost double our herd to accommodate all the orders flooding in—but still, I know my parents worry about money. Winterizing the farm stand was a big project, plus our house is ancient and always needs repairs and so do our cars, plus college is hovering on the horizon for me, and Dylan and Ryan, my twin brothers, aren't all that far behind. On top of that there's a new employee to pay, the guy my parents hired after I got the scholarship to Colonial Academy and couldn't help out as much as I used to.

I still feel guilty about that, even though they tell me not to.

I'm earning my keep today, though, that's for sure. And so is Emma. Josh Bates, our farmhand, has the weekend off so he can spend Thanksgiving up in New Hampshire visiting his family. They live near my aunt and uncle, which is how my parents found out about him. Josh graduated from the University of New Hampshire a couple of years ago with a degree in dairy management and was looking for some hands-on experience at a goat farm.

The bells over the door jangle again, and while Emma goes over to greet the new customer, I grab my jacket and duck out the back door. Crossing the field we use for a parking lot on my way to the barn, I wave to my brothers, who are helping my dad spread sand on the walkways again. They did a really good job yesterday pitching in with the plowing and shoveling. Mom says they're growing up, and it's true. They used to be totally useless, but I've noticed they've both gotten a lot more responsible now that they're in fifth grade.

My dad's the real hero of the weekend, though. He's been up at the crack of dawn two days in a row juggling his regular chores with all the extra stuff we had to do to get ready for our harvest festival. Yesterday he ran the snowblower practically nonstop. No sooner were the driveway and parking area clear than he had to start all over again. It was what Mr. Graves, my classics teacher, would have called a Sisyphean task. We've been studying Greek myths this fall, and Sisyphus was this king who tried to trick the gods, and ended up getting punished for it by being forced to roll a boulder uphill for all eternity, only to have it roll down again every time right before he reached the top.

The snow finally stopped late yesterday afternoon, and the snowblower's back in the garage again today. Even though the sun is out it's still cold, though, and I wrap my jacket tightly around me as I make a dash for the barn. Inside, I dawdle for a bit with Sundance and Cedar, my pet goats. I don't get to spend as much time with them as I used to, and I feel guilty about that, too.

I hear mewing behind me and turn around to see Elvis, our black barn cat, slink into the stall. Behind him totter a trio of kittens, a tiger-striped male, a gray female with white boots and bib, and a coal-black male who looks just like his daddy.

Heather Vogel Frederick

"Hey, everybody," I say softly. "Did you come to say hi? Where's your wife, Elvis?"

Elvis twitches his tail and blinks at me. I lean down and scratch him behind the ears, and he twines himself around my legs with a rumbling purr. "Your turn for day-care duty, is that it? Good job, Dad."

Scooping up the little female kitten, I carry her with me to the storage room. There are only two boxes of blackberry jam left, and I make a mental note to let my mother know the supply is dwindling fast. We made a ton of it last summer, but it's our most popular flavor after Concord grape, and we'll probably run out this weekend.

Giving the kitten one last nuzzle, I set her down and zip my coat, then heft one of the boxes and head back to the farm stand.

"You just missed Megan and Becca," says Emma, as I set it on the counter. "They stopped in to buy some grape jelly. Becca's grandmother wants to take some home to Cleveland with her."

"Shoot! Are they still coming over tonight?" Emma and I have been planning a sleepover for the four of us.

"Yup. They were on their way to the Concord Museum to see the Family Trees exhibit, then they're heading into Boston for lunch and more shopping."

"More shopping?" I pretend to look shocked at this news, and Emma giggles. There's no such thing as too much shopping when it comes to Megan and Becca.

"That reminds me, I should get the boys over to that exhibit," says my mother. "You always loved it when you were their age, Jess."

"I still do," says Emma. "My mother and I went last week."

Family Trees is a big fund-raiser for the museum, and one of Concord's most popular holiday traditions. Each tree—and there are a couple dozen of them of all shapes and sizes on display inside the museum—is decorated to represent a different children's book, which is featured beside it. It's really cool, and every year the lineup changes. The last time I went, they had some of my old favorites like *A Little Princess* and *The Borrowers* and *The Cat in the Hat*, along with new books I'd never heard of but ended up wanting to read after seeing the trees. One of my favorites was *Betty Crocker's Junior Cookbook for Boys and Girls*, because the tree was decorated with miniature cooking tools like rolling pins and pie plates and things, along with small measuring cups and teaspoons and tiny fake food.

"You should get your mom to do a *Betsy-Tacy* tree some year," I tell Emma. "She's on the museum board, right? I'll bet she could get Mrs. Chadwick to help her."

Before she can answer, the pocket of her jeans vibrates. She reaches in and pulls out her cell phone. "It's Darcy," she reports, reading the text message. "He wants you to call him."

I grab two jars of jam and stack them on the almost-empty shelf. "Why doesn't he just call me himself?"

Emma's fingers fly across her cell phone keypad. She pauses briefly, waiting for her brother's reply, then looks up. "He said you didn't answer."

"What?" I pat my coat pockets and the pockets of my jeans. Duh.

Heather Vogel Frederick

Of course I didn't answer. My cell phone is in my bedroom, where I accidentally left it. "Okay, tell him I'll call him in a minute when I'm finished here. Did he say what he wants?"

"No," she replies, shaking her head and sending her long curly hair flying. Emma used to wear her hair short, but she grew it out last year while she was in England. It's just a little past shoulder length now, and it looks good. She's wearing her contact lenses today, too. She finally got them when we started high school. Half the time she wears her glasses anyway, though—I guess they're just easier. She used to have purple ones, but her new frames are dark, almost the same shade as her hair. They make her look older, more sophisticated.

Emma lounges by the woodstove while I finish my task, taking advantage of the lull in business to warm herself with a mug of hot apple cider. She looks especially cute today in her jeans and borrowed farm boots and cable-knit red sweater.

"Can I use your phone?" I ask when I'm done arranging the jam jars.

She hands it over and I text her brother: IT'S JESS. LEFT MY CELL IN THE HOUSE. WHAT'S UP?

He texts me back instantly. GOING SLEDDING AT NASHAWTUC. STEWART 2. CAN U AND EMMA COME?

I relay the message to Emma, and my mother turns and smiles at us. "Sledding?" she says. "That sounds like fun."

Emma and I exchange a glance. Nashawtuc Hill is the best sledding spot in Concord, but we promised to help out here all day.

I shrug. "It's too cold."

"Yeah, it probably wouldn't be any fun," adds Emma. Loyalty is one of her best qualities. "We'd rather stay here with you."

"Really?" My mother looks surprised to hear this. "You'd both rather spend your entire Saturday here instead of having fun with your friends?"

"I love helping out at Half Moon Farm!" Emma exclaims, her brown eyes brimming with sincerity.

My mother laughs. "Emma Hawthorne, you are a terrible liar!" She stretches out her hands with the palms turned up. "Hmm. Farm store or sledding?" she says, looking from one to the other, as if she's pretending to weigh the choices. She grins at us. "Sorry to disappoint you, girls, but I vote sledding."

"Really?" I ask hopefully.

"Really," my mother says. "I don't know what I would have done without you two this morning, but I think I can handle it from here. One condition, though—would you mind taking the boys? They've worked hard this weekend too, and I think they deserve a break."

I make a face. My little brothers might be growing up, but they're still pests. It's a small price to pay for an afternoon of freedom, though. "Okay."

"Good girl. Now go grab some lunch and get changed, and I'll ask your dad to give you a ride."

As we trot across the yard to the house, I turn to Emma. "Savannah says that in Gstaad, they have toboggan runs that go for miles—I mean kilometers. And there are buses at the bottom to take you up

Heather Vogel Frederick

to the top again. It sounds really cool. And she and her parents always have fondue afterward."

"That's nice," Emma replies coolly. She hates it that I'm going to Switzerland for Christmas, even though she's trying really hard not to let it show.

What was I supposed to do when Savannah asked me? Say no? I'm quiet as we climb the stairs to my room, where we change out of our jeans into ski pants. Emma has to borrow an old pair of my dad's because she's a lot taller and sturdier than my mom and me. We're both petite.

Emma has no business being jealous. She got to live in England for a whole year. I'm just going for seven measly days. I know what it's like to feel left out, though, so I've been trying not to rub it in. Still, I'm really excited about this trip. Switzerland! It's a place I've dreamed about ever since I read *Heidi* back in elementary school. I have a vivid picture of it in my mind, but I keep wondering what it will really be like. Will the alps look like the White Mountains, near where my aunt and uncle live? Do people actually yodel? Will there be cows and goats running around everywhere?

I glance across my room at Emma, who's scowling. There's only one way to deal with her when she's like this. It's time to talk books.

"Don't sulk," I tell her. "Please. When Betsy got invited to Milwaukee for Christmas in *Betsy in Spite of Herself*, Tacy was happy for her. She didn't sulk."

Emma sighs gustily. "I'm not sulking! Not really. I'm just

disappointed that we're going to miss spending Christmas Eve together two years in a row."

"Whose fault was that last year?"

She gives me a sheepish grin. "I know, I know. But still."

"Yeah, I know."

Ever since we were little, our families have gotten together on Christmas Eve for dessert. Sometimes Emma and her family come to Half Moon Farm and my mom makes gingerbread with homemade whipped cream and caramel sauce, and sometimes we go over to the Hawthornes' and Mr. Hawthorne makes something fancy, like a bûche de Noël or a trifle. And then we all go to church to see the Christmas pageant.

"So, do you want to go with me to see Mr. Mueller tomorrow?" I ask, changing the subject. "Someone brought in an owl the other day."

Walter Mueller is a wildlife rehabilitator here in Concord. I'm his apprentice. Helping him counts as community service for school, but that's not why I'm doing it. I'm doing it because I totally love it. Last year I helped him with a fox that had been hit by a bicycle. I love animals anyway, and helping ones that are hurt like that, or lost, or orphaned—well, there's no feeling in the world quite like it.

"Sure," says Emma, who I can tell is relieved not to have to hear any more about how totally awesome Switzerland is going to be.

"I promised to help exercise the horses at Colonial this weekend too," I tell her. "Maybe we can stop by afterward and take Blackjack and Cairo for a ride." Emma's not much of a rider, but Cairo is a sweetheart, and we'll most likely be in the indoor arena in this weather.

"Will we have time before the filming at Cassidy's?"

I shrug. "Yeah, we should." Mrs. Sloane-Kinkaid has invited the book club and our friends to help out with the *Cooking with Clementine* holiday special tomorrow.

After we're changed, Emma and I make sandwiches for ourselves and my brothers, and half an hour later we pile into my dad's truck. My mother raps on my window as we start to pull out of the driveway. I roll it down.

"I'm counting on you to watch out for your brothers," she tells me. "Tobogganing can be dangerous."

"Mo-om!" protests Dylan. "We're not babies!"

"I know you're not, honey," she assures him.

"Kids have been sledding on Nashawtuc Hill since the dawn of time," my father reminds her. "Including this kid."

My dad grew up here in Concord. Right here at Half Moon Farm, in fact.

"Yeah," I add. "What he says."

My mother gives me a look. "Don't sass me."

"Okay, okay, I'm sorry! I promise I'll keep an eye on them."

"Thank you." She leans in and kisses my cheek. "Have fun!" She waves as we head off down the driveway.

The parking area at the base of Nashawtuc is crowded. I spot Darcy standing by the Hawthornes' old station wagon as we pull in, and my heart starts beating a little faster.

I still can't believe that Darcy Hawthorne actually likes me. I've known him all my life, and for most of that time he was just Emma's big brother. Then a few years ago everything changed, and I started to notice how cute he was, and how warm his brown eyes were, and how funny and kind he could be. And his smile! Darcy has the best smile.

But I never, ever thought he'd think of me as anything but his little sister's best friend. And for a long time he didn't. And then all of a sudden last summer, he did.

"Hey, Jess," he says, crossing the parking lot to open my door.

"Hey."

He reaches for my hand, and I take it as I hop down onto the snowy ground.

"Glad you could make it." He smiles down at me, and I smile up at him, and the two of us stand there for a moment beaming at each other.

"Darcy and Jess, sitting in a tree, k-i-s-s-i-n-g," chant my brothers from the back seat.

"Shut up!" I tell them, but I'm not really mad.

"Call me if you need a ride home," says my dad, grinning as they clamber out.

"I can drive everybody back, Mr. Delaney," says Darcy.

"That would be great, Darcy. Thanks."

As he heads off, Emma looks around the parking lot. "Where's Stewart? I thought you said he was going to be here."

"He was a second ago," Darcy replies. He shades his eyes against

Heather Vogel Frederick

the sun, which seems to be out to stay now, and squints at the hill. "There he is—over with Third and Ethan." He points them out. "Looks like they're all heading for the top."

"Tell them to wait up!" Darcy calls after Emma as she jogs off. Dylan and Ryan are right behind her, making a beeline for Third's little brother Andrew.

A tiny shiver of happiness goes through me, the way it always does when I'm alone with Darcy. He slips his arm around my waist, and I lean my head against his shoulder. He's tall and I'm short, so I barely reach it. He doesn't kiss me or anything. Darcy never kisses me in public, like when we're out on dates at the movies and stuff, which is fine by me. We're both kind of private about that part of our relationship. Plus, I hate it when couples get all gooshy, as Cassidy puts it. Or what is it that Betsy Ray and her friends call it? Oh yeah, *spoony*. Emma and I love that word. It's perfect, even if it's from 1910.

Darcy and I cross the parking lot and pull the toboggan out of the back of his station wagon, then start up the hill after our friends. It's a long slog to the top. The storm the news has been calling the Thanksgiving Weekend Surprise dumped nearly a foot of snow on Concord yesterday. We stick to the path that's been worn by the other sledders off to the side of the main hill, but the sun has warmed the packed snow just enough to make it a little slick, and I keep sliding backward.

"Come on, Jess, you can do it!" Darcy teases, giving me a push from the rear.

When we finally reach the top, Third pounces on Emma and me. "Where are Becca and Megan?"

"Are you kidding me?" I reply. "Where do you think?"

Third's face falls when we tell him they've gone shopping in Boston. "Who'd choose shopping over this?" he asks, sounding disgusted, and Emma and I look at each other and burst out laughing.

"Race you to the bottom!" says Ethan.

"You're on," Darcy calls back, towing our sled into position.

Ethan, who was short and kind of tubby back in elementary and middle school, joined Alcott High's wrestling team last year. He grew a bunch too, and now he's almost as tall as Darcy and Third and really wiry. Third takes a seat on the front of the toboggan, and my little brothers and Andrew Bartlett climb on behind him. Ethan squats down and readies himself to give them a shove.

I climb onto our toboggan behind Darcy, meanwhile, clasping my arms around his waist. Emma's behind me, and Stewart braces himself with his hands on her back, waiting for the signal to start.

"On your mark, get set, go!" cries Third, and Ethan and Stewart give both sleds a running start. They hop on as we lurch forward, and we hang for one long second on the near-vertical roller-coaster drop that's the top of Nashawtuc Hill. I hold on for dear life as we plunge downward, then whoop and holler with my friends as we rocket toward the bottom, the wind whipping past us as the sleds pick up speed. Halfway down we hit a bump, and instantly we're airborne. I scream and grab Darcy even tighter, feeling Emma's arms do the same

Heather Vogel Frederick

around me. When we touch down, Ethan and Third and my brothers flash past us, pumping their arms in victory. Our toboggan, meanwhile, skids and turns on its side, tumbling us all out into the snow. I lie there for a moment, laughing as I try to catch my breath.

Megan and Becca are totally missing out. No shopping trip could possibly be as fun as this.

My brothers and Third's little brother Andrew holler for more, and we all get to our feet and collect our sleds. The next hour flies by in a blur of ever-faster runs and laughter and snowball fights and heart-pounding climbs back up to the top. I do as I promised and keep an eye on my brothers, but they don't seem to need a whole lot of supervision. Plus, it's not as if they're about to wander off. They're having the time of their lives hanging out with the high school boys.

"Next one's the tiebreaker," says Ethan, as our two sleds coast to a stop again side by side in the field at the bottom of the hill. "Losers buy dinner for everyone from Pirate Pete's."

"Hope you brought your wallet, man, because you are going *down*!" There's a gleam in Darcy's eye as he says this. Emma's brother loves a challenge, especially one that involves sports. "Gimme a second, though, would you? I need some water."

He heads for the parking lot, and Emma and I turn to climb the hill, leaving the boys to drag the heavy sleds. When we reach the top we stand there, panting, as we survey the view.

"We have a Crowd," says Emma suddenly.

"What?" Emma does this a lot—blurts out something random.

Usually it's related to a book. I'm used to it by now, but it can be unnerving to people who don't know her. Especially when they have no clue what she's talking about.

"You know, like Betsy and Tacy. A Crowd—a bunch of friends we hang out with."

I nod. "Welcome to Deep Valley," I tell her, and she grins.

"So if you had to pick, which one of the guys do you think is a Tony, and which one is Joe?"

My eyes narrow as I watch our friends below. "Well, I think Stewart and Darcy are both Joes. I don't know if we have a Tony, though. Zach, maybe?"

"Nah, Zach is Herbert Humphreys."

I start to laugh. "Oh, I *loved* the HHAS, didn't you? When I read that, it reminded me exactly of us back in elementary school."

The HHAS—the Herbert Humphreys Admiration Society—was a club Betsy and her friends founded, back when they were little and all had huge crushes on this kid named Herbert.

"I think Becca Chadwick is a one-woman ZNAS," I tell Emma.

"I don't know, Jess, I think maybe Cassidy's a member too."

"Really?"

She nods. "Something's changed between her and Zach. Watch them tomorrow at the TV filming—you'll see."

Way down at the bottom of the hill, a little figure in red waves to me. It's Maggie Crandall. I wave back. Her parents were my house parents back in eighth grade. They're incredibly nice, and they really helped me that first year at Colonial Academy when I was homesick and didn't feel like I fit in. Especially Mrs. Crandall. I still babysit now and then for Maggie, who's three now. I don't have as much time as I used to, though. I'm juggling a lot this year, between MadriGals, my school's a capella group, and the equestrian team, plus helping Mr. Mueller with his foster animals. Not to mention all my classes.

I'm taking mostly junior- and senior-level courses this year, which is hard, but I love it, especially calculus and AP Physics, my two favorite subjects. I like classics, too. English, not so much. That's more Emma's thing, and I'm just okay at it. I'm working hard at my singing this year too. I washed out in the solo auditions for regionals last year, and I want a chance to redeem myself. I was talking to Becca's grandmother about it at our book club meeting the other night, and she said she'd loan me her copy of the *Betsy-Tacy Songbook*. She says I should think about "Dreaming," one of her favorite songs, for my audition piece.

Becca is going to bring the music over tonight so I can look it over this weekend. I make a mental note to remember to practice "Silver Bells," too—the MadriGals are supposed to sing it at the tree lighting in Monument Square next week.

The boys stagger up over the brow of the hill, and we all take our places again.

"On your mark!" shouts Darcy.

I can tell he wants to win this last run, and not because of the pizza, either. The only person I've ever met who's more competitive than Darcy Hawthorne is Cassidy Sloane. The sun has dipped behind the trees on the horizon, and the wind has picked up. I close my eyes and clasp my arms around Darcy's waist and snuggle against the back of his jacket in an effort to keep warm.

Ethan starts the countdown, and a split second later both toboggans are flying down the hill again.

"Lean forward!" Darcy shouts at us, and as we do I feel our sled surge ahead. Faster and faster it goes, passing my brothers and their teammates.

"Yeah!" shouts Darcy, pumping his fist in the air. "Suckers!"

We hit the bump midway down and go flying again. Right on cue, Emma and I both scream, just as we have on every run so far today. We land again, hard. This time we hit an icy patch, though, and the toboggan wobbles. Darcy struggles to keep us pointing straight ahead, but he pulls too hard on the rope and overcompensates. Behind me, Emma screams again as the sled spins out of control, then veers across the hill and right into the path of our friends. A second later we're upended into the snow.

Everyone scrambles to get out of the way of the oncoming toboggan, but somehow I'm caught in the rope. As I tug on it, I hear my brothers hollering at me. There's real fear in their voices. I fling myself to the side at the last minute, but my entangled leg gets slammed between the two sleds.

For a moment, I don't feel anything at all. And then a noise comes out of me unlike any noise I've ever heard myself make before.

In a flash, Darcy is at my side. "Don't move," he says, as I struggle

Heather Vogel Frederick

to sit up. His face is as white as the snow I'm lying on.

"My leg," I mumble.

"I know." He looks stricken. "I'm so sorry."

Sorry? I want to ask him why, but I can't form the words. I'm confused. I can't think straight. My leg hurts.

Mrs. Crandall runs over to us and drops to her knees beside me in the snow. "Jess, honey, everything's going to be okay."

I gaze at her, puzzled. Why wouldn't it be? Then, in a flash of panic, I struggle to sit up again. Something must have happened to my brothers. "Dylan! Ryan!" I call wildly, as Mrs. Crandall grabs my shoulders and presses me gently back down into the snow. "What happened to them? My mother is going to kill me."

"Your brothers are fine," Mrs. Crandall reassures me. "Lie still now."

Darcy takes off his jacket and spreads it over me. I give him a wobbly smile and he tries to smile back, but it falters. In another moment Emma is beside us too, along with Mr. Crandall. He's on his cell phone, a serious expression on his face.

"Your parents are on their way," he tells me, slipping it back into his pocket.

I hear the distant wail of an ambulance, and I realize suddenly why everyone's so concerned. It's not my brothers, it's *me*. I make one more effort to sit up, but the searing pain in my leg renders me quickly horizontal again.

I need to see my leg. I crane my neck, but Mrs. Crandall and Emma and Darcy are deliberately blocking my view. Shifting a little,

I manage a quick glimpse, then sink back into the snow again, feeling faint. The lower part of my left leg is sticking out at a weird angle.

I've seen a leg like that before. *Where?* The pain is making me foggy.

Lydia! The fox I helped rehabilitate last year. The one who was hit by a bicycle. Her leg looked just like that.

I start to cry.

Lydia's leg looked like that because it was *broken*.

"This is all my fault," I hear Darcy tell Mrs. Crandall. "I never should have agreed to a race." He squeezes my hand. "Does it hurt badly?"

Worse than anything I've ever felt before in my life, I think, but I don't tell him that. Swiping my jacket sleeve across my tear-drenched face, I manage to whisper, "That's not why I'm crying."

Darcy looks puzzled. Emma knows why I'm crying, though. I can see it in her eyes.

I'm crying because I can kiss the trip to Switzerland good-bye.

Heather Vogel Frederick

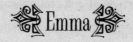
Emma

"For a girl who wants to be a writer, it might be educational to spend Christmas in Milwaukee."
—Betsy in Spite of Herself

I stare at Jess's left leg, which is propped on the sofa in the keeping room at Half Moon Farm. Sugar and Spice, her family's two Shetland sheepdogs, are snuggled up on either side of her like furry bookends, looking appropriately mournful. They're also keeping a sharp eye on the strange beast wrapped around Jess's leg. It's a cast—a light blue one. Blue is Jess's favorite color.

"I still can't believe you broke your leg," I tell her.

Jess nods sadly. "Me neither."

She's been unusually quiet since I got here, and I'm beginning to wonder if maybe her parents were wrong about her wanting company tonight. Maybe I should go home. It's hard to tell if Jess is so listless because her leg hurts, or because she's upset that her trip to Switzerland got canceled. A little bit of both, probably.

"It's kind of like in *Downtown*, isn't it?" I ask.

Jess's forehead wrinkles. "Huh?"

I know she hates it when I do this, but I can't help it—for me, life and books are intertwined, and one is always reminding me of the other. "You know, in *Betsy and Tacy Go Downtown*, when Betsy has that tobogganing accident."

She grunts. "Except she didn't break her leg, she just sprained her ankle."

"Enter Mrs. Ray," says Mrs. Delaney, who must have overheard us from the kitchen. She bustles in carrying a tray with a couple of mugs—Half Moon Farm's hot cider, from the smell of it—and a big bowl of popcorn. "And Betsy's mother is absolutely right, by the way—none of us mothers like tobogganing. Too risky." She nods at Jess's leg. "I rest my case."

She sets the tray down on the coffee table and nudges Spice out of the way as she squeezes in next to Jess on the sofa. "How are you doing, honey?" she asks, reaching over and smoothing Jess's blond hair.

Jess lifts a shoulder. "Okay, I guess."

"I know you're disappointed about the trip, but you do understand that it's absolutely out of the question, don't you?"

Jess grunts again.

"Your father and I just don't think it would be good for you—that long international flight, and traipsing through airports on crutches—"

"That's what wheelchairs are for," mutters Jess.

"Be reasonable, sweetheart. It's just too much! You need to focus

Heather Vogel Frederick

on getting plenty of rest and not overdoing things for the next six weeks. Don't you want your leg to heal properly?"

"Savannah said I could come along anyway, even if I can't ski." Jess is not giving up without a fight. She can be really stubborn when she wants to.

Her mother sighs. "The answer is no, Jess. You're staying home for the holidays. I'm sure you'll be invited again sometime."

My face is arranged to look properly regretful, but it's a struggle to keep from smiling. Jess will be here in Concord with me over winter break!

The thing is, between Jess attending Colonial Academy and me living in England last year, plus both of us having boyfriends now, the two of us just don't spend as much time together as we used to. We're still best friends and everything, but I really miss "us"—I miss just hanging out having fun. Winter break will be the perfect opportunity for that.

My cell phone buzzes again. I don't even have to look to know it's a text from my brother.

After the accident this afternoon, Darcy drove me and the twins back to our house while Jess's parents went with her in the ambulance. I've never seen my brother so upset. He was planning to skip foot-ball practice—well, football conditioning, because nobody, not even tough-as-nails Coach Elliott, would make a team practice outside on a weekend like this one—but my parents made him go, to try and take his mind off things. He was still at the gym when Mr. Delaney stopped by to pick up Dylan and Ryan.

"I'm happy to keep the boys overnight for you if you'd like," my mother told him.

"Thanks, Phoebe, but it's really not necessary," he replied. "Jess is going to be just fine. She's a very fortunate girl—it's a simple break, and they had her leg set and in a cast in no time."

"What about our sleepover?" I asked.

Mr. Delaney shook his head regretfully. "Not going to happen, Em. Shannon wants to make sure Jess gets plenty of rest, which definitely won't happen at a sleepover. And we're not sure about the TV filming tomorrow either—she wants to go, of course, but we're going to wait and see how she's doing in the morning."

"Okay," I said, but I couldn't keep the disappointment out of my voice.

"Shannon did say it's fine if you and Megan and Becca still want to come over later and watch a movie, though," Mr. Delaney continued. "Jess could definitely use some cheering up, as long as you're not too rowdy."

I left home before my brother returned from practice, and he's been texting me nonstop ever since I arrived here at the Delaneys'. Jess lost her cell phone someplace—she thinks probably it was in the pocket of the ski pants she was cut out of at the emergency room.

"Darcy's worried that maybe you're mad at him," I tell her, glancing at his latest message on my phone and grabbing a handful of popcorn.

"What?" she says, finally showing signs of life. "Are you kidding me? Of course I'm not mad at him!"

Heather Vogel Frederick

I point at her leg. "He thinks this is all his fault."

"Maybe you should call and talk to him," her mother suggests.

"Can't he just come over?" Jess replies. "He could watch the movie with Emma and Megan and Becca and me."

A worried pleat appears between the wings of Mrs. Delaney's dark eyebrows. "I'm not sure, honey. Are you feeling up to it?"

Jess nods vigorously. "Absolutely. Please, can he?"

"Well, I guess there's room for one more. But I'm going to kick everybody out right after the movie, okay?"

"Okay."

As she heads back to the kitchen, the keeping room door flies open and Jess's brothers tumble in, carrying Magic Markers. "Can we sign your leg now?" asks Dylan.

"You said we could as soon as Emma got here," adds Ryan.

Jess nods. "Emma gets to go first, though."

"How come?" Dylan demands.

"Because she's my best friend." Jess smiles at me. I smile back, relieved to see that she's acting more like herself. I guess the prospect of seeing Darcy again did the trick.

"But we're your brothers!" Ryan protests.

"BFBB," says Jess loftily, passing me a Magic Marker.

Best friends before boyfriends. And brothers, too, apparently.

Dylan's eyes narrow. "What does that mean?"

"None of your beeswax," Jess tells him. I bend over her leg and start to write.

Violets are red,

Roses are blue,

You broke your leg,

You Rupert, you.

I sign it and add a little heart after my name.

Dylan peers over my shoulder and grins. "Rooooopert Loooomis!" he crows.

"Mooooo," adds Ryan, and the two of them collapse on the floor laughing.

Jess and I smile at each other. "In a weird way, I kind of miss Rupert," she says.

"Yeah, I know what you mean."

Rupert Loomis is this guy I met in England last year. He lived in the same village that I did, and we went to the same school. He's kind of hard to describe. Before Rupert, I thought Kevin Mullins was the biggest dork I'd ever met. But Rupert isn't just a dork; he's in a category all his own. Darcy called him Eeyore, because he has this deep, mournful voice and kind of shuffles around all the time. Rupert lives with his great-aunt, which might be part of the reason he's so weirdly old-fashioned. He's at boarding school this year, which I think will be really good for him. I don't know if it's had much impact yet, though, judging by the mail he's been sending me. He writes these long, formal letters, handwritten in real ink from a real fountain pen, on paper engraved with his family crest. There's

Heather Vogel Frederick

nobody in Concord like Rupert, that's for sure. He's one of a kind.

"Boys!" Mrs. Delaney pokes her head back into the room, and the dogs prick up their ears. "I think I hear a car in the driveway. Go see who it is."

Sugar and Spice race out of the room on the twins' heels. A minute later the four of them race back in again, followed by Megan and Becca and Mrs. Wong. Megan's mother isn't in the room two seconds before she spots *Rudolph the Red-Nosed Reindeer* on the coffee table.

She frowns. "Girls, you're not planning to watch that silly old thing, are you?"

Megan's mom gets kind of nuts this time of year. She hates what she calls the "headlong rush toward Christmas." I agree with her at least partly, because I can't stand it when stores start playing holiday music at Halloween either. But what with the snow and everything, Rudolph seemed like the perfect choice for tonight. Jess and I have watched it together every year since we were practically in diapers. We love everything about it—the clunky animation, the goofy songs, Yukon Cornelius and that ridiculous Abominable Snowman, and especially Hermie, the elf who wants to be a dentist.

"Of course not," I tell her, whisking it out of sight. "The twins got it out, didn't you, boys?"

I give them Winona eyes, and for once they get the message.

"Yeah, it was us," says Dylan, managing to look a little hangdog. Ryan nods too.

"Thanksgiving is a time to be grateful for all the good things in our lives," says Mrs. Wong.

"I'm grateful for Rudolph," says Ryan with a mischievous smile, and I see the corners of Jess's lips quirk up.

"Thanksgiving is a wonderful noncommercial holiday," Mrs. Wong continues, warming to her topic. "It's not just the welcome mat to the Christmas season."

"You mean we shouldn't wipe our feet on it?" asks Dylan, wide-eyed with feigned innocence.

"That's my point exactly, boys!" exclaims Mrs. Wong. "Savor it, don't step on it."

Megan looks like she's counting to ten under her breath. She gets embarrassed by her mother, but we all just think she's funny.

Especially the twins, who chase each other around the room shouting, "Savor it, don't step on it!" This gets Sugar and Spice all riled up, and they race around in circles, barking, until Mrs. Delaney shouts at them all to knock it off. As the boys charge out the door, the dogs hop back up onto the sofa next to Jess again, panting.

"Lily, why don't you join me in the kitchen while I heat up some more cider," suggests Mrs. Delaney.

Mrs. Wong isn't done being Mrs. Wong, though. She reaches into the backpack she uses for a purse and produces a small amber bottle. Holding it up, she says, "You might add some of this to Jess's food while her leg is healing. It's flaxseed oil. Very beneficial. It has lots of vitamins and omega-three oils—fifty percent more than fish oil, in fact, and no fishy aftertaste."

"Ah," says Mrs. Delaney politely. I can tell she's trying not to smile. "Yes, that fishy aftertaste is off-putting, isn't it?"

Behind Mrs. Wong's back, Jess is waving her arms wildly at her mother and mouthing the word *NO*. Becca and I are doubled over in silent laughter. By now, the muscles in Mrs. Delaney's jaws are twitching as she struggles to keep her composure.

I take pity on her and change the subject. "How was Boston?" I ask Megan and Becca.

They flop onto the chairs across from Jess and me.

"Amazing," says Becca. "We spent most of our time hunting for vintage at Sweet Repeats—you know, that consignment shop on Newbury Street we like? And then Gigi and my grandmother took us to tea at the Four Seasons."

"Fancy," says Mrs. Delaney. "How did it compare to the Pump Room in Bath?"

"Nothing compares to the Pump Room, but it was still pretty awesome," Becca replies. "And they had their holiday decorations up already too. See?" She pulls out her cell phone and taps on the screen, then passes it to Jess and me.

"Wow," says Jess, looking at the picture. "Cool tree." I nod in agreement.

Mrs. Wong shakes her head. "Two whole days of shopping," she says mournfully. "Whatever happened to spending a quiet Thanksgiving weekend with your family?"

Mrs. Delaney winks at us. "Come on, Lily, bring your flaxseed oil and your lovely self out to the kitchen and I'll fix you some hot cider." She shuts the door firmly behind them, and the four of us explode with laughter.

"Flaxseed oil?" Becca gasps. "That's *disgusting!*"

"Tell me about it," says Megan, who's been pretty quiet since she got here. "She's sneaking it into everything at our house these days. I caught her drizzling some on my cereal this morning."

Jess shudders, and I look over at her. "Maybe you should drink a little before Darcy gets here. You look like you could use a few vitamins."

"Darcy's on his way over?" Becca's voice rises an octave. "We need to do something fast—you look awful!"

It's true. Jess's face is pale, there are dark circles under her eyes, and her hair is kind of matted down on one side. She could really use a shower. Still, I wouldn't be quite so blunt. Not that a little thing like that ever stopped Becca.

"Thanks a bunch!" snaps Jess. "In case you forgot, I just broke my leg!"

"Quit whining," Becca replies. "This is your boyfriend we're talking about. We need to get you fixed up." She gives Sugar and Spice a stern look and points to the floor. "Move, doggies."

Jess's shelties obediently hop down off the sofa. What is it about Becca that makes everybody—dogs included—jump to do her bidding? Is it some queen bee thing? Or former queen bee thing?

Heather Vogel Frederick

"The first thing we have to do is get you out of that hideous outfit you're wearing and into something prettier," Becca orders, frowning at Jess's old green turtleneck. It's the same one she had on earlier today when we went tobogganing. "I know we can't do anything about those sweatpants, but you must have nicer tops." She looks over at Megan. "Fashion intervention time. Go see what you can round up in Jess's closet. And maybe bring down some accessories, too."

The minute Megan leaves the room, Becca lowers her voice to a whisper. "Simon broke up with her last night," she tells us.

"*What?*" I gape at her. "Really?"

Becca nods. "She's trying to hide it, but she's really upset. Be extra nice to her, okay? And don't tell her I told you—she doesn't want a whole lot of people to know yet."

Jess and I exchange a glance. Poor Megan! No wonder she's looking subdued. I can't imagine how I'd feel if Stewart did that to me.

Becca cocks her head and gives Jess a once-over. "Bring me Jess's hairbrush, would you, Emma?" She wrinkles her nose. "And better bring a toothbrush, too."

"Hey!" Jess says again. "Cut me a little slack!"

Becca smiles and reaches for her purse. "You'll thank me when it's over," she says, pulling out a small zippered bag full of makeup.

Upstairs, Megan is rummaging in Jess's closet. She takes one look at my face and sighs. "Becca told you, didn't she?"

I nod guiltily. "I'm so sorry, Megan."

She turns away. "It's hard, you know? He told me in an *e-mail,* Emma!"

I cross the room and put my arm around her shoulder. She leans her head against mine for a minute. "I really, really like Simon," she says softly. "And I'm really, really mad at him for doing this to me."

"I understand." Sometimes that's all you can say when a friend is hurting.

"I keep thinking maybe he'll change his mind," Megan continues.

"Maybe he will."

She shrugs. "Maybe. But probably not." She straightens up. "No point stewing about it tonight, right? We're supposed to be here to cheer Jess up, not the other way around."

"There's plenty of cheer to go around," I tell her. "Feel free to take your share."

That gets a hint of a smile. "Thanks, Emma."

Back downstairs, Becca doesn't even turn around to look at me, just snaps her fingers and holds out her hand. I slap the hairbrush into it, of course. Like I said, there's something about Becca that commands obedience. Her mother's the same way. My dad says Mrs. Chadwick was an army general in a former life.

"Take off that revolting thing you're wearing and put this on," Becca tells Jess, nabbing the fresh top from Megan. "You should never wear that shade of green—it makes you look like you're nauseous. Hurry! I think I hear a car in the driveway."

Jess does as she's told too, naturally.

Heather Vogel Frederick

"Much better," says Becca approvingly.

The pink sweater that Megan picked out gives Jess a little color, and so does the blush that Becca's already applied to her cheeks. Jess's hair, which she usually wears in a thick braid down her back, is loose, and Becca brushes it so that its soft waves fall over her shoulders, then hands her the toothbrush, which I've already spread with toothpaste.

"Spit bowl!" Becca orders, and I dart into the kitchen.

When Jess is finished, Becca takes the toothbrush and bowl from her and hands them to me.

"What am I supposed to do with this?" I ask grumpily, holding it at arm's length.

She ignores me and passes Jess the earrings that Megan brought downstairs—a pair of silver hoops with pink beads threaded on them. As a final touch, Becca reaches over and adds a sheer layer of pink lip gloss. "What do you think, girls?" she asks, leaning back and surveying her handiwork.

Jess bats her eyes at Megan and me. She hardly needs mascara, because she has amazingly long eyelashes. I'm as envious of them as Betsy Ray is of her little sister Margaret's. Some people have all the luck.

"Puny," I tell her, which is the Ray family's hired girl Anna Swenson's favorite word of praise. "Very puny."

"Definitely puny," says Becca, smiling at me. For a moment I'm surprised that she picked up on the literary reference. But then I remember that Becca read the Betsy-Tacy books first. I guess sometimes I underestimate her.

There's a knock at the back door, followed by the sound of male voices in the kitchen, and a split second later the keeping room door opens and my brother comes in. To my surprise, Stewart is with him, along with Ethan and Third.

"It looks like the Crowd is gathering," says Mrs. Delaney, who comes in behind them with the twins. She whisks the spit bowl out of my hand and levels a glance at Jess, whose cheeks are glowing even pinker now that my brother is here. "I guess I don't have to ask how you feel about the extra company. Well, the more the merrier, right? There's certainly plenty of cider to go around, and I'll make another batch of popcorn."

"Don't forget the flaxseed oil!" I add, cracking Jess and Megan and Becca up again.

The boys don't get the joke, but they're too busy hovering around Jess to care. Darcy lowers himself gingerly onto the couch beside her and gives her a hug, and then he and the other boys take turns signing her cast. When they're done, my brother whispers something in her ear—I can't hear what—and she nods and smiles up at him. He puts his arm around her shoulder and pulls her close, kissing the top of her head.

That's the most PDA I've ever seen between the two of them, and it gives me an odd feeling. It's still kind of weird to think of my brother as my best friend's boyfriend. I know Becca feels the same way when she sees me and Stewart together—I've seen the look on her face.

The boys beg to hear about the ambulance ride, and then they take turns telling us all the gross details about the times they've broken

Heather Vogel Frederick

their arms or legs or collarbones or fingers or whatever, and then we bring in more chairs and pillows for the movie. Stewart settles into the oversize armchair next to me. We're a little squished, but I don't mind. It's not a hardship being close to Stewart.

We let Dylan and Ryan watch the movie with us, which is a mistake because they're so wound up from the day's excitement that they can't sit still, and they keep jumping up and showing off. We have fun anyway, singing along as loudly as we possibly can to drown them out, and saying all the lines we can remember, and my brother does his hilarious "NOBODY wants a CHARLIE in the box!" impression when Rudolph and his friends get to the island of misfit toys.

I'm so glad to be home again! Living in England last year was amazing, and I loved every minute of it—staying in Ivy Cottage, with its stone walls and thatched roof; riding the red double-decker bus to school every day in Bath; all the trips we took, to places like the Lake District and London and Scotland and everywhere else; and especially the friends I made. Even Rupert. But Dorothy is right, there's no place like home. Concord is where I belong. It's my Deep Valley, and this is my Crowd!

The phone rings out in the kitchen just as the movie is finishing.

"It's for you, honey," says Mrs. Delaney, bringing the receiver in to Jess. "It's your aunt Bridget."

"Hey, Aunt Bridget," says Jess. I can tell her aunt must be worried about her, because Jess keeps saying, "No really, I'm fine," and then she's quiet for a bit, and then—

"MOM!" she hollers, bringing Mrs. Delaney running from the kitchen.

"What is it?" she cries. "Is it your leg? Are you okay?"

"Aunt Bridget wants us to come to New Hampshire for Christmas!" Jess tells her, her eyes sparkling with excitement.

"Oh, for heaven's sake, you nearly—here, give me that phone." Her mother takes the receiver out to the kitchen, and we hear the low murmur of her voice. She reappears a minute later in the doorway.

"Well? Can we?" begs Jess.

"I have to check with your dad when he gets back in from the barn, but I don't see any reason why not. Since Josh took Thanksgiving off, he's scheduled to work that weekend, and I think he's ready to try handling things all by himself around here." She smiles. "It would be fun, wouldn't it? I can't think of a better place to spend Christmas than with your aunt and uncle and your cousin Felicia."

Jess looks over at me and pretends to stick her finger down her throat. She's not particularly fond of Felicia.

"Besides," her mother continues, "I don't think we've taken an actual vacation over the holidays since we inherited the farm."

"See? Who needs Switzerland?" says my brother, tousling Jess's hair.

Trust him to be supportive. Mr. Perfect Pants is making me feel like a big Grinch for feeling so deflated. Jess won't be here in Concord with me for winter break after all. I don't say anything, of course. After all she's been through today, Jess deserves a little happiness.

"I hate to break up the party, but I think it's time to call it a night,"

Heather Vogel Frederick

says Mrs. Delaney. "You all have a big day tomorrow, and Jess needs to get her rest if she's going to make it to Clementine's filming."

We mill around for a while finding our coats and saying good-bye to Jess and the Delaneys and one another, then head outside to the cars. Stewart must have worked some sort of magic or made a deal ahead of time with my brother, because everybody else piles into our family's station wagon for the ride home, and I end up with Stewart all to myself.

"Milady," he says, opening the door of his father's sedan with a sweeping bow.

"Stop it!" I protest. "You're acting like Rupert Loomis."

He grins. I still can't believe that Stewart thought I liked Rupert. That only lasted until he actually met him, fortunately.

"How come you're driving your dad's car?" I ask. Stewart usually borrows his mother's car when we hang out.

"Um," he says, a funny look on his face. "I guess—that is—my dad needed the SUV. He had this thing he had to go to."

"Oh," I reply. "Okay." It's not like Stewart to be evasive, but I figure he has his reasons. Mrs. Chadwick's birthday is coming up, so maybe it has something to do with that.

We drive along in silence for a while, the headlights revealing snow piled up in drifts on either side of the nearly deserted streets. It feels strange, not like Thanksgiving at all.

"So have you written your column yet?" I ask him. Stewart is the editor of our school newspaper this year, and the editor always gets to write a column on any subject that strikes his or her fancy. Stewart's having fun with it, and it turns out he's really good at writing humor.

"Uh-huh," he says.

"What's it about?"

"The pitfalls and perils of filling out college applications."

"Sounds good," I tell him. "I can't wait to read it."

He smiles at me. "I'll give it to you tomorrow to take a look at."

Stewart and I always edit each other's work. We can trust each other to be honest without being harsh. My dad says you have to have at least one person, besides your editor, who's willing to be straight with you about your writing. Stewart's that person for me, and I'm that person for him.

As he pulls into our driveway, I snicker.

"What?" he says.

"Remember that night a couple of years ago when we were standing here, and my brother and Kyle Anderson drove in and aimed the headlights right at us, then honked and cheered?"

Stewart gives me a rueful grin. "Yeah. I'd finally worked up the courage to try and kiss you that night, and Darcy scared me off for months." He shuts off the engine and turns to face me. "I'm not too scared now, though."

His lips are cold, and I know mine must be too. Plus, my nose is starting to run. We break away and both of us start to laugh.

"So much for romance," says Stewart, reaching into the glove compartment for a tissue.

Heather Vogel Frederick

"It's freezing out here!" I reply in mock indignation, taking it from him and wiping my nose. "Sorry, but it's way too cold for spooning."

"For *what*?"

"Uh, spooning. It's from—"

"Let me guess. Betsy-Tacy, right?"

I nod. Stewart shakes his head, but he's smiling. He gets the way my mind works, because his works the same way. We've talked about it, and both of us agree that we can't help it—when we read a book, it's like we're actually living in the world that the author has created, and we start viewing our lives from the point of view of the characters.

That's what's so great about books, though, the way a writer can make a character seem so real to you. And that's what's so great about having a boyfriend who really understands that.

Stewart leans over and gives me another quick kiss. "See you tomorrow at Cassidy's."

"Okay. Don't forget your sweater."

"Not a chance. You're going to faint when you see it."

I smile at him. "Not if you faint first." Cassidy's mom's TV special this year is going to feature fun Christmas party themes—white elephant gifts, holiday karaoke, ugly sweaters, that sort of thing. We're supposed to wear the wildest, most hideous Christmas sweater we can find.

I hop out of the car and wave good-bye, then slip inside the back door. Pip, our sweet golden Labrador, hears me enter and scrabbles across the kitchen floor in a lather of excitement. You can always count on your dog to be the first to greet you when you come home.

For a moment, I half expect to see Melville trail in behind him, but of course he doesn't. Our cat's been gone since early October. My father found him sleeping in a patch of sun in his office one afternoon, only he wasn't sleeping. Mom told us we shouldn't be sad, that Melville had a long and happy life just like Mrs. Bergson, but I really miss him a lot. We all do. Pip is great company, but he doesn't snuggle the way Melville did. He's way too big to fit in my lap, for one thing—not that that stops him from trying.

Surprisingly, it's my mom who misses Melville the most. He was always kind of my dad's cat, but after he was gone my mother moped around for weeks. She still hasn't let us put his kitty basket away. It's by the radiator in the living room, filled with Pip's chew toys. At least Melville waited until after we came home from England. It would have been much harder to lose him while we were away.

I lean down and scratch Pip's ears, then kiss him on the nose. "I'm glad you're not going anywhere, boy. Especially not to dumb old New Hampshire for Christmas."

I hear voices in the living room, and I hang up my jacket and go to check in with my parents. They're having a spirited discussion about the recent crop of Jane Austen mash-ups—novels mixing her plots with werewolves and vampires and zombies and stuff. My father loathes them and calls them "an abomination," but my mother, oddly enough, since she's the real Jane Austen freak in the family, loves them. She says it's a fresh and fun way to keep Jane relevant, and to keep young readers interested in her books.

"If they read the mash-up, they're eventually going to want to read the original," she says. "Otherwise, they're not going to get the jokes, and everybody wants to be in on the jokes."

I tell my parents that Darcy will be home as soon as he's done dropping everybody off, and assure them that Jess is fine.

"Well, except for the fact that she's going to New Hampshire for Christmas," I add morosely.

"How fun for her!" exclaims my father.

I lift a shoulder. "Yeah, but not for me."

My mother gives me a keen look. "You were looking forward to hanging out with her this year, weren't you?" she says, and I nod. My mother's always been able to read me like a book.

"Do you want to hang out with us?" asks my father, patting the sofa cushion beside him. "We could watch a movie."

I smile and shake my head. "No thanks," I tell him. "I think I'll go read."

The truth is, I just feel like being alone for a while. And the best place to be alone is in my bedroom.

I love my room. I love the old-fashioned wallpaper covered with yellow roses that my mother and I hung after we read *Anne of Green Gables*, and I love the bird's-eye maple bookcase filled with all my favorite books, just waiting there on the shelves for me like old friends. And Mrs. Bergson's skates! She wore them when she won the Olympic gold, and she left them to me when she passed away. They don't look like much, but they're one of my most treasured possessions. Mom and I found this cool old curio cabinet at a flea market, and the silver blades glint at me from behind its glass doors, reminding me of the special friendship that Mrs. Bergson and I shared.

More than anything, though, I love the rolltop desk that used to belong to Mom's grandfather. It's the perfect desk for a writer, because it has all sorts of little drawers and compartments for supplies. Plus, if I don't want anybody messing with my stuff, I can pull the top closed and lock it with a key.

Mom has started calling it "Uncle Keith's trunk" in honor of the Betsy-Tacy books, after the trunk that Betsy Ray's mother gives her to use as a desk in *Betsy and Tacy Go Downtown*. Unlike Betsy, though, I don't actually write at my desk very often. Mostly, I write curled up on my bed, just as I'm about to do now.

I turn off my cell phone, which is a trick I learned from my dad. It works wonders. Without the constant interruptions of text messages and calls, I can focus a lot better. It's just me and my pen and paper and a steady stream of thoughts.

I have to finish my boring article about our high school's boring cafeteria renovation so that I'll be ready to swap it for Stewart's column tomorrow, plus I owe letters to Rupert and to Bailey Jacobs, my pen pal from Wyoming. Then, if there's still time, I might work on some poetry, or the story I started last week.

But first, some inspiration.

I read the opening stanzas of Tennyson's New Year's poem "Ring Out, Wild Bells," which I stumbled on in *Betsy in Spite of Herself*. I tracked the rest of it down in a book on my mother's poetry shelf.

Heather Vogel Frederick

Ring out, wild bells, to the wild sky,
The flying cloud, the frosty light;
The year is dying in the night;
Ring out, wild bells, and let him die.

Ring out the old, ring in the new,
Ring, happy bells, across the snow:
The year is going, let him go;
Ring out the false, ring in the true.

There's more, but the first bit is my favorite, especially the first stanza. It gets me every time. I love the way a poem can pierce my heart like that—all it takes is just the right words in just the right order and *bang!* I'm a total goner. I puzzle over it for a while—is it the repetition of the word "wild" that sings to me? Or the alliteration of "flying" and "frosty"? I can't exactly put my finger on it. There's a mystery to poetry, which is part of what makes it so irresistible.

I set the poem aside finally and rifle through the piles on my desk—even with all the drawers and compartments, I can't always manage to keep things organized—until I find the notebook that I keep for things I want to remember. Fragments of poems like this one, or great quotes about writing, or names for characters or bits of dialogue I overhear or passages from books that I'm reading—stuff like that. Lately, most of those passages have been from the

Betsy-Tacy books, because I've spent so much of my fall with them. I've read the entire series twice.

I still can't believe I'd never heard of these books. Finding them was like finding buried treasure. I've loved all the books that our book club has read—especially *Pride and Prejudice,* which is probably my all-time favorite—but Betsy's world is almost like an alternate reality. Some books you feel like you could walk into and instantly be friends with all the characters, and that's how the Betsy-Tacy books feel to me. Not that I couldn't be friends with, say, Elizabeth Bennet, but I'd probably be a little intimidated by her wit. Betsy, on the other hand, well, let's just say that anyone who has a weakness for "fresh new notebooks and finely sharpened pencils" is a friend of mine.

If Betsy showed up at Alcott High, we'd work on the school newspaper together, and we'd hang out and debate the relative merits of Tony and Joe, and she'd stress about the space between her front teeth and her straight hair that she's always desperately trying to curl with her Magic Wavers curlers, and I'd stress about my curly brown hair that I'd so much rather was thick and blond like Jess's or silky straight like Megan's, and about whether I'm getting chunky again because I'm not skating as much this year as I used to, now that Eva Bergson is gone.

And then we'd go out for a banana split at Heinz's. Or in Concord's case, at Kimball's Farm.

Plus, Betsy is a total kindred spirit because she longs to be a writer, the same way I do. And she articulates that longing—she talks about it and thinks about it. Or at least Maud Hart Lovelace makes her talk

Heather Vogel Frederick

about it and think about it. Like in *Heaven to Betsy,* when Betsy wonders what life would be like without her writing. I glance down at the sentence I added to my notebook last month: "Writing filled her life with beauty and mystery, gave it purpose ... and promise."

That's *exactly* how I feel.

There's another Betsy quote from *Betsy and Joe* on the opening page of my notebook, as a reminder: "She had already discovered that poems and stories came most readily from the deep well of solitude."

The deep well of solitude. I lie back on my pile of pillows and gaze around my room, filled with contentment. The lamp by my bed casts a deep pool of light, setting the yellow roses on the walls aglow. This is my deep well of solitude, right here.

Turning the pages in my notebook, I savor more of my favorite bits. Maud has a gift for quick descriptions, like when she writes about the "snowy Niagara" of an old man's beard. Just two words, but they instantly bring to mind a picture of that flowing white beard. Perfect! And when she describes Mrs. Ray as "slim as a breeze," or the letters that fly back and forth between Betsy and her friend Tib "like fat, gossipy birds." I look over at my bedside table, where Bailey's latest letter to me from Wyoming is awaiting my reply. Perfect again! And another time, in *Betsy and Tacy Go Downtown,* she writes, "Like a kettle boiling over, the room foamed with laughter."

I close the notebook with a deep sigh. Maybe, just maybe, if I work hard enough at it, I'll be a great writer someday like Maud, and like Jane Austen and Louisa May Alcott and all the other authors I admire.

I glance at the clock. It's nearly ten o'clock. I'd better get a move on. I open up the netbook my friends got me last year when I went to England so we could video-chat, and plod my way through the article about the cafeteria renovation. There's just no way to spark up such a dull topic, so I have to lower my literary standards and settle for accuracy, which is something at least. After that, I type a short letter to Rupert (short because I don't want to encourage him too much) and print it out, and then I write another letter to his aunt—handwritten this time, because she's kind of old-fashioned and I want to make a good impression, especially since she's looking into getting a story of mine published. Finally I write a "fat, gossipy bird" to Bailey, filling her in on the weekend's activities. I don't put it in an envelope yet, though—I'll add some more tomorrow night, after the ugly sweater party. I'm sure there will be some fun details to share with her from that.

By the time I'm done, it's ten thirty. I hear Darcy and my parents come upstairs, and then a soft tap on the door. My mother pokes her head in.

"Don't stay up too late, sweetie," she says, as Pip pushes his way past her and heads for his dog bed in the corner. "You want to look fresh for Clementine's show tomorrow."

"I won't, Mom," I assure her, and she blows me a kiss and closes the door again.

But I've still got the itch to write. So I do, adding a new chapter to the story I've been working on this fall, about an English village and all the odd characters who live there. After that, I fiddle with a poem that's been

Heather Vogel Frederick

giving me fits. I can feel it circling my mind like a bright fish that I can see but can't quite catch. It's frustrating, but that's the way it goes with poetry, at least for me. Sometimes, all a writer can do is keep fishing.

When I finally crawl under the covers and turn out the light, it's really late, after midnight, and the house is completely silent. I lie there in the dark, thinking about my to-do list—that's another way Betsy and I are alike, we both love to make lists—which includes shopping for Secret Santa gifts. Eventually I roll over and pull the comforter up under my chin, and just as I'm about to drift off, I remember my cell phone. I decide to check it, just in case Stewart called. I grope around on my nightstand for it and turn it on. Nothing from Stewart, but there's a text message from Jess: AUNT BRIDGET CALLED BACK. WANT TO GO TO NEW HAMPSHIRE WITH US FOR CHRISTMAS?

I sit bolt upright in the dark. My fingers start to fly across the keypad, but then I stop. Jess just broke her leg; she needs her sleep. I can't text her now. I'll have to wait until morning. And I'll have to wait until morning to ask my parents, too.

I hug my knees in excitement. Christmas in the White Mountains! That would be so amazing!

There's just one thing, though.

We've always spent Christmas together as a family. It's my mom's favorite holiday, and kind of a big deal at our house.

There's no way my parents are going to let me go. Not in a million years.

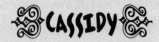

CASSIDY

"It was fortunate that November was cold, with snow on the ground and an icy bite in the air, for the Rays had to create some early Christmas spirit."

—*Betsy and Joe*

"Allegra! I'm open!"

My teammate's saucer pass lands on my stick perfectly. I fake left, dodging the Yankee Clipper defense. The blades of my skates slice across the ice, their driving rhythm echoed in every beat of my heart. The roar of the crowd fuels my will, and I push myself even harder, feeling the adrenaline kick in as I race toward the far end of the rink. The Lady Shawmuts are ahead at this tournament, and if we win this one, we take home the trophy.

And I really, really want that trophy.

The sound of the crowd fades away as I draw closer to the goal. My world shrinks to one thing and one thing only: taking the shot. The Clipper wing rushes me, but I brush her off and circle around, watching for my opening. There it is! I fire a snap shot, smacking down so hard on the ice I feel the impact in my bones. The puck goes flying, and the

Heather Vogel Frederick

goalie launches herself toward it . . . reaches for it—and misses! It's in!

"Yes!" I jab my stick in the air and glance at the clock. My goal tied the score; all we need is one more to win. It's going to be tough to do with less than a minute to go, though.

Our coach gives the signal for a time-out. The ref blows the whistle, and I skate over to join my teammates, glancing up into the stands as I pass our cheering section.

"Way to go, Cassidy!" shouts my sister.

My whole family is here, along with Courtney's boyfriend, Grant, who waggles the tassels on his red-and-white-striped scarf at me. Chloe is dressed in our team colors too, and she's bouncing up and down on Stanley's lap, waving her red-and-white pennant wildly.

My baby sister has been really, really good this weekend. Tournaments can be pretty grueling; we've been here since early Friday morning. Fortunately, there's an indoor pool at the hotel, and between games my mom and stepfather have taken turns going back with her for swims, naps, a little TV—whatever it takes to keep her happy. It can't be easy for a toddler to sit still for hours and hours, watching a bunch of people she doesn't know play hockey.

It can't be easy for anyone who's not a complete hockey nut, actually. None of my book club friends are here this weekend, although two of my Chicks with Sticks players came down with their families to watch their older sisters compete. Little Katie Angelino spots me and comes rushing down to the edge of the rink, and we high-five each other through the Plexiglas barrier as I pass by. Katie's doing really well this fall. Last year, when she first joined the club, she could barely stand up on her skates, but now she's one of my rising stars. I've nicknamed her "The Mosquito" because she's scrappy and strong and persistent, and I'm encouraging her parents to let her try out for a Pee Wee team.

Emma texted me last night about the tobogganing accident. Poor Jess. I know how much she was looking forward to her trip to Switzerland. Emma told me about Megan and Simon, too. Bummer. I haven't heard a word from Megan directly, though, or from Becca. Not that I expected to. I know they've been busy with their shopping spree. I don't do shopping. I'm allergic to malls—all those stupid crowds, and stupid stores, and trying on stupid clothes. It's a big fat waste of time, as far as I'm concerned. Time I could spend doing things I'd much rather be doing. Like playing hockey.

"Nice job!" says Zach Norton, slapping my helmet as I glide to a stop beside him.

"Thanks." He hands me a water bottle, and I take a long swig. I'm not exactly sure what's going on with Zach these days. He's been spending a lot of time at the rink in Concord this fall, watching me coach Chicks with Sticks, and sometimes we hang out afterward. I thought he was cool with us just being friends, but then he went and volunteered to come along to the tournament this weekend as equipment manager. Which is great and everything, since our old one quit, but it seems a little over the top.

Maybe I'm just being too sensitive, though. He's certainly been taking his duties seriously, and he's not treating me any different from the rest of my teammates, which is good. Coach Larson doesn't put up with boyfriend drama, and when Zach volunteered, she was a little suspicious at first, even though I told her we were just friends.

My right elbow is feeling the effects of that last hit, and I massage it as I listen to her pep talk. She cuts a glance over at me and frowns, and when she's done she comes over to check me out.

"I'm fine," I insist. "It's just a little tender."

She slaps me on the back. "Okay, then, let's show 'em how it's done."

She jerks her chin toward the far side of the rink, where the scouts are sitting in the stands in the corner. I knew they'd be at the tournament—there's usually at least a couple at every tournament—but this weekend they're out in full force. It's a little nerve-racking. College is still a couple of years away, of course, but this is when the recruiters start to sit up and take notice.

I haven't thought too much about where I might want to go, but the University of Wisconsin is a definite possibility. I can see myself as a Badger. One of the coaches at last summer's skills clinic was a Badger, and she talked up the program there. UNH is another possibility, and so is Boston University. Courtney thinks I should try for a school in California, so I can be near her. A lot of my teammates are shooting for one of the Ivy League schools, but I don't have the GPA for that.

Mom's always harping on me to keep my grades up, and they've actually improved a lot since I started high school. I had so much going on last year, between elite hockey and coaching Chicks with Sticks and all the ice dancing I did, that it forced me to be really disciplined about homework and studying. The habit stuck, and I'm doing a lot better in school this year. I'm liking it more too. My electives rock, for one thing—especially photography—and my guidance counselor is looking to see if there's a way I can do an independent study in sports management, and get credit for coaching. That was Stanley's idea.

When my mother first started dating Stanley Kinkaid a few years ago, I didn't like him. I mean *really* didn't like him. I did everything I could to bust up their relationship. When I look back on it now, I cringe to think about what a brat I was. I made fun of Stanley all the time and picked fights with him, even when he went out of his way to do nice things for me, like take me to a Bruins game for my birthday.

Stanley hung in there, though, and gradually we became friends. He may not be all that much in the looks department—he's shorter than my mother, for one thing, and bald as an egg, although I agree with my mom and Courtney that he has really nice eyes and a great smile—but he's supersmart, and super supportive. Without Stanley, there wouldn't be a Chloe, which is impossible for me to imagine now. And Stanley got behind Chicks with Sticks from the start, plus he was the one who talked my mother into letting me try out for the Lady Shawmuts.

The whistle blows, and we line up for the face-off. The Clippers have the puck, but we have the will to win. In ten seconds flat Allegra Chapman whisks it away from them and sends it over to me. We pass it back and forth between us as we head back down the ice toward the goal, careful not to get overconfident. I've made that mistake plenty of times before, and so has she.

Heather Vogel Frederick

"SHAW-MUTS! SHAW-MUTS! SHAW-MUTS!" chants our cheering section.

Allegra and I lock eyes. Time for our special double-trouble play. We split off toward opposite sides of the rink, dividing the defense. Then I double back, and a second later so does she. This next part is a little bit tricky—a blind pass. If I cue the Clippers as to what I'm doing, it's all over. Looking straight ahead and glaring at the defenseman rushing my way, I rely on my peripheral vision to locate Allegra, then fire the puck to her without so much as a glance in her direction. Bingo!

She receives it handily, and I spring forward. We have the element of surprise on our side now. The Clippers hesitate ever so slightly; they hadn't anticipated this. They rush over in Allegra's direction just as she passes the puck back to me. Now we've got them on the run, and they're mad. I surge forward, making it look like I'm driving for the goal. Determined not to let us trick them again, the Clipper defense charges me, leaving Allegra wide open. It's the perfect setup. One more quick flick of my wrist sends the puck back to her, and we're home free. She puts it away, and the rest, as they say, is history.

Our fans leap to their feet, hollering their heads off. My family rushes down to the edge of the rink, and as I skate over to greet them, my little sister's face splits into a grin from under her white knit hat. She waves her red-and-white pennant wildly, shouting "SHAWMUTS!" at the top of her lungs.

"Get used to it, monkey-face," I whisper to her. My mother hates it when I call her that. "You'll be out here soon too, if I have anything to say about it."

I'm going to turn my little sister into a hockey player if it's the last thing I do. We need another jock in the family.

Because of our schedule, I have to skip the postgame pizza party, which is lame, but at least I'm going home with a shiny new trophy. Mom already has my stuff packed, so all I have to do is hop in the shower and we're ready to go. Zach climbs into the backseat of the minivan and plunks himself down next to me. In all the excitement of our win, I forgot he was driving home with us. Coach sprang him from his post-tournament duties so he can make the filming in time.

"Great game," he says, giving my knee a squeeze.

Startled, I pull my leg away. But the press of his warm hand lingers, and I can feel the blood rushing to my face. I flick a glance at his profile. Same old Zach. Same old blue eyes and shaggy blond hair that has driven all the girls in Concord wild since they were Chloe's age. Not me, though. Never me.

At least not until now.

Something about Zach seems different to me lately. But what? The way he looks? I don't think so. Maybe it's the way he smells—clean and masculine, with a hint of aftershave, or maybe just deodorant. He smells—well, good. So good that I'm tempted to lean over and take a deep sniff. Except that would be really, really weird.

I turn to my sister instead and ignore him for the rest of the ride home. Zach doesn't seem to mind and spends the trip talking to Grant.

Heather Vogel Frederick

"See you soon," my mother says when we drop him off at his house. "Don't forget to wear your sweater."

Zach grins. "No way, Mrs. Sloane-Kinkaid. I have that prize in the bag."

He waves to the rest of us, his gaze lingering on me a split second longer than on anyone else. This should annoy me, but instead it makes me happy for some reason.

Courtney leans over and whispers in my ear, "He likes you."

"Shut up!" I whisper back furiously, hoping my mom and Stanley can't hear. "He does not!"

She nods at me, her eyes dancing. "Uh-huh. And I think you like him, too."

I jab her in the shoulder. My sister still knows how to push my buttons.

Forty-five minutes later, I'm dressed in my Christmas finery and standing in the front hall as instructed.

"Nice," says Fred Goldberg, the show's producer.

"Thanks," I reply, flicking one of the jingle bells that dangle from the Christmas tree on the front of my sweater. It's knit in an eye-watering shade of red, which looks absolutely hideous with my hair. That's the whole point, of course. It was totally worth every cent of the five dollars I paid for it at Goodwill.

"I'll have you know I gave up a perfectly good Thanksgiving week-end to do this," Mr. Goldberg calls up to my mother as she heads down the stairs.

I'm actually thinking the same thing, even though I understand why my mother planned it this way. Grant is majoring in film and television at UCLA, and he was really interested in a behind-the-scenes peek at what goes into making an episode of *Cooking with Clementine*. Between Thanksgiving, my hockey tournament, and the red-eye that he and my sister are catching back to L.A. later tonight, there was really only this one brief window of opportunity.

"Anything for a ratings boost," my mother replies. "Which, may I remind you, are higher this season than for any of our other seasons so far."

"Show-off."

"Grinch."

She and Mr. Goldberg tease each other a lot.

"Be still my heart!" he says as she reaches the bottom of the stairs and he gets a closer look at her sweater. It's easily the most ridiculous thing I've seen so far. My mother looks good in just about anything, but even she can't rock this one. For one thing, it's brown, which is not such a great color on her. Plus, who ever heard of a brown Christmas sweater? Basically she's wearing a giant reindeer head, complete with padded fabric antlers sewn to the tops of the shoulders and an actual lightbulb on the end of Rudolph's nose, which is located somewhere in the region of her belly button.

Mr. Goldberg gapes at it, horrified and delighted, as it blinks on and off. "Where on earth did you find it?"

"Rummage sale," says my mother smugly. She pokes her head into the living room, which is crowded with TV film crew members, and

Heather Vogel Frederick

claps her hands. "Let's go, people! Time to liven this place up!"

She crosses to the stereo and puts on some Christmas music to get us all in the mood. The doorbell rings, and I go to answer it. Murphy, who is wearing a Santa hat, follows at my heels, barking furiously. He hates filming days. Too much bustle and confusion, and too many things to bark at.

"Ho-ho-ho," says Third as I open the door. He has on a garden-variety Santa sweater, but there's such a huge grin on his round face and he looks so pleased with himself that I take pity on him and tell him it's awesome and that I'm sure he's going to win the prize.

Murphy and I escort him to the living room, where Courtney and Grant are setting out platters of cookies. They're wearing Santa sweaters too—only theirs are matching Mr. and Mrs. Santa sweaters.

"Awww," I coo. "How sweet!"

"Shut up, Cass," says Courtney, swatting at me.

I evade her easily, but Grant is quicker. "Let's ring those jingle bells of yours," he says, grabbing me and tickling me.

"Knock it off!" I tell him, squirming away. But I'm laughing—I like Grant. He's easily the nicest of Courtney's boyfriends so far. And he likes sports, too. He's on the UCLA tennis team, which earns him major points in my book.

"Ta-da!" says a voice behind me. I turn around to see my stepfather making a grand entrance. He's wearing a white shirt and a neon-red-and-green plaid sweater-vest, plus a bow tie in a clashing black-and-yellow plaid. He looks horrible, and I give him a round of applause.

He's got my little sister by the hand, and even though she slept in her car seat almost all the way home, I can tell she's still a little cranky. She's rubbing her eyes with her free hand and tugging at the sparkly snowflakes on her white sweater. I reach for her and swing her up into the air, then twirl her around the room.

"Let it snowy, let it snowy, let it snowy—for Chloe," I sing along with Sinatra, my improvised riff perking her up a little.

When my mother first came up with the idea for this episode, I thought it was really lame, but now that things are underway, I can tell we're going to have fun.

The Chadwicks and the Wongs arrive next. Mr. Chadwick and Becca's grandfather and Mr. Wong all took the conservative route, choosing black, gray, and navy sweaters with boring snowscapes and skiers on them. Like Third, they look pleased with themselves, though, so I ooh and aah appreciatively.

The moms got more into the spirit of things, even though Mrs. Wong somehow managed to find a holiday sweater with a message: a big planet Earth floating on a blue background with PAX written underneath it.

"That means 'peace,'" she informs us. "Get it? Peace on *Earth*?"

My stepfather is behind her, grinning broadly at me. I ignore him. "Yeah, Mrs. Wong, I get it. Cute."

Gigi links her arms through Becca's grandmother's and drags her into the living room. "We're the candy dish sisters!" she announces to no one in particular. Her black sweater has a red-and-white-striped

Heather Vogel Frederick

candy cane in some hideously shiny fabric on it, and Mrs. Gilman is wearing a red sweater with huge pouffy silver candy kisses all over it.

"KISS KISS KISS!" shrieks Chloe when she sees it. Chloe loves candy kisses.

"Anytime, sweetie," says Becca's grandmother, taking her from me. She and Gigi give her tandem kisses, one on each cheek.

"Are you getting this?" my mother says to the cameraman, who nods.

"Wait a minute, you're already filming?" says Mrs. Chadwick, whipping out her lipstick. She's stuffed into a white mohair sweater that makes her look kind of like a baby polar bear.

"Not officially," my mother tells her. "Just some preliminary stuff."

I inspect the sequined swirls on the front of Mrs. Chadwick's sweater and realize that they're meant to be ornaments. "Cool design," I tell her.

"Cool bells," she replies, and Chloe leans over suddenly, almost toppling out of Mrs. Gilman's arms as she reaches out to jingle one of them.

I cast a critical glance at Becca and Megan. Obviously, they spent way too much time on this assignment. The sweaters they're wearing are only marginally ugly—in fact, they're almost cute, especially the fluffy little sheep on Megan's—and I notice that they both made sure to choose really flattering colors. I shake my head in disgust. What exactly about the words "ugly sweaters" did they not understand?

"Are the boys here yet?" asks Becca, craning to see past me.

Duh. Of course. It's not that they didn't understand the assignment, they just chose to ignore it. I should have known. "Just Third so far," I tell her.

"Oh," Becca replies, not trying to hide her disappointment. "Do you think the others will come?"

I shrug. "Guess we'll have to wait and see."

I'm surprised any of the guys agreed to be involved, actually. For some reason, though, the idea of an ugly sweater party totally hooked them.

Third comes galumphing over and grins at Becca. "Hey, guys," he says.

"Hey," says Becca, without enthusiasm.

Poor Third. He's a great guy, and it's obvious he's got a crush on Becca. He's barking up the wrong tree.

The doorbell rings again, and I leave them standing there to go answer it. For the next fifteen minutes, a steady stream of friends passes through the door. Soon our living room is aglow with sweaters sporting Santas and sleighs and snow-capped trees and piles of presents. If I never see the colors red and green again, it'll be too soon.

Kevin Mullins turns up, even though I'm pretty sure he wasn't invited. "Is Jess here?" he squeaks. He's as tall as I am now, but his voice hasn't changed yet, and if I close my eyes he could pass for Dylan or Ryan. Or Hermie, the dentist-elf from *Rudolph the Red-Nosed Reindeer.*

"Nah, not yet," I tell him. "Great sweater."

It's forest green, and must be a size XXL, which on skinnybones

Heather Vogel Frederick

Kevin is hilarious. The thing hangs d███ ███████████

the sleeves up so many times to make th██ ██ ████████

wearing life preservers on his wrists. Th████ █████ █████

stocking on it, with an elf peeking out of t██ ███████████

"Why don't you go perch on the mant███ ████████████████

blend in."

He blinks at me behind his thick glasses. "██████ ████ squeaks.

"Never mind," I tell him. "Go get some punch."

So far, I'd say the prize should go either to him or to Emma, who

showed up in the red snowman sweater she wore to a party we had

back in seventh grade. It's kind of the opposite of Kevin's, because it

looks like she shrunk it in the dryer. The bottom hem barely reaches

to the top of her midriff, and the cuffs only come to her elbows. It's

hilarious, actually. Especially since her mother is wearing a match-

ing one.

"And to think I spent good money on these, thinking they were

cute," says Mrs. Hawthorne, plucking ruefully at the front of hers.

"Tuck your turtleneck in, Emma. Your belly button is showing."

The Delaneys made their own. They're wearing matching navy-

blue sweaters, and Jess and her mother sewed a big shiny silver letter

onto the front of each one. When they all stand in a line, it spells

"M-E-R-R-Y."

"Now that's original!" says Mr. Hawthorne, who like my stepfather

opted for a vest. His belongs to Mrs. Hawthorne, though, which is

really funny. I saw her in it at story time when I took Chloe to the

ek. She recognizes it too, and toddles over to pat the
lying around on it.

ch is the last one to arrive. All I can say when I open the door is,
Oh. My. Gosh."

"Told you so," he says smugly, striking a pose.

His sweater is a truly awful shade of olive green with a wide band
of white stretching around the chest. Across it is a line of skating mice,
or rats maybe, each one holding a hockey stick and wearing a bright
orange Santa hat.

"It's revolting!"

"I thought of you the second I saw it," he replies.

"Gee, thanks."

He reaches over and flicks one of the jingle bells. "Nice job at the
tournament today."

"You already told me that."

"It's worth telling you again."

My mother comes down the hall carrying a tray loaded with presents—prizes for the winners. Zach's sweater stops her in her tracks.

"Good heavens," she says. "You weren't kidding. I actually feel
faint." She leans dramatically against the doorjamb, then grins. "Give
me a hand with these, would you?"

Zach takes the tray and we follow her into the living room. She
pauses in the doorway, happily surveying the crowd. Her cheeks are
flushed and her eyes sparkling—my mother eats this stuff up. I hope
someday I have a job I love as much as she loves hers.

"Okay, everyone," she says. "Time to take your places!"

The crew worked wonders this morning getting everything set up. The tree is decorated and lit, glowing in the curve of the front window. There's a punch bowl on the table to the left of the fireplace, and platters of cookies and appetizers are scattered around the room.

Out of the blue I feel a pang. I really miss Mrs. Bergson! She would have loved a silly party like this one. It still seems strange not to have her with us at book club meetings, or at my Chicks with Sticks practices. It's like she just stepped out of the room, and should be back any minute.

"As you all know, we're here to tape my 'Home for the Holidays' special," my mother says. "I want you all to act as natural as possible, and just try and ignore the cameras. When we start rolling, I'll talk a little about how to host an ugly sweater party, and then I'll come around the room to take a look at each of you. After we award the prizes, we'll take a quick break and then move on to karaoke. Any questions?"

Emma's hand shoots up. I swear she'll be thirty and still raising her hand to ask a question. She just cannot break the habit. "So you want us to hang out and eat snacks and talk and stuff like we'd normally do?"

My mother nods. "Exactly. My goal is for us to convey the happy buzz of a holiday party, so everybody just buzz, buzz, buzz, okay?"

Emma's eyes slide over to mine at this unfortunate choice of words. "Buzz, buzz, buzz" is what we used to say to each other in middle school, when Becca was in the middle of her queen bee phase.

She and her posse, which included Megan back then—we called them the Fab Four—used to make our lives miserable. Becca's improved a lot, but she's still not my favorite person in the world. There's still too much *Chadwickius frenemus* in her, as Jess would say. That's Jess's secret Latin name for Becca, because she's kind of a frenemy.

Fred Goldberg glances at his watch. "All right, everyone, places! Time's a-wasting here. Get ready to eat, drink, and be merry in three—two—one . . . ACTION!"

He points to the cameraman, and as the light on the camera turns from red to green, Zach grabs my hand and pulls me over toward the punch bowl, where Ethan, who like Third also went with a Santa-themed sweater, is standing talking to Megan and Becca. Becca's face flushes as she spots our clasped hands.

"Hey, guys," I say coolly, ignoring her as I slip my hand out of Zach's to serve myself some punch. "How about that Thanksgiving game? Did we send Acton home with their tail between their legs or what?"

That sets the boys off, and I stand there sipping my punch and eating cookies and listening to them go over it play by play. Then, just as my mother and the cameramen get to us, Becca turns to me and says sweetly, "So Cassidy, how's Tristan?"

The conversation comes to a screeching halt. My face goes beet red. *Chadwickius frenemus* strikes again! Zach looks at me intently, but this is definitely not the sort of thing I want to talk about in front of him, and especially not on national television.

Behind the cameraman's back, my mother is gesturing at me

Heather Vogel Frederick

urgently, using two fingers to stretch up the corners of her mouth in a smile. I bare my teeth obediently at Becca in a grin. "Fine, thank you for asking."

She flicks a glance at Zach, then hits me with another zinger. "Are you two still going out, then?"

I hesitate, weighing my response. If I say no, that implies that Tristan and I were dating and stopped, which isn't true. We never dated, officially, we just kind of hung out. And I'm not sure that last night in England at the dance really counts. Yes, he chased me across the lawn at Chawton House. And caught me. And then—well, let's just say there was a bit of spooning involved, as Betsy Ray would put it. But I'm certainly not about to tell Becca that. I haven't told any-body about it. And the truth is, I haven't heard much from Tristan since. Which is okay, really. I've been busy with hockey, and he's been busy with his European ice dancing competitions.

If I say yes, on the other hand, what will Zach think?

If I'm being honest with myself, I guess my sister is right, and I do kind of like Zach Norton. I've spent so many years telling everybody that I don't, though, and that we're just friends, that it would be kind of embarrassing to acknowledge the truth.

Especially here, and now. It's not a truth I'm about to share with Becca, who obviously also likes Zach, and who obviously really, really resents the fact that he's maybe a little interested in me.

Mumbling something about needing some air, I retreat to the far side of the room, leaving my mother to deal with the fallout.

Courtney comes over. "What's going on?"

I lift a shoulder.

"Why is she looking at you like that?"

Across the room, Becca is trying to drill holes in me with her glare.

"Who knows?"

We take a quick dinner break—turkey enchiladas, served buffet-style in the kitchen—before filming the next segment. I was sure the Christmas karaoke would be a dud, but it isn't at all. Ethan and Third and Stewart, who is also wearing a Santa sweater, only his is beyond awesome because it's just a black sweatshirt with a fuzzy Santa toilet seat cover sewn onto the front of it—bill themselves as the Three Santas and belt out a hilariously off-key "Jingle Bell Rock." The book club moms plus Gigi and Becca's grandmother all line up for "Silver Bells," complete with embarrassing dance moves and a lot of swaying back and forth at the chorus. Darcy Hawthorne, who in my opinion deserves the Most Boring award for his green-and-black plaid sweater with a Scotty dog on the front, manages to coax Kevin into warbling "Frosty the Snowman." We're all practically in tears by the time he's done, we're laughing so hard.

It's Jess, though, who really brings us to tears.

I don't know much about music, but I know a heart-stoppingly beautiful voice when I hear one. The room grows quiet as she stands there on her crutches and sings "White Christmas." I actually get chills. I know it's Thanksgiving weekend, but that's the perfect song for an afternoon like this one, what with the snow outside and everything.

Heather Vogel Frederick

"How come you didn't sing?" Zach asks me, after Jess is finished.

"Me?" I give him a look. "That would be because I have a voice like Darth Vader with laryngitis. Trust me, you don't want to hear me sing."

It's past Chloe's bedtime when we finally wrap. Emma just manages to edge Kevin out for the grand prize for ugliest sweater, winning a gift certificate to the swanky Patriot Shoppe ("so you can trade in that horrid thing for something beautiful," my mother tells her). Kevin is happy with his runner-up prize, though, a sparkly light-up star ornament. He promptly presents it to Jess, who turns beet red. Kevin is so clueless. Darcy just laughs. He likes Kevin, plus he knows it's not like there's any real competition there.

There's a flurry of activity as the crew packs up the equipment and our guests all leave. My book club friends and their moms linger to help with the dishes, and I follow Courtney upstairs to her room, where I plunk myself down on her bed to hang out for a bit while she finishes packing for her flight back to L.A.

"So tell me about Zach," she says, picking up a shirt from the pile on her bed and folding it.

I shrug. "There's nothing to tell."

"Becca seems to think there is."

"Becca is a moron."

My sister laughs. "She's a lot smarter than you think—she's obviously caught on to the fact that he likes you."

I can feel my face redden. I'm skating on thin ice here. Boys are not a topic that Courtney and I have covered much before. There's never been a need to. "You think so?" I ask casually, picking at a loose thread on the bedspread.

She gives me a sideways glance. "I know so." She places the shirt in her suitcase, then sits down beside me. "I wish you could see his face when he looks at you," she tells me. "He lights up like a Christmas tree."

I bite my lip. My own face is easily as red as my ugly sweater by now. This is really embarrassing.

Courtney stands up again. "So what's your game plan?" she asks briskly, picking up another shirt.

I breathe a sigh of relief. Terminology I can deal with again. "Um, I don't have one?"

"You should. Boys need a little encouragement."

This is news to me. "Really?"

She nods. "Sure. They're often surprisingly shy, despite all their macho sports talk. That's why they stick together the way they do, you know. Sometimes you need to cut them out of the herd and let them know you're interested."

I laugh. "You sound like one of those nature programs." I drop my voice to a whisper and do my best to mimic an Australian accent. *"G'day, mate! Today we're observing the double-breasted seersucker. See how he flocks together with the other males of his species and ducks for cover in the brush. Let's watch the female as she approaches from his blind side—oh, look! She's nabbed him."*

Courtney grins. "Exactly! My point is, don't be afraid to let Zach know that you like him."

"I'm not," I tell her, but that's not entirely true. All this stuff comes easily to her—boys have liked Courtney since she was in kindergarten—but it's mostly unknown territory to me. That evening at Chawton House with Tristan last summer hardly counts.

"Time to go!" Stanley calls from downstairs.

"You'll figure it out," says Courtney, zipping her suitcase shut. "Everybody does. And remember, you can always call me to talk about it, okay?"

"Okay." I help carry her bags downstairs to the front hallway, where everyone is gathered to say good-bye. "Thanks," I tell her, when it's my turn to give her a hug.

Courtney squeezes me back. "You're welcome. I love you, Cass."

"I love you, too."

After she and Grant and Stanley leave, my mother puts Chloe to bed, then comes into the kitchen to join the rest of us.

"Whew," she says, stepping out of her shoes and sagging against the doorway. "This has been one long day."

"What you need is a nice hot cup of tea," says Gigi. "I'll put the kettle on."

My mother crosses the room and perches on one of the island stools next to Jess, who is drying a pile of silverware. "How are you holding up, honey?"

"Fine," Jess replies. She points to the R on her sweater. "Very merry," she adds, rolling her Rs.

"Sorry to hear about Switzerland," my mother continues. "But Concord's a nice place to be over the holidays."

"Actually, I'm not going to be in Concord," Jess tells her. "I'm going to be at my aunt and uncle's in New Hampshire."

"How fun!"

"We're all going," adds Mrs. Delaney as Gigi sets out a row of mugs on the counter. She picks out a teabag and plops it into one of them. "It's our first Christmas away from the farm as a family since the twins were born."

"How about you, Phoebe?" my mother asks, leaning forward to take a mug too. "Does your family have plans too?"

"No, we'll be here in Concord," Mrs. Hawthorne replies. She pauses, glancing over at Emma, who is suddenly on full alert by the sink, fixing her with Winona eyes. Mrs. Hawthorne smiles. "Yes, dear? Was there something that you wanted?" She turns back to my mother. "All of us will be here in Concord except for . . ."

Emma drops to her knees and clasps her hands dramatically.

". . . my lovely daughter, who's going to be joining the Delaneys in New Hampshire."

Emma lets out a squeal. "Really, Mom?"

Mrs. Hawthorne nods. "Really. Your dad and I talked it over, and while we'll certainly miss you, it's a lovely opportunity and we don't see any reason you shouldn't go."

Heather Vogel Frederick

Emma starts hopping up and down in excitement. Jess waves her dish towel in the air and lets out a whoop.

"Sheesh, they act like they're still in preschool," Becca mutters to no one in particular. I ignore her, still stinging from our run-in by the punch bowl.

Mrs. Delaney takes a sip of tea. "And how about your cruise, Lily? When do you leave?"

"We'll be flying to Fort Lauderdale on the twenty-first, and sailing on the twenty-second."

"That sounds heavenly!"

Mrs. Wong nods. "We chose Paragon Cruise Lines for their environmentally sound practices. Their ships are the greenest on the seas and have greatly reduced their carbon footprint. Did you know, for instance, that most cruise ships generate twenty-one thousand gallons of sewage a day?"

This little factoid leaves everybody speechless. And more than a little uncomfortable. Megan looks like she wants to sink through the floor.

"Paragon, on the other hand, has a state-of-the-art wastewater treatment system, and the capacity to dry, sterilize, and offload inert sewage for recycling."

"Boy, Mrs. Wong," I tell her, "you sure make the Caribbean sound like a lot of fun!"

Everybody cracks up at this, even Mrs. Wong.

"And how wonderful that you'll be traveling with the Chadwicks," says Mrs. Hawthorne, looking over at Becca's mother.

Mrs. Chadwick's face goes rigid. "Actually, we're not—" she begins, but stops as her mother puts a hand on her arm.

"Yes, isn't it?" says Mrs. Gilman. "We're all looking forward to the trip so much."

Mrs. Chadwick blinks. "But I thought—"

Her mother pats her arm, then leans over and I hear her whisper, "A little Thanksgiving gift from your father and me," just as Becca starts to squeal.

"What was that about preschoolers?" I ask her under my breath, but she ignores me.

"So much for 'Home for the Holidays,'" remarks Gigi. "Maybe you should call your TV special 'Gone for the Holidays,' Clementine."

My mother laughs.

"I guess you'll be holding down the fort here in Concord all by yourselves, then," Mrs. Wong says to her.

"Mmm," says my mother. "Actually, we may be out of town too."

I whip around and stare at her. "Really?" She hasn't mentioned anything to me about it. "Where?"

"We'll talk later."

"Ooh, I smell a mystery trip!" says Mrs. Hawthorne.

"So everyone is heading out of town, then?" says Becca's grandmother. "Life really does imitate art, doesn't it?"

"What are you talking about, Mother?" asks Mrs. Chadwick.

"It's just like Betsy's Christmas trip in *Betsy in Spite of Herself*."

"Only, no one's going to Milwaukee," says Emma.

Heather Vogel Frederick

I fidget my way through the rest of the party cleanup. Finally everyone leaves, and I pounce on my mother. "So what's this about a trip?"

She pats the stool next to her. "Come sit by me." I pad across the kitchen to join her, stepping carefully over Murphy, who's sacked out in front of the fridge. "Grant has invited Courtney to spend Christmas with his family in Santa Barbara."

"Is she going to go?" Like the Hawthornes, our family has never spent the holidays apart.

My mother nods. "Of course. It's important to her. But I'm wondering how you'd feel about flying to California then too."

I frown. "All by myself?"

"No—all of us. We'd see Courtney, of course, and meet Grant's family, and maybe spend a few days in Laguna Beach."

"That sounds like fun."

My mother gives me a sidelong glance. "There's another reason that Stanley and I would like to go too."

She pauses, and I look at her expectantly.

"Stanley's had a job offer from a big accounting firm in L.A. He's flying out next week for an interview."

If she had told me he was booked on the next shuttle to Mars, I couldn't have been more surprised. I sit there, too stunned to speak. "You mean we might be moving back to California?" I finally manage to ask.

My mother tucks a strand of hair behind her ear. "It's a possibility."

"But I thought he liked his job in Boston!"

"He does," says my mother. "This is a pretty amazing job offer, though, and he wants to at least check it out."

"What about your job?"

"I can film *Cooking with Clementine* anywhere." She looks at me anxiously. "It wouldn't be all that bad if we went back, would it? Courtney would be nearby, and you'd like that, wouldn't you?"

I stare down at my hands, which are lying limply on the granite countertop. When we first moved here to Concord five years ago, all I could think about was getting back to California. Now, though, Concord is home.

Leave this house, and my hockey team? I've just barely gotten into the groove with the Lady Shawmuts. And Chicks with Sticks! I'd miss those little girls so much. I'd miss all my friends at Alcott High, too— especially my book club friends.

And then there's the whole Zach Norton situation.

Final score: Cassidy Sloane—a big fat question mark.

Heather Vogel Frederick

"Betsy dreamed about going away from Deep Valley, but she didn't for a moment suspect that around a bend in her Winding Hall of Fate a journey was actually waiting."

—*Betsy in Spite of Herself*

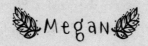

Megan

"The trunk stood open in Betsy's room, and slowly it was being filled . . . not only with clothes. The Crowd brought tissue-wrapped bundles to put in it. And Betsy had to buy or make Christmas presents to take along, as well as to leave behind."

—Betsy in Spite of Herself

"I hope that's everything," says my dad, wedging the last of our suitcases into the trunk of the car. He stands back, shaking his head in disbelief. "How is it that your mother and I managed to get everything we needed into one bag each, and you two have five between you?"

Gigi and I exchange a glance. My parents just don't understand about clothes.

"We had to put the presents somewhere, didn't we, Megan?" says my grandmother.

My dad breaks into a grin. "Oh, so your suitcases are full of presents for me, are they? Well now, that's another story."

We all climb into the car, and as we pull out of the garage and head down the driveway, I suddenly lean forward. "Dad," I say, tapping him on the shoulder, "can you hold on a sec?"

"Please tell me you didn't forget anything, like another suitcase."

I shake my head. "Nope, I just want to check the mail." He brakes, and I hop out and run over to the mailbox. *Please, please, please let there be something from Simon!* But there isn't; it's empty.

My mother gives me a sympathetic glance as I slide back into the car. Gigi reaches over and pats my knee. They both know how hard these past few weeks have been for me. I keep going over everything in my mind, trying to figure out what went wrong and what I could have done differently. The whole thing is just so weird, and so not like Simon. Plus, everywhere I go and everything I do reminds me of him, and all the fun we had together last year here in Concord. There's nobody like him at Alcott High. Heck, there's nobody like him anywhere. Simon is just about perfect.

Well, except for the fact that he dumped me. Via e-mail.

"You remembered your Secret Santa presents, right, sweetie?" my mother asks as we pull out onto Strawberry Hill Road. It's pitch-black out still, and the headlights reflect off the snowbanks lining both sides of the road.

"Yup. Got 'em right here." I point to the brown paper bag at my feet. After we found out that the entire book club was scattering for the holidays, Mrs. Hawthorne suggested we bring our gifts to the bon voyage breakfast this morning. We were supposed to wrap them, put them in a paper bag, and then staple it shut along with a card with the recipient's name typed on it, so our handwriting wouldn't give anything away. Our moms are going to be in charge of distributing the gifts while we're on our trips.

Heather Vogel Frederick

"I'm sorry we won't all be together here in Concord over the holidays, but at least we have New Year's Eve to look forward to," my mother continues. It was her idea to have a book club party and the Big Reveal then, instead of waiting until later in January.

"And we have right now to look forward to, too," says Gigi. "Only true friends would throw a going-away party this early in the morning."

A few minutes later we turn into the driveway at Half Moon Farm. My father parks in the lot by the barn.

"Brrr," I say as I get out of the car. "It's freezing!"

"Hang in there just a few more hours, Megs," says my dad. "It's supposed to hit eighty in Miami today."

He puts his arm around me, and we crunch across the snow-covered field toward the Delaneys' back door, where we're greeted by Sugar and Spice. They come running around the corner of the house and do what Jess and her family call the "happy sheltie dance"—twirling in circles and barking excitedly.

Mrs. Delaney welcomes us with hugs and asks the twins to take our coats. "Oh, and give your Secret Santa bag to Michael, Megan. He's in the keeping room."

I head for the little room off the kitchen that serves as the Delaneys' family room, where I add my paper bag to the pile on the coffee table. Mr. Delaney, who's been poking at the fire, straightens up when he sees me.

"Hey, Megan! Excited about your trip?"

I nod.

"I know you're going to have a great time. It's going to be warmer where you're going than it is where we're going, that's for sure."

"Yeah, but the White Mountains sound fun too."

"Absolutely," he replies, bending down to poke at the fire again.

Half Moon Farm has a fireplace in just about every room, because that's how they used to heat houses back in the 1700s, when it was built. I love Jess's house. It's so different from mine. Ours is nice and everything, but Half Moon Farm is unique. It's not just the house itself, either—it's the whole spirit here. The Delaneys are so relaxed. There are always dogs and kids running around, and sometimes chickens, too, in the spring and summer whenever someone forgets and leaves the back door open. Jess's house is a little messy and crazy, but that's part of why I love it. My parents are hyper about messes of any kind. We hardly even use the one fireplace we have, for instance, because we have white carpet and white furniture and they're afraid we'll get soot on something. Things have eased up a bit since Gigi came to live with us—not the clean part, because she's just as tidy as my mom and dad are—but she painted one wall in the living room red and bought bright throw pillows for the sofa, so there's a little more color, and lately she's been dropping hints that our house could use a cat.

I'd love that. The thing is, it gets a little lonely being an only child. I finally gave up on ever getting a brother or sister, and even though having Gigi around makes a big difference, a pet would be awesome.

Heather Vogel Frederick

Jess pokes her head in the door. She's still got her pajamas on under her hoodie. I'd still have mine on too, if I wasn't going anywhere this morning. "Hurry up, guys!" she says. "Everybody's waiting. We don't want you to miss your flight."

Her father and I follow her back to the dining room, which is decorated very simply. There are lots of fresh evergreens on the mantel—there's a fireplace in here, too, of course—and they smell great, like winter. Mrs. Delaney lit the candles in the chandelier, and the room is bathed in their soft glow. Emma and Cassidy and their families are milling around the buffet that's set up on the table.

"Go ahead and get started," Mrs. Delaney tells us. "The Chadwicks should be here any minute."

Sure enough, as I'm taking my plate into the living room there's a knock at the front door, and Sugar and Spice launch into their ecstatic spirals again.

"Caribbean, here we come!" cries Mrs. Chadwick, doing sort of a cross between a hula and a cha-cha as she enters the room. She must have raided her fashion stash from her "new and improved Calliope" phase a couple of years ago, because she's busted out the animal prints again. For the flight, she's chosen a leopard-print tracksuit, along with an enormous straw sun hat and sunglasses. Becca and Stewart look appropriately mortified at this parental fashion disaster. I just hope my seat isn't anywhere near hers on the airplane.

If Mrs. Chadwick is practically bouncing off the walls with excitement, by contrast Mr. Chadwick seems quieter than usual. Not that he's ever super flamboyant—Mrs. Chadwick takes up enough oxygen in a room for both of them—but still, he doesn't seem like his normal cheery self.

"Is everything okay with your dad?" I ask Becca.

"What do you mean?" she replies sharply.

"Um," I say, "I mean, I guess he doesn't seem all that excited about the trip."

"He's fine," snaps Becca. "Leave him alone."

I stare at her, taken aback at her response, and she sighs.

"Listen, Megan," she says, "I can't talk about it right now, okay? Maybe later."

So I was right—there is something going on. "Okay."

After everybody's eaten, all the guys head outside to transfer our luggage into the Sloane-Kinkaids' minivan and the Hawthornes' station wagon for the trip to the airport. We're going to leave our cars here at the farm while we're gone.

"All right, girls, gather round!" says Mrs. Hawthorne. "It's time for the quickest book club meeting in history! These folks have a plane and a ship to catch."

We join her in the living room, where she gives us each a handout. "You'll be receiving some 'Fun Facts to Go' later, in an e-mail," she announces. "But here are a few questions for you to think about over the holidays. Pop them into your suitcases and take a look when you have a minute, and we'll discuss them at our final Betsy-Tacy meeting on New Year's Eve."

Heather Vogel Frederick

"I'd like to talk about that get-together," says Mrs. Delaney. "I had an idea for it the other night."

We all look at her expectantly.

"I was reading ahead in *Betsy Was a Junior*—"

"You're hooked!" cries Mrs. Chadwick happily. "I knew it! I told Mother once you started reading you'd want to read the whole series! Wait until I tell her. She'll be thrilled."

Jess's mom smiles. "Guilty as charged. There's no way I could leave Betsy hanging halfway through high school—I've got to find out what happens to her, and especially what happens with Tony and Joe. Anyway, I thought it might be fun to lift a page straight from that book for our grand finale. Remember the Okto Deltas?"

"That dumb club the girls start?" asks Becca.

I guess she read on past *Betsy in Spite of Herself*, too. I haven't had a chance to yet, although I'm as hooked as Mrs. Delaney. I've been really busy this month sewing stuff for the cruise. There weren't a whole lot of spring and summer things available at the mall, since it's the middle of winter, and I wanted to have just the right clothes to bring along. There's this reception with the captain tonight after sailaway, plus a formal dinner on Christmas Eve, and there's a teen dance club on board too, and I needed a couple of outfits for that as well.

"I guess it is a little silly," agrees Mrs. Delaney, "but I loved reading about the progressive dinner they planned."

"What's a progressive dinner?" asks Cassidy, sounding wary.

"They're really fun," Mrs. Delaney explains. "You start at one person's house for appetizers, then move on to another one for salad, and another one for soup, and so on through the entire meal. Anyway, I was thinking maybe we could do that on New Year's Eve—what do you think?"

"Fabulous!" says Gigi. "I love it!"

Mrs. Sloane-Kinkaid nods vigorously, sending her trademark mane of blond hair—artfully highlighted to look the same way it's looked since those years when she was on the cover of *Vogue*—rippling around her shoulders. "Great idea, Shannon—count me in."

"Me too," says Mrs. Chadwick, and my mother nods in agreement as well.

Mrs. Hawthorne makes a note on her calendar. "It's settled then. A New Year's Eve progressive dinner and book club meeting."

"Shall we invite dads and brothers, too?" asks Mrs. Delaney. "Or just make it a hen party for the Sistren, as Betsy might call it?"

A quick show of hands favors including our families.

"Our menfolk can make themselves scarce when it's time for official business," says Mrs. Hawthorne. "Now, who wants to sign up for what?"

While our moms work out the details of the grand finale dinner, Becca and I go to find our coats. Jess's little brothers come rushing past us as we're rooting around in the hall closet, and they head for the stairs, giggling.

"Boys!" calls Mrs. Delaney, who has incredibly good mom radar. You have to, Gigi says, when you have twins. "What are you up to?"

Heather Vogel Frederick

"Nothing," they chorus.

"It doesn't sound like nothing. Come in here, please."

They slink into the living room, protesting their innocence.

"You didn't hide a chicken somewhere, did you?" Mrs. Delaney asks.

They shake their heads.

"Last week they put one in the pantry," she explains to the rest of us. "I nearly fainted when I went in to get some flour."

I try to imagine what my mother would do if she found a chicken stashed somewhere in our house. I start to smile. Across the room, Cassidy gives Dylan and Ryan a thumbs-up. She would. Cassidy loves practical jokes. I'm really going to miss those jokes if she ends up moving back to California. She told us about her stepfather's job interview, but I guess they haven't made a decision one way or the other yet.

"No toads or spiders anywhere?" Mrs. Delaney asks Dylan and Ryan. "No snakes in my underwear drawer? No plastic wrap over the toilet seat?"

The twins shake their heads again.

Mrs. Delaney looks at them, unconvinced. "Well, okay then, I guess," she says reluctantly. "Why don't you show our guests how charming you can be, instead of running around like wild animals? Where are your recorders?"

As the boys dash off, Mrs. Delaney turns back to us. "They're actually playing recognizable songs now. The new music teacher at Emerson Elementary is fabulous."

We're all putting on our coats when the twins stampede back

down the stairs. They start to serenade us with "Jingle Bells," then switch to "Here Comes Santa Claus" when they see Mrs. Hawthorne sorting through the brown paper bags filled with Secret Santa gifts.

"Very appropriate choice, boys," she says as she distributes the bags to all the moms for safekeeping.

"These are for you," says Emma, handing envelopes to Becca and me. We look at them curiously.

"What are they?" asks Becca.

"Train letters!" Emma's face falls when it's clear that neither of us have any idea what she's talking about. "From *Betsy in Spite of Herself*, remember? When Betsy's friends all come to the train station to see her off to Milwaukee, and they give her letters to read on her trip?"

"Oh yeah!" I tell her. "I totally forgot. That's really sweet of you." I give her a hug and so does Becca.

"Sorry we don't have anything for you," she says.

"That's okay," Emma replies. "I hope you have a great time on your cruise. We can't wait to hear all about it."

"And I hope you and Jess have fun in New Hampshire," I tell her.

Cassidy looks over at Jess. "Maybe if you and Emma are lucky, there'll be gnomes in the basement of your aunt and uncle's inn."

"You finally read the books!" cries her mother, slapping her a high five.

Dylan and Ryan put down their recorders. "Gnomes? What gnomes? You mean like hobbits or something?"

"Don't get all excited, guys," Jess tells them. "Cassidy's talking about this book we read. One of the characters has a grandfather who keeps his garden gnomes in the basement over the winter."

"That's stupid," says Dylan.

"What was up with that, anyway?" asks Becca. "They were kind of creepy. Do your aunt and uncle have creepy gnomes, Jess?"

Jess shakes her head. "Nope," she replies. "No gnomes."

"No gnomes is good gnomes," says Mr. Hawthorne, poking his head in the front door, and everybody groans.

He grins. "Sorry. Couldn't resist. And on that note, the Delaney/Hawthorne limo service is ready to depart."

Four hours, two airport terminals, and one taxi ride later, we arrive at the Port of Miami. Going from cold and snowy Concord to sun-drenched Florida feels surreal. Almost as surreal as the *Calypso Star*.

"Whoa," says Stewart, gaping up at the skyscraper of a cruise ship that looms over the terminal. "Are we going on *that*?"

"What were you expecting, a rowboat?" asks Becca scornfully.

My parents have taken me on a cruise before—we went to Mexico a few years ago—but I've never been on a ship this size, and I'm as impressed as Stewart. The *Calypso Star* is really, really gigantic.

"It's brand-new—the biggest in the fleet," says my father proudly, as if maybe he had a hand in building it. "There's a bowling alley, an ice rink, a rock-climbing wall, an indoor movie theater *and* an outdoor movie theater—"

"—plus it's the greenest ship ever designed," my mother reminds us, like anybody but her cares.

"—and a water slide and a SurfRider," my father continues, ignoring her.

"I can't wait to try that," says Stewart, squatting down and holding out his arms in a surfer pose.

"Get up, you dork!" Becca snaps, looking around anxiously. "Someone might see you!"

Stewart grins at me as he straightens up. He knows I can't wait to try it, either. I was at Emma's house one day when he came over, and he showed us a video clip on the cruise ship website. I have no idea how the SurfRider works—I guess there's a machine that makes fake waves somehow—but it looks incredibly fun.

"There's a spa, too, right?" asks Becca.

"You bet," says my dad.

Once we're aboard, we rendezvous with Becca's grandparents, then head for the lunch buffet where we're supposed to wait while our luggage is delivered to our cabins. As we cross the lobby, I practically run into Stewart, who stops smack-dab in the middle of the atrium to gape up at the three-story Christmas tree.

"Awesome," he says, taking a picture. "Wait until I show Emma."

It is awesome, and so is the buffet. There are platters of fresh fruit, about a dozen different kinds of salad, every sandwich known to man, cookies, cake, ice cream, and all the soda and lemonade a person could ever want to drink. My dad made arrangements for a big table to be reserved for us, and as we take our seats, Gigi and Becca's grandmother and our moms all start poring over the brochure listing the activities for the week.

Heather Vogel Frederick

"Look, Megan! They have cookie decorating," says Gigi. "Maybe we'll get some ideas for Pies & Prejudice."

I smile politely, but there is absolutely no way I'm going to waste my time on a cookie decorating class. Not when there are things like a teen pool party, dances, an eighties movie night, and a surfrider competition to choose from. With any luck, Becca and I will hardly see our parents.

Stewart turns to his grandfather. "Grampie, did you see that they have Scrabble competitions?"

Becca looks over at me and mouths the word *Dork*, making me giggle. The laughter gets caught in my throat when I remember how much Simon loves Scrabble too.

No, no, no! I tell myself sternly. *You will not think about Simon Berkeley!* It's hard, though. Everything reminds me of him. But I really, really don't want to spend this entire vacation moping.

"There's a towel animal class," Becca's grandmother announces.

"What's a towel animal?" asks Becca.

Her grandmother gives her a mysterious smile. "Just you wait and see—you're in for a treat."

"They're pretty awesome," I add. "That class might actually be fun."

"Mother, do you want to try scrapbooking?" says Mrs. Chadwick. "Or make-your-own Christmas ornaments?"

My mother pounces on this idea. "That's what you girls should do! It would be perfect for your final Secret Santa gifts. And homemade is always better than store-bought."

"Oh, darn," says Becca, trying to sound sincere. "There's an ice-skating party for teens at the same time. What a shame, Mrs. Wong."

I kick her under the table, and she kicks me back.

"I almost forgot. I have something for everyone," says my father, reaching into his tote bag. He pulls out eight walkie-talkies. "Our cell phones won't work once we're out of sight of land, and this is a big ship."

"Sweet," says Stewart, grabbing one and switching it on. "Houston, we have a problem," he drawls.

"Will you grow up already?" Becca looks around to see if anyone at the nearby table heard him. Anyone male and cute, that is. But of course no one is paying us the least bit of attention. They're all busy being as excited as Stewart.

"Now, kids, we don't want you leaving your cabin without your walkie-talkies, okay?" my mother says. "We always want to be able to get ahold of you."

"Sure," says Stewart.

Becca and I nod reluctantly and stash ours in our purses.

"Don't forget to turn them on," says Mrs. Chadwick, who has eyes like a hawk.

"Oops," says Becca, kicking me under the table again. Our big plans for freedom on this cruise are fast being scuttled.

Our parents lay down the rest of the rules: We're on our own for breakfast and lunch, so we can sleep in as late as we want, but we're expected to show up at our reserved table every night for dinner, and we need to be back in our cabins by eleven p.m. unless

Heather Vogel Frederick

we're with an adult, or unless we have special permission.

"Agreed?"

"Agreed," we chorus.

A few minutes later the steward comes by to tell us our cabins are ready. Becca and I are staying with Gigi; Stewart will be with his parents; and my parents and Becca's grandparents have cabins to themselves. Our staterooms are all in the same corridor, though.

Becca and I can't stop giggling as we make our way up two flights of stairs and then down a long corridor toward the rear or "aft" of the ship, as her dad calls it.

"This is so exciting!" she whispers.

"I know! I know!" I whisper back.

Gigi swipes her card key and goes in first. "Very nice," she says, looking around. "We'll be comfortable here."

The room is bigger than the last teeny cruise ship cabin I stayed in, thanks to my dad. He wanted to make sure Gigi was comfortable, so he upgraded us. There are two beds, plus a foldout sofa where Becca will sleep. The sofa's in a separate sitting area that also has two armchairs and a small coffee table, plus a desk that doubles as a vanity, with one of those lighted mirrors. On the wall above the built-in dresser is a flat-screen TV with a DVD player. There aren't enough closets for three of us, but that's to be expected. The bathroom makes up for it, though— it's a good size, with a walk-in shower.

"Look at the view," says Becca with a sigh, opening the balcony doors.

I step outside to join her. The marina is spread out below us, and beyond it, Miami. Skyscrapers and palm trees sway in the warm breeze, stretching up toward an impossibly blue sky.

"Pinch me," says Becca. "It was twenty-seven degrees when we left Concord this morning!"

I smile at her. "I know. Awesome, huh?"

The loudspeaker in our room crackles, then announces the lifeboat drill. We grab our bright orange life jackets and head for the aft dining room a few decks down.

"Nice look, Megan," says Stewart, as my dad makes us line up for a group picture.

"Shut up."

"We would have made Fashionista Jane's Fashion Faux Pas list for sure," Becca whispers, referring to the disastrous blog I started last year.

"I miss Fashionista Jane!" I whisper back. I promised my mother I wouldn't try blogging again, though, at least not for now.

Back in our stateroom, we stow our life vests away and unpack, putting our clothes into the drawers and closets and leaving what doesn't fit in our suitcases, which we shove under the bed.

"You haven't even opened that one," I tell Gigi, pointing to her last suitcase.

"Never you mind that one," she says airily. "I want you two to shoo for a while. Go for a swim or something and don't come back for at least an hour."

Becca and I do as we're told, changing into bathing suits and

Heather Vogel Frederick

cover-ups and flip-flops. Finding the pool isn't as easy as it sounds. The ship is just as big on the inside as it is on the outside, and we take a few wrong turns. Fortunately, we run into Stewart, who is on his way to the library—Becca rolls her eyes at this—and he points us in the right direction.

We emerge on deck finally, where we stake out two lounge chairs with our towels and magazines, then hit the water slide to cool off. Afterward, we grab sodas, slather on sunscreen, and settle in, turning our faces up to the sky.

"Heaven," says Becca with a contented sigh.

"Bliss," I agree.

"Wait until our friends back at Alcott High see our tans. They're going to be so jealous."

"Mmm-hmm."

A calypso band is playing Christmas carols, and the steel drums give the familiar music an exotic lilt. I hum along, feeling slightly giddy. This is already so much fun!

"May I join you two bathing beauties?"

Becca and I open our eyes to see her grandmother standing beside us.

"Sure, Gram, grab a chair," says Becca.

"Nice suit," I tell her. It's one of those kind that older ladies like, with the little skirt attached, but it's nicely cut in a retro Hollywood style with a sweetheart neckline, a halter tie, and ruching across the front. I love the fabric, too—gold swirls on a black background. I reach for my sketchbook, then remember I left it back in our stateroom.

"Thanks," says Mrs. Gilman. "Gigi helped me pick it out that day we all went shopping in Concord." She pulls a book out of her tote bag, waving it at Becca. "Perfect reading for a cruise, now that I've staked out my deck chair, right?"

Becca looks at the title and laughs.

"What's so funny?" I ask.

Mrs. Gilman peers at me over her sunglasses. "Haven't you read *Betsy and the Great World* yet?"

"Um, not yet."

"You have to! It's my favorite!"

"I thought *Downtown* was your favorite," says Becca.

"They're all my favorite. But yes, if I absolutely had to choose, it would be *Downtown* first, and then this one. Betsy goes on a transatlantic cruise to explore Europe—what could be better than that?" She takes a seat and opens to the first page. "I'm going to pretend the *Calypso Star* is Betsy's ship *Columbic*, and that we're heading for the Azores instead of Antigua and Martinique."

While Becca's grandmother settles in with Betsy and Becca settles in to read the latest issue of *Flashlite*, I lie back in my chair and people-watch from behind my sunglasses. There are a lot of families on this cruise, many of them with little kids, but I spot a fair number of teenagers, too, including some cute guys. Becca spots them too. I can tell by the way she's checking them out from behind her magazine

After a while, I close my eyes. It's been a really long day—my mother woke me up at four a.m.—and the music is soothing, and before long I fall asleep. Next thing I know, the ship's whistle is blowing.

"What?" shouts Becca, startled. She must have fallen asleep too. "Are we sinking?"

"Shut up, you idiot," I tell her. "We haven't even left yet. That's the signal for sail-away."

Sure enough, the ship is starting to move. People drift toward the railings to watch, and Becca and her grandmother and I slip on our cover-ups and flip-flops and gather our things to join them. Daylight is beginning to fade, and the city lights are twinkling in the distance. As we clear the shelter of the harbor, the breeze picks up. I fish my towel out of my tote bag to drape around my shoulders. The three of us stand there for a few minutes, watching Miami retreat on the horizon.

"I could stay here all night looking at that view, but I suppose we should get dressed for the captain's reception," says Becca's grandmother finally.

We manage to find our way back to the corridor where our staterooms are, only getting turned around once.

"Uh-oh, Gigi's been busy," I say, spotting our door.

The entire thing is wrapped in shiny green paper, and there's a big red velvet bow on it too, along with a fake gift card that says HAPPY HOLIDAYS!

"Surprise!" says Gigi, flinging open the door.

"No fair! You girls are in the fun cabin!" says Mrs. Gilman, following us inside.

Our stateroom has been transformed. I can't believe my grandmother managed to fit all this stuff in her suitcase. There's an artificial tree perched on the dresser, complete with tiny ornaments and lights, and a strand of multicolored twinkle lights have been strung up around the top of the walls. Battery-powered candles line the coffee table, there's a wreath on the bathroom door, and she even hung our Christmas stockings on a clothesline stretched across the mirror.

"Just like home," she says happily.

"Better than home," I tell her, giving her a hug. "Home stays put. We get to go to the Caribbean."

Becca's grandmother shakes her head. "You make the rest of us look like slackers," she complains, and Gigi laughs.

"I have plenty to go around," she replies, rummaging in her suitcase. She pulls out an extra strand of twinkle lights and a huge cardboard candy cane and hands them to her.

"Good heavens," says Mrs. Gilman. "What else do you have in there, a sleigh?"

My walkie-talkie crackles. "Dad to Megan."

I look over at Becca and make a face. This is going to get old quick. "Megan here," I reply.

"We're picking you girls up for the reception in twenty minutes."

Mrs. Gilman scurries off to change, and Becca calls dibs on the shower. Fortunately, she makes it quick, and somehow we both manage to be dressed by the time my parents knock on the door.

Heather Vogel Frederick

"Wow, it looks like Santa made a house call," says my dad, glancing around the cabin.

"Mother, for heaven's sake!" my mother protests. "Part of the reason for this trip was to get away from all the excess of the holidays."

Gigi raises her eyebrows. "Excess? What excess? It's just a few lights and a wreath." She turns to my father. "Nice tie, Jerry."

I look over at him and nod in agreement, then almost keel over when I notice that my mother is wearing actual high heels.

"Mom!" I exclaim, pointing to them.

"I know, I know," she says with a sigh. "Mother made me buy them."

My mother is morally opposed to high heels. She says they're a symbol of the objectification of women, and that nobody but a fool would go around with something that uncomfortable on their feet.

"They're perfect." My mother is wearing the red silk *qipao* that I made her for her birthday last year. It's become her go-to dress for everything fancy. I used this fabulous vintage fabric that Gigi brought me from Hong Kong when she first came to live with us. The dress is designed in the classic, formfitting Chinese style, with a high mandarin collar and a mid-thigh slit up the side. It looks great on my mother.

"See, Lily?" says my grandmother. "Didn't I tell you those shoes were just the thing? Our resident fashion expert just awarded you her seal of approval."

"You get an award too, Gigi," I tell her. My grandmother always looks fabulous. Tonight she's wearing cropped black velvet pants with black high-heeled sandals and a black V-neck silk top. I particularly like the wide band of sequin-spangled white satin around the neckline, and make a mental note to sketch it later.

Becca and I picked out our outfits for tonight weeks ago. She's wearing a minidress that she found at Sweet Repeats in Boston. It's hot pink, which is a great color on her, and it's covered in this cool retro pattern of swirls.

"Groovy," says her grandmother, slipping in behind my mom and dad.

"Very retro," Gigi agrees. "Good choice. You look like Twiggy."

"Who?"

"A famous model way back when," Becca's grandmother tells her.

I made my own dress, "a Wong original," as my mother calls it. It's a mini too, but black and strapless. My dad looks at Becca and me and places his hand on his heart.

"I don't know if I can handle all this beauty," he says.

"Better get used to it," says Gigi, slipping her arm through his.

My father offers his other arm to my mother, and we follow them out into the hall where the rest of the Chadwicks are waiting.

"Hand me my sunglasses, would you?" whispers Becca when she spots her mother.

Mrs. Chadwick has on a full-length dress with a gold chain-link belt and gold sandals. If it weren't for the color, which is somewhere between apple and kill-me-now-before-my-eyes-explode lime green, the dress wouldn't be all that bad, because it's nicely cut, and artfully disguises her, uh, curves. The dress may be flamboyant, but she

Heather Vogel Frederick

certainly isn't. At least not tonight. There's no sign of the bubbly Mrs. Chadwick who got on the plane with us this morning.

Mr. Chadwick is quiet too, which makes me wonder if they've been arguing or something. I hesitate before asking Becca, though. She practically bit my nose off this morning.

"Is everything okay with your parents?" I whisper finally, curiosity getting the better of me.

She flicks me a glance. "Yeah. No. I can't talk now. Maybe later."

We follow my dad up a few decks and then all the way to the rear of the ship. The big, expensive suites are back here, including the penthouse where the reception is being held. We go through the receiving line and are greeted by the ship's officers, all in full uniform.

"*Bonsoir, mademoiselle,*" says Captain Dupont, bending low over my hand. "Welcome to the *Calypso Star.*"

"*Bonsoir,*" I reply, feeling at least twenty-five. I wonder if I look it. I hope so.

The penthouse suite has its own open-air courtyard, with a small pool and a not-so-small Christmas tree. Overhead, the stars are out, along with a full moon. The soft strains of holiday music drift over to us from a jazz combo in the far corner.

An older gentleman in a tuxedo makes a beeline for Gigi and asks her to dance, and our parents and Mr. and Mrs. Gilman quickly follow, leaving Becca and Stewart and me standing by the tree. Stewart pulls a notepad and pen from his suit-coat pocket.

"What are you doing?" asks Becca sharply.

"I thought I'd see if I could interview the captain, or some of the officers," he replies. "For my newspaper column."

"Stewart! Not here—you'll embarrass us!"

"Calm down, I will not." He saunters off, leaving us to sip sparkling cider and nibble hors d'oeuvres and hope that someone besides our dads asks us to dance.

All of a sudden I see Becca stand up straight and suck in her stomach. "Don't look now, but I think I'm about to meet the love of my life."

I turn around and spot a guy about our age in a white dinner jacket talking to some of the ship's officers. He has the same dark hair and chiseled features as the captain, and when the captain says something and they both start to laugh, their dark eyes crinkle in exactly the same way.

Captain Dupont sees us watching them. He smiles at us, then puts his hand on the younger guy's shoulder and murmurs something in his ear. His son—it's got to be his son, unless the captain has a brother who's way younger than him—nods and heads across the courtyard in our direction.

"Here he comes, here he comes, here he comes!" squeals Becca under her breath.

"*Bonsoir*," says the boy, inclining his head in a brief, courtly bow just as his father did in the reception line. "I am Philippe Dupont, son of Captain Dupont." If his voice were a color, it would be midnight blue—and that accent!

Becca cocks her head and gives him her most alluring smile, the

Heather Vogel Frederick

one I've seen her practice a hundred times in her mirror at home. "I'm Becca Chadwick," she murmurs.

"*Enchanté, mademoiselle,*" says the captain's son, then turns politely to me.

"*Bonsoir, Philippe. Je m'appelle* Megan Wong," I tell him, overwhelmingly grateful that I listened to Gigi and switched from Spanish to French this year.

There's a moment of hesitation as we all realize there's only one of him, and two of us. And then Philippe extends his hand. To me.

"*Voulez-vous danser avec moi, Mademoiselle Wong?*" He smiles, and something stirs inside me as we step out onto the dance floor.

Maybe there's life after Simon Berkeley after all.

❧ Jess ❧

*"Whenever I see whipped cream, all my life,
I'll think of Milwaukee."*
—*Betsy in Spite of Herself*

"On the count of three, okay?" says Emma, and I nod. "One, two, three!"

We both rip open the Secret Santa gifts we found on the end of our beds this morning. My mother must have put them there while we were sleeping. We've been finding one a day ever since we arrived here at the Edelweiss Inn.

I stare down at my latest gift, frowning. It's a set of Downhill Buddies hand and foot warmers, the kind you tuck into your ski boots and ski gloves. This strikes me as a little mean—didn't my Secret Santa remember that I had to cancel my trip to Switzerland?

I toss them onto the floor beside the growing pile of other strange gifts I've gotten so far, including the word-a-day calendar, the purple nail polish that I'll never use because I hate nail polish and because purple is my least favorite color, and the dog dish—sort of cute, but Sugar and Spice don't like to share their food.

Heather Vogel Frederick

This whole Secret Santa thing is turning out to be kind of a bust.

"What did you get?" I ask Emma. She looks unhappy too.

"Is someone trying to tell me something?" she replies, tossing over a DVD. The cover shows a sinewy girl with a blond ponytail and a blindingly white smile pretending to do a crunch. The title screams *Rockin' Rudy's Rockin' Hard Abs!* Emma looks down and pats her tummy. "Am I that out of shape?"

"You're fine," I assure her. "Your Secret Santa is lame. Mine is too—check this out." I hold up the Downhill Buddies package.

Her mouth drops open. "Are you kidding me? That's really mean!"

"I know."

"Just for the record, I'm not your Secret Santa," Emma tells me.

"I'm not yours, either."

"So who picked these gifts for us?"

I shrug. "Becca, maybe? She's the only one of us who can sometimes be a little, you know—"

"*Chadwickius frenemus?*"

"Exactly. She can't have picked both of our names, though," I muse, looking from her present to mine and back again.

We're still puzzling about this when my mother taps on the door. "Glad to see you're rising and shining, girls!" she says, poking her head in. "It's almost time for breakfast, and then—"

"Nestlenook!" I cry.

Nestlenook is a resort near here that turns its small lake into what they call a "Victorian Skating Park" every winter. It's really cool.

My face falls as I remember my leg. No skating for me today. My mother notices my expression and gives me a sympathetic look. "You'll have fun anyway, sweetheart, I promise. I think you and I need to try out one of those heated Austrian sleighs of theirs."

She's been hyperventilating about those sleighs ever since we got here and Aunt Bridget showed her the brochure.

Emma helps me wrap my cast in a garbage bag and duct tape it closed. Taking a shower is a bit of a production, but Uncle Hans and Aunt Bridget put us in one of the inn's handicapped rooms, so there are handrails for me to hold onto once I hop into the big shower stall, and a bench to sit on if I want, so I manage. Afterward, I get dressed while Emma showers, and then we make our beds.

This was one of Mom's rules for coming to the Edelweiss, because she didn't want us creating extra work for the staff. Actually, Emma's the one who's been doing most of the work, since it's kind of hard for me to maneuver in my cast. I hop around gamely for a bit until she finally shoos me out of the way.

I grab my crutches and go over to the window to check on the weather. The Edelweiss Inn is built on a hillside overlooking the Mount Washington Valley, and the view is breathtaking. Outside, the early morning sun sparkles on the snow-frosted evergreens that dot the property, and in the distance I can clearly see the peaks of the White Mountains. It's going to be a beautiful day.

This might not be some fancy resort in Switzerland, but I have to admit it's pretty fabulous, even if it is as familiar as an old ski boot.

The Edelweiss was designed to look like a Bavarian chalet, with white stucco walls and dark wood balconies and shutters, and a sharply peaked roof with a deep overhang that offers protection from the heavy winter snows. All the upstairs rooms have window boxes. They're empty now, but come summer Aunt Bridget will fill them with red geraniums. For the holidays, Uncle Hans outlined the eaves and windows with white lights. It looks magical at night.

"That takes care of that," says Emma, fluffing up the last pillow and surveying the room with a critical eye. She's trying to be a super-conscientious guest. "Ready?"

"For breakfast, or for Felicia?"

My cousin is the only drawback to this vacation so far. We've never gotten along all that well. Mom says she's going through an awkward phase, but she's been saying that since Felicia was five. The weird thing is, though, that Felicia and Emma have really hit it off.

I follow Emma out of our room and down the long hallway to the lobby. My uncle Hans, a big, broad-shouldered man with sandy hair and the ruddy complexion of someone who spends a lot of time out-doors, flashes a smile from behind the front desk when he sees us.

"*Guten Morgen!*" he says.

"*Guten Morgen!*" we chorus back.

My uncle is from Bavaria. He met my mom's sister Bridget when she was a visiting professor at the University of Munich. After they got married they moved here to the White Mountains because Aunt Bridget wanted to live near family, and Uncle Hans wanted to be able to ski. The inn was really run-down when they bought it, but it's gorgeous now. They put a ton of work into renovating it. It was worth it, though, because everybody who comes here falls in love with the place, and families come back year after year. There's a special feeling at the Edelweiss. It's so cozy—*gemütlich*, Uncle Hans calls it—with all the dark wood paneling and comfy overstuffed chairs and sofas and the big stone fireplace in the living room. It's the best place in the world just to hang out and relax.

"Did you sleep well?" asks my uncle.

We both nod.

"*Sehr gut*," he says. "Very good." He winks at me. "I have it on good authority that there are gingerbread *Pfannkuchen* on the menu this morning."

Emma has picked up enough German in the last few days to know the word for pancakes when she hears it, and she practically swoons at this announcement.

"You'd better hurry, though, before Dylan and Ryan eat them all," teases Uncle Hans.

Emma and I race off to the dining room. Well, she races; I limp along behind on my crutches. I will be so glad to get rid of these things. I can't wait to be able to walk normally again, and to run, and ski, but most of all to ride. I haven't been able to exercise Blackjack since the accident.

"Morning, glories," says my father as we take our seats at the table. He looks more relaxed than I've seen him look in ages. My parents work really, really hard on the farm.

Heather Vogel Frederick

"Pass the pancakes, please," says Dylan.

I whisk the platter out of his reach. "Pig! We haven't even had any yet." I slide two onto my plate and hand the platter to Emma, who helps herself to a couple as well before passing them to my little brother.

There's homemade applesauce to go with the pancakes, as well as eggs, sausages, and all kinds of cereal and granola. Best of all, there's Edelweiss Inn's famous cocoa. Uncle Hans special-orders this amazing chocolate from Germany, which he grates by hand and then melts over a double boiler before adding steamed milk. I drink pots of it every time I come here. With homemade whipped cream, of course. *Mit Schlag,* as my uncle calls it. A lot of things on the menu here are served *mit Schlag.*

"My pants aren't going to fit if I keep this up," says my mother, who doesn't sound too worried about the prospect. She adds another dollop of whipped cream to her mug.

"Could you pass the applesauce, please, Jess?" says Emma.

I look across the table at her and snort.

"What?"

I point to my upper lip. She's wearing a whipped cream mustache. Dylan and Ryan instantly grab their cups and give themselves matching ones too.

We all get the giggles, and a minute later my entire family has whipped cream mustaches. Aunt Bridget and Felicia come into the dining room just then, carrying more platters of food.

Aunt Bridget laughs. "Behave yourselves!" she scolds, but her eyes are twinkling. "I want people to think I have normal relatives!"

My cousin doesn't laugh at all. She just shoots me a disgusted look and gives our table a wide berth.

That's the thing about Felicia. She's kind of a snob. She's bilingual, of course, having grown up with Uncle Hans as her father, and she likes to show off that fact whenever she can. She also likes to show off the fact that she's a year older than me and has spent a lot of time in Europe what with her dad being German and her mother teaching medieval history. Aunt Bridget takes Felicia along on all her research trips.

I know it bugs my cousin that she lives in this tiny little town in New Hampshire instead of someplace like New York or Paris or Rome, and it about kills her that I got a scholarship to a top-ranked school like Colonial Academy. Felicia likes to brag about the fact that she scored high enough on her IQ tests to qualify for MENSA, that genius society. Unfortunately, she also scores really high at making people feel stupid. She's a master of the smirk that says, *I can't believe you didn't know that*. I try never to do that to people, and I'm just as smart as she is, only in a different way. Where I'm more into math and science, Felicia is all about English and history. Which is probably why she and Emma are getting along so well.

After breakfast, Emma and I go out to the kitchen to see if we can use my cousin's laptop. There's no sign of her, though, so we head for the library instead. The Edelweiss Inn doesn't have cable TV or Wi-Fi— Uncle Hans wants to make sure that guests unplug and relax—but there's a computer terminal available so people don't feel completely

Heather Vogel Frederick

cut off. Cell phone reception is spotty here too. I haven't been able to call or text Darcy much, and it's the same for Emma and Stewart. So we're stuck with dashing off the occasional e-mail on the computer in the library, or on Felicia's laptop on the rare occasions that she deigns to let us use it.

We're in luck; the terminal in the library is free.

"You go first," says Emma, and I take a seat and lay my crutches on the floor while she circles the room, checking out the titles of the books on the shelves.

There are two e-mails waiting for me, a brief one from Darcy— he misses me and hopes I'm having fun—and a cautious one from Savannah, who is trying to pretend like Switzerland isn't all that great. She's a terrible liar, though, because it's easy to read between the lines and tell that she's having a fabulous time. Especially since she mentions some guy named Andreas, like, twenty-seven times.

"Your turn," I tell Emma, gathering up my crutches.

I flip through a magazine while she's reading her e-mail—it's probably from Stewart because she keeps laughing—and when she's done, we go back down the hall to our room to brush our teeth and grab our jackets and everything else we'll need for Nestlenook.

"I'll meet you in the lobby," Emma tells me, rooting around in her bedside drawer for her notebook. "I've got to write something down before I forget it."

Leaving her to her poem or story or whatever's buzzing around in her head, I close the door behind me.

"Hans, Jonas is here!" My aunt's voice floats down the hall, and as I approach the lobby, I see a lanky boy standing by the reception desk. His face looks vaguely familiar.

"You must be Jess," he says when he spots me. "I've heard a lot about you."

"You have?" I cock my head, trying to place him. Where have I seen him before? "Oh, you're Josh's brother!"

I'd forgotten that Half Moon Farm's hired hand was from around here.

Uncle Hans comes up behind us and drapes his arms around our shoulders. "I've arranged for Jonas to be your escort today," he informs me. "He'll be keeping a close eye on you and make sure you stay safe around all that ice."

I can feel my face flushing, though whether from embarrassment or anger, I'm not sure. Probably both. My uncle hired a *babysitter* for me?

"I can manage on my own just fine," I tell him stiffly.

Uncle Hans gives me a mischievous grin. "Of course you can, but you'll have so much more fun with a handsome young man to keep you company." He slaps Jonas on the back and heads back toward the kitchen, just as Felicia comes in.

She's changed out of her waitressing uniform, the traditional Bavarian dirndl that she and my aunt and the other kitchen staff wear when they're on duty, and she's changed her hair, too. It's dark, like Aunt Bridget's, but unlike my aunt, who wears hers loose around her shoulders, Felicia has piled hers on top of her head in some complicated braid thing. It's probably a medieval hairstyle—I wouldn't put it past her to have researched it on the Internet.

"Sir Jonas," she says, dropping a deep curtsy. Did I mention that in addition to being a card-carrying member of MENSA, my cousin is also kind of socially awkward? Jonas must be used to it, though, because he doesn't even blink.

"Milady," he replies, inclining his head politely.

Felicia turns to me. Her eyes are a piercing blue, like Uncle Hans's. "Where's Emma?"

"In our room. But she's—" I don't get a chance to finish telling her that Emma wants some time alone before Felicia is off like a shot, leaving me standing there feeling irritated. I might as well be part of the furniture as far as my cousin is concerned.

I turn back to Jonas. "You really don't have to do this," I tell him.

He laughs. "Don't worry about me. It'll be fun."

For you, maybe, I think sourly. *For me, not so much.* But I follow him out to the driveway, where my mother is standing by one of the vans. When she sees Jonas, she does a double take.

"You have got to be related to Josh Bates," she says.

Jonas grins. "I'm his baby brother."

"Pretty big baby," my mother replies, gazing up at him. He laughs.

The front door of the inn swings open, and Felicia and Emma appear, laughing about something. They come over to join us, and Emma's forehead crinkles when she takes a look at Jonas.

"Are you—"

"Yep," says Jonas, answering her question before she even asks it. "He's my brother."

As he and Emma and Felicia start talking, I pull my mother aside. "Mom!" I whisper furiously. "Did you hear what Uncle Hans did?"

"No, what?"

"He *hired* Jonas to babysit me today!"

My mother smiles. "Lucky you—he seems like a really nice guy. And what a sweet thing for your uncle to do. Hans is always so thoughtful."

"Thoughtful? Mom—it's humiliating!"

"Sweetheart, I don't understand what the big deal is. Jonas is just going to keep you company. That way Emma and the rest of us can, uh—" She pauses and bites her lip.

So that's it, I think, feeling as if my face has been slapped. I've just been a big wet blanket all week, have I, keeping everyone from having fun? And now, with me out of the way and safely in Jonas's care, nobody will have to think about me. Especially not Emma.

I glance over at her just as Felicia whinnies nervously at something Jonas has said. Emma laughs too. I don't get it. How can she stand my stupid cousin?

"Has Emma been complaining about me to you?" I ask my mother.

She sighs. "Of course not. And that's not what I meant at all. It's just that I've noticed what a good sport she's been about hanging out here with you while the rest of us have gone skiing and sledding, and this will give her a chance to stretch her legs today, that's all."

When I don't say anything, she continues, "Look, I know you're sick of that cast, honey, and that you're going a little stir-crazy from all the forced inactivity, but please don't be a drama queen. Your aunt and uncle have been incredibly generous to us this week. They know how hard we work all year on the farm, and they've gone all out to see that we have a really good time. That *everybody* has a good time, including you and including Emma. Could you please just try to be diplomatic about this thing with Jonas?"

I'm quiet for a moment. "I'll try."

"That's my girl."

I'm silent on the ride to Nestlenook, mostly because everybody else has plenty to say. My dad is talking to Uncle Hans, my mother is fishing Jonas's life story out of him, and Emma and Felicia are debating the relative merits of Jane Austen and Charlotte Brontë, tossing around terms like "leitmotif" and "gender relations" as they discuss which book is better, *Pride and Prejudice* or *Jane Eyre*. Nobody seems interested in anything I might have to say, so I just sit and stare out the van window. It's a pretty ride, at least, and I've always liked watching for the covered bridge in Jackson. I poke Emma with one of my crutches as we pass it.

"Awesome!" she says, whipping out her camera and snapping a picture. Then she dives right back into her conversation with Felicia.

Stung, I pull my jacket closer around me and hunch down in my seat. Forget BFBB, it looks like the latest rule is NFBBF—new friends before best friends. Fine. Emma can have her shiny new toy.

My gaze wanders over to Jonas instead, who's telling my mother all about UNH. He has dark hair and gray eyes, like his brother, but his smile is broader and his nose a little narrower. His hands are different too—less blunt, with long, slender fingers. He's definitely cute.

Not that it matters. I'm taken. And I slip my cell phone out of my pocket and look at pictures of me and Darcy just to prove it.

A few minutes later we pull into the parking lot by Nestlenook's frozen lake. Emma's eyes widen as she gazes out the window. Before I can stop myself, I lean over and murmur, "Deep Valley, right? Didn't I tell you?"

She nods.

Felicia looks at us sharply. "Deep Valley? Wait a minute, isn't that from those dumb Betsy-Tacy books?"

"They're not dumb!" I tell her. "They're really good. We've been reading them for our book club."

"Are you kidding me?" She gives me a look of deep disdain. "I read those back in elementary school."

Emma laughs uneasily. "Well, these days our club is mostly just an excuse to get together with friends, you know, Felicia? We let our moms pick the books to keep them happy."

I gape at her. *Traitor!* After she's spent the past four months gushing about how much she loves Maud Hart Lovelace, too! Is she so worried about impressing Felicia that she won't even stick up for our book club?

Before things escalate further, Jonas reaches over and opens the van door, then climbs out. "Can I give you a hand, Jess?"

"I'm fine," I snap, then promptly trip over my crutches in my haste to get away from Emma and Felicia.

Heather Vogel Frederick

"Whoa, careful there," he says, catching me and setting me down gently onto the snow-covered parking lot.

"Um, thanks," I tell him. I take a deep breath, trying to calm my racing pulse. There's nothing like falling into the arms of some guy you barely know to make your face turn red.

"Perfect day for skating," he says, looking around.

It's true—and this is a perfect spot for it. We have a pond that we skate on back at Half Moon Farm, but Nestlenook's is easily three or four times the size of it, and at least twice the size of the rink back in Concord. It's also ridiculously picturesque. There's an arched bridge that spans one of the narrow spots, and since it's Christmas, it's been decorated with garlands of evergreens and a big wreath with a red bow. There are Victorian gas lamps lining the pathways, and in the middle of the lake is a small island where a hut with a fireplace offers skaters a chance to warm themselves and drink hot chocolate. Plus, there are sleigh rides. It's like something out of a Dickens novel. Or Deep Valley, no matter what Felicia thinks.

"Mind your step," says Jonas, handing me my crutches and watching as I place them under my armpits. "The parking lot is pretty slick."

The twins burst out of the second van and race for the frozen lake.

"Boys!" calls my mother. "Watch out for other guests!"

They ignore her, of course, and she shakes her head, then joins Emma and Felicia in trailing Jonas and me as he leads us toward one of the benches near the bridge.

"How's this?" he asks me.

Catching my mother's warning glance, I resist the urge to tell him I'm not ninety and don't need to be hovered over. I nod, and he spreads a blanket on the bench. I lower myself down onto it, then stack my crutches underneath where they won't be in danger of tripping anyone. Especially me. I don't need to be catapulted into Jonas Bates's arms again today. Once was more than enough.

"Would you like another blanket?"

"Really, I'm fine," I assure him.

"Come on, Emma, let's go skate," says Felicia.

I shoot Emma the best Winona eyes I can muster, hoping she'll pick up the mental message I'm telegraphing—*Don't ditch me for your new best friend!* But she doesn't even glance in my direction.

"Sure!" she tells Felicia, and the two of them dart off.

"Mrs. Delaney?" says a voice, and I turn to see my father coming down the path, skates in hand. "May I have the pleasure of your company?"

My mother smiles at him, and I feel a pang of regret for all the things I thought and said earlier. Of course I want everyone to have fun—especially my parents! They both look so happy out here in the cold air and the sunshine.

My mother looks over at me. "Do you want me to stick around for a while, sweetie?" she asks gently, and I know she's thinking of our earlier conversation.

I shake my head. "No, Mom—go have fun. I'm fine."

My parents lace up their skates, then step onto the ice and glide away, holding hands.

Heather Vogel Frederick

"Your folks sure are nice," says Jonas. "My brother thinks so too."

"Yeah," I reply. "They really are."

We're quiet for a bit, watching everybody swoop and twirl on the lake in front of us. I feel more than a bit awkward sitting here with him. I'm not as shy as I used to be, but sometimes it still kicks in. Then a horse-drawn sleigh approaches the bridge, and I pull out my cell phone and snap a picture. "I didn't know they use Belgians here!" I exclaim. "That's so cool—we have two at home."

"I know," says Jonas. "Led and Zep, right? Man, I love those names."

I grin. My father named our horses after Led Zeppelin, his favorite rock band. "You should hear what my mother calls our chickens," I tell him. My mother named our flock after her favorite country music stars.

"My brother already told me," Jonas replies, smiling back at me. "A little bit country, a little bit rock and roll is the way it plays at Half Moon Farm, right?" He holds out his hand. "Give me your cell phone and I'll take a picture of you with the bridge in the background."

I give him an even bigger smile, and he snaps a shot and gives me a thumbs-up. "That turned out great," he says, handing my cell phone back. "You should send it to your boyfriend."

I look at him, surprised. "Let me guess, your brother again?"

He nods. "Yeah. He's told me a lot about you guys. He really likes your family."

"We really like him, too. He's a big help on the farm." And I find myself telling him all about winning the scholarship to Colonial

Academy, and how it meant I couldn't help out as much at home, and how guilty I felt about it and everything. Jonas is a good listener, and a good talker, too. It turns out we have a ton of stuff in common, like the fact that we both hate horror movies, plus we both love music and animals. He's in the veterinary premed program at UNH, and when I tell him about my wildlife rehabilitation apprenticeship, his eyes light up.

"I would love to learn more about that," he says.

"You totally should. Come down and visit your brother, and I'll take you over to meet Mr. Mueller."

I ask him about college, and find out that he's on the UNH swim team and that like me, he sings in an a cappella group too.

"What piece did you choose?" he asks, when I tell him about MadriGals, and my upcoming solo audition.

"This song called 'Dreaming.'"

He shakes his head and says he's never heard about it, so I explain about the Betsy-Tacy connection.

"Were those the books you three were arguing about back in the van?"

I lift a shoulder, embarrassed that he overheard us. We must have sounded like a bunch of five-year-olds. "Yeah, sort of. I shouldn't have snapped at Felicia like that. It's just that she's so, well, you know." My voice trails off.

He laughs. "She's a good kid. But I know what you mean. She's a little, uh, O.D.D., as we say in our family."

Heather Vogel Frederick

I frown. I've heard of A.D.D. before, but this must be some new condition. "O.D.D.?"

He shoots me a mischievous glance. "Odd."

I burst out laughing.

"Glad to see you two are getting along," says my mother, swooping to a stop on the ice in front of us. My father is with her, and they're still holding hands. Sometimes parental PDA can be embarrassing, but not today. Today it's perfect. "Have you seen the boys?"

I point to the island.

"Ah," she says. "The gazebo. I should have guessed. Wherever there's food."

"Or hot chocolate," adds my father. "Speaking of which, I could use some myself. Shall we?"

They skate off again.

"Can I get you some?" Jonas asks. "Or maybe a pillow to sit on? I think I saw one back in the van."

"No thanks, I'm fine. Really." The corners of my mouth tug upward in a smile. "I'm not ninety, you know."

He smiles back. "I noticed."

Uh-oh, I think, feeling a little flutter. Jonas is flirting with me. And maybe I'm flirting with him a little too. There's definitely a spark between us.

I gaze back out at the skaters on the ice, trying to shake it off. Jonas would be easy to like, but I already have someone. A fabulous someone named Darcy Hawthorne. Betsy Ray and her sister Julia may be able to juggle more than one boy at a time, but it's way too complicated for me. Besides, I'm crazy about Darcy. Darcy is my Joe.

But what happens when a Tony shows up on your doorstep?

Directly across from us, on the other side of the lake, Emma is showing off for Felicia. I watch her do a little jump and then spiral to a stop, her curly brown hair flying out from beneath her bright pink wool hat. For all the complaining she's been doing about not getting enough exercise, she hasn't lost her touch on the ice.

She sees us watching and slips her arm through my cousin's, and the two of them skate over to us.

"This is the most amazing place I've ever been to in my life!" Emma says.

"It's pretty great, isn't it?" Jonas agrees. "I've been skating here since I was a kid."

"Lucky you," Emma tells him. She's glowing from the exercise, and she looks really pretty with her snapping brown eyes and her cheeks all pink from the wind and cold. "Do you know they have their own Zamboni here?"

Jonas laughs. "Do I know it? I drive it!"

"No way!"

He nods. "Oh yeah. I help out on the weekends whenever I'm home, and over winter break. Maybe I can give you all rides later."

"Sounds like fun," I say.

"C'mon, Emma, let's go get some hot chocolate," says Felicia, and once again they skate off without a backward glance.

Heather Vogel Frederick

Does Emma have to look like she's having such a good time? I think, aware that I'm being petty but not caring. I've barely had time to talk to her since breakfast, and I was so looking forward to sharing Nestlenook with her. I knew it was exactly the kind of place that she'd love, and I was hoping we'd get to hang out together, and maybe take a sleigh ride or something.

Out of the corner of my eye I notice Jonas watching me, and quickly rearrange my face into a more pleasant expression.

"Executive decision," he says, leaning over and reaching for his backpack, which is underneath the bench with my crutches. "We need hot chocolate too. I'll go get us some, okay?"

"Okay," I tell him, and he pulls his skates on and laces them up.

"Mit Schlag?" he asks.

I nod. I could use a whole lot of *Schlag* right now.

Later, after a spin in the sleigh with my parents—Emma chooses to keep skating—Jonas does what he promises and gives us rides on the Zamboni. My little brothers nearly wet their pants with excitement, and even my father gets a kick out of it when it's his turn. Getting me across the ice and up into the seat is a bit of a project, but it's worth it in the end, because it's really fun. I take lots of pictures for Darcy. He's on the hockey team at Alcott High, but even he's never ridden on a Zamboni. For some reason, the best part for me is looking out behind us at the stretch of smooth, clean ice the machine leaves in its wake.

"It's kind of mesmerizing, isn't it?" says Jonas, hollering to be heard above the roar of the engine.

I nod, laughing. Catching sight of Emma and Felicia standing together on the island, I wave. Emma waves back. Felicia leans over and whispers something in her ear. Emma's wave falters.

Jonas was supposed to be finished babysitting me after the skating party, but when we get back to the Edelweiss, Aunt Bridget invites him to stay to dinner, and he accepts. Afterward Uncle Hans gets a game of charades going. Felicia picks Emma and Jonas for her team, and I get stuck playing with my parents and the twins and some family from Pennsylvania. We lose, of course. Emma and Felicia think so much alike they can practically finish each other's sentences, and together they're unstoppable.

"Cheer up," Jonas tells me, after my team goes down in flames. "Let's go see if they have any good music."

He steers me over to the piano, where we find some holiday sheet music on the rack. Jonas plays pretty well—better than me, that's for sure—and we start singing "Here We Come A-Caroling" and before long everybody in the room wanders over to join us, including Emma and Felicia. We follow up with a medley for the little kids—"Santa Claus Is Coming to Town," "Frosty the Snowman," and "Rudolph the Red-Nosed Reindeer," which sends my brothers scurrying for their recorders to accompany us.

"Here's a good one," says Jonas, pulling out the music to "Baby It's Cold Outside." "Sing it with me, will you? It's a duet."

I shrug. "Sure."

"Uh, just the first verse, okay?" says my mother, with a significant

Heather Vogel Frederick

nod in my brothers' direction. "Little pitchers. Some of those lyrics are a little sophisticated."

"Gotcha, Mrs. Delaney," says Jonas.

We really ham it up for the audience, with me playing the part of the reluctant date ("I really can't stay . . . I've got to go away")—the one the directions on the sheet music calls "the mouse" and Jonas the part of "the wolf," the guy who's trying to coax her to stay ("Baby it's cold outside"). Halfway through I notice Felicia whispering to Emma again, but I ignore them and concentrate on the song. We get a big round of applause when we finish.

Felicia, who can't stand it when I'm in the spotlight, offers to recite something "suitable for the occasion," as she grandly puts it. "It's from 1513—"

The Middle Ages, I think sourly. Of course. Her specialty.

"—and it's by Fra Giovanni." She clears her throat and strikes a pose, one hand extended toward the ceiling like she's onstage in a Shakespeare festival. "A Christmas Prayer," she announces. I don't dare look over at Jonas. Emma, on the other hand, is rapt.

> I salute you! There is nothing I can give you which
> you have not;
>
> but there is much that, while I cannot give, you can
> take.

No heaven can come to us unless our hearts find rest
in it today. Take Heaven.

No peace lies in the future which is not hidden in
this present instant. Take Peace.

The gloom of the world is but a shadow; behind it,
yet within our reach, is joy. Take Joy.

And so, at this Christmas time, I greet you, with the
prayer that for you, now and forever, the day breaks
and the shadows flee away.

Felicia finishes with a flourishing curtsy, and there's a polite round
of applause.

"I think some hot chocolate is in order after that," says Uncle
Hans, ever the genial host.

"*Mit Schlag?*" says my mother hopefully.

"*Aber natürlich*. But of course."

"I'd better get going," says Jonas, putting on his coat. "I'll see you
tomorrow."

Uncle Hans has another outing for us all up his sleeve, and he's
arranged for Jonas to keep me company once again. This time, though,
I don't mind at all.

Heather Vogel Frederick

"See you!" I call back.

He says good-bye to my parents, and to Uncle Hans and Aunt Bridget, and waves to Emma and Felicia. Pausing in the doorway of the sprawling living room, he turns back toward me and mouths the letters O-D-D, pointing surreptitiously at my cousin. I double over in silent laughter.

Back up in our room I notice that Emma's really quiet.

"Did you have fun today?" I ask her, determined to be friendly. It is Christmas, after all.

"Yep," she says. The word comes out short and clipped.

"Nestlenook is awesome, isn't it?"

She nods and climbs into bed, then punches her pillow.

"Just like what you'd imagine Deep Valley to look like, don't you think?"

No answer.

I sigh. "Emma, what is it? What's bugging you?"

"You know exactly what's bugging me," she says coldly, reaching over and snapping off the light.

"I do not!" I protest. "I'm completely in the dark here—well, so to speak." I pause, waiting for her to giggle. That's exactly the kind of dumb pun that usually makes Emma laugh. But she doesn't, and I sigh again. "Look, all I know is that you've spent the entire day ignoring me and bonding with stupid 'watch me recite medieval poetry' Felicia."

"Like you'd even notice if that was the case."

"What are you talking about?"

"Never mind," she says. "I don't want to talk about it. Felicia said you'd deny everything anyway."

"But—"

"Can we just go to sleep? I'm exhausted. I haven't skated that much in ages."

I lie there, listening to her breathing. I don't know whether to laugh or cry. This is turning into a horrible vacation. I have a crummy Secret Santa, a broken leg, and on top of everything else my best friend has been snaffled away by my repulsive cousin.

Things can't possibly get any worse.

Heather Vogel Frederick

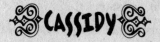

CASSIDY

"She tried to imagine not living in Deep Valley."
—*Betsy in Spite of Herself*

There's one thing California has that Concord doesn't: waves.

I look back over my shoulder, spot a gnarly one heading my way, and throw myself onto my board, paddling furiously as the water surges toward me. The wave lifts me up and shoots me forward and I ride it in toward the beach, whooping at the top of my lungs all the way. A few yards over, my friend Hannah Blum watches from her own board, grinning. Boogie boarding is baby stuff to her—she competes in longboard events all over Southern California and even Hawaii—so today is just about having fun.

On our final ride we let the wave carry us all the way to shore. Hannah slips nimbly off her board as we surge into the shallows, but I miscalculate and stay on a few seconds too long. As I hop off, the swirling water knocks me off balance and I stumble, ending up on my hands and knees in the sand. Hannah laughs as she grabs my hand and pulls me to my feet.

"Serves you right, you sponger!"

Real surfers make fun of boogie boarders, and "sponger" is the nicest of their names for them.

My friend looks at her watch. "We'd better head back. It'll be dark in another couple of hours, and I promised Mom I'd help with dinner."

We slip off our fins and splash onto the beach, then up the stairs to where we parked. Wriggling out of our surfing wetsuits, we towel off and pull on dry sweatpants and sweatshirts, then hop into her VW Beetle for the short drive back up the Pacific Coast Highway.

It's been really fun staying with the Blums. Hannah's older sister, Danita, is one of Courtney's best friends, and Mrs. Blum and my mom were good friends when we lived here too. I'm having a great time with Hannah. She's two years older than me, and although we were never close friends at elementary school—for one thing, two years is a huge gap when you're little, and for another, most of my friends were hockey players—we were always friendly, and I have good memories of the times our families spent together.

It's weird seeing someone you haven't seen for five years, though. We've both changed a lot since then. Hannah's taller, though not as tall as me, of course. Hardly any other girl I know is as tall as me. She used to wear her dark hair long back when we were at Canyon Elementary, but now it's short, in kind of a pixie style. Hannah says she cut it ages ago when she got serious about surfing. She was tired of it always

Heather Vogel Frederick

flopping in her eyes. My hair, on the other hand, has bounced back and forth between long and short over the years, and now I'm wearing it sort of in the middle, just long enough to pull back in a ponytail when I'm playing sports.

We stash our boards and gear in the garage, and I follow her into the house. "Smells good!" I call out to whoever's in the kitchen. "I'm starving."

"Me too!" echoes Hannah, who's one of the few girls I've met—well, besides hockey players—who has an appetite like mine and isn't afraid to show it. I hate it when girls pretend like they never eat a thing, and just have, like, a piece of lettuce for lunch. What's the point of that? Is it supposed to impress boys or something?

"Latkes again, just for you," Mrs. Blum calls back.

I groan. "Oh man, I never want to leave!"

Tonight is the fourth night of Hanukkah, and the Blums have been really nice about including us in their celebrations. We got here a couple of days ago and had dinner with the Blums on the second night of Hanukkah, but last night we went out for Mexican with other friends here in town. I'm looking forward to watching the whole candle-lighting ritual again tonight.

Hannah and I shower and change and then head for the kitchen to join my mother and Mrs. Blum.

"Where's Chloe?" I ask.

"Dani's playing with her downstairs in the family room," says Mrs. Blum, who is grating potatoes.

Hannah's older sister is totally in love with Chloe, and the feeling is mutual. Chloe's been following her around like a puppy ever since we got here. Hannah, on the other hand, says she doesn't do babies, which was how I always felt until Chloe came along. All that drool and mess! Now I just say I don't do *other* people's babies.

Not that Chloe is a baby anymore. She's officially a toddler now that she's walking, Mom says. It's hard to believe that she's going to be two next summer.

"Would you girls set the table, please?" asks Mrs. Blum, who is slim and dark-haired like Hannah. "We'll be ready to go as soon as our menfolk return."

Mr. Blum took Stanley to the marina down in Dana Point this afternoon to show him his new boat.

Dad always kept our sailboat in Dana Point too. I've been thinking a lot about him since we arrived in Laguna Beach. I've been back here a couple of times since he died, but never at this time of year. Christmas was my father's favorite holiday. When he was traveling on business, he used to bring back ornaments from all over the world for my mother. Hannah and I drove by our old house earlier today, and it gave me a weird feeling to see some other family's Christmas tree in the front window.

That's another reason it's been nice to be here at the Blums' this week. Their blue-and-white Hanukkah decorations are really low-key, and there's nothing to remind me of Dad. It's not that I don't want to remember him—I definitely do, and I think about him often, like every time I look at the Laguna Lightning jersey that's hanging on the wall in my room. Dad helped coach my Pee Wee team back when we

Heather Vogel Frederick

lived here, and Mom had his jersey framed for me. The thing is, though, I want my memories of my father to be on my terms, and not sprung on me unexpectedly, like when I get blindsided in a hockey game.

Hannah and I set the table using her family's best china and silver, along with the white tablecloth and blue napkins that Mrs. Blum set out for us. We have to make a contest out of it, of course—what can I say? we're both überjocks—and I'm laughing so hard by the time we finish that my legs are weak. Still, I manage to plunk down the last fork a split second before Hannah does.

"Here," she says, tossing me one of the foil-wrapped chocolate coins that are sitting in a dish on the sideboard next to the gleaming silver menorah. "A little Hanukkah gelt for the winner."

"Thanks," I reply, unwrapping it. "I could use a little something to tide me over until dinner."

There's a low rumble underfoot from the garage door. "Dad's home," Hannah announces. "Shouldn't be long now."

The aromas coming from the kitchen are sheer torture. I'm practically drooling by the time we all gather around the table a few minutes later for the Hanukkah blessings.

The Blums softly recite the Hebrew words, and my mother and Stanley and I watch respectfully as Mrs. Blum takes the *shamash*—the "helper" candle smack dab in the middle of the menorah—and uses it to light four more candles, one to mark each night of the holiday so far. When she's done, she moves the menorah to the window, to remind everyone passing by of the miracle of Hanukkah.

Home for the Holidays

I knew Hanukkah was called the Festival of Lights and everything—I'm not a complete ignoramus—but I had no idea where it got that name, or what miracles had to do with it. Mr. Blum explained everything to us at dinner the first night we were here. Turns out there were these guys called the Maccabees, who were fighting these Greek invaders, and when they finally beat them—which was pretty miraculous in and of itself, since they were just a tiny handful of soldiers going up against one of the mightiest armies on earth—the first thing they wanted to do was rededicate their temple, which the invaders had trashed. The only problem was, when it came time to relight the menorah, they could find only one jar of oil whose seal was unbroken, barely enough to last one day. I guess they couldn't use just any old olive oil, it had to be guaranteed to be pure. Amazingly, that measly little jar burned for eight days, long enough for them to go get a new supply. So that's why Hanukkah lasts eight days, and that's why families like the Blums light a candle each night of the holiday, to celebrate the miracle of the oil.

Chloe, who is sitting in a high chair, looks at us with big round eyes as we all hold hands and sing. Well, the Blums sing—we just hold hands. They sing "Ma'oz Tzur," which Mr. Blum tells us means "Rock of Ages" in Hebrew. It has a different melody from the "Rock of Ages" hymn I've heard at our church, though.

By the end, Chloe is banging on the high chair tray with her spoon, singing along tunelessly at the top of her little lungs and making everybody laugh.

"Sorry, everyone," says my mother. "I think somebody's hungry."

Heather Vogel Frederick

"I know I am," says Mr. Blum. "Dig in!"

Dinner tastes as good as it smells. There's chicken and rice and vegetables, along with latkes, of course. Another Hanukkah tradition is to eat some kind of food fried in oil. Latkes are scrumptious little potato pancakes, and Mrs. Blum made applesauce to go with them.

For dessert, there are *sufganiyot,* these awesome homemade jelly doughnuts, another one of those fried-in-oil foods. I woof down four of them before my mother puts a stop to it.

Hannah's parents distribute presents to everyone, us included. Just fun little things, nothing major like at Christmas. Tonight Chloe gets a dreidel, and I get half a dozen rolls of hockey tape in assorted colors and designs.

"Thanks, Mr. and Mrs. Blum," I say when I open the box. "I can guarantee you the pink camo will be a big hit with Chicks with Sticks."

Mrs. Blum smiles. "Your mother told me about the hockey club you started," she says. "I think it's wonderful."

It's really sad, but the things Hannah's parents have given me have been a whole heck of a lot better than the stupid stuff I've gotten from my Secret Santa.

The big joke since I arrived is what a loser my Secret Santa is. Hannah thinks the whole thing is hilarious, because so far, the gifts have been downright embarrassing. Not my sort of thing at all—fashion magazines, perfume, earrings, a sparkly headband—this morning I even got underpants. Underpants! And not just regular ones, either. These were pink and lacy. I'd be laughed out of the locker room if I showed up at hockey practice wearing them.

"Oh, I almost forgot," says my mother. "Mrs. Hawthorne e-mailed me earlier. She sent along something for you." She passes me a piece of paper.

"What's in it?" asks Hannah, as we head down the hall to her room.

"Fun facts," I tell her.

"Huh?"

She sits down next to me at the foot of my bed, and I explain about how that part of our book club works. Curious, she looks over my shoulder as I read the list.

FUN FACTS "TO GO" ABOUT MAUD

1) Maud Hart Lovelace attended the University of Minnesota ("the U" in the Betsy-Tacy books), but came down with appendicitis her freshman year and went to her grandmother's home in California to recuperate. She loved the warm climate, and later in life she and her husband retired there.

2) While at her grandmother's, Maud wrote and sold her first short story—"Number Eight." She got ten dollars for it from the *Los Angeles Times Sunday Magazine*.

3) Although Maud enjoyed writing for the student newspaper at the U, she wasn't all that keen on college otherwise, and

Heather Vogel Frederick

she dropped out to spend a year in Europe. Her time there would later become the basis for *Betsy and the Great World*.

4) Shortly after the outbreak of World War I, Maud met Delos Lovelace, a handsome reporter for the *Minneapolis Tribune*. Their marriage was both a love affair and a working partnership, as they wrote a number of novels together. Maud did the historical research while Delos worked out the plots. Then they divided up the chapters to be written, swapping when they were finished so they could edit each other's work.

5) Maud and Delos enjoyed each other's company so much that they sometimes had difficulty settling down to work. "We would get up as early as five a.m., have breakfast and talk," Maud once told a reporter, adding that they had to set an alarm for eight o'clock to remind themselves to quit visiting and start writing!

6) Maud always considered herself a midwesterner, even though for many years she lived in and around New York City and later retired to Claremont, California. Reminiscing to a fan about her life in the Big Apple, she wrote, "My favorite spot in the whole city was always the Public Library at Fifth and Forty-second. I did research on so many books there. There is a room . . . where authors, properly identified, are permitted to work. Their

typewriters, and the books and magazines which they are using may be left there for days and even weeks (unless especially requested by an indignant patron, in which case a page comes and asks politely if one can part with them for a few hours and one graciously accedes). I almost lived there."

7) The Betsy-Tacy series started as bedtime stories that Maud told her daughter Merian about her growing-up years in Mankato. By the time Maud was ready to write about the high school years, Merian was a teenager herself. "She brought the atmosphere of high school into the house, helping to refresh my memory," Maud explained to another reporter. "When she comes home from school she'll grab the copy I've written right out of my typewriter. And she's very frank, too. If she doesn't like what I've written she'll tell me, and I usually change it."

"Is that Maud?" asks Hannah, pointing to the photos on the second page of Mrs. Hawthorne's e-mail.

"I guess."

"I like this one of her in the white dress, where she's sitting perched on the arm of her husband's chair."

"Yeah." My heart skips a beat. Delos Lovelace looks a lot like Zach Norton.

"Who are these people?" Hannah says, pointing to two pictures at the bottom of the page labeled "Betsy and Tacy, best friends forever."

Heather Vogel Frederick

We read the captions. The first one, which is an old black-and-white photo, says "Maud and Bick (Betsy and Tacy), age 10." The other one is a color shot of two older ladies wearing matching dresses. The caption reads "Maud and Bick, age 70." I recognize Maud right away by her gap-toothed smile.

Mrs. Hawthorne has added a note underneath the two photos, and Hannah reads it aloud.

"Maud Hart Lovelace immortalized her lifelong friendship with Bick Kenney in her Betsy-Tacy stories. If you had to pick a best friend to honor in that way, who would you choose?" She flops back onto her bed and crosses her arms behind her head. "Easy. Taylor Lane."

"Who's she?"

"Not a she, a he," she replies.

"Really? You have a guy for a best friend?"

Hannah nods. "We've been best friends since sixth grade."

Zach and I used to be really good friends too. Not quite best friends, but close. Now, though, things are more complicated.

"How about you?" asks Hannah. "Who would you choose?"

I have to think about this for a minute. I've never really had a best friend. Not in the way that Jess and Emma are best friends, or Megan and Becca. My book club friends and my hockey teammates are my closest girlfriends, but I like them all equally. Well, except maybe Becca. She's a rung or two lower on the friendship ladder.

Then I remember the night of the ugly sweater party, when Courtney and I had that talk about Zach, and I think of all the other times she's been right there for me when I needed someone to confide in and give me advice. "I guess I'd have to say my sister."

"Yeah, Danita's pretty cool too. Especially now that we're older. We used to fight like cats and dogs when we were growing up."

I grin. "Courtney and I did too."

The next morning I awake to find another Secret Santa gift waiting for me on the bedside table.

"Open it!" urges Hannah, sitting up in her bed and watching in gleeful anticipation. My lame Secret Santa gifts have provided a lot of entertainment this week. For her, anyway.

Scowling, I eye the package. It's bigger than yesterday's, so it's probably not underwear, but I'm still pretty sure I'm not going to like whatever's inside.

"Hurry up!" urges Hannah. "We can squeeze in one more session at the beach before you have to go if we get a move on here."

Reluctantly I tear off the paper. At first I think maybe it's a fishing tackle box, but what fisherman would be caught dead with a pink tackle box? Then I lift the lid and a bunch of tiered trays unfold, each one filled with different kinds of makeup: sparkly eye shadow, half a dozen different colors of blush, other powders I don't recognize, a bunch of little pots of lotion, plus wands and applicators and tweezers and junk. Oh, and lip gloss. A lifetime supply of it.

Hannah starts to laugh.

I shake my head in disgust. Does my Secret Santa come from outer space?

Heather Vogel Frederick

Something like this could only be Becca's doing. *Chadwickius frenemus* rides again. This must be her secret revenge for the fact that Zach Norton likes me better than he likes her.

I close the useless box and slide it over onto Hannah's bed. "You keep it," I tell her.

"What am I supposed to do with it?" she says, still laughing. "I don't wear that stuff either."

Which is true. And which is probably why the two of us have gotten along so well. If my family does end up moving back to California, at least I know I'll have one ready-made friend waiting for me.

I end up tossing the makeup kit into my suitcase. I can rewrap it and give it to Courtney for a Christmas present. She'll like it. I can give her the underpants, too.

After our final boogie-boarding session and a brunch of leftover latkes, it's time to leave.

"It's been so good to see you and your family again, Beth," says my mother, hugging Mrs. Blum. "Thank you for everything. I'll keep you posted on our decision."

Hannah and her mother help us out to the rental car with our suitcases, then stand in the driveway talking with us while Stanley straps Chloe into her car seat.

"If you end up moving to L.A., I'll make a real surfer out of you," Hannah says.

"It's a deal, but you have to let me teach you how to play hockey, okay?"

We wave good-bye and hit the road, heading north along the ocean. It's gorgeous out, sunny, light breeze, low seventies, the kind of winter day that gives Southern California its fabulous reputation. As I stare out the window at the familiar scenery, Concord with its snow and cold seems like a distant dream. It's almost as if we never left Laguna.

Still, I'm not sold on the move. Not that Mom and Stanley have confirmed it. "We're still thinking things over," they keep telling me when I ask them about it. I'm trying really hard to be a good sport—I'm not a little kid anymore, and I know they have a lot of things to take into consideration, not just me. If Stanley does decide to take the job, I could probably find a new hockey team. Still, I'd really, really miss Concord. It took me a long time to adjust to living there, but now it feels like home.

My mother and I went for a walk on the beach the other night and talked about it a little bit.

"People are kind of like hermit crabs," my mother said, poking at one with her toe. "Hermit crabs are nomads, moving from shell to shell, just like people often move from house to house. A house is just a shell, really. But home—home you carry with you wherever you go. Home is in here." She touched her hand to her heart. "It's what you put inside your shell."

I understand what she meant. The thing is, though, I really like our shell on Hubbard Street.

I stare out the window, my thoughts drifting. I know it's Christmas Eve and I should be feeling the holiday spirit, but if I could wish for

Heather Vogel Frederick

a holiday miracle of my own right now, I'd wish us back in Concord. California likes to do everything in a big way, and Christmas is no different. All that over-the-top stuff felt normal when we lived here, from "Surfin' Santa" blaring all over the place to fake snow on fake trees to all the lights and parades and hoopla at Disneyland (which Chloe loved), but now I'd swap all the flashy trappings for the simplcity of a colonial New England in a hot second. Dad would have *loved* Concord at Christmastime.

We pass Crystal Cove, one of my favorite spots on the planet, and then continue on toward Newport Beach. When I see the sign for Balboa Island, I suddenly lean forward and tap my mom on the shoulder. Even though I'm stuffed full of latkes, and even though we're going to be eating dinner with Grant's family in Santa Barbara in a few hours, I have a sudden craving for a frozen banana.

"You can't be serious," says my mother, but she must be in a good mood—though whether from lunch or the prospect of moving back here or just the general holiday spirit, I can't tell—because she doesn't even hesitate. One quick U-turn later and we're on the road that leads over the arched bridge to Balboa.

The streets are jammed with cars, and we drive around for a bit looking for a parking spot, then stroll up the sidewalk to my favorite frozen banana stand.

"Looks like everybody else had the same idea," says Stanley.

That's the thing that's not so great about Southern California. It's really crowded here. Everywhere, all the time. Roads, beaches, amusement parks, restaurants, hiking trails, you name it. Everybody's always out, having fun in the sun. My father always used to say that's the price you pay for living in paradise.

We manage to snag a bench, and Mom places our order at the take-out window.

"Oh, man," says Stanley, as he takes his first bite. The top of his bald head goes pink, which it always does when he's happy. Maybe today it's just sunburn, though. It's hard to tell.

I give him a smug smile. "Told you so." What's not to like about a frozen banana dipped in chocolate and chopped nuts?

Chloe is enchanted with hers, too. Two seconds after mom hands it to her, she's a chocolate-covered mess. Little kids really know how to enjoy food. They play with it, they squish it in their hands and smear it in their hair, they wipe it all over their face, and they never worry about it spilling on their clothes or about what people might think. There are times I wish I could still eat like a toddler.

Smiling at her, a memory flashes to mind of me at her age, or probably a little older. When we lived in Laguna Beach, my father used to drive me over here once in a while as a special dad-and-daughter treat. He had separate rituals for me and Courtney—with her it was always doughnuts. But coming to Balboa was ours, and it always brings back happy memories whenever I visit. Mom tried making frozen bananas at home for me once, after Dad died and we moved to Concord and I was feeling homesick. She thought it might cheer me up, but it wasn't the same, and she never tried again. There's something about the sun

Heather Vogel Frederick

and the crowds and the ocean breeze and the ferry ride afterward that's part of the experience, and that makes it about more than just something to eat.

It's kind of like going to Kimball's Farm for ice cream with my book club, something I'd really miss if we leave Concord.

After giving Stanley a guided tour of the downtown, we take the teeny ferry to the other part of the island. Riding the ferry is one of my favorite parts of going to Balboa. Seriously, it's like a toy. Only three or four cars at a time can go on it.

I roll down my window once we're aboard and stick my head out, sniffing the air greedily as I look out at the familiar harbor. Maybe it wouldn't be so bad to live here again. Beside me, Chloe bounces her legs against her car seat, singing her own version of the song on the radio: "*Jingle, jingle, jingle, jingle, jingle, jingle BELLS!*" The other ferry passengers smile in amusement.

I pull my head back in and lean over to give her a kiss. She really is the cutest thing on two legs. I can't believe I ever thought Chloe was—what did Betsy Ray call it when her little sister Margaret arrived?—oh yeah, a "perfectly *unnecessary* baby." Our family would not be complete without Chloe. That would be like a hockey team without its goalie. Or its mascot, maybe. Chloe's our mascot.

Dad would have loved her too.

We don't linger because we still have a long drive ahead of us, and before long we're on the road north again. My stomach gurgles, rebelling against all the sugar and grease I've stuffed into it these last few days. Mrs. Wong would have a fit if she could see me. So would Coach Larson, for that matter. I haven't been on the ice once all week. I've managed to squeeze in a couple of runs, and then there was the boogie boarding, of course, but still, I'm going to be wicked out of shape by the time we get home.

Chloe and I eventually doze off, although it's more like a sugar coma in my case, and when I wake up a couple of hours later, my stomach is upset. Plus, my mother's all in a dither for some reason about meeting Grant's family, and she gives me the "you'd better be on your best behavior" lecture as we get closer, glancing in the rearview mirror for emphasis.

"Sure, Mom," I tell her, yawning. I'm still wondering what she's all worked up about when we pull into the Bells' driveway a short time later.

Grant's parents seem perfectly nice—they're older than Mom and Stanley, both silver-haired in that distinguished-but-youthful California way—so I can't imagine that's what set her off, and they go on and on about what a great girl Courtney is, so that can't be it either.

"Where are the kids, anyway?" my mother asks, as we stand in the driveway chatting.

Mrs. Bell smiles. "They went for a hike. Grant promised they'd be back by dinnertime. How about we get you inside and settled before they arrive?"

The Bells live in a beautiful house. It's set way up on a hill, with views of Santa Barbara and the ocean beyond. It's made of adobe, with

Heather Vogel Frederick

one of those red tile roofs and lots of wrought iron. Spanish Colonial, my mother calls it. Plus, there's an inner courtyard with a fountain. My mother goes gaga over it. She's kind of an architecture nut.

I trail inside with my suitcase behind Stanley and Mr. Bell. They're talking about Stanley's job interview, and I strain to listen. I catch only a few words: "great opportunity . . . big upheaval . . . weighing the choices."

Since my stepfather flew out for his interview a couple of weeks ago, there have been a lot of closed-door discussions between him and my mother. So far, all they've said is that the interview went well and the accounting firm is interested in him, but that they want to think about it some more. Then nothing. Total radio silence. It's driving me crazy. If we're going to move, I want to know. I don't want it sprung on me at the last minute again. When we moved back east, Mom didn't even discuss it with Courtney and me. We just came home from school one day and found her packing everything up in boxes. I want more time to prepare this time around, to say good-bye to everything—my Chicks with Sticks kids, my school, my house, my friends.

Especially my friends. Well, except for my lame Secret Santa. *Chadwickius frenemus.*

"I'm putting you in here with your sister, Cassidy," says Mrs. Bell, holding open the door to one of the bedrooms. "And Clementine, you and Stanley and Chloe are right here across the hall."

I toss my suitcase on the bed, glance in the mirror to make sure I don't have frozen banana still stuck to my face the way Chloe does, then head down the hall, following the sound of laughter. Mom and Mrs. Bell are in the kitchen. Their laughter stops abruptly as I walk in.

"Uh, is there anything I can do to help?" I ask politely, shooting my mother a suspicious glance. I hope they weren't talking about me.

"That's so sweet of you to ask," says Mrs. Bell, "but Christmas Eve around here is pretty casual. The table's already set. We're having oyster stew and salad and popovers, and there might be a treat or two for dessert, you never know." She smiles at me.

I smile back. I'm warming right up to Grant's mother.

"You can put those presents under the tree," my mother tells me, pointing to a couple of tote bags that are leaning against the wall.

"It's going to be so much fun to have a little one around tomorrow morning!" exclaims Mrs. Bell. "It's been years since we've had a baby in the house."

"You say that now, but just you wait," my mother replies. "Chloe's a handful."

As she and Mrs. Grant start discussing popover recipes, I drift out of the kitchen and head for the living room. I kneel down in front of the Christmas tree by the fireplace and start unloading the presents my mother brought.

Of course I have to look at the tags. My mother's handwriting is on most of them, but two that are addressed to me draw me up short. One is from Zach, and the other, surprisingly, is from Tristan. I sit back on my heels when I see it. Tristan's had a heavy round of competitions

Heather Vogel Frederick

the past couple of months, and I haven't heard much from him lately. Not that we've stayed in super-close touch since he went back to England—it's nothing like Megan and Simon—but between an e-mail now and then and the photos we both post online and the occasional video-chat, we've kept up on what each other is doing. To take the time to send a present, though—that seems significant somehow. Hefting it, I can tell it's a book. The one from Zach is smaller, but still heavy. What the heck did he get me, a hockey puck?

Now I'm feeling guilty that I didn't get anything for either of them. Should I have? But what? And why would I, anyway? It's not like I'm dating either of them.

Can a girl even date two guys? Would I want to if I could? Suddenly, things feel like they're getting too complicated. I wish there was a guidebook, or rules listed somewhere about this kind of thing. Hockey has guidebooks; hockey has rules. You can practice for hockey. You can't practice for real life.

Glancing over my shoulder to make sure that no one's watching—Mom and Mrs. Bell are still yukking it up in the kitchen, and Grant's father and Stanley are out taking Chloe for a walk—I slide my finger under the tape on one end of Tristan's present and slip the book out of its wrapping paper. It's a biography of Jayne Torvill and Christopher Dean, the British Olympic gold medalists. They're Tristan's ice-dancing idols. I glance inside the front cover, hoping he inscribed it.

He did. It says "To Cassidy, who rocks the ice no matter which skates she's wearing. Fondly, Tristan." I trace the word "fondly" with my fingertip, feeling a flutter in my stomach. I'm going to have to talk to Courtney about this later.

Slipping the book back into the wrapping paper, I retape the end and add it to the stack of presents under the tree. Then I pick up the little box from Zach. I sniff it. Nothing. I shake it. Nothing. Double-checking to make sure I'm still safe from prying eyes—Mom hates it when I do this—I wiggle the ribbon off and unwrap it.

I laugh out loud. Zach really *did* get me a hockey puck!

But not the usual kind. This one is made of glass, or crystal maybe, and there's a diamond pattern cut into the outside edge that catches and reflects the lights on the tree. I hold it in my hand, staring at it. My name is engraved across the surface, along with a single star.

It's gorgeous.

There's no card, no note, just this simple, stunningly beautiful *thing*. Hearing the scrape of chairs in the kitchen, I stuff it back in its box and rewrap it as quickly as I can, then stick it way toward the back of the pile under the tree. By the time my mother and Mrs. Bell appear, I'm out in the courtyard sunning myself.

I can't stop thinking about the two presents, though. Zach must have gone to a lot of trouble to get that crystal puck made for me. Does that mean something? And what about the book from Tristan? Especially that word "fondly." It's not quite "love," but it's definitely more than "sincerely" or "your friend."

I fall asleep in the sun thinking about it all, and when I wake up, Mr. Bell is lighting a fire in the big adobe outdoor fireplace. There's still

Heather Vogel Frederick

no sign of my sister and Grant yet. Mrs. Bell brings out a tray of egg-nog and blankets to tuck around us as we stare at the flames. She must have put some music on too, because a familiar carol melody floats through the open French doors from the living room, soft as a whisper. Mr. Bell plugs in the strands of lights strung through the potted trees. I start to relax. The Bells' house isn't Hubbard Street, but everything about Christmas here is simple and perfect, just the way it should be.

And then my sister and Grant walk in.

"Hi, everybody!" says Grant. "Merry Christmas!"

"Merry Christmas!" we all chorus back.

The two of them stand there by the living room doors, holding hands. Courtney's face is flushed with happiness. Grant clears his throat.

"We have something to tell you," he announces. "I just asked Courtney to marry me, and she said yes. We're engaged!"

There's a moment of stunned silence, and then everybody scrambles up from their seats and rushes over to hug them. My mother is crying. Mrs. Bell is crying. Chloe sees them crying and she starts crying too. Even Mr. Bell and Stanley look like they might cry. I stare at them all, aghast.

What is wrong with you people? I want to shout. My sister can't be *engaged!* She's only four years older than I am!

I knew Courtney liked Grant—was *fond* of him even—but when did that turn to love? How could this happen without me knowing about it?

I look over at my mother, who is showering Courtney with kisses.

Can't she put a stop to this? Doesn't my sister have to get permission or something? Then it dawns on me—my mother knew this was coming, or at least suspected it! And so did Mrs. Bell. That's why my mother was so worked up in the car earlier, and why the two of them were whispering and laughing in the kitchen this afternoon. They must have known something was up.

My mother should have told me. She knows how much I hate surprises, especially life-altering ones like this. Why did she just let the news come as a shock?

First a move, now an engagement. I can hardly breathe.

Final score: How the heck should I know? The only thing I know is that as soon as we get back to Concord, I'm going straight to Dr. Weisman's office again. There's only so much change a person can handle in one lifetime.

Heather Vogel Frederick

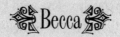

Becca

*"'Life,'" she said, "'is complicated . . .
for a woman, at least.'"*

—*Betsy in Spite of Herself*

"She's a beauty, isn't she?"

Philippe pats the steering console and beams at us. Megan and I both nod, trying to appear enthusiastic. It's hard, though—the captain's son has been droning on nonstop about the *Calypso Star* and her state-of-the-art this and highly advanced that ever since our private tour started two hours ago.

"She has a GPS navigator, of course," he continues proudly, "but did you know that she also has two fiberoptic gyro compasses?"

Beside me, Megan murmurs appreciatively. I stifle a yawn. Not that I really need to hide it. For one thing, Philippe is too busy dragging us across the room—I mean the bridge, which is the proper name for the ship's control room—to view something called a maneuvering panel. For another thing, when he does manage to pry his eyes off his precious ship, the only one he's really noticing is Megan.

Which shouldn't come as a surprise, after all. Lately it seems I'm practically invisible to guys, except for Third, who doesn't count.

It's not as if I'm desperately in love with Philippe, but it would be nice to think maybe he's just a little bit intrigued. I can't help it—when there's a cute boy around, I like to be noticed. Is that such a bad thing?

What I really want to know, though, is how someone so good-looking can be so incredibly dull. Philippe is so gorgeous I can hardly take my eyes off him. All that tousled dark hair! Those smoky gray eyes and dimpled chin! He's a total knockout. Until he opens his mouth, that is.

The first part of the tour, when he took us down to the galley where the chefs prepare the food for the passengers, was actually pretty interesting. Gigi joined us for that part, because she was dying to get a look at the kitchens. It's incredible how much food they have stored away on the *Calypso Star*, and how many people work pretty much around the clock to feed the thousands of passengers onboard. I especially liked getting to go inside the refrigerators—they were about the size of the Wongs' living room back home—and visiting the dessert station, where there were literally hundreds, if not thousands, of beautiful treats being prepared.

Gigi about went nuts at that stop, asking the pastry chefs a zillion questions and snapping pictures of everything.

"Research," she told us. "I might want to add a few things to the menu at Pies & Prejudice."

But all this technical stuff? Honestly, if I never hear another thing about bow thrusters and gross tonnage and engine output it will be too soon.

Heather Vogel Frederick

I swallow another yawn and glance over at Megan. She must have a serious crush, because she's still pretending to hang on Philippe's every word. Even when he gets all excited telling us about how environmentally friendly the ship is, with its garbage incinerators and recycling program, and sounds just like her mother.

Finally Captain Dupont crosses the bridge to join us. I think maybe he saw my last yawn. "Philippe," he says, "your enthusiasm is *admirable*"— he pronounces it in that adorable French way, with the accent on the last syllable—"but don't you think perhaps it's time to offer the *mademoiselles* some refreshments?" He gestures to a table in the corner, where a steward is setting down a tray of chocolate-covered strawberries and sodas.

Philippe dutifully steers us over to it.

He tries to make small talk but can't resist wedging in a few more not-so-fun facts about the ship, including the incredibly exciting news—not!—that there are 810 miles of electric cable in her hull.

I resist the urge to ask, "What's a hull?" and instead glance at my watch. "Omigosh, look at the time!" I exclaim, nudging Megan with my elbow. "We'd better get going. We have an appointment in the spa, and I have a few more presents to wrap before dinner."

Christmas Eve is a big deal aboard the *Calypso Star*. For starters, there's a fancy formal dinner, and our families have been invited to sit at the captain's table, thanks to Philippe. Afterward there's eggnog and caroling in the atrium, some big Broadway-style Christmas extravaganza in the theater, a teen skating party at the rink, and a midnight chocolate buffet. Plus, our families are both planning to open presents tonight. That was Gigi's idea, so that we won't have to try and cram it in tomorrow morning before disembarking at the cruise line's private island for a day on the beach.

"I will escort you to your destination," says Philippe politely.

Megan and I thank his father and leave the bridge, heading down the hallway to the stairs leading to the spa deck. Megan and Philippe are chattering away, and I try not to be jealous, really I do, because it's Christmas and everything and because I am capable of being a mature, sensitive person when I set my mind to it, but it's hard because it's obvious that Philippe is really interested in Megan more than he is in me. Probably because she's pretending he's the most fascinating creature on the planet.

I tried to at first, too—really tried, but my eyes glazed over after a while as Philippe droned on about latitude and knots and the electric propulsion plant. Julia Ray would have rallied to the occasion. She always does. One of the questions Mrs. Hawthorne asked us to think about for our next book club meeting on New Year's Eve was which character we admire the most and would most like to be. I picked Julia. She has the magic touch with boys. They're always following her around, bringing presents, and proposing. A girl could learn a thing or two from Julia Ray.

"Until tonight, *mademoiselles*," says Philippe when we reach the spa. He's speaking to both of us, but looking at Megan, of course. It's been like this all morning.

"This is the life, isn't it?" says Megan a few minutes later, taking a

Heather Vogel Frederick

sip of her mango smoothie. We're wrapped in thick terrycloth robes and lying on deck chairs in the spa, waiting for the attendants to come get us.

"I guess."

She looks over at me. "What's wrong?"

"Nothing."

"Hey—it's me. I know when something's bugging you."

I put my magazine down. Might as well get this out in the open. After all, if you can't talk to your best friend, who can you talk to? "It's stupid, I know—but it's just that Philippe obviously likes you better than me."

Megan's dark eyebrows nearly take flight. "Is *that* what you're sulking about?"

"I'm not sulking."

Megan sighs. "Fine. But you like Zach, remember? And in case you forgot, Simon broke up with me a month ago. Gimme a break, please, this is the first time in weeks that anyone's even noticed I'm alive."

"At least someone's noticing! I might as well be invisible these days."

"It's not as bad as that," she says. She gives me a mischievous smile. "Third likes you."

I let out a snort. "Great. Just what I want to be—a Third-magnet."

"I think he's kind of cute."

"You take him, then."

"C'mon, Becca! There are tons of guys our age on this ship. And don't tell me you haven't noticed. I've seen you checking them out."

I have to smile at this. I guess I'm not as sly as I think I am.

"How about that guy from Texas we met at the barbecue—Brock or Bryan or something like that?"

"Brody?"

"See? I knew you noticed him."

I lift a shoulder. "Well, it's not like he's noticed me."

"Time to trot out the la de da, then," Megan says.

"La de da?"

"You know—what Julia Ray calls pouring on the charm. Using your womanly wiles. Remember?"

I make a face. "I don't think I have any."

"Sure you do. All girls do. What do you think I've been doing with Philippe?"

"Looking at his cute face while trying not to hear what's coming out of his boring mouth."

Megan looks shocked.

I grin at her. "You have to admit it's true."

The walkie-talkie in my purse crackles before she can reply. I pull it out and press the transmit button. "Yes?"

"Mom to Becca."

I roll my eyes at Megan. "Yes, Mom?"

"Just thought you'd want to know that your brother and grandfather advanced to the semifinals in the Scrabble competition!"

I hold up my index finger and circle it in the air. Megan giggles. "Wow, Mom, that's great."

Heather Vogel Frederick

"Are you girls having fun getting bee-yoo-ti-fied?"

"Yup."

"Well, we'll see you at dinner. Over and out."

I turn to Megan. "Okay, I'll give it a try. With the la de da, I mean."

"Go, Becca! That's more like it. Brody won't stand a chance."

"You can start by calling me Rebecca," I tell her.

"Huh?"

"I need an alter ego," I explain. "An alias. 'Becca' just doesn't cut it in the la de da department."

"But you hate it when your mother calls you Rebecca!" Megan protests.

"That's because it's always attached to my middle name, which means she's mad at me." I lean back in my chair and sip my smoothie thoughtfully. *Rebecca*. Yes. It's perfect. "It'll be like playing a part onstage," I explain to Megan.

She shrugs. "If you say so."

The attendant comes in and beckons to us, and two minutes later we're settled into our spa chairs with our fingers and toes soaking in warm, bubbly water. There's nothing like a mani-pedi to cheer a person up.

"Would you girls like to choose your nail polish?" asks the manicurist, holding out a tray. "We have some fun holiday colors."

Megan goes for a brilliant red called Fun Fun Rudolph. My hand hovers over a sparkly green that would go perfectly with the outfit I'm planning on wearing this evening, until I turn it over and look at the name: Wintergreen with Envy. No, thank you. Don't need that reminder. I'm having enough of a struggle with what my mother calls "the green-eyed monster" as it is.

Torn between Santa's Baby, a really pretty pink, and Making Spirits Bright, a festive plum, I ultimately choose Making Spirits Bright. It sounds like something I could use a jolt of right now. Besides, *Rebecca* is nobody's baby. She's a woman of the world.

My brightened mood—and fingers and toes—quickly sour again the minute Megan and I return to our stateroom, though. Two packages are waiting for us, one on the end of Megan's bed, and the other on the coffee table in front of the sofa.

"Looks like our Secret Santas stopped by," Megan says.

"Whoopee." So far, my Secret Santa has been a complete dud. I know exactly who it is, too. Who else but Jess would give me a book about stargazing (like maybe she thought I'd be doing that on the ship instead of hanging out in the teen disco?), a CD of some stupid opera singer, and stationery with horses on it? Nothing I'm ever in a million years going to use again. I gave most of it to Stewart. But even he didn't want the stationery.

Megan's presents haven't been so bad. Mostly stuff anybody would be glad to have, including a pair of really pretty beaded earrings, some Motor Mouth lip gloss, and bubble bath. No wonder she's so eager to unwrap the latest offering.

"Nice," I tell her, as she rips the wrapping paper off and holds up a really cute stuffed bear dressed as a cheerleader. I almost bought one

Heather Vogel Frederick

just like it for myself a couple of weeks ago when I saw it in the window of the Concord Toy Shop. Megan sets it on the shelf above the desk with all our towel animals and takes a picture.

The towel animals have been one of the best parts of this cruise. Every night when we come back to our room, there's a different one waiting for us. Our steward makes them out of twisted and folded towels, and they're really amazing. So far we've found a dog, a swan, a mouse (made from a washcloth), a pig wearing Gigi's sunglasses, and a monkey. The monkey nearly scared me half to death. It was hanging by its little towel arms from the ceiling, and I wasn't paying attention when I came into our cabin and walked right into it.

"Open yours," Megan urges.

Reluctantly I pick up my present and unwrap it. "Are you kidding me?" I blurt when I see what's inside.

"What is it?" asks Megan, craning to see.

"Nothing." I crumple the wrapping paper and toss it into the trash, wadding the present in beside it.

"Oh come on, it can't be that bad."

"Really?" I snap. I fish it out and hold it up. "My Secret Santa gave me a framed photo. Of a *goat*."

Megan starts to laugh.

"It's not funny!" I yell, which makes her laugh even harder.

I toss the picture into the wastebasket again. If this is Jess's idea of getting even with me for calling her "Goat Girl" back in middle school, all I can say is, it's pretty lame. Not to mention mean.

Our stateroom door opens, and Gigi breezes in. My grandmother is right behind her.

"Hello, girls!" she says. "How was the spa?"

Megan displays her glowing fingers and toes.

"Ooh," says Gram. "Very nice. Let's see yours, too." I show them off, and she nods. "Positively puny, as Anna Swenson would say. You both look very Christmasy."

Christmasy is the last thing I'm feeling at the moment. Murderous is more like it. Jess Delaney is going to get an earful from me when I get back to Concord. Rebecca isn't the type of person who puts up with stuff like that.

"We have mail, ladies," says Gigi, passing out sheets of paper. "From Phoebe Hawthorne. Fun Facts to Go."

My grandmother sits down on the sofa and beckons to me. "Let's look at them together."

Forcing myself to smile, I join her. Time to try and shake off my sour mood. There's no point in spoiling everybody else's evening. Gram and I scan the list, then look at the photos that Mrs. Hawthorne attached.

"Oh, wow," says Megan, who's sitting on the end of her bed next to Gigi. "Look at that white dress Maud is wearing! Don't you just love the collar and those lacy sleeves? The big hat, too. I'd kill for an outfit like that!"

"I'd kill for the guy beside her," says my grandmother.

"Gram!"

She laughs. "I'm serious—look at him! Delos Lovelace was a catch."

"Don't you think he looks like Zach Norton?" Megan asks me.

"Maybe, if Zach had a mustache and a crewcut." Megan's right, though, Maud's husband does look a lot like Zach.

"So which character was based on him again?" asks Megan. "Was it Tony or Joe?"

"It was—"

"Shhh!" my grandmother puts her hand over my mouth. "No spoilers, please. Remember? Megan hasn't read *Betsy's Wedding* yet."

Gigi points to the pair of pictures at the bottom of the page. "I like these two best," she says. "Maud and Bick are adorable as ten-year-olds, and even more adorable at my age, don't you think?"

I have to admit they are pretty cute, for a pair of older ladies. And they sure look happy.

"You can just tell they love life, can't you?" says Gram.

"Look at the detail on their dresses!" says Megan. "They're so stylish!"

"What, older ladies can't be stylish?" Gigi teases.

Megan swats her. "You know what I mean. Don't you love that black crisscross ribbon at the neckline, and the single big black button on their jacket pockets?"

Gigi nods.

"What's that stuff on their hats?" I ask, squinting.

"Netting," Gram replies. "It's like a little see-through veil that you could pull down to make a fashion statement. My mother used to have hats like that, and gloves like they're carrying too. No self-respecting woman went anywhere without gloves back in those days. Right, Gigi?"

Megan's grandmother nods.

"How come Maud never got that gap in her teeth fixed?" I muse. "I sure would have."

"Oh, I think it gives her character," says Gram. "Plus, it gave her something to pass along to Betsy Ray."

"It just adds sparkle," says Gigi, who has plenty of sparkle herself.

My grandmother reads Mrs. Hawthorne's question for us aloud: "Maud Hart Lovelace immortalized her lifelong friendship with Bick Kenney in her Betsy-Tacy stories. If you had to pick a best friend to honor in that way, who would you choose?"

Megan and I look at each other and grin.

"Ha!" says Gram. "I thought so."

"What's this?" asks Gigi, leaning over and plucking the goat picture out of the trash.

My grin fades. "Um, nothing."

"Doesn't look like nothing. Don't you want to keep it? Such a nice frame."

I take it from her wordlessly and set it on the coffee table, and the four of us head off to join up with the others. But between the stupid goat picture that will not die and the fact that Philippe and Megan can hardly take their eyes off each other, dinner is pretty much ruined. And Brody is nowhere in sight. So much for Rebecca. I'm feeling so sorry for myself by the time dessert is served that I'm seriously considering just going back to the cabin and spending the rest of the evening by myself, watching a movie or something.

"You're missing out on the best cake ever," says Stewart, shoving

Heather Vogel Frederick

his plate closer to me. "It's chocolate volcano torte with raspberry drizzle. Try a bite."

"No thanks."

"Stop moping and be nice to yourself. It's Christmas Eve!"

The fact that my dorky older brother is feeling sorry for me and trying to cheer me up makes me even more depressed than I already am. I take a grudging bite.

"Good, huh?"

I nod.

"Told you so."

Like my mother, Stewart is convinced that chocolate has magical properties, and maybe it's true, because I'm feeling a teeny bit better by the time we all get to the atrium for the caroling party. The uptick in my mood doesn't last long, though.

"Isn't this fun?" says Megan, slipping her arm through mine. Her dark eyes are sparkling and her pale skin is flushed, but I'm not sure if her obvious excitement is because of the holiday spirit or because of Philippe, who's standing across the expansive open area with his father and the other ship's officers, but whose gaze keeps straying back toward her. How can he help it? She looks fabulous in her red silk sheath dress.

Fun for you, maybe, I think, not bothering to reply. I tug at the hem of my own dress, which is made of navy velvet with spaghetti straps. It's a bargain-basement special, which is all I could afford this year. It's okay, but it pales in comparison to Megan's.

I make a halfhearted attempt to spot Brody-from-Texas and maybe try and unleash some la de da, but it's impossibly crowded in here, and I quickly give up.

A steward comes by with a tray of eggnog. I sip mine, gazing upward at the crowded balconies. All four stories of the atrium are encircled by balconies, each one filled to the brim with passengers eager to join in the singing. Captain Dupont steps forward and makes a few welcoming remarks, then signals the jazz combo by the Christmas tree. As they strike up "Deck the Halls" and everyone starts to sing, I can hear the voices above us drifting down.

Something else drifts down to us too.

"Whoa," cries Stewart, delighted. "Snow!" He sticks out his tongue and grabs a flake with it, then makes a face.

"It's fake, you moron," I tell him. "We're in the Caribbean."

"I knew that," he retorts, stung.

The snow is pretty, but it doesn't do much to improve my mood, nor does the Christmas "Extravaganza," which is glitzy and peppy in a Rockettes kind of way. It's not the music and dancing so much as the fact that toward the end I see Philippe reach over and take Megan's hand. She looks really happy, of course, but what about me? I stare down at my fingernails. I should have gone with Wintergreen with Envy.

"See you at the rink," says Philippe as he drops us off at our stateroom afterward.

"He seems like a nice boy," says Mrs. Wong, watching him stride away down the hall. "I like him."

Of course she does. Philippe probably gave her his lecture about the *Calypso Star*'s environmentally friendly incinerator.

"Time for presents!" says Gigi.

Thinking maybe this will finally jolt me out of my gloom, I grab the pile I wrapped earlier and head down the hall to my parents' cabin.

Due to my dad's job situation, I know not to expect much—we actually sat down before the trip and talked about it, and decided just to do stocking stuffers for one another this year—but still, it's hard not to get my hopes up. I still have my fingers crossed for a car of my own. Christmas is the time of year for miracles, right? Maybe my dad got a job and didn't tell us.

He didn't.

My parents really tried. Our stockings are bulging, and my mother wrapped each of the little gifts in our stockings individually. I like absolutely everything they got me, from the fancy soap and candles to the silver hoop earrings and lip gloss and gift card for music downloads. Stewart stuck in a small box of my favorite chocolates, which was really nice of him, and Gram managed to find all sorts of Betsy-Tacy stuff: refrigerator magnets and bookmarks and Post-It Notes and stationery and stuff like that. She gave us all joke gifts, too, in honor of the Ray family's tradition in the Betsy-Tacy books. Mom gets a beautifully wrapped onion, just like Mrs. Ray used to get every year, and for Dad and Stewart and Grampie, there are lumps of fake coal. I find mine near the bottom—a yo-yo with a gift tag that says, "From Yo-Yo."

"Is this a joke, too?" asks Stewart, holding up the card he got from

Mrs. Wong. I pull one out just like it. Megan's mother gave us each a certificate that says she donated a flock of chickens in our name to some kids in Cameroon.

"Stewart!" scolds my father. "That was very generous of Lily, and you need to be sure and thank her." But his lips are quirked up in a smile. It's really hard not to poke fun at Mrs. Wong sometimes.

Stewart grins. "Sorry."

Finally, there's just one thing left—the bulge in the toe. I already know what it is, because Mom always puts chocolate oranges in our stockings at Christmas. But when I reach down to fish it out, my fingers close around another small envelope. Out of the corner of my eye I see my grandmother watching as I open it.

I see the money first. "Thanks, Gram!"

"You shouldn't have," says my mother, frowning at the crisp bills. "This cruise was present enough."

Grampie winks at me. "It's just a little pocket money, Calliope. No need to get your knickers in a twist. Your mother and I thought the kids might like to buy some souvenirs to bring home to their friends."

"Thanks," Stewart tells them. He got a matching envelope too.

Mine is a little different, though. In addition to the bills, there's another piece of paper. I pull it out. It's a handwritten gift certificate that says: *GOOD FOR ONE SPRING BREAK TRIP TO DEEP VALLEY!*

"Now that you're finally a Betsy-Tacy fan too, I thought you might be curious to see where it all started," Gram says, beaming. "I've got it all planned out. We'll both fly to Chicago, then take the train to Minneapolis.

Heather Vogel Frederick

It may not be quite as glamorous as Betsy's train trip to Milwaukee, but it will still be fun. From there, we'll rent a car and drive out to Mankato."

I manage a smile, even though Mankato, Minnesota, is not exactly at the top of my list of dream spring break destinations. "Thanks, Gram," I tell her again, giving her a hug.

Afterward, I head back to my own cabin with my haul. Megan is twirling around the room, or as much as a person can twirl in a cruise ship cabin.

"You'll never guess what I got for Christmas!" she says.

"Philippe had himself gift-wrapped," I reply sourly.

"Becca!"

"Rebecca," I correct her.

She flaps a long slim envelope at me.

"Fine. What did you get?"

"Gigi's taking me to PARIS for spring break! My parents finally agreed to let me go!"

Tears spring to my eyes. Paris? I'm going to Minnesota, and she gets to go to *France*?

"Awesome," I say flatly, and turn away.

Megan stops twirling. Her smile fades. "Did you hear me? I'm going to Paris! It's what I've dreamed of my entire life!"

"Yup." I know I'm being unfair to her, but I can't help it. It's been a roller coaster of a day, and this feels like the last straw. Why did my father have to lose his stupid job, anyway? And why did we have to come on this stupid cruise with the stupid Wongs? Being with them is like getting my nose rubbed in the fact that my family is broke. The Wongs have absolutely everything. Especially Megan. A new crush, talent bursting out her ears, and now a trip to Paris. This is the worst Christmas ever.

She takes a step toward me, then hesitates. "I thought you'd be happy for me."

"I am, okay? Quit bugging me."

"Fine," she snaps. "Be that way."

She stomps off to the bathroom to get changed, leaving me to stew in my own juice. Green-eyed monster juice. I feel absolutely miserable right now. Grabbing a tissue, I wipe my eyes and blow my nose, then cross the room to the mirror over the dressing table and give myself a good talking-to.

"You stop this right now!" I whisper, sounding scarily like my mother. "Megan is your best friend. She deserves every speck of happiness she gets, and you know it."

My reflection looks back at me, chastened.

I hear the bathroom door open and turn around. "Megan, I'm sorry," I tell her. "It's great you're finally getting to go to Paris. I'm happy for you, really."

"You don't look all that happy," she says, sounding somewhat mollified.

I sigh. "I am. It's just—"

"Just what? Please tell me this isn't about Philippe."

"No, it's not that," I reply, shaking my head. I sit down on the sofa. "I mean, it sort of is, but it's more than that. I guess because it's Christmas

Heather Vogel Frederick

and everything. Maybe I was hoping for a miracle, I don't know. The thing is, there's something I haven't told you."

"Is everything okay?"

I shake my head. "My dad lost his job a couple of months ago."

Megan stares at me wide-eyed. "Omigosh, why didn't you tell me?"

"You know my mom. She doesn't want Concord to know that a pillar of the community and our perfect family might have a problem. She and my dad asked Stewart and me to keep it quiet, until after the holidays at least."

"That totally explains why your father hasn't seemed like himself lately," says Megan.

"Partly it's because he's tired," I tell her. "He's been job hunting all day, and delivering pizzas at night for Pirate Pete's to help tide us over."

"Really? Eye patch and everything?"

I nod. "Really. It's humiliating."

Megan laughs. "No, it's not—they have great pizza. Besides, it's just temporary." She sits down on the sofa beside me. "Is there anything we can do to help?" she asks softly. "I have some money in the bank from Bébé Soleil, and—"

"*No,*" I say sharply. Sheesh, like I'd take money from her college fund.

"At least let me tell my parents. I know they'll want to help."

I shake my head.

"It seems kind of silly not to let your friends know," Megan continues. "They're the people you most want standing by you when there's trouble. You'd stand by me, right?"

Home for the Holidays

She's got a point. "At least wait until we get home before you say anything," I tell her. "My parents don't want to spoil the trip for everybody, you know?"

Megan gets up and goes over to the dresser. Opening one of the drawers, she takes out a present. "Maybe this will help cheer you up."

I open it. "A Wong original!" I exclaim, holding up the pale blue silky top that's inside and regretting my uncharitable thoughts earlier. "I love it!"

"I thought maybe you'd like to wear it to the party at the rink tonight," she says. "It's got these really full sleeves that will billow out while you're skating. They're very—" she gives me a mischievous look—"*Rebecca*. Loads of la de da. I think it would look supercute paired with that white fleece vest of yours."

"I have something for you, too," I tell her, pulling my suitcase out from under the sofa and fishing out a small, brightly wrapped box.

"They're perfect!" she exclaims, holding up the pair of silver snowflake earrings it contains. "Especially for tonight. I'm putting them on this instant. Thanks, Becca—I mean Rebecca."

I give her a hug. "And thank you—for putting up with me today, and for listening to me just now."

"What are best friends for?"

We change, then stop by my parents' stateroom to pick up Stewart. As we pass the Internet café, Megan pauses.

"You guys go on ahead, I need to send an e-mail real quick," she says.

"Simon?" I ask.

Heather Vogel Frederick

She gives me a mysterious smile and shoos us off to the rink, where we find Philippe waiting for us. His face falls when he sees that Megan isn't with us, but he brightens again when I tell him she'll be along shortly.

"Shall we go ahead and get our skates, Becca?" he asks me.

"Um, it's Rebecca actually."

"*Ah oui, bien sûr*, Rebecca." Philippe inclines his head.

Stewart gives me a funny look. I haven't sprung my new, more glamorous self on my family yet.

"*Excusons-nous*," says Philippe, cutting in front of a group of kids about my age. One nice thing about hanging out with the captain's son is that you always get to go right to the head of the line.

One of them has his back to us, and when he turns around I see that it's Brody from Houston. I give him a dazzling Rebecca smile.

"Hey!" he says, sounding annoyed. "No cuts!"

"VIP guests," murmurs Philippe, ushering Stewart and me forward.

There's an excited buzz behind us as everyone starts speculating who we are. I stand up straighter, hoping I look like a celebrity. *Rebecca the glamorous and mysterious*. We collect our skates, and as we go over to one of the benches to put them on, I spot Brody watching me curiously. I waggle my fingers at him. He reddens, then waves back.

Hooked!

Now to reel him in.

"You are having an enjoyable Christmas Eve, I hope?" Philippe asks politely, as we step out onto the ice.

"*Oui*," I reply, trotting out one of the few words in my French vocabulary.

Philippe smiles and rattles something off in rapid French. I stare at him blankly for a second, then take a deep breath. *You can do this*, I tell myself. It's time for Rebecca to make her grand entrance. I'll practice on Philippe before springing some la de da on Brody. No harm in that. Philippe can be my guinea pig.

I laugh a tinkling little laugh. Stewart gives me another odd look, but I ignore him. I put my hand on Philippe's arm. "I just adore French accents," I tell him.

He looks a little startled as I tuck my arm through his. "Uh, *merci*."

We start to skate, and my eyes flick over to Brody.

"Did you know that this space doubles as a nine-hundred-seat arena?" Philippe asks me, gazing lovingly around the rink. "It's a remarkable feat of engineering."

"Really?" I reply, aiming for Megan's tone of breathless fascination. "Tell me more."

Philippe seems taken aback at my sudden interest, but quickly recovers. As he launches into a detailed inventory of the rink's many features, including the control room beneath it, I pretend to hang on his every word. Out of the corner of my eye I see Brody. He's still watching us. I hold my arm out, letting my sleeve billow.

"What's wrong with your arm?" my brother asks, swooping by.

I drop it hastily, scowling at him. I glance over at Brody again, but now he's talking to some girl with a strawberry-blond ponytail. How

Heather Vogel Frederick

dare he ignore Rebecca! What would Julia Ray tell me to do if she were here? I wonder. Try again, most likely. *You can do this, Becca*, I tell myself again. I'll need to borrow Philippe, though. Assuring myself that it's for a good cause and that Megan won't mind—it's just a role in a play, right?—I steer him in Brody's direction. As we skate by I say loudly, "Any chance you could give me a private tour of the rink's control room?"

That definitely gets Brody's attention.

Philippe frowns. "Tonight? But the skating party is just starting and—"

"Just a quick one? We'd be back in a few minutes. No one would even know we were gone."

"But I—"

Suddenly, as if a switch has been flipped deep inside me, Rebecca takes over. My mouth opens of its own accord, and her words come out. Words I didn't even know I knew. *"S'il vous plait,* Philippe?" she says. "Please?"

Rebecca speaks French?

Philippe inclines his head politely. "How can I resist when you ask so charmingly?" he replies. "As you wish."

We take our skates off again and stash them under the bench. I glance over my shoulder as we start to leave and waggle my fingers at Brody again, feeling the power of Rebecca. *I'll bet he thinks I'm some Hollywood starlet*, I think. *He'll be falling all over himself asking me to skate when we get back.*

Conscious of Brody's eyes on me, and using the swaying of the ship and my teetering heels as an excuse, I take Philippe's arm again as we exit the rink. Just as we pass through the door, the ship gives a lurch and I stumble. Philippe reflexively reaches out to steady me, putting his arms around me as he pulls me back to my feet. We stand there for a split second in a close embrace, so close I can feel the thud of his heart. Before I can step back, I hear a sudden, sharp intake of breath behind me.

I turn around.

Megan is standing there, a stricken look on her face.

Philippe releases me instantly. I almost fall over when he does, and have to grab the handrail against the wall.

Megan doesn't say a word; she just turns and runs.

"Megan!" cries Philippe, and jogs off down the hallway after her.

Stewart comes up behind me. "What's going on?" he asks. "Where did you guys run off to?"

"It's nothing," I tell him sharply. "Nothing happened."

I follow him back to the rink, but the skating party has lost its sparkle. Trying to ignore the terrible pit in my stomach, I lace my skates back on and glide halfheartedly around with Stewart. I don't even look at Brody. Rebecca seems to have vanished.

"Can I ask you something?" says my brother after a while.

"Sure."

"What would you think about me deferring college admission and doing a gap year instead?"

I stop in my tracks and gape at him. "What?" All Stewart's talked about since he was in elementary school was going to college.

He shrugs. "It's not that big a deal. The thing is, I overheard Mom and Dad discussing things, and it turns out she's planning to drop out of the landscape design program." He gives me a sidelong glance. "I don't think she should have to do that, do you? I mean, she's so close to finishing and everything."

I'm too stunned to say anything, still trying to wrap my mind around the idea of Stewart not going to college. "What would you do?" I ask finally.

"I don't know. I can live at home and get a job or an internship or something." He grins. "Maybe *Flashlite* will hire me full-time."

My brother does some occasional modeling work for the teen fashion magazine.

"It's okay, really. I'm sure it will be fine," he continues, but it sounds to me like he's trying really hard to convince himself of that fact.

All of a sudden I feel terrible. The only person I've been thinking about through this whole layoff situation is myself. I didn't worry about how my dad felt when he started delivering pizza, I worried about what people would think of me. Here's my brother, facing the biggest disappointment of his life, and is he thinking about himself, and whining and complaining? No. He's thinking about Mom, and what's best for her.

I am a selfish pig.

"Stewart, everything's going to be fine," I tell him. "You'll see. I bet you end up winning an amazing scholarship or something."

He looks over at me. "You think?"

"Of course! Colleges should be falling all over themselves to get you. You're smart, and you're talented—you're one of the best people I know." It feels weird to be giving my brother a pep talk, but seeing the way he perks up, it also feels really right.

"Thanks."

We circle the rink again, and my thoughts return to Megan and Philippe. All of a sudden I hear Rebecca's voice whispering inside my head: *You didn't do anything wrong. It wasn't what it looked like. Besides, you and Megan talked about this—you were only playing a role for a few minutes, that's all. Philippe was just your guinea pig.*

But Rebecca's explanation sounds suspiciously like an excuse.

My stomach tightens as I wonder how I'm going to explain everything to Megan. I keep waiting for her and Philippe to reappear, but they don't.

"I'd better go," I say to my brother finally.

"What about the midnight buffet?" he protests. "I went up earlier to scout it out—they've got these amazing sculptures made out of chocolate."

I shake my head. I couldn't eat anything. Not now. "I'm going to bed," I tell him. "It's been a really long day."

"Suit yourself," he says, pulling out his walkie-talkie. "I'll see if Grampie wants to go."

Heather Vogel Frederick

It's dark inside our stateroom. I tiptoe in, using the night-light in the bathroom to guide me.

"Megan?" I whisper.

There's no answer. I can tell she's there, though, because I can see the lump under the covers on her bed. There's no sign of Gigi. She's probably at the chocolate buffet with everyone else.

"Megan?" I repeat.

"Go away," she mumbles.

"Nothing happened," I tell her. "Remember that guy from Texas? Brody? Well, I was just practicing a little—you know, like we talked about in the spa, playing a role onstage . . ." I falter, my voice trailing off. Rebecca's explanation sounds feeble as the words come out of my mouth. "It's not what you think," I finish lamely.

"It's exactly what I think and you know it, *Rebecca*. Go away. I hate you."

I flinch, feeling like I've been slapped. *Fine*, I think. *Be that way.*

If she doesn't want to talk to me, I don't want to talk to her. I slip into the bathroom to change into my pajamas, then cross the room to the sofa, which the steward remade into my bed while we were gone. There's something on my pillow. I freeze when I see what it is: a towel coiled up to look like a snake.

Crawling under the covers, I lie there miserably in the dark, listening to Megan sniffle. I don't move, and I don't say a word. I can't. What could I possibly say that would make her feel better? She wouldn't believe me anyway.

On the other hand, what kind of a horrible person lets her best friend cry herself to sleep?

The same kind of person who thinks only of herself when her family is in trouble, that's who.

A snake.

Emma

"As early twilight gathered outside the windows she thought of the Christmas Eve ritual at home going on without her . . . and was swept by homesickness."
—*Betsy in Spite of Herself*

"All aboard!"

The conductor waves to the engineer, and the old steam locomotive whistle blows as we start chugging out of the North Conway station.

"Wouldn't Clementine love this!" says Mrs. Delaney, leaning out the window and snapping a picture of the little building. Built in 1874 with towers and turrets and lots of Victorian gingerbread trim, the station looks like it would feel right at home in Cassidy's backyard.

"Mom!" Jess protests. "Close the window! It's freezing out there!"

The whistle blows again, and we all settle back in our seats. I love trains. I've never ridden on one like this before, though. Mostly just the commuter rail from Concord to Boston, or Amtrak to New York, although last year in England we traveled by train a lot. But there's something special and terribly romantic about an old steam locomotive.

Speaking of romantic, my gaze wanders across the aisle, where Jess is sitting next to Jonas. They're deep in conversation, and as I watch the two of them I feel my temperature rise again. I can't believe she's doing this! Jess, of all people!

Last night was the closest the two of us have ever come to an out-and-out fight, and even though I'm still mad at her, I woke up feeling a little guilty. The thing is, I was so tired from all that skating at Nestlenook that I could barely keep my eyes open, and I wasn't in the mood to try and talk things out. And by the time I got up this morning, Jess was already dressed and gone. Later, when I saw her at breakfast, she was so stiffly polite to me we might as well have been total strangers, which really hurt.

Still, she's my best friend, and I probably should make an effort to find out from her what's going on. I want to be willing to give her the benefit of the doubt. Not that there's much doubt any longer, I think, glancing across the aisle again. Felicia is right; there's something going on between Jess and Jonas.

Felicia didn't join us for the excursion today. She's back at the inn with Jess's aunt, helping prepare for tonight. Everybody keeps telling me that Christmas Eve is a big deal at the Edelweiss. It's a big deal at my house too, and right now I'm beginning to wish I'd stayed home.

"See ya later, North Conway!"

Jess's little brothers are sitting across from me, kneeling on their seats with their faces pressed against the window. They can barely contain their excitement. North Conway's Christmas tree train is not

Heather Vogel Frederick

exactly the Polar Express, but it's a pretty good runner-up.

"Lovely countryside, isn't it?" says Mrs. Delaney, leaning over the back of my seat.

I nod.

"Bridget told me they started taking their guests on this excursion a few years back, and it was such a big hit that it's become an annual event."

I nod again. "I can see why."

When we first got to the Edelweiss, I wondered why they didn't have a Christmas tree up. There were plenty of other holiday decorations, including the big nutcracker soldier who stands guard over the candy dish on the reception counter in the lobby. But no tree. Jess explained that the inn has a lot of German traditions, and when her uncle was growing up in Germany, people didn't put their tree up until Christmas Eve. His parents always kept it as a big surprise for him and his brothers, and he likes to do the same thing for his guests.

The twins bounce in their seats again, their faces shining as they stare at the passing scenery. I look out the window, too, and as the train wends its way through the snow-covered forests of the White Mountains, I lean back and allow myself to be lulled by the swaying motion and the rhythmic clack of steel against rails. My thoughts drift back to England. Living there was exotic and wonderful—there's nothing like the English countryside—but there's just as much beauty here, too. I love New Hampshire! I watch as we chug past tidy little villages tucked into the foothills, each with its white-spired church anchoring the village green, and past ice-frosted rivers that glitter in the sun in their rush toward the Atlantic.

Jess's laughter draws me out of my reverie. I glance over and see that her cheeks are pink and her eyes sparkling. She looks really pretty—and really happy, too, I think glumly.

She's supposed to be dating my *brother.* It's going to kill him if he finds out that she likes someone else. And where is my loyalty supposed to lie? Jess and I are best friends, but Darcy is family. How could Jess put me in this position, making me feel torn between the two of them?

"Wanna play gin rummy, Emma?" asks Dylan, and even though it's the last thing I feel like doing, I nod and say yes. Maybe it will help keep my mind off my dilemma.

The hour-long trip passes quickly. When we arrive at our destination, a huge horse-drawn hay wagon is waiting at the platform to take us to the tree farm. I watch as Jonas carefully boosts Jess aboard, then passes her crutches to her and climbs in beside her. They're sitting so close their shoulders are touching. Of course, I'm wedged in too, beside the twins, but that doesn't count. Jess could move over if she wanted to.

"Isn't this fun?" says Mrs. Delaney, and I rearrange my face into a smile.

"Yeah." Fun couldn't be further from the truth, though. Right now I'm still wishing I could go home.

"How about you, Jess? Isn't this just like something out of a dream?"

Heather Vogel Frederick

"*Dreaming, dreaming, of you, sweetheart, I am dreaming . . . ,*" warbles Jonas, and Jess laughs, hearing this snippet from her solo audition piece coming from his lips.

Nightmare is more like it, I think, looking away. The wagon rumbles forward, and Jess's uncle starts singing, "*Dashing through the snow.*" Everybody but me joins in.

At the Christmas tree farm there are two sleds waiting, one for the tree we'll be cutting down, and one for Jess. Jonas picks her up and carries her over to it, and Dylan and Ryan make a big show of helping him pull her around. I trail along miserably behind as we all troop off on a well-worn path leading into the woods.

"We must look for just the right tree," Jess's uncle tells us. "Not too big, not too small, not too wide and not too narrow. The one who finds it gets a special prize." He winks at Dylan and Ryan, who drop the rope to Jess's sled and race off ahead of us.

Everybody but me is in a good mood, enjoying the sun sparkling on the snow. Mr. and Mrs. Delaney are holding hands. Some of the little kids start a snowball fight, which their parents quickly squelch. Jess is still studiously ignoring me, which makes me equally miserable and mad. I scuff along feeling like Scrooge. *Bah, humbug!*

Jess's brothers win the tree-finding contest with a beautiful Douglas fir that's about eight feet tall and perfectly shaped.

"*Ausgezeichnet,*" says Uncle Hans. "Excellent." He reaches into his pocket and pulls out two golden dollar coins and tosses them each one.

He lets them help cut the tree down, and then he and Mr. Delaney and Jonas tie it to the second sled. After we hike back, we have about half an hour left to poke around in the tree farm's tiny shop before our train leaves to go back to North Conway. I wait until Jess and Jonas are done shopping before I go inside. The less I have to watch them flirting the better.

Predictably, most of the souvenirs are tacky, but they have some nice ornaments, and I still haven't found just the right thing for Becca. To be honest, I'm feeling a little stumped. For one thing, I'm pretty sure she's my Secret Santa, too—who else would send such a pointed message with that exercise DVD?—and she's done such a crummy job of it I don't feel inspired to put all that much effort into her final gift.

I don't find anything for her, but I linger by an ornament that would be perfect for Jess. After some hesitation I decide to go ahead and buy it. I can always give it to Cassidy if I don't end up giving it to her.

The train whistle blows as I'm at the cash register, signaling us all to get back on board, and I hurry back to my seat. I barely have time to take off my jacket before the conductor comes through, announcing that lunch is served.

"Wow," says Mr. Delaney as I follow him into the dining car. "This is amazing."

The old Pullman car has been completely restored, and the bright murals on the ceiling, richly upholstered booths, and linen-covered tabletops give it the look of a fancy restaurant.

"Wow is right," says Mrs. Delaney. "The snack car on Amtrak doesn't quite compare, does it, Jess? I'll bet this is just like the dining

Heather Vogel Frederick

car Betsy ate in when she took the train to Milwaukee."

"Mmm," Jess murmurs, sliding into a booth and putting her napkin on her lap. Her mother slides in across from her, and Jonas and Mr. Delaney join them, leaving me stuck with the twins.

"May I join you?" asks Uncle Hans, and I nod and move over to make room for him. He quickly manages to take my mind off Jess and Jonas, regaling the boys and me with funny stories and jokes. It turns out he's a big fan of steam trains, and he tells us a bit about the excursion train's history too, as we're waiting to order.

I start feeling a little better. Besides Uncle Hans's company, there's something about eating in a dining car that makes me feel incredibly grown-up. It's like a scene out of an old movie. "Swell-elegant," as Mr. Ray would say. The waiter brings our food, a pumpkin-barley soup that would be great for Pies & Prejudice—and in fact I hear Mrs. Delaney asking for the recipe, so I'm guessing she's thinking the same thing—plus chicken pesto wrap sandwiches and salad. There are also freshly baked shortbread cookies—cut in the shape of Christmas trees, naturally—for dessert, along with tea, coffee, or hot chocolate.

"Hot chocolate," I tell the waiter. "*Mit Schlag*. With whipped cream."

Uncle Hans roars with laughter. "Already fluent in German, after just a week!" he exclaims. "But then Jess told me you're a clever girl."

I glance across the dining car at her, wondering what she'd say about me now.

Back in North Conway, we transfer to the vans for the drive back to the Edelweiss, stopping briefly to drop Jonas off at his house.

"See you later tonight!" he calls to Jess, and she waves.

When we get to the inn, Mr. Delaney helps Jess's uncle untie the tree and lift it off the top of the van, and then all the little boys, Jess's brothers included, swarm around to carry it inside. After it's placed on its stand in the library, Uncle Hans shoos everybody out, closing the doors firmly behind him.

Earlier this morning, before we left, he and Jonas taped brown paper over the glass panes in the French doors, to keep out prying eyes. That doesn't stop Dylan and Ryan, though, who hang around for a while, hoping to get a peek at the proceedings, but they eventually give up and go off with some other kids to play a board game.

Aunt Bridget pokes her head out from the kitchen. "You girls might want to take a nap," she tells the rest of us. "German Christmas Eves can be late ones, and you'll want to be rested up."

"Sounds good," says Mrs. Delaney, heading upstairs.

I hesitate, wondering if maybe now is a good time to try and talk to Jess. But she's clearly not interested in my company, and instead makes a beeline for the piano, where she starts picking out the melody to "Dreaming."

Dreaming of who, that's the question, I wonder bitterly, and stalk down the hall to our room.

There are two sheets of paper on my bed, along with a sticky note from Mrs. Delaney that says *Book club stuff!*

The list of fun facts sounds so much like my mother that I find myself blinking back tears. Why did I ever think it would be a good

Heather Vogel Frederick

idea to spend Christmas Eve anywhere but at home with my family?

The pictures of Maud and her friend Bick only make me feel worse. Especially the one of them in the matching dresses, when they're seventy. That was supposed to be Jess and me! Lifelong friends, BFBB, inseparable. But now there's this stupid wedge between us.

I look at the question underneath the pictures. Which friend would I choose to immortalize in a book? Jess, of course. She's the Tacy to my Betsy. Only now I don't know who she is, or what we are. I stare at the pictures miserably as a tear trickles down my cheek.

I desperately need to talk to someone. First, though, I need to blow my nose. Grabbing a tissue, I dry my eyes and make myself presentable, then reach for the tote bag by my bed that contains my journal and a couple of books and head back toward the lobby to find Jess's aunt.

"Of course you can use the phone," she says when I ask. She takes me into the small office behind the front desk, then closes the door to give me some privacy. I can't help it; I get choked up again when I hear my mother's voice.

"Is everything okay?" she asks, sounding concerned.

"Yes," I tell her, then, "No!" I wail. "I want to come home!"

There's a pause on the other end of the line. I can hear the clatter of pots and pans in the background—my father must be in the kitchen fixing Christmas dinner, which we always have on Christmas Eve. I feel another stab of homesickness. I can practically smell the roasting turkey, and hear the crackle of the fire they've probably lit already in the living room.

"Sweetheart, what happened?" my mother asks.

I tell her how much I miss her and Dad and Darcy and Pip, and although I stop short of sharing Felicia's suspicions regarding Jess and Jonas, I tell her that Jess and I aren't getting along very well.

"I see," says my mother when I'm finished explaining how Jess has been giving me the cold shoulder. She's quiet for a moment. "Friendships can be so complicated at your age. At any age, really."

I hiccup softly into the receiver, wiping my nose on my sleeve.

"I guess you're just going to have to give Jess some space, sweetheart. You two have been cooped up together day and night for a whole week, and that can be a strain on any friendship. But I'm sure you'll sort it all out eventually." She swings into mom pep talk mode. "Right now, honey, it's Christmas Eve. See if you can pull yourself together and make an effort to be cheerful—as your gift to the Delaneys. It was so kind of them to invite you along."

"I know," I reply. "It's not like I'm trying to be a Scrooge."

"Of course you're not," my mother tells me. She pauses, then adds, "Remember when Betsy and her boyfriend break up right before Christmas, and Betsy realizes that unless she rises to the occasion and stops moping around, she's going to make the holiday miserable for everyone else?"

"Y-e-s," I say slowly. My mother thinks in books, the same way I do.

"Well, just hang in there, okay?"

"Okay."

We talk for a while longer, and I tell her about Nestlenook, and the train ride to the Christmas tree farm, and by the time I hang up the phone I'm feeling a lot better.

I wander into the living room. Soft holiday music spills from hidden speakers somewhere, and there's a fire crackling in the stone hearth. Guests are clustered in the rocking chairs and sofas around it. Dylan and Ryan and other kids are laughing over some game they're playing at a table in the corner. There's no sign of Jess. I figure she must be in the kitchen, because I can hear muffled voices and the clatter of pots and pans, and smell the aroma of dinner being prepared. I take a deep breath. The Edelweiss isn't home, but it's still a pretty nice place to be on Christmas Eve.

Snagging an afghan from one of the sofas, I head for the window seat at the far end of the room. I need some inspiration. Didn't I jot something down about Christmas music, something I just read in *Betsy Was a Junior*? I rummage in my tote bag for my book of inspiring quotes, and flipping through it, I find what I'm looking for: "Carols were being practiced by the choir. Betsy wondered what gave these songs their magic. One strain could call up the quivering expectancy of Christmas Eve, childhood, joy and sadness, the lovely wonder of a star."

I sigh. Sheer poetry.

Hungry for more literary comfort, I open the slim volume that I brought downstairs with me—Dylan Thomas's *A Child's Christmas in Wales*. My father reads this aloud to our family every Christmas Eve. Since I can't be there tonight to hear it, I figure I'll read it myself. In my mind I can hear my father's voice wrapped around the opening words:

"One Christmas was so much like another, in those years around the sea-town corner now and out of all sound except the distant speaking of the voices I sometimes hear a moment before sleep, that I can never remember whether it snowed for six days and six nights when I was twelve or whether it snowed for twelve days and twelve nights when I was six."

I love Dylan Thomas and the lilting rhythms of his prose. As I fall headlong into the book, the room fades away, and soon I'm as oblivious of my surroundings as I am of the wave of homesickness that had threatened to engulf me. Reading is the antidote to a great many troubles.

I emerge eventually, still a bit woolly-headed from my visit to snowbound Wales, and tucking the book back into my bag, I grab my journal. I didn't write in one for a few years, after Becca stole the one I kept back in sixth grade and read aloud this poem I'd written about Zach Norton. Talk about humiliating. It seems like ancient history now, and even a tiny bit funny, although it still makes me squirm to recall how mortified I'd been. At any rate, last year when we went to England I decided it was time to start keeping one again. I'm glad I did, because already some of my memories of our year there are starting to fade.

My eye falls on another quote in my inspiration book, this one from *Betsy in Spite of Herself*: "It was pure romance to sit at a table spread with glossy linen and eat a delicious meal while looking out at a flying white landscape."

Heather Vogel Frederick

I decide to start with lunch on the Christmas tree train, and after that I write about yesterday's outing to Nestlenook. I haven't been skating all that much since we got back from England. Now that Mrs. Bergson is gone, it's made me a bit sad to go to the rink in Concord. But yesterday reminded me how much I love to skate. There's nothing like that feeling of flying over the ice, and outdoors is so much better than being inside a rink. Sometimes Jess and I skate on her pond back home, but that's like a teaspoon compared to Nestlenook, plus the Delaneys don't have a Zamboni at their disposal to keep the surface smooth.

I try to capture in words all the sights and sounds from yesterday—the way it sounded under the bridge when the sleigh passed over, the thunder of the horses' hooves mingled with the brighter notes of the jangling bells; the way the blue bowl of the sky arched overhead; the way the air filled my lungs, so cold that it hurt; the way the enticing scent of hot chocolate drifted from the little gazebo on the island. I describe the Edelweiss Inn, too, and how much it reminds me of *Betsy and the Great World*, when Betsy travels to Oberammergau, the village in the mountains of Bavaria.

When I'm finished, I flip back idly through my journal to this time last year, remembering Christmas Eve at Ivy Cottage in England. I could never have imagined back then that the Winding Hall of Fate, as Betsy calls it, would find me at the Edelweiss Inn this year, instead of at home in Concord.

I'm feeling much calmer by dinnertime, and I decide to make an effort to sit with Jess. At the last minute, though, Felicia squeezes in between us. She's off duty tonight as a waitress, because Christmas Eve dinner is served buffet-style.

"How was the trip to the Christmas tree farm?" she asks me, casting a significant look in Jess's direction.

"Um, fine," I reply. I don't really want to talk about Jess and Jonas, though. It will only make me gloomy again, and I promised my mother I'd try and keep my spirits up. So I quickly change the subject.

After dinner, Jess's aunt and uncle invite us to join them in front of the library. It's time for the unveiling of the Christmas tree! A current of excitement runs through the room, and as the adults take out their cameras, Uncle Hans calls the younger kids to the front of the crowd.

"Can you all say *'eins, zwei, drei'*?" he asks them, and they parrot back his words.

"*Sehr gut!* You are now responsible for the countdown. Ready?"

Dylan and Ryan and the other kids nod, and Jess's aunt dims the lights. A hush falls over the room and then, at Uncle Hans's signal—

"*Eins, zwei, drei!*" the children cry.

Uncle Hans flings back the doors to the library. "*Fröhliche Weihnachten!*" he cries. "Merry Christmas!"

An audible gasp goes up from the gathered guests. There are real candles on the tree! They glow so beautifully, so softly, that it takes my breath away.

"Merry Christmas!" we chorus back.

Heather Vogel Frederick

Then we form a semicircle around the tree, and taking hold of one another's hands, we sing "O Tannenbaum"—"O Christmas Tree"— stumbling over the unfamiliar words on the slips of paper that Felicia has been busy handing out.

In Germany it's traditional to open presents on Christmas Eve, so the Delaneys decide to go with the flow. Families take their piles of presents and retreat to various corners of the sprawling living room, and pretty soon all you can hear is the tearing of wrapping paper and squealing of little kids. My parents sent along several presents from home for me to open, including *Emily of Deep Valley* and *Carney's House Party*, two of the Deep Valley books I don't have yet, and *The Synonym Finder* from my father. He adds a reference book every year for my "writer's shelf," as he calls it, a tradition he started back in sixth grade, when he slipped Strunk and White's *Elements of Style* into my stocking. There's one more present too—a small box from Stewart. Inside is a heart-shaped locket.

"How romantic!" says Mrs. Delaney.

I open it and start to laugh. So much for romance. Inside are pictures of Pip and Yo-Yo, our familys' dogs. The card is signed "Love, Stewart," though, which is nice.

Jess gets a new riding helmet, a pair of suede boots, several books, and from my brother, a silver charm bracelet with a little heart dangling from it. *Poor Darcy*, I think when I see it. He's in for a rude awakening.

Becca's grandmother sent both of us a canvas tote bag with a picture of Betsy Ray on one side and another one of my favorite Betsy-Tacy quotes on the other: "Betsy returned to her chair, took off her coat and hat, opened her book and forgot the world again."

Jess gives me a fleeting smile when she opens my present. It's a scoop-necked cashmere sweater I got for her in England last summer before we came home. It was on sale, and I had some leftover birthday money, and it looked like it would be perfect for her. Especially the color—a dreamy pale blue. I had visions of her wearing it to audition in.

"Thanks," she says politely.

"You're welcome," I reply, just as politely.

Her mother gives us a funny look.

"Where's your present for Emma?" she asks, and Jess shrugs.

"Around here somewhere, I guess."

It isn't, though. There's no present at all for me from Jess. I try not to show how much this hurts, but it's almost impossible, and her mother gives us another speculative look.

Uncle Hans claps his hands. "The vans will be leaving for the Christmas Eve service in the village in ten minutes!" he announces, and a number of families scurry off to get their coats, including us. But just as we're heading through the lobby, the phone at the front desk rings.

"*Ja*," says Uncle Hans. "I understand. Don't worry—we know all the words."

He hangs up and looks over at us. "That was the minister. Our organist can't make it. His car broke down."

Heather Vogel Frederick

"Maybe we can help," says Mrs. Delaney, whispering something to the twins.

Half an hour later, we're all seated inside the small church. I'm finally next to Jess—not that it does me any good at the moment. This isn't the time or place to try and talk to her.

The door at the back opens, and Jonas and his parents step inside. Jonas smiles and waves as they slip into a pew a few rows behind us. Jess smiles back. I don't.

The service is as simple and beautiful as the evergreens and white candles that grace the altar. The minister reads the nativity story from the Gospel of Luke, and then Dylan and Ryan march up to the front with their recorders. The boys look solemn and unnaturally clean.

Mrs. Delaney leans over to Jess and me and whispers, "I fixed their hairs," which gets a faint smile out of Jess and a chuckle out of me. Betsy and Tacy's friend Tib always says this, because she's German, and the German word for "hair" is plural.

The twins accompany us manfully if not exactly tunefully as we sing "Away in a Manger" and "O Little Town of Bethlehem" and "It Came Upon a Midnight Clear."

We finish with "Silent Night," this one a cappella, and as we sing the tale of a babe born in a faraway stable two thousand years ago, I pause for a moment, listening as the haunting melody spirals up to the church rafters. A shiver goes down my spine.

It's magic—pure Christmas magic.

I glance over at Jess, wondering if she feels it too. Her eyes are closed; her face alight with joy. The quiet beauty of the old carol has clearly cast its spell on both of us. As I watch her, I feel something else: a rush of love.

I can't be mad at Jess. She's my friend and always will be. It's as simple as that.

There's more magic in store too, for afterward, the church doors swing open to reveal—

"Snow!" Dylan cries in delight, grabbing his brother's arm. The two of them race out into the parking lot, where they stand with their heads flung back, smiling up at the sky.

The congregation flocks out to join them, and the boys throw their arms out and start twirling through the falling flakes. I feel like twirling too.

"Deep Valley," Jess murmurs beside me.

We smile at each other, real smiles this time, and I feel more of the anger and hurt of the past couple of days draining away.

"Can I talk to you when we get back to the inn?" I ask, and she nods.

"I've been wanting to talk to you, too."

Jonas comes over to say good-bye, and gives us both hugs as he wishes us a Merry Christmas. I try not to look as he's hugging Jess. I don't want to spoil the magic.

Back in our room, I close the door and lean against it. Jess hobbles over to her bed and puts her crutches down, then takes a seat. "You first," she says. "You're the one who's mad."

"You're the one who hasn't been talking to me."

Heather Vogel Frederick

"Because you're mad," she says. "It's only logical."

"Jess! This isn't a math equation! This is my brother we're talking about."

She wrinkles her brow. "Darcy? What does he have to do with anything?"

"What do you mean, what does he have to do with anything? He has *everything* to do with *everything!*"

Jess still looks baffled. "I still have no idea what you're talking about."

"I'm talking about you and Jonas."

"Me and Jonas?" She stares at me in disbelief. "What about me and Jonas? You mean you think—"

"Come on, Jess," I tell her. "Even Felicia noticed."

"So that's what you two were whispering about at Nestlenook!" she says. "You think I like him?"

"Don't you?"

She crosses her arms over her chest. "Of course I like him, Emma. Jonas is smart, and funny, and he likes music and animals, and yeah, maybe we flirted a bit, but—"

"Ha! I knew it!"

"But I happen to be dating your brother, and I would never do that to Darcy. Don't you know me better than that?"

I shift uncomfortably. "Well, I thought I did, but Felicia said—"

"Felicia, Felicia, FELICIA!" Jess's voice rises. "Why would you take her word for anything, anyway? And while we're on the subject of Felicia, is it any wonder I spent so much time with Jonas? I mean, besides the fact that my uncle hired him to hang out with me, which you seem to have conveniently forgotten? You ignored me, Emma! You completely and utterly ignored me. What was I supposed to do? Sit and twiddle my crutches while you ran around hanging on my stupid cousin's every word?"

I'm silent, stung by her accusation.

After a while, Jess sighs. "I hate it that we're arguing," she says gloomily.

"Me too," I reply.

I look out the window. I can see from the reflection of the Christmas lights that it's still snowing. Where's the magic now, I wonder? And then it occurs to me that maybe what I'm looking for isn't out there somewhere, but in here, right inside of me, in the form of those two little words it can sometimes be so hard to say.

"I'm sorry," I tell her.

"I'm sorry too," Jess replies, and the relief in her voice is audible.

"You're absolutely right," I continue. "I shouldn't have ignored you, and I shouldn't have misjudged you. I was an idiot."

"You're not the only one. I made things worse by giving you the cold shoulder." Jess stands up and hops across the room to the dresser. "I have something for you, by the way. Two somethings, in fact."

"Really?" Jess has a present for me after all!

She passes me a package that can only be a book, plus another little bag.

I smile when I see it. "I have something else for you, too," I tell

Heather Vogel Frederick

her, reaching under my bed and pulling out an identical bag. We both shopped for each other at the Christmas tree farm.

"Open the big one first," she says.

I unwrap it. "Oh," I breathe. "Oh, wow."

"It's a really old edition," she tells me. "I was up in the attic at home a few months ago and found it in a trunk. Mom said I could give it to you. She knows how much you love it."

Jane Eyre. I run my finger across the title, then open the cover. "Gosh, Jess, I don't know if I can accept this. It could be valuable."

"Nothing is more valuable to me than your friendship," she says fiercely. "I don't ever want to fight again, okay?"

"It's a deal. And thank you—this is beautiful. I love it."

We open the other bags at the same time and burst out laughing. We got each other the exact same ornament—a tiny red sleigh with two girl elves inside. On the side, written in glittery ink, are the words: *Friends are the sisters you choose for yourself.*

I cross the room to give her a hug. "I hated being mad at you!"

"Me too," she replies.

"Are you hungry?" I ask her.

"Need you ask?"

"Let's go find something to eat. We can have a picnic up here in our room, Betsy-Tacy-style."

We change into our pajamas, pull on our robes and slippers, and make our way as quietly as we can down the hall to the kitchen. We put together a tray of cold roast pork, homemade applesauce, and gingerbread—*mit Schlag,* of course—and as we start to head back, I pause in the lobby.

"Do you mind if I check my e-mail real quick?" I ask Jess.

"Go ahead. I'll check mine when you're done."

I log on. I have two e-mails, one from Stewart (Merry Christmas! See you in three days!) and one from Megan. I suck in my breath as I read the subject line.

"Jess!" I whisper urgently. "Check this out!"

She swings herself over to where I'm sitting, and I tap the subject line with my finger, which reads: *EMERGENCY MDBC MEETING!*

"Uh-oh," says Jess. "That doesn't sound good."

We scan the contents together:

> Sistren! The Chadwicks need our help. No one is
> supposed to know this, but Mr. Chadwick got laid
> off from his job a couple of months ago. They're
> going through a really tough time.

"That explains why I saw Mr. Chadwick driving down Main Street with a Pirate Pete's sign stuck to the roof of his car," says Jess.

"You did?"

"Uh-huh."

"When?"

"A few weeks ago."

"Why didn't you tell me?"

She shrugs. "I meant to, because I thought it was a little weird, but it was right before finals, and I had a lot on my mind. I guess I forgot."

We continue to read:

> Becca's worried. If Mr. Chadwick doesn't find a job soon, Stewart might not be able to go to college next year, and Mrs. Chadwick will have to drop out of her landscape design program.

Stewart not go to college? My heart sinks. I can't believe he didn't tell me.

> Here's my snoggestion: I think the Chadwicks need a Secret Santa. What if we surprised them at our New Year's Eve party with some practical things to help tide them over and cheer them up until Mr. Chadwick finds another job?

> Gigi's totally on board, and I'm going to talk to my parents later tonight. If we all put our heads together, I'll bet we can come up with some great ideas. Let me know what you think.

It's signed Love, Megan.

"A Secret Santa for the world's worst Secret Santa," I say glumly.

Jess pokes me in the back. "Becca's not that bad. Besides, this is about the whole Chadwick family, not just Becca."

"I know. You're right."

Jess shoves her crutches under her arms and starts down the hall. "Grab the food," she says. "We've got some brainstorming to do!"

"To go from Before Christmas to After Christmas was like climbing and descending a high glittering peak. Christmas, of course, sat at the top. The trip down was usually more abrupt and far less pleasurable than the long climb up, but not this year. For this year, the After Christmas held Mrs. Poppy's party."

—*Betsy and Tacy Go Downtown*

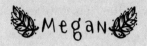
Megan

"*Parties came thick and fast in
Deep Valley during holiday week.*"
—*Heaven to Betsy*

"I hope you all appreciate what a big sacrifice I'm making," says Mrs. Hawthorne, opening the rear door of my mother's hybrid sedan and extending her hand to my grandmother.

Gigi grasps it as she climbs out. "We certainly do," she says. "Will Mr. Darcy ever get over the shock of you deserting him for our humble party?"

Emma's mother always spends New Year's Eve watching *Pride and Prejudice*—the six-hour one with Colin Firth as Mr. Darcy. She's making an exception this year because of our book club's progressive dinner.

"He'll survive," Mrs. Hawthorne assures her. "Besides, I promised I'd spend all day tomorrow with him instead." She tucks Gigi's hand into the crook of her arm as my dad climbs out of the car behind her. The three of them start across the icy driveway. "Go ahead and park over there," Mrs. Hawthorne calls over her shoulder to me, pointing to a spot on the far side of the garage that's been shoveled smooth.

"Okay," I call back, shifting into drive and nudging the gas pedal.

"Watch out for Pip," my mother says sharply, as if maybe somehow I couldn't see the large, furry shape bounding straight for us.

"Sheesh, Mom, I'm not blind!"

"There's no need to get snippy."

Driving with my mother is no fun at all. Even though I've had my learner's permit for a while now, she's still incredibly nervous whenever I'm behind the wheel, and jumps at every little thing I do, or don't do.

I manage to park without (a) squashing the dog, (b) hitting the side of the garage, or (c) disgracing myself in some other unforeseen way. Still, my mother breathes a huge sigh of relief when I turn off the engine, as if she's just returned to earth from a dangerous mission in space. I don't know how she's going to survive when I actually get my license.

As the two of us head for the back door, I feel my stomach twist into a knot. I haven't seen Becca—make that Rebecca—since we got back to Concord.

The last few days of the cruise were awful. Becca and I weren't talking to each other, and hiding it from our families wasn't easy. She took a sudden interest in Scrabble and skipped most of the beach day to attend the final competition and cheer on her brother and grandfather. I, on the other hand, spent most of my time hiding out in the

Heather Vogel Frederick

spa reading fashion magazines and dreaming about Paris. I even went to the towel-animal class with my mother and Gigi.

I avoided Philippe, too. I was too embarrassed to talk to him.

Besides, to be totally honest, I wasn't all that into him anyway. It was just that having somebody—anybody!—interested in me felt really good after being dumped by Simon. And it was especially nice to have that somebody be so handsome. But Philippe and I had absolutely nothing in common. Looking back, I'm feeling a little guilty that I pretended to be so interested in his stupid ship. A little la de da can get a person into a whole lot of trouble.

"Come in, come in!" says Mrs. Hawthorne. "Welcome to the first stop on the official New Year's Eve Betsy-Tacy Progressive Dinner!"

She takes our coats and looks me up and down. "Wow, Megan, look how tan you are! I can tell you had a great time."

I smile automatically and nod, peeking over her shoulder into the living room. I wish my first postcruise encounter with Becca wasn't so public, but the rest of the group is already here, chowing down on appetizers. Pip bounds past me and makes a dive for the plate of bacon-wrapped somethings on the coffee table. Jess's little brothers leap up and fling themselves on him, and fortunately, they're able to stop him before he can do any damage.

"Nice save, boys," says Mr. Hawthorne, grabbing the dog by the collar and towing him out of the room.

Mrs. Hawthorne pours my mother and me some punch, and I squeeze in beside Emma on the sofa while my mother goes over and perches on the arm of my dad's chair. The Hawthornes' house is really small, so we're all kind of squished together here. Not that anybody minds—Emma's house is one of the coziest I know. There's something about all the shelves full of books and the comfy furniture and colorful art on the walls that's really appealing. I even like their pink kitchen, although I'm not sure I'd want to paint ours that shade.

Gigi has a been given a place of honor in the armchair by the fire, and Darcy and Stewart and the twins are sitting on the floor by her feet. Cassidy's on the floor too, leaning against her mother's legs. Chloe is in Cassidy's lap, eating a cracker. I carefully avoid looking at Becca, who is perched beside her dad on the fireplace's brick hearth. Out of the corner of my eye I can tell that she's just as carefully avoiding looking at me, too.

"Did you hear anything more from Simon?" Emma whispers to me.

I shake my head regretfully.

"Too bad," she says, squeezing my arm. Then she looks down at it and pushes up her sleeve. "Man, check out that tan! I look like the belly of a fish next to you."

I smile and fix myself a little plate of appetizers—a stuffed mushroom, some carrot sticks and dip, a few crackers, couple of the bacon-wrapped things (scallops, as it turns out), and what looks like a little bundle tied with a green ribbon. I bite into it. The outside is crunchy, and the inside is creamy and delicious.

"Aren't those good?" says Cassidy, piling a bunch more onto her plate. "I can't stop eating them."

Heather Vogel Frederick

"Nick, are these wonton wrappers?" asks Mrs. Sloane-Kinkaid, holding one up.

Emma's father does all the cooking in her family. He nods. "Yup, with brie inside, and just a smidge of cranberry chutney. What do you think?"

"Fabulous!" Cassidy's mother tells him. "You deep-fried them, right?"

He nods again. "I thought maybe the green onion 'ribbon' was a bit much, but that's what the recipe called for, and I thought, oh, what the heck. Might as well go whole hog. It's New Year's Eve, after all."

"They're perfect! I'm stealing the idea from you for one of my shows."

"Help yourself."

We do, and the pile on the platter rapidly disappears.

"So how does this thing work tonight?" asks Darcy. "When we're finished eating here, we head off to the next stop?"

My mother reaches into her purse and pulls out a sheaf of hand-outs. "I've got it all planned out," she replies. "I made maps for every-one."

Of course she did. My mother is nuts about maps.

"Half of you left your cars at Clementine's, right?"

Heads bob up and down around the room.

"Good. We'll walk up to the Chadwicks' next for soup, then to Clementine's for salad. From there we'll caravan to the Delaneys' for the main course, and back to the tea shop for dessert. After that, you'll

simply walk back to wherever your cars are parked and drive home."
She looks around the room, obviously pleased with herself. "I thought
it might be nice to celebrate the holiday by reducing our carbon footprint."

Only my mother could make a New Year's Eve party sound like a
chemistry test.

"Thank you, Lily, for your earnest and thoughtful planning," says
Mrs. Hawthorne, who is good at being diplomatic. "You are a true citi-
zen of the world. Now before we move on to the Chadwicks', I'd like to
propose a toast."

We all reach for our punch cups.

"To all our dear friends who are gathered under our roof tonight—
may the new year bring you peace and prosperity!"

"Hear, hear!" echoes Mr. Hawthorne, clinking his punch cup
against Gigi's.

Across the room, I see Mr. and Mrs. Chadwick's eyes meet at the
mention of the word "prosperity." They still don't know that we know
about him losing his job. Becca or no Becca, the surprise we have in
store for them is going to be the best part about tonight.

I clink my punch cup against Emma's and Stewart's as Mrs.
Hawthorne continues.

"When we were planning this party," she says, "the other mothers
and I thought it might be fun to mix a little book club business in with
the merriment."

Emma stiffens at the words "the other mothers." She's convinced

Heather Vogel Frederick

this always means trouble. Maybe it does, because Dylan and Ryan both groan.

"Hush, boys," says Mrs. Delaney. "Just think—if it weren't for our book club, we probably wouldn't be here right now, eating this yummy food. In fact, we might not even all be friends."

The room falls silent as we consider this prospect. It's true, I guess, but it's hard to imagine. We've been together for nearly five years. Well, most of us. I flick a quick glance at Becca, who's carefully studying the mushroom on her plate.

"Another toast!" says Mr. Delaney, and we raise our punch cups again. "To the Mother-Daughter Book Club, the tie that binds us all together."

We drink to that, too.

"It's just a tiny bit of book club business I was referring to, boys," says Mrs. Hawthorne. "We thought it would be fun to answer one book club question at each of our stops tonight, and then do the Big Reveal for the person whose house we're at, so they can find out the identity of their Secret Santa. That way, their new ornament can go right onto the tree."

"Are we supposed to answer the questions too?" asks Darcy.

His mother looks at him over her glasses. "If you're qualified to do so." Reaching into the pocket of her sweater, she pulls out a slip of paper. "With no further ado, then, here's the first one: Which Betsy-Tacy character are you most like, and why?"

"I'm out," says Darcy cheerfully. "Not qualified."

"That's easy," says Emma. "Betsy Ray, because she wants to be a writer."

Her mother nods. "Same for me, but because of her love of books."

"Aren't you Miss Sparrow?" asks Mrs. Chadwick, frowning.

"Too obvious," says Mrs. Hawthorne. "I love Miss Sparrow, but just because she's the town librarian doesn't mean she's the character I most identify with."

"But the question wasn't which character you most *identify* with, it's which one you're most *like*," Mrs. Chadwick replies, clearly not willing to let it go.

"Fine," says Mrs. Hawthorne with a sigh. "I'll be Miss Sparrow. Who are you, Calliope?"

"Mrs. Poppy," Emma whispers to me, and I nearly choke on my stuffed mushroom.

"Isn't it obvious?" says Mrs. Chadwick, looking around the room. She seems a little puzzled by our grins. "I'm Mrs. Ray."

"I would have pegged you for Mrs. Muller," says Mrs. Delaney mildly.

Mrs. Chadwick shakes her head. "Not me at all," she says. "She's so strict."

Emma and I grin at each other.

"I think you're Mrs. Kelly," Cassidy's mother says to Mrs. Delaney.

"Except I don't have ten children."

"No, but you have twins, and that counts as double at least, I'd say."

Everybody laughs.

Heather Vogel Frederick

"In that case," says Jess's mother, "I feel free to nominate you to be the glamorous Aunt Dolly."

Mrs. Sloane-Kinkaid inclines her head. "How very generous of you, Shannon. I graciously accept."

"And I see Lily as Miss Clarke," says Mrs. Hawthorne. "Remember? The Deep Valley High teacher who assigns the essay on 'Conservation of our Natural Resources.'"

"Touché," says Mrs. Wong. "I accept."

"What, no Marmee moment this time around?" says Emma's father.

The first year of our book club, our mothers almost got into an argument about which of them was most like Marmee in *Little Women*.

"Nope," says Mrs. Hawthorne cheerfully. "No Marmee moment. How about you girls, though? Who do you think you're most like, Jess?"

"Julia, because she loves music."

Mrs. Sloane-Kinkaid nods thoughtfully. "I see a lot of Julia Ray in Courtney, too. Julia's such a good big sister to Betsy, the same way Courtney's a good big sister to Cassidy. Right, Cass?"

"Yeah," says Cassidy. "Most of the time. Except when she goes off and gets—"

Her mother gives her a warning look.

"Who do you see yourself as, Cassidy?" asks Mrs. Hawthorne.

"She's Winona," says Emma. "Or maybe Tacy, because she's not interested in boys."

Becca snorts at this pronouncement, and Cassidy gives her the stink-eye.

"I didn't ask you, daughter mine," Mrs. Hawthorne tells Emma. She looks expectantly at Cassidy.

"I guess maybe Tacy, because she has red hair," Cassidy replies. "Or Tib, because she skates and plays basketball."

"I think you're more of a Bonnie Andrews," says Becca.

"That's an interesting choice," says Mrs. Hawthorne. "What made you think of her for Cassidy?"

Becca shrugs and looks down at her plate, but she can't keep the smirk off her face.

Emma leans over to me. "Bonnie stole Tony from Betsy in *Heaven to Betsy*, remember?"

Uh-oh, I think, hoping Cassidy doesn't pick up on this. There could be trouble otherwise.

Sensing an undercurrent, Mrs. Hawthorne wisely moves on. "How about you, Megan?" she asks, turning to me.

"Miss Mix," says Emma, and her mother sighs. Emma gives me a guilty look. "Sorry."

"I know she's Deep Valley's dressmaker and everything, but I think I'm more like Tib," I tell her. "Remember how she made all her own clothes? She was always sewing something."

"And Midge Gerlach, the real Tib, became a dress designer in Chicago when she grew up," says Mrs. Chadwick triumphantly. "There's a fun fact for you."

Heather Vogel Frederick

"Fascinating," says Mrs. Hawthorne. "Okay, Megan, then you're Tib for sure."

"And my daughter is Carney," says Mrs. Chadwick. "She's so fun-loving and popular."

Now it's Cassidy's turn to snort.

"Hey," says Jess. "We forgot Gigi."

Everyone looks over at my grandmother.

"Mrs. Poppy," she replies. "I'm definitely Mrs. Poppy." We all burst out laughing. My tiny little grandmother is about as far as you can get from enormous Mrs. Poppy. She looks at us, wide-eyed. "I'm serious! I may not look like her, but Mrs. Poppy loves to throw parties and have fun."

"True," says Mrs. Hawthorne. "Well done. Okay, it's time for the first Big Reveal. Would Emma's Secret Santa please stand up?"

Emma looks expectantly at Becca. This strikes me as a little odd, but even odder is her reaction when I set down my plate and cup and rise to my feet.

"*You* were my Secret Santa?" she exclaims, clearly shocked.

I shrug. "Yeah. Didn't you guess?"

She gives me a funny look. "Nope. Never in a million years."

I fish in my purse for the small package I tucked inside. It wasn't hard to find the perfect ornament for Emma.

She takes it from me kind of hesitantly.

"Well," prods her mother. "Aren't you going to unwrap it?"

Emma looks reluctant as she unties the ribbon. "Oh," she says when she sees what's inside, sounding surprised again. "It's—it's wonderful. Thanks, Megan."

"You're welcome."

"What is it?" asks Stewart.

Emma dangles it in front of him. "A miniature book of poetry," she says. "Shakespeare's *Sonnets*. And there's a note inside from Miss Sparrow." She reads it aloud: 'To Betsy: You're at the age when poetry sinks in.' That's what Miss Sparrow tells her in *Betsy in Spite of Herself*."

"Cool," says Stewart.

"A gift from Deep Valley's librarian to a librarian's daughter," says Mrs. Chadwick, nodding approvingly. "Well done, Megan."

Emma crosses the room and hangs it on the tree, then turns and smiles at me. She still looks a little puzzled, though. "Thanks again, Megs—I love it."

"What about Phoebe's present?" says Mrs. Sloane-Kinkaid. "Or did someone forget?"

Mrs. Delaney raises her hand. "Guilty as charged. Sorry, Phoebe, you'll just have to wait until we get to our house."

"No problem," says Mrs. Hawthorne.

"All right, everyone—time to move this party along!" says Mr. Hawthorne, clapping his hands. "If you wouldn't mind clearing your dishes and taking them to the kitchen before you grab your coats, the management would be most appreciative."

I file out of the living room and down the hall behind Emma and

Jess. They're whispering about something; I can't quite tell what. I do manage to catch Becca's name, though, and mine. Jess pauses by the kitchen doorway, leaning on her crutches, while Emma crosses the room to the sink, carrying their cups and plates. I scoot up behind her and give her a nudge.

"What's going on?"

She swivels around. "Uh, nothing," she replies. She flicks a glance at Jess though, so I can tell this isn't true.

"Yes there is."

"It's no big deal," says Emma. "Really."

"You're acting weird. Didn't you like my Secret Santa presents?"

"Yeah. Sure. They were great." But her voice is flat and expressionless.

Hurt, I open my mouth to say something else, then close it again. Brushing past Jess, I go back down the hall for my coat, and a minute later I'm out on the sidewalk, my breath making frosty puffs of white in the cold air.

Gigi tucks her arm through mine. "Isn't this fun?" she asks, giving me a squeeze. "I can't wait until the grand finale, can you?"

"Uh-huh," I tell her. But I'm not really looking forward to the rest of the evening. Between what's going on with Becca and me, and whatever it is that's bugging Emma, something's brewing. This New Year's Eve party has the potential to be a disaster.

❦Emma❦

"The rambling white house at the end of Hill Street
was full of greens and Christmas cheer. The Crowd
played games, and the refreshments— as always
at the Kelly house— were superabundant."

—*Heaven to Betsy*

I puzzle over the Secret Santa surprise all the way to the Chadwicks'.

"I just don't get it," I tell Jess, who's gamely pegging her way down the sidewalk beside me. Because of Jess's crutches, we're taking up the rear of the procession, right behind Stewart and Darcy, who are energetically dissecting the Boston Bruins' latest game. "I was so sure it was Becca! And now—well, now I don't know what to think."

"Yeah, I know," she replies. "It doesn't make sense that Megan would give you all those snarky gifts and then pull a switcheroo with that fabulous ornament."

"Exactly!"

We mull it over some more, but aren't any wiser by the time we reach the Chadwicks' house.

"Hey, you guys," says Cassidy, galloping over to us as we step inside.

She's giving Chloe a piggyback ride, and she lowers her voice to a conspiratorial whisper. "Is it just me, or have you noticed that Megan and Becca are acting a little weird tonight?"

Jess and I crane our necks in tandem, trying to see over the knot of parents clogging the front hall.

"Way to attract attention, dudes," says Cassidy in disgust.

Chloe's teeny voice pipes up, "DOODS! DOODS!" She's echoing everything Cassidy says these days, which is adorable. I feel a pang when I think of her moving away to California too. I'd miss Chloe almost as much as Cassidy if they end up leaving Concord.

"Just keep an eye peeled, and see if you think I'm crazy," Cassidy continues. "It's like they're going out of their way not to talk to each other or even look at each other."

Jess and I exchange a glance. Been there, done that, glad it's over.

"Maybe I'm wrong," Cassidy continues. "See what you think."

We nod as Mrs. Chadwick comes over and closes the door behind us. "Now that everyone is here," she says in a loud voice, "I'd like to welcome you to the second stop on our Betsy-Tacy New Year's Eve progressive dinner!"

"We really should make it an annual tradition," says Gigi, her dark eyes sparkling. "This is fun."

"The only problem with that," says my mother, "is that it would mean permanently giving up my celebration with Mr. Darcy, and I'm not sure I'm ready for that."

My father slips his arm around her waist. "Am I not a worthy substitute?" He pulls her under the mistletoe hanging from the hall chandelier and gives her a resounding kiss.

"KISS!" shrieks Chloe, pointing at them. "KISS, KISS, KISS!"

"Nicholas! You're scaring the children!" scolds my mother, pretending to be angry with him.

My father waggles his eyebrows and grins. "Nonsense. I'm just getting into the spirit of things. Mistletoe abounds in Deep Valley, and I seem to recall Maud Hart Lovelace penned several holiday snogging scenes in her immortal tomes."

My mouth drops open. "Did *you* read the Betsy-Tacy books, Dad?"

He shrugs. "You and your mother gushed over them so much, I had to see what all the fuss was about. A little girly for my taste, but overall, quite delightful."

"I wouldn't exactly call them 'snogging scenes,' dear," my mother says primly. "The word 'spooning' would be more appropriate in this case."

"Were kisses involved?" my father demands, waggling his eyebrows again.

"KISS, KISS, KISS!" cries Chloe again, twirling around the hallway.

"Well, yes," my mother concedes.

"I rest my case." He lunges for her again. She squeals and dodges him, pretending to hide behind Mr. Wong.

"My turn," says Jess's father, pulling Mrs. Delaney under the mistletoe. Things get a little crazy after that, with Mr. Wong kissing Mrs. Wong, Stanley Kinkaid kissing Cassidy's mother, and Cassidy and Gigi both kissing Chloe, who's still shrieking, "KISS, KISS, KISS!"

Heather Vogel Frederick

Mrs. Chadwick makes a big show of crossing her arms and tapping her foot. "If you are all *quite* finished, the soup is getting cold," she says sternly.

"Calliope?" says Mr. Chadwick.

"Yes, Henry?"

"I believe the soup could use one more thing."

Mrs. Chadwick frowns. "And what would that be?"

"A SPOON!" He swoops in for a kiss, much to the delight of the rest of us. We whistle and clap and cheer him on. All except Becca, that is, who looks totally disgusted. Not that I don't sympathize. Parental spooning is downright embarrassing.

"Really, Henry," says Mrs. Chadwick reproachfully, when she finally manages to disentangle herself. Her cheeks are pink and she looks pleased, though. "As I was saying, help yourselves to soup, and then bring it into the living room. We have a little surprise for you."

"Another one?" jokes my father.

Mrs. Chadwick gives him a look.

As everybody heads down the hall toward the dining room, a pair of arms slip around me from behind. It's Stewart.

"Where do you think you're going?" he says softly, pulling me back toward the chandelier.

I don't usually like PDA—I'm private about all that stuff. But for one thing nobody's looking, and for another, well, it's New Year's Eve. Plus, kissing Stewart is the perfect antidote to last year's disastrous under-the-mistletoe kiss from Rupert Loomis, the one I was tricked into by Annabelle "Just Call Me Stinkerbelle" Fairfax. Which reminds me—

"Stewart!" I gasp, breaking away.

"What?"

"I totally forgot to tell you—I got a letter from Rupert's aunt today."

His eyebrows shoot up. "You did? What did she—hey, wait a minute, how come kissing me reminded you of Rupert?"

"It didn't!" I pause, then give him a sheepish smile. "Okay, maybe it did. It's not you, though, it's the circumstances." I point to the mistletoe. "Really."

"Whew," he says, pretending to wipe his brow. "That's a relief. I thought maybe I was losing my touch. So what did she say?"

"That there's a good chance *Stinkerbelle and the Fairies* is going to be published."

"Emma!"

"Wait—don't get too excited. She said she can't promise me anything yet, but she showed it to one of the editors at Loomis and Sons, and they really liked it. She should know more in a few weeks."

"What do you mean, don't get excited? That's fantastic news! Congratulations!"

"Thanks. But I'm not telling anybody yet besides you and my parents, and maybe Jess. I just don't want to have to explain if nothing comes of it, you know?"

He nods. "I totally understand, Em. But still, congratulations!" He kisses me again, and we head back to the dining room.

Mrs. Chadwick made Gigi's Thai Butternut Squash Soup. I'm really glad, because it's my favorite thing on the menu at Pies & Prejudice. Well, besides all the treats, of course. I always order it when Mom and I go to lunch there. I love how creamy it is, and I especially love the topping, a crunchy-tangy mix of chopped peanuts, cilantro, and grated lime peel. Yum.

We carry our mugs into the living room and find a spot on the floor next to Jess and Darcy. I smile at Jess, and she jangles her charm bracelet at me, sending the little heart on it flying. I'm really glad that whole thing with Jonas Bates was a figment of my imagination. She and my brother just seem to fit together like two puzzle pieces.

Mr. Chadwick flips on the TV, then slips a disc into the DVD player. He dims the lights as calypso Christmas carols start to float from the speakers.

"What's going on?" asks Mr. Delaney. "Please tell me there isn't some Betsy-Tacy dance I wasn't warned about."

Jess leans over to me. "Dance of the Maypole Maidens?" she whispers, and I nearly choke on my soup. That was her father's only—and totally disastrous—attempt at hosting book club, back when we were in sixth grade.

Mr. Chadwick laughs. "Nope. No dancing on the menu tonight. Calliope's parents put together a slide show of our cruise, and we thought you all might like to see it."

"Ooh, yes, please!" says Mrs. Sloane-Kinkaid.

Across the room from me, I notice a funny look on Becca's face.

"Don't worry, it's brief," her father continues. "Nothing worse than having to sit through slide shows of other people's vacations, in my opinion."

"Count me as weird, then," says Mrs. Sloane-Kinkaid. "I love looking at other people's slides."

A title fades in on the TV screen: *The Chadwicks and the Wongs and the Great World.*

"I can tell your mother had a hand in this, Calliope," says my mother.

Mrs. Chadwick laughs. "No point trying to deny that, is there, Becca?"

I watch her and Megan. I'm beginning to think that Cassidy is right. Something's up. Usually the two of them are joined at the hip, kind of like Jess and me. Well, Jess and me when Darcy and Stewart aren't around. But tonight they're sitting on opposite sides of the room, and Megan's been sticking to Gigi like a burr.

The first slide comes on. It's Stewart, gaping up at the ship. He looks like a total dork. Everybody laughs.

"It was big!" Stewart protests.

"So's your mouth," my brother tells him.

The twins think this is hilarious and collapse on the floor, howling.

"Look at those bathing beauties!" says Mrs. Delaney as a picture of Megan and Becca by the pool flashes on-screen.

One after another, the slides follow in quick succession: Stewart and his grandfather, frowning in concentration at the Scrabble board.

Heather Vogel Frederick

Stewart and his grandfather, triumphantly holding up a trophy. Mrs. Wong and Mrs. Chadwick, bent over their scrapbooks. Gigi showing off her stateroom door, which has been wrapped to look like a Christmas present. Buffet tables. Stewart on the surfrider. Stewart wiping out on the surfrider, which sends the twins into gales of laughter again. A three-story Christmas tree, with huge crowds of people milling around.

"That was Christmas Eve, remember?" says Mrs. Chadwick. "Check this out—they made it snow."

The next slide proves her right.

"Ooh," chorus the twins. "How'd they do that?"

"Soap flakes," says Mr. Chadwick. "Right, Stewart?"

Stewart shudders and makes a face. "Yep. They didn't taste so good."

There are lots of pictures of Megan and Becca: Megan and Becca getting pedicures; Megan and Becca all dressed up for a party or something; Megan and Becca bowling, skating, swimming, sunbathing, and snorkeling in water that's impossibly blue.

"Stop!" groans Darcy. "You're torturing us! I want to be there right now!"

"Who's that?" asks Jess, as a pictures of a good-looking guy in a white uniform comes up. On one side of him is Becca, and on the other, Megan.

"The captain's son," says Gigi. "Isn't he handsome? And so polite—very French." Megan's grandmother loves anything French.

"His name was Philippe, and Megan had a crush on him," says Mrs. Wong.

Megan's face goes beet red. "Mom! I did not!"

Another picture appears. Philippe is pointing at something in this one, and it looks like he's giving a lecture. Megan and Becca are both listening intently.

"What's he talking about?" I ask.

Mrs. Chadwick looks expectantly at Becca, who shrugs and doesn't reply, so Mrs. Chadwick turns to me. "The ship. He was very proud of it."

"He certainly was," says Gigi, her dark almond eyes twinkling.

I see Megan and Becca exchange a glance, and then Becca looks away, scowling. Cassidy shoots me another *I told you so* look.

Mr. Chadwick turns the lights back up as the last slide—an early-morning shot of the Miami harbor—fades to black.

"Wow, what a trip." Mrs. Sloane-Kinkaid sighs. "That's a memory to treasure for a lifetime."

"Yes indeed," agrees Mrs. Wong. "Right, Megan?"

Megan just grunts, and Cassidy gives me and Jess Winona eyes again.

"So," says my mother, "is it time for the next question?" She fishes in her pocket again and reads it aloud: "Would you like to live in Deep Valley? How is it different from Concord?"

Jess sighs happily. "I'd love to live in Deep Valley. All those parties and picnics and dances and fun."

Heather Vogel Frederick

"We have plenty of fun here in Concord, don't we?" says her mother.

"I know, but it's different somehow."

"That's because it's a book," says Cassidy.

"Yeah, but it was based on real life," Jess replies stubbornly.

We talk for a while about fictional versus real places, and the choices authors make in writing about those places.

"There don't seem to be any really serious problems in Deep Valley," says Mrs. Wong, "aside from the occasional squabble over a boy. Everybody's so happy all the time."

"Just the way I like it," says Jess. Her family had a couple of rough years back in middle school, when her mother moved to New York for a while to pursue her acting career, and then when they almost lost the farm.

Megan and Becca both vote for Concord, and I'm undecided. "Deep Valley because I want to go to high school with the Crowd and hang out with Betsy talking about writing, Concord because I already have my own Crowd, and I have Stewart to talk to about writing."

"Awwww," says Darcy, and I flick a peanut at him.

Stewart swats me with his napkin. "So are you saying the character I'm most like is Betsy?"

I grin at him. "If the shoe fits."

He pretends to be insulted. "Couldn't I at least be Tony or Joe? Or maybe Cab Edwards?"

His mother's mouth drops open. "Stewart Chadwick!" she exclaims. "Have you been reading the Betsy-Tacy books?"

He shrugs sheepishly. "What can I say? I got curious."

My brother thinks this is hilarious. "Ooh, Chadwick, wait until we get to the rink tomorrow. I'm going to tell the guys that you joined the Mother-Daughter Book Club."

"Darcy," says my mother severely. "If you keep this up, I'll tell everybody about your Little Mermaid pajamas."

"WHAT?" shriek Dylan and Ryan.

Darcy hates it when my mom teases him about this. When he was little, he desperately wanted to be Ariel when he grew up. He had the pajamas, the movie poster, the CD and DVD, and he knew all the songs by heart.

"I think you just told them, Mom," I say.

She grins and turns to Cassidy. "How about you, Cassidy? Deep Valley or Concord?"

"Deep Valley for sure, at least in the winter. They're always out on the ice."

"That's Minnesota for you," says her mother. "But seriously, what else draws you to Deep Valley?"

I look at Cassidy, who still hasn't said whether she's going to be moving or staying, and I wonder whether the appeal of Maud Hart Lovelace's world is its sense of permanence. Sure, the characters grow and change over the years, but most of the changes are happy ones, and there's an abiding sense of stability in the books.

"But seriously," Cassidy replies, "I'm still hungry. Can we move this dinner party along?"

Heather Vogel Frederick

"Cassidy Ann!" her mother scolds.

My mother flaps her hand. "Not to worry. Let's skip to the next Big Reveal."

"How about we start with a mom this time?" suggests Mrs. Wong. "Is there a present here for Calliope?"

My father holds up a brightly wrapped box. "This was on the hall table."

He passes it to Mrs. Chadwick, and she opens it. Her face softens when she sees what's inside.

"A gnome!" she cries in delight. "A little garden gnome!"

The small creature is wearing blue overalls and a pointed blue hat, and he's pushing a wheelbarrow full of flowers. The card reads: *For Grossmama Muller from Grosspapa Muller*—Du bist mein Blümchen, Mama.

"What's a bloom-shin?" asks Ryan.

"A flower, right, Jess?" their mother replies, and Jess nods.

"Who's it from?" asks Mrs. Chadwick, and Mrs. Sloane-Kinkaid raises her hand. "Thank you, Clementine. It's delightful, and so appropriate for my work."

"I had to get Wolfgang to help me with the German," Cassidy's mother tells us, referring to her old friend and colleague who's now the fashion director at *Flash* magazine.

"And now it's Becca's turn," says my mother, as Mrs. Chadwick happily hangs her ornament on the tree. "Do you have a guess as to the identity of your Secret Santa?"

Becca glances at Jess, and I see the muscle in her jaw clench. She shrugs.

"Well then, would Becca's Secret Santa please reveal herself?"

I hop to my feet. "It was me!" I announce proudly, glad in a way that it turned out to be Megan who gave me all those crummy presents, and not Becca. I feel better now about the time I spent making her ornament. Reaching into my purse, I pull it out and hand it to her.

She takes it from me and stares at the wrapping paper, then opens it. She looks puzzled when she sees what it is: a tiny pennant with DEEP VALLEY HIGH printed on it in felt letters.

"Read the card," her mother urges.

"'To Betsy from Joe: Wish I could join you at the game this weekend, but I have to work. Cheer our team on for me, okay? Your friend, Joe.'"

"Good job, Emma!" says Mrs. Chadwick. "It's perfect. Hold it up, darling, so I can get a picture for Gram."

Becca gives the pennant a feeble wave.

"What do you say?" her mother prompts.

"Thanks, I guess," Becca replies.

"What do you mean, you *guess?*" snaps her mother. "Where are your manners?"

Becca glares at her. "What I mean is, one good gift doesn't make up for a bunch of crummy ones."

I stare at her, shocked.

"Rebecca Louise!" thunders her mother.

Heather Vogel Frederick

"It's true, Mom! She gave me some really mean stuff."

"Well, maybe that made up for all the stupid stuff you gave *somebody else*," says Cassidy.

"What stupid stuff? I didn't give anybody stupid stuff!" says Becca, her voice rising. She looks around at us all. "You don't like me—you never have. I thought it was Jess, but now I see you were the one behind it, Cassidy. You probably gave Emma the whole idea for the goat thing."

"Goat thing?" I look at her blankly.

She whirls around to face me. "Don't play dumb. You and Jess and Cassidy ganged up on me, I know you did!"

"Rebecca Louise!" her mother repeats. "What's gotten into you?"

"You want to know how Concord is different from Deep Valley?" Becca's face is flushed with anger. "I'll tell you how it's different—people pretend to be your friends here when they really aren't, that's how. They hate me, Mom! They always have. I'll never be part of their little circle, their *Sistren,* and this just proved it."

She looks over at Megan, who's gone pale beneath her tan. "I wish I'd never joined this stupid book club!" And with that Becca throws down the pennant and stomps out of the room.

Nobody moves.

I look over at Jess and Cassidy. Now what?

CASSIDY

"Later Betsy and Tacy had a serious hour alone. They made their New Year's resolutions, and when she got home Betsy wrote them down. Never had she made such serious, such sobering resolutions. She resolved to work harder at school, to read improving literature, to brush her hair a hundred strokes every night, not to think about boys . . ."

—*Heaven to Betsy*

My mother marches down to the end of our upstairs hallway and yanks on the door leading to the turret. Flinging it open, she flips on the light and points to the stairs with one perfectly manicured finger. "*Go!* Now! All of you!"

I hesitate, but only for a split second. It's pretty hard to defy my mother's Queen Clementine voice, especially when it's combined with the evil witch mother eye of death. Make that five evil witch mother eyes of death: Mrs. Wong, Mrs. Hawthorne, Mrs. Delaney, and Mrs. Chadwick are all lined up along the hallway behind her, glaring at us. It's like face-off time at the rink.

Heather Vogel Frederick

I slink through the door sheepishly. Emma and Megan and Becca and Jess are right behind me.

"And don't you dare come down until you've sorted this mess out!" my mother calls up the stairs after us. "Ridiculous, girls your age acting this way." She slams the door shut.

In the confusion after Becca's meltdown, our mothers pounced on Emma and Jess and Megan and me, wanting to know what had happened. We tried to explain, but since we were still kind of in the dark too, it was complicated. Tempers flared. Voices were raised. Stanley invited the dads and brothers to go on ahead with him and Chloe to our house, and they were only too happy to escape.

After they left, my mother threw up her hands. "You girls are *not* going to ruin the party for the rest of us," she sputtered. "You need to sort this out, and you need to sort it out now."

"But we didn't *do* anything, mom!" I protested.

"Well, someone made Becca unhappy about something, and I suspect there's more than enough blame to go around," said Mrs. Wong.

The other mothers and Gigi all nodded.

"Dr. Weisman taught me long ago the importance of making the punishment fit the crime," my mother continued. "So here's what we're going to do, if you other moms agree. Since it's New Year's Eve, this is a perfect time to make a fresh start. Out with the old and in with the new, as they say. You girls will come with me while you tend to your daughter, Calliope. Bring her along as soon as you can. And then, while those of us who are adult enough to act like adults—as opposed to bratty teenagers *pretending* to be adults—enjoy the wonderful cucumber-pomegranate salad I've prepared, you five girls will sit together until you sort this out. You're old enough to do it by yourselves this time, without our help, or our interference."

Mrs. Hawthorne nods. "I heartily agree, Clementine. You girls got yourselves into this mess, and you can get yourselves out."

And that was that, and now here we are.

"I feel like Rapunzel," grumbles Jess, stumping up the turret stairs behind me. She emerges into the small, circular room and plops down on the window seat, leaning her crutches against it.

Emma wraps her arms around herself and shivers. "It's freezing up here!"

"That's why my mom chose it," I reply morosely. "I heard her say so to Mrs. Wong. She figured the less comfortable we were, the less time we'd waste squabbling."

I can hear the wind whistling through a crack in one of the diamond-paned windows, and I put a pillow over it and open the grate at the base of the window seat. We keep it closed unless someone's up here, because my mother says there's no point heating rooms we're not using. "It'll warm up before too long," I tell my friends. "Well, a little, at least."

Becca doesn't say a word. Her mascara is still kind of smeared from her tears, and she's got a grim expression on her face.

"Who wants to go first?" I ask.

We all look at each other. Nobody replies.

Heather Vogel Frederick

"Well, I for one don't intend to stay up here all night," I tell them. "I'm starving, and I want the rest of my dinner."

"You're always starving," says Becca.

"Shut up!"

"Make me!"

"C'mon, guys," says Emma. "You heard what they said, we have to sort this out." She sighs. "Okay, I'll start. I'll confess, I thought my Secret Santa gifts were from you, Becca."

"Whatever."

"I thought it was some kind of mean joke you were playing. I'm sorry."

"Of course you thought it was me," Becca says stiffly. "That's my whole point. You don't like me, and you never have."

"That's not true!" Emma protests. "I do like you." Her gaze falters, though.

"Like I said," says Becca bitterly.

"To be honest," I tell her, "my gifts were weird too, and I figured it must have been you, because you're mad about Zach."

Becca's face flushes. "How's this for honesty?" she snaps. "Emma doesn't like me because I'm more popular at school than she is. And maybe because I'm a cheerleader and everybody loves to hate cheerleaders, right?"

"I think maybe you're forgetting middle school," Emma says in a tight voice.

"Middle school?" Becca's voice rises dangerously, and I start to worry that we're in for another meltdown. "That was *ages* ago, Emma! Give me a little credit for maybe growing up a little since then." She glares at her, then turns to Jess. "Jess, you don't like me because you're Emma's friend, and you're loyal."

"And loyalty's a bad thing?" I can't help pointing out.

Becca whips around to face me. "And *you*—you don't like me because I've had a crush on your boyfriend since kindergarten, and because you know that I think if you'd just tell him you're not interested, maybe he'd finally be interested in me."

I'm speechless. She pretty much nailed it. Well, except for that last bit about Zach. The thing is, I finally figured out that maybe I am interested, and maybe I do like him back. But I'm not about to tell her that. At least not now. She doesn't give me a chance to anyway, because she's already moved on.

"And Megan," she continues. "Well, Megan—"

"I don't like you because of Philippe," says Megan coldly.

"I did you a favor," Becca retorts.

"That wasn't for you to decide!" Megan leaps to her feet. "He liked me, Becca—*me*, not you! And you couldn't stand that, so you went and ruined it."

"I knew it!" I say triumphantly, turning to Emma and Jess. "Didn't I tell you guys something was up between these two?"

"Who's Philippe?" asks Jess.

"That cute guy in the picture on the cruise ship, right?" says Emma, and Megan nods.

Heather Vogel Frederick

"So what happened?" I ask, and our heads all swivel toward Becca, who stares stonily out the window.

"*Rebecca* is what happened," says Megan bitterly. "Becca decided she needed an alter ego. Someone with more la de da. Someone who turned out to be a big traitor."

"It was your idea!" Becca tells her.

"It was not!" Megan retorts.

"Let's get back to Philippe," says Emma. "What was the deal?"

"On Christmas Eve," Megan continues, "I left Miss La de da Rebecca with Philippe for just a few minutes, and when I came back she was draped all over him."

"It wasn't a big deal!" Becca protests. "It was an accident. I wasn't trying to steal him or anything."

"You mean unlike Bonnie Andrews?" I tell her, and she blinks at me. Score! "Oh yeah, I read the book."

"You knew how much it meant to me to have someone pay me a little attention, after my breakup with Simon," Megan tells her. "I told you that very same day, remember? What you did really hurt."

"Like I said, it was an *accident*," Becca repeats. "The boat lurched and I fell and—oh, what's the point? You're determined not to believe me anyway. But you were the one who told me to use some la de da, remember? The whole Rebecca thing was a game we made up, that day we were in the spa."

"You made it up," says Megan shortly.

"Fine. I made it up. Look, I'm sorry. I never should have used

Philippe as my guinea pig. And I certainly never meant for things to end up the way they did."

Megan regards Becca for a few seconds. "Well," she says, not sounding completely convinced, "it still hurt my feelings."

"And that's exactly the problem," says Emma, leaning forward. "Sometimes you don't think about our feelings when you do stuff and say stuff, Becca."

Becca inspects her fingernails.

"And sometimes you still do mean things," I add.

She looks up sharply. "Name one."

"How about trying to sabotage me at the ugly sweater party?" I reply.

Becca shrugs. "That was so not a big deal."

"It was to *me*, though, and that's Emma's whole point. You deliberately tried to embarrass me on national TV!"

Becca gives me an icy look. "Let's not even go there," she retorts. "Or have you forgotten about Carson Dawson?"

Back in seventh grade, the rest of the book club and I tried to play a little prank on Becca during one of my mom's TV show filmings, to get even for her reading Emma's diary. Unfortunately, it backfired, and this famous TV show host was the one we ended up accidentally pranking. We were in trouble for weeks.

"Oh, gimme a break! Talk about dredging up middle school! That was years ago! Are you still mad about that, *Rebecca*?"

We glare at each other. I sit down and put my head in my hands.

Heather Vogel Frederick

We're not getting anywhere. We'll be up here all night at this rate. Something's gotta give, and somebody's got to be willing to give a little. I guess it might as well be me.

"Look, when I mess up out on the ice, my coach doesn't pull any punches. If she doesn't tell me where I've gone wrong, how will I ever learn to be a better hockey player? I do the same thing with my Chicks with Sticks girls, you know? So here's the thing. I have a lot of faults. I've got a temper, and I'm not always very patient, and sometimes I make jokes at other people's expense—including yours. I apologize for that. But I have good points too, and so do you. Here's the stuff I like about you," I tell Becca, ticking the list off on my fingers. "You're really creative. You're fun, and you're funny, and you've got amazing drive. You know how to get things done." I pause for a moment, hoping some of that sank in. "Now here's the stuff that I don't like about you: You're snarky, you gossip, and you can be manipulative."

Becca is still quiet. She's listening, though, I can tell.

"And the whole name-change thing? Dude. Stupid, if you ask me."

"Which I didn't," snaps Becca.

I sigh. "Anyway, like Emma said, I shouldn't have leaped to the conclusion that I did, either, about the Secret Santa gifts. I should have figured there'd been some sort of mix-up. You all know me too well for any one of you to buy me a sparkly headband and pink underpants."

Jess starts to giggle. "Those were for Megan," she says. "I was her Secret Santa. They're French underpants, by the way. From Josephine's. I thought she'd like them."

"I would have!" Megan cries.

I grin at her. "You still can. I was going to give them to Courtney when we were out in California, but I forgot. They're in my suitcase, down in my room. And by the way," I tell Jess, poking her in the arm, "I don't care if they're French. I still hate them."

Emma looks around at us all. "So if Megan was my real Secret Santa, then who got the gifts she bought for me?"

Megan ticks them off on her fingers. "Let's see, for starters there was that word calendar thing, and a cute dish for Pip that I found at the Concord Pet Shoppe, and some of those great hand and foot warmers for you to use when you go skating. I think they're called Downhill Buddies?"

Emma and Jess exchange a glance. "Duh," says Emma. "Why didn't we figure that out? Okay, so Jess got my stuff. Who was supposed to get the ab workout DVD and the sports bottle and little pedometer and stuff that I got?"

"Cassidy," says Becca. "I was her Secret Santa."

"Man, what a mess," I say, shaking my head.

"And who got the gifts I meant for you to have, Becca?" says Emma. "Let's see, there was Motor Mouth lip gloss, some cute earrings, bubble bath—"

"I did," says Megan, turning to Becca. "I've used the lip gloss already, but you can have the bubble bath and the earrings. Which were nice, by the way, Emma—thanks."

"I'm confused," says Becca in a low voice. "Who gave me the goat picture?"

Heather Vogel Frederick

I hold up my hand. "I did—except it was supposed to be for Jess! It's a picture of Sundance. I took it for my photography class this fall."

"Aww," says Jess. "I would have liked to have seen it."

"I'll print you another one." All of a sudden I slap my forehead. "Ladies, we have completely overlooked something here!" My friends look at me expectantly. "We've been sabotaged! Blindsided! Checked into the boards!"

Nothing but blank stares.

"Somebody needs time in the penalty box," I tell them. "We've been *pranked*. This wasn't random—someone switched our Secret Santa gifts!"

Light dawns as my friends get what I'm saying.

"But who?" says Emma. "I suppose Stewart might have thought it would be funny, but it's not really his type of thing."

"And I don't think Darcy . . . oh." Jess's voice trails off. "Those weasels!"

"What weasels?" asks Megan.

"Dylan and Ryan, who else? Remember how they were all wild and giggly that morning at the bon voyage party, and my mother thought they'd been up to something? They switched the tags on our gift bags."

"Oh, man! Of course!" I shake my head, disgust mixed with admiration. You've gotta admire a good prank. "They are so going down! What we need is a plan, girls. But first, I have something for all of you."

I creep down the stairs, but nobody is standing guard. I hear laughter coming from the living room. My stomach rumbles hungrily. Soup and a few appetizers is not enough fuel for all six feet of me. I dash into my room and grab the pile on my desk, then race back upstairs to the turret.

"Sorry, Jess, yours is in the trash incinerator of the *Calypso Star*," I tell her as I hand the packages around the room.

"You mean the environmentally friendly, state-of-the-art green incinerator of the *Calypso Star*," says Megan, smiling slyly at Becca.

Becca smiles back. "I told you I did you a favor! You have to admit it too. Philippe was kind of a Phil Brandish, don't you think?"

For the second time in the same day, I actually get a literary reference. I finally finished *Betsy in Spite of Herself* while we were on the plane back to Boston, and Phil Brandish is this rich, good-looking, but completely brainless and car-crazy guy Betsy convinces herself that she likes for a while.

Megan nods. "Only instead of a red sports car, he had an entire cruise ship to brag about."

"Dreaming, dreaming, of your big cruise ship I'm dreaming . . . ," sings Jess.

"Knock it off," Megan tells her, but she's smiling. She opens her package. It's a fun shot of her with her mother and Gigi at Pies & Prejudice on the day that it opened. The three of them are standing out front, arms linked. Gigi is in the middle, and they're all wearing white aprons and ruffled hats like the woman in the sign over the shop.

Heather Vogel Frederick

"I love it!" she tells me. "Thank you!"

Emma opens hers next. It's a black-and-white photo I took of her and Mrs. Bergson last year, when she was home for spring break before Mrs. Bergson died. They're at the rink, and they're both laughing at something one of them said.

"Oh, Cassidy," says Emma, her eyes filling with tears. "It's beautiful. I know right where I'm going to put it too."

"In the cabinet with her skates?"

Emma nods. She leans over and gives me a hug. "Thank you."

"You're welcome." I turn to Becca and hand her the last package. "I've got one for you, too, believe it or not."

Inside is a picture I took of her at the Thanksgiving Day game. I was using my telephoto lens, and she didn't see me take it. It's a great shot. I was kneeling on the ground looking up, and I caught her in midleap with her knees bent back, her pom-poms flying in the air, and her arms flung high. The best part is the look on her face, though—just sheer joy. She's totally in the moment. I know the feeling; every athlete does. It's why we love sports.

Becca stares at the picture. Then she looks up at me and smiles, the same joy-filled smile that I captured in the picture. "Thank you, Cassidy."

"You're welcome," I reply.

She reaches into her purse and pulls out a small box. "Here," she says, shoving it into my hands. "I wasn't going to give it to you, but I just changed my mind."

I open it and start to laugh. It's a glass ornament with sparkles on it. A banana split. The tag reads: *For Betsy Ray, our best customer.* It's signed *Heinz's Restaurant.*

Becca grins. "I picked it because you eat like a horse, just like Betsy and Tacy and Tib and their friends," she says. "And you never gain weight, either."

"Speaking of which, let's go get something to eat," I reply. "I'm—"

"STARVING!" my friends all shout.

Final score: The Mother-Daughter Book Club—one zillion points.

Heather Vogel Frederick

❦ Jess ❦

"There were presents for everyone, beautiful presents, and joke presents too."

—*Betsy and Tacy Go Downtown*

"I'm so glad you sorted things out, sweetheart," says my mother, smiling as she arranges a platter of twice-baked potatoes. "There's no point carrying old grudges into the new year. Much better to start off with a clean slate, isn't it?"

I nod.

"Did you check on Mrs. Hawthorne's, um, ornament?" she asks, lowering her voice and glancing over her shoulder. Not that anyone can hear her. The party's reached a fever pitch, and everyone is talking and laughing in excited anticipation as they hunt for their name cards at the tables we've set up in the dining room.

"Yup," I reply. "Ready and waiting." After the disaster at the Chadwicks', our moms decided to postpone the rest of the ornament exchange to our house.

She gives me a conspiratorial smile. "This is going to be fun."

I smile back, hardly able to contain my glee. She has no idea.

Cassidy came up with the plan, of course. She always has the best ideas when it comes to pranks. I'm really, really going to miss her if she moves to California. Our book club just won't be the same.

"You look like the cat who swallowed the canary," says my father as I follow my mother into the dining room.

"Something like that," I reply, setting down the dish I'm carrying and pretending to flap my wings. Across the table from me, Emma and Cassidy explode in giggles.

My mother calls for everyone's attention. "For your dining pleasure tonight, we have grilled salmon—wild-caught and certified sustainably harvested, of course, Lily," she adds, before Mrs. Wong even has a chance to open her mouth. "And from our own organic garden, maple-roasted carrots with thyme and twice-baked potatoes."

"I've never had supper this late before," says Ryan, who is bouncing in his chair with excitement. I glance at the clock on the mantel, surprised to see that it's almost nine. I don't think I've eaten this late before either.

My father asks us all to hold hands as he says grace, giving thanks for a year full of good things. "I'd also like to give thanks for the fact that our daughters managed not to kill one another tonight," he adds at the end, and everybody laughs.

"Seriously," he continues, "there's so much to be grateful for. Rare indeed are friendships that span a number of years, as ours have. We've weathered many changes, and we'll weather many more

Heather Vogel Frederick

as our sons and daughters grow up and fly the coop—"

Megan lets out a snort at this, and I have to bite my lip not to laugh.

"—but hopefully they'll always fly back again too, especially at the holidays."

"Dig in, everyone!" says my mother.

As Cassidy happily plows into the mound of food on her plate, Emma gives her a mischievous glance. "Why don't you tell everybody about the ornament you got?"

"What made you think of that?" Cassidy retorts.

Emma eyes her plate. "Oh, nothing . . ."

"What Emma is trying to say is that I'm a pig," Cassidy announces cheerfully. "And Becca gave me a banana split ornament to prove it. It was addressed to Betsy from Heinz's Restaurant."

"How perfect!" says Mrs. Hawthorne. "I mean, not perfect that you're a pig—which you're not, by the way, just an active girl with a healthy appetite—but perfect because it's so Betsy-Tacy."

"The Deep Valley girls do love their ice cream, don't they?" says Mrs. Chadwick. "I'll have to swing by tomorrow and take a picture of it, Cassidy. I'm making a scrapbook of this evening's festivities to share with my mother, and she's very eager to hear how our ornament exchange turned out."

"Speaking of which," says Mrs. Hawthorne, "isn't it time for Jess's Big Reveal?"

"Um, sure," I say, with a quick warning glance at my friends. We decided not to tell anybody yet about the Secret Santa mix-up and our suspicions as to the twins' involvement, because otherwise it would mess up our plan for revenge.

Cassidy stands up. "It was me!" she says, handing me a small box.

"Really? I never would have guessed." I smile at Megan.

Opening the box, I take out a graceful silver musical note on a silver cord. There's a note inside to Julia from Betsy. *Dear Julia— Please take this with you as a reminder of home as you begin your adventures in the Great World. We know you're going to become a famous singer!*

"Thanks, Cassidy," I tell her. I've been practicing "Dreaming" ever since we got back from the Edelweiss Inn, but I'm still nervous about next week's solo audition.

She gives me a thumbs-up. "You're going to nail that audition, I just know it."

I smile at her. I wish I had Cassidy's confidence. That's another thing I'm going to miss if she moves away—her pep talks.

My mother taps her glass. "While everyone's finishing up—and please help yourself, there's plenty more—we'll keep things moving along here." She picks up a small box from the pile of presents in the center of the table and passes it to Mrs. Sloane-Kinkaid. "This one is for you, Clementine."

Cassidy's mother opens it and draws out what looks like a long, hollow metal rod with holes in it. Whatever it is has been dipped in glittery silver sparkles.

"What the heck is that?" asks Cassidy.

"Um, let me read the card," her mother replies. She scans the note, and her puzzled expression vanishes. "Ha!" she says. "Very clever. 'To Betsy from her Magic Wavers: Merry Christmas from one who's stuck on you. Looking forward to another year together.' It's a curler," she explains, dangling it in the air. "Remember how Betsy always agonized over her straight hair?"

"It's from me," says Mrs. Wong, looking pleased with herself. "Homemade."

"I never would have guessed," says Mrs. Sloane-Kinkaid, winking at the rest of us. "It's perfect, Lily, and perfectly hilarious."

"You're due an ornament too, Lily," says my mother, passing another little box to Megan's mother.

Inside is a tiny horse and buggy. Mrs. Wong passes it around as she reads the card: "'*To Betsy from Old Mag. I may not be as up-to-date as you'd like, but my carbon hoofprint can't be beat. I'm more economical, get great gas mileage, and you can fertilize your roses with my emissions.*'"

Mrs. Wong laughs so hard that she starts to cough, and Mr. Wong has to pat her on the back.

"It's from me," says Mrs. Hawthorne with a grin. "I couldn't resist."

Gigi reads her card before opening her box. "'*Bon voyage, Betsy! I can't wait to hear all about your adventures in the Great World! Don't forget to pack your la de da! Love, Julia.*'"

Across the table, Becca and Megan smile at each other.

Gigi opens the box and takes out a small Eiffel Tower. "How perfect! Thank you."

"I thought you'd like it," says Mrs. Chadwick.

"You didn't get one yet, Mom," says Dylan, who's been keeping careful track.

"You're right, I didn't," my mother replies. "Let's see what we have here—oh, look! This one is for me!" She passes it to him. "Would you like to open it for me while I open the envelope?" My brother takes the box as she slips the card out and reads it to us: "'To Betsy from Tacy: Here chickabiddie, chickabiddie! Remember when we caught the hen and put it in a box and tried to train it to lay eggs? I'm glad our friendship was more of a success. Love, Tacy.'"

Across the table, Cassidy gets a mischievous glint in her eye.

"Buck, buck, buck, bugaw!" she clucks softly, cracking Emma and me up. I'll definitely miss Cassidy's sense of humor if she moves to California.

My mother's smile broadens as she looks inside the box. "How lovely," she says, taking out a large decorative egg. It's covered with a delicately painted design of flowers and birds.

"The egg is a symbol of good luck in Hong Kong," says Gigi.

"I love it," my mother tells her. "Thank you!"

"And how appropriate for Half Moon Farm," adds my father. "One thing we have plenty of around here are chickens."

My friends and I are all giggling now, and my father looks at us all, puzzled. "What's so funny?"

Heather Vogel Frederick

I shake my head. "Nothing, Dad."

My mother taps her water glass again. "There's one last orna-ment—Phoebe, I blew it back at your house as far as the element of surprise goes, and I've blown it again because I left your gift in the keeping room. Jess, would you mind getting it, please? The rest of us can adjourn to the living room for predessert after-dinner mints."

I manage to keep a straight face as I push back my chair and reach for my crutches. "Darcy, can you give me a hand?"

"You bet." He follows me out of the dining room, through the kitchen, and out the back door. "Where the heck are we going? I thought your mom said it was in the keeping room."

"It will be in a minute," I tell him, wishing I'd grabbed my coat. The wind is bitingly cold. "I will be so glad to get this cast off," I grumble as we cross the yard to the barn.

"Two more weeks, right?"

"Feels like forever." I flip on the light in the tack room, revealing two cardboard boxes—a large one and a small one. I quickly close the smaller one before Darcy can see what's inside, but he does a double take when he sees what the big one contains.

"Uh-oh," he says. "What are you and your friends up to?"

"I need you to not ask any questions, okay?" I transfer the boxes carefully into two separate oversize gift bags. "What I need you to do is carry these inside, and put the little one in the keeping room. That's the one from my mother. The big box is from Cassidy and Emma and Megan and Becca and me. Your mother's getting ours first."

He grins, shaking his head. "Man, you are in trouble already. You'll be grounded for weeks!"

"I'll risk it."

"Hey, Jess," he continues, his voice softening. "Cassidy's right, you are going to nail that audition."

I sigh. "I hope so."

"I know so. You're amazing, and the song sounds amazing the way you sing it." He pulls his cell phone out and looks at the time. "Hey, guess what? It's midnight."

He grins at my startled look. "Midnight somewhere, right?" he adds. "Do you mind if I wish you Happy New Year a little early? I'd rather not do this when everybody else is around."

I feel a prickle of anticipation as he reaches for my crutches and sets them down. "You won't be needing these," he says, slipping his arms around my waist and pulling me close. I lean in and rest my cheek on his chest, enjoying the warmth of his hug.

"Happy New Year," he murmurs, kissing my hair.

"Happy New Year back," I reply.

Darcy marches a line of soft kisses down the side of my face. He kisses my eyelids and my cheeks, lingering on the tip of my nose before his lips finally come to rest on mine. I put my arms around his neck and kiss him back. I *love* Darcy's kisses.

"We'd better go back inside," I tell him after a while. "Everybody will wonder what's taken us so long."

"I think they can probably guess," he says, grinning at me again.

Heather Vogel Frederick

He hands me my crutches and picks up the gift bags, and I swing my way out of the barn and across the yard toward the house, feeling giddy and breathless.

"Hurry up, Jess!" calls Cassidy from the living room, as we come through the back door. "I want dessert!"

"That's a big surprise," I call back, and everybody cracks up at this.

"Sorry, no banana splits on the menu tonight," says Gigi. "You'll have to settle for chocolate fondue."

A cheer goes up from the living room at this, and I have to say I feel a wave of relief. Entrusting the Wongs with dessert carried a certain element of risk—none of us will ever forget Mrs. Wong's tofu cheesecake—but Megan assured us that Gigi would come through.

Darcy puts the smaller box in the keeping room as instructed, then follows me into the living room with the bigger one. My mother raises her eyebrows when she sees it.

"That's an awfully big box for an awfully little—," she starts to whisper.

"Just throwing Mrs. H off track, Mom," I whisper back, as Darcy sets it down on the coffee table.

"Ah. Good thinking. Phoebe will never guess what's inside."

I shake my head, biting the inside of my cheek to keep from laughing out loud. Her words are truer than she could ever imagine.

Mrs. Hawthorne opens the card. "Oh, look!" she says. "It's to Miss Sparrow from the Kelly family. How fun."

Mrs. Chadwick reaches for her camera as Emma's mother starts to read: "'This tiny reminder of England comes from our house to yours, to warm both your hearth and your heart.' My goodness, how poetic. I can't imagine what it could be. I'm sure it will look lovely on our tree, though."

Out of the corner of my eye I see Becca and Megan clutch each other. Emma is literally covering her mouth to keep from screaming with laughter, and Cassidy's knee is bouncing like a jackhammer.

Mrs. Hawthorne lifts the box out of the gift bag and opens the lid.

"BWACK!" A chicken explodes from within. Mrs. Hawthorne shrieks and lurches back against the sofa.

For a minute, it seems like everybody's shouting at once as the indignant hen—Carrie Underwood, one of my mother's prized new Buff Orpingtons—flaps her wings and clucks furiously, scrabbling around on the coffee table as she tries to elude my father's grasp. Chickens are notoriously difficult to catch, and Carrie is particularly wily. Which is why I picked her, of course.

"BOYS!" shouts my mother, as Carrie hops down from the table and dives under Mr. Wong's legs. He lifts them high in the air, squawking nearly as loudly as the chicken.

Dylan and Ryan, who have been gleefully joining in the chase, stop in their tracks. My mother's face is like thunder. She points to the front stairs. "GO TO YOUR ROOMS! NOW!"

"But Mom—"

"NOT ANOTHER WORD!" she cries. "I've HAD it with you two and your chicken pranks!"

"But—"

"But NOTHING! UPSTAIRS! You're both grounded for a MONTH!"

My little brothers' mouths drop open. Dylan looks like he's going to cry. Cassidy looks over at me and raises her eyebrows. I shake my head. Let them dangle a bit longer.

"You heard your mother," my father warns them. "Best do as she says." He shakes his head sadly. "I'm very disappointed in you two. This was a very unkind and thoughtless thing to do to our guest. You've scared her half to death. The rest of us too."

Dylan and Ryan start to slink from the room, glancing sorrowfully at Mrs. Hawthorne as they pass the sofa. She's fanning herself vigorously, still breathless from the shock. All of a sudden she lets out a snort, which quickly turns to a giggle, and then full-blown laugh. She laughs so hard she cries.

"What I want to know is," she finally gasps, "what on earth does a chicken have to do with England?"

"Well, for Pete's sake, Phoebe, I didn't really mean to give you a *chicken!*" says my mother, exasperated. "Obviously there was a mix-up." She glares at the boys, then tilts her head, her scowl deepening. "Wait a minute—how did you two—Jess?" She looks over at me. "Didn't you suspect something when you brought the box in from the barn?"

"She was too busy spooning," says Cassidy.

"Cassidy Ann!" exclaims her mother as my face goes beet red.

Cassidy grins. "Just giving her an alibi, Mom. I couldn't help noticing that Darcy is covered in lip gloss."

Darcy swipes at his face. "Let me help you with that," says Stewart, reaching over and dabbing at it with a napkin. Darcy swats him away, but he's grinning.

"That's my boy," says Mr. Hawthorne proudly. "Chip off the old mistletoe block."

"What about the chicken?" says Mr. Wong, who's still holding his feet well above the floor. Megan's father isn't exactly the barnyard type.

This sets us all off again, and the living room echoes with laughter as the chicken hunt resumes. My father finally corners the runaway hen by the piano.

My brothers, meanwhile, are lingering hopefully in the doorway.

Cassidy and I exchange another glance, and I nod this time, finally ready to let the little weasels off the hook.

"I have an announcement to make," says Cassidy, rising to her feet. She crosses the room and stands over my brothers—towers over them, really—folding her arms across her chest and staring down at them. Her face is expressionless. They look up at her fearfully, wondering what's coming next. "You two," she says, "have ... been ... PRANKED!"

Emma and Megan and I all erupt in whoops and hollers, and Becca does her touchdown cheer.

"What?" says my mother, mystified. "Why? I don't get it."

"Dylan and Ryan switched all our Secret Santa gifts," I tell her finally, when I'm able to stop laughing. I explain about the mix up and its aftermath. "It was just a little payback." I glance over at Mrs. Hawthorne. "Sorry, Mrs. H."

Heather Vogel Frederick

"No harm done," she says. She looks down at the card she's still holding. "But does this mean I don't get an ornament?"

"What's the matter, Phoebe," says my father, "you mean you don't you want a CHICKEN on your Christmas tree?" He pulls the squawking bird out from behind him and thrusts it toward her, setting off another round of shrieks and flapping wings.

"Michael Delaney!" cries my mother. "You're as bad as the boys! I mean the girls! I mean—oh, for heaven's sake, get that bird out of here!" She collapses on the couch and puts her arm around Mrs. Hawthorne. "Jess, would you please go get Phoebe her real present?"

Darcy and I duck out of the room.

"That went well," he says.

"Everything but Cassidy's dumb smooching comment."

"Nobody cares, Jess. They know you're my girlfriend."

I love it when he says that I'm his girlfriend. It makes me feel— happy. Really, really happy. "Yeah, I guess."

He tugs my braid. Darcy Hawthorne will probably be tugging my braid until I'm ninety. "So what's in the other box, a goat?"

I give him a mischievous smile. "Pretty small goat," I reply, handing him the box. "You'll just have to wait and see."

Things have settled down a bit by the time we return. Carrie Underwood has been banished to the chicken coop, my brothers are back in my mother's good graces, and Mrs. Hawthorne has regained her composure. She smiles as Darcy gives her the box, but I notice she still opens it gingerly.

"Oh!" she cries in delight. "Oh my!" Reaching in, she lifts out a kitten. Our barn cat Elvis's daughter, the little gray one with the white paws and bib. Around her neck is another gift tag, and Mrs. Hawthorne practically swoons when she reads it aloud: "'For Miss Sparrow from the Kelly Family: Please take care of Lady Jane Grey for us while we're out at Murmuring Lake for the summer.'" How utterly perfect!"

"You mean *purr*-fect," says Dylan, rolling his *r*'s.

Mrs. Chadwick snaps a picture. "Mother won't believe this."

"We know that nothing will ever replace Melville in your hearts," my mother tells Mrs. Hawthorne, "but a house as cozy as yours deserves a cat."

Mrs. Hawthorne nuzzles the kitten. "She's beautiful, Shannon. Thank you."

"Can I hold her too, Mom?" asks Emma, and her mother hands the kitten over.

"Hello, Lady Jane," coos Emma. "Pip is going to be beside himself when he sees you! He's been wanting a pet of his own."

"Me too," says Megan, holding out her hands. Emma surrenders the furry bundle, and Megan kisses it on the nose.

"The perfect accessory for a fashion designer," says Gigi. "Don't you think so, Lily?" She gives Megan's mother a sly look, and Mrs. Wong sighs.

"Mother, we've talked about this before. No pets."

"Oh, but look at how cute she is. A kitten is more like a family member than a pet."

Heather Vogel Frederick

Mrs. Wong shakes her head.

"She is pretty cute," says Mr. Wong, reaching over and stroking the kitten's ears.

"We have two more to give away," says Mrs. Delaney.

Mrs. Wong sighs again. "We'll see," she says finally, which is almost always mom-code for "No way."

The kitten makes the rounds of our living room. By the time she gets to me, she's pooped from all the excitement, and she snuggles against my chest and goes to sleep, purring.

"Dreaming, dreaming, of your sweet paws I'm dreaming," I sing softly to her.

"This is the best New Year's Eve ever," says Emma. "I wish it could go on and on. I love happy endings!"

"It's not over yet," says Cassidy. "There's still dessert."

Mrs. Sloane-Kinkaid shakes her head. "I swear you have a hollow leg."

"You know who else liked happy endings?" says Mr. Hawthorne.

"Who?"

"Charles Darwin."

Mrs. Chadwick frowns. "What does Charles Darwin have to do with Betsy-Tacy, Nicholas?"

"Nothing at all," replies Mr. Hawthorne. "Just a random fun fact." He pulls the little notebook he always keeps with him out of his shirt pocket. "I came across this quote the other day while I was reading a new biography of him. Let me see, yes, here it is. Darwin once wrote,

'I often bless all novelists. A surprising number have been read aloud to me, and I like all if moderately good, and if they do not end unhappily—against which a law ought to be passed.'"

"I agree," I say firmly. "It should definitely be a law. Let's make a book club New Year's resolution: nothing but happy endings."

Gigi springs to her feet. "Speaking of happy endings," she says, "who's ready for chocolate fondue?"

❧ Becca ❧

"Ring out the old, ring in the new . . . Betsy."

—*Betsy in Spite of Herself*

"Welcome to Heinz's Restaurant!" says Megan's grandmother, throwing open the door to her tea shop.

Pies & Prejudice has been transformed. A HAPPY NEW YEAR! banner obscures the tea quote on the far wall, and there are silver balloons and streamers dangling from the ceiling, along with a glittering disco ball.

The tables have been pushed together to make two long ones, and the yellow-and-white color scheme has been replaced by sophisticated black and white—tablecloths, napkins, chair cushions, everything. I'm betting Megan had something to do with this. It looks really cool—especially with the black-and-white tiles on the floor. Mr. Wong must have been on the decorating committee too, because there's a big flat-screen TV set up on the hutch, and a slide show of pictures taken at various events over the past year is playing on it. Cassidy at the rink with Tristan. Mrs. Bergson. Our trip to England last summer. Darcy making the winning touchdown at the Thanksgiving Day game. Megan winces slightly as a picture of Simon flashes on-screen, and I reach over and give her a sympathetic squeeze.

"Cell phones, please, check your cell phones here," says Mrs. Wong, coming around the room with a basket. "This is a cell-phone-free establishment."

My mother gives me a nudge, and I reluctantly relinquish mine. So does Megan. Our parents are all alike—they're always trying to get us not to talk or text so much, especially at dinner.

We mill around for a bit, looking for our place cards. The adults are all at one table, and the girls plus my brother, Darcy Hawthorne, and the twins are at the other. Megan and I are seated next to each other, across from Cassidy.

"Yum," says Cassidy happily, looking at the spread. Both tables are outfitted with their own fondue pots and fondue forks, along with platters of pound cake, marshmallows, strawberries, pineapple, bananas, and other fruit.

"Just a quick announcement!" says Mrs. Wong, as we all pick up our menus. "Mother and I would like to let you know that here at Heinz's we serve only fair-trade chocolate, and the fruit is, of course—"

"Organic!" our table choruses.

Mrs. Wong looks chagrined.

"Did you design this?" I ask Megan as I open the menu.

She nods. "With a little help from Emma."

Megan's got great design sense, not only when it comes to clothes, but everything else as well. She was the one who came up with the logo for our baked-goods business last year, for instance—the one that's now on the sign outside the shop.

On the front of the menu is a drawing of an old-fashioned ice cream parlor, complete with the words "Heinz's Restaurant" arched over it. At the bottom is the address: "Main Street, Deep Valley, Minnesota."

The best part is the fake ads, though. There's a border of them all around the inside of the menu—Deep Valley High Class of 1910, Bob Ray's shoe store, the Melborn Hotel, Magic Wavers curlers, singing lessons with Mrs. Poppy, that sort of thing. On the back cover is a collage of artwork by Lois Lenski and Vera Neville, who illustrated the series.

"Good work, girls," says my mom, tucking hers into her purse. "Mother will love this. I'll add it to the scrapbook."

"Here's a question for the book club," says Mr. Hawthorne. "What do you think it is that makes these Betsy-Tacy books worth reading, all these years after they were published?" He glances around the room at us. "From a novelist's perspective, it's a fascinating question. I can't help but wonder if people will be reading my books decades from now with the same kind of enthusiasm that you're reading Lovelace's."

"Girls, do you want to field that question?" asks Mrs. Hawthorne, adding in a stage whisper, "Put your hand down, Emma! Let someone else have a turn."

We all look at one another. Cassidy shrugs. "I can tell you what I think, I guess. For me, they're just real stories about real girls. It's kind of like things change, but they don't, you know? I mean, it's 1910, they get all excited about the first automobile in town, they pouf up their hair in this weird style—"

"It's called a pompadour," says Megan.

"—and wear long dresses and stuff, but I think I could really be friends with someone like Betsy."

"Yeah, anybody who thinks geometry is 'about as much fun as going to the dentist' is a kindred spirit," I add.

"Wait a minute, I liked geometry!" says Jess.

"You would," I retort, but I smile to make sure she knows I'm just joking.

"So what you're saying is that it's the insides of the characters—their emotions and feelings—that you connect with, not the time period in which a book is set?" Emma's father continues.

We all nod, and Mr. Hawthorne takes his notebook out of his shirt pocket again and jots something down, which makes me wonder if maybe we're going to be in his next book.

"Enough talk! Time to eat," says Gigi.

Even though I'm so full of salmon and potatoes and soup and everything else I can hardly move, somehow I manage to load up a few forkfuls of goodies and dip them into the luscious melted chocolate.

A few minutes later Stanley Kinkaid taps his knife against his water glass. "Clementine and I would like to make an announcement!"

This is it, I think. The decision on California!

Across the table from me, Cassidy calmly dips her fondue fork into

Heather Vogel Frederick

the pot again. If she's nervous, she sure isn't showing it. They must have told her already.

Deep down, I'm really hoping she goes. I have to admit I'd miss her—we're about as different as two people can be, but I admire her spunk, and book club would never be the same without her, that's for sure. Still, if Cassidy moves back to California, I might finally have a chance at Zach Norton.

"Clemmie?" says her stepfather, turning to Mrs. Sloane-Kinkaid. "Would you like to do the honors?"

Cassidy's mother raises her glass. "A toast to my beautiful daughter Courtney, who got engaged on Christmas Eve!"

There's a collective gasp around the table.

"*Engaged?* Really, Clementine!" says my mother, ever the wet blanket. "Isn't she awfully young for such a major life decision?"

Cassidy's mother is unflappable. "That's right, Calliope, she is. But I wasn't all that much older when I met her father, and at any rate the plan is for them both to finish school first. Grant is a senior and will be graduating this year, and then he's heading to law school. He wants to be an entertainment lawyer. Getting his degree should keep him busy while Courtney is finishing up at UCLA."

"There's no love like young love," says Gigi.

What about California? I think, looking over at Cassidy, who is poker-faced. Chloe is sitting on her lap, smeared all over with chocolate. She's getting sleepy now, her eyes drooping as she leans back against her big sister. I'll definitely miss Chloe if they move.

"It's so romantic, getting engaged on Christmas Eve," says Emma, sighing. She turns to Cassidy. "Don't you think?"

Cassidy doesn't reply.

"What did the ring look like?" Jess asks her.

Cassidy frowns and stabs her fondue fork into a piece of banana. From the looks of it, she's not too thrilled at the idea of her sister getting married, even if the wedding is a few years away. "I can't remember."

"It's platinum," says her mother. "A beautiful vintage art deco setting that belonged to Grant's great-grandmother."

A chorus of sighs go up around both tables from all the females. The dads shake their heads, and Darcy and Stewart look downright uncomfortable. I think all this talk about weddings is making them nervous.

"So many changes ahead," says Mrs. Delaney. "Stewart and Darcy heading off to college next year, Courtney getting engaged—and how about California? Have you made a decision on the job, Stanley?"

Here it comes, I think. Finally.

Mr. Kinkaid glances over at Cassidy. "Would you like to tell everybody?"

She nods and passes Chloe to him, then pushes back from the table and stands up. I have to tilt my head back to see her face. There's just such a *lot* of Cassidy Sloane.

"My family has decided—" she begins, and I cross my fingers under the table as she pauses dramatically.

"—to stay here in Concord."

Heather Vogel Frederick

Everyone cheers but me. I just sigh and uncross my fingers.

All the noise startles Chloe, who starts to cry. Cassidy takes her back from her stepfather and hugs her close. "No, no, monkey-face, it's okay. It's good news!"

"Don't call her monkey-face," says her mother automatically.

Cassidy sits down again. "They made me promise not to say anything," she tells us.

"We decided a couple days ago, but thought it would be fun to wait and tell you all tonight," Stanley explains.

"A New Year's Eve present," says Gigi.

"Exactly," says Mrs. Sloane-Kinkaid.

I try and look on the bright side. Now that they're staying, I'll still get to babysit Chloe. That's a definite plus. And it's not a sure thing with Zach and Cassidy, is it? She hasn't said anything one way or the other, and there are always twists and turns in the Winding Hall of Fate. Maybe I still have a chance.

"There've been a lot of changes under our roof these past few years," Cassidy's mother continues. "First David's passing, then the move across the country and the TV show, and—"

"Don't forget me and Chloe," says Mr. Kinkaid.

"I could never forget you and Chloe," she replies, leaning over and kissing his cheek. "At any rate, we decided it would be better for our family if we stay put for a while, at least until Cassidy's finished high school."

"Speaking of change," says Mrs. Hawthorne, "do you realize it's been almost five years since we started this club? A lot has happened since that very first meeting."

"I happened!" says Gigi, which makes everybody laugh.

"You certainly did, Mother," says Mrs. Wong. "And the tea shop happened too."

"So did Mrs. Bergson," says Emma loyally.

"A toast to Mrs. Bergson!" cries Mrs. Hawthorne, and we all raise our punch cups in her memory.

"And I joined the Lady Shawmuts and started Chicks with Sticks," says Cassidy.

"And we moved to England," says Emma.

"And I went to boarding school," says Jess.

"And don't forget the fashion show," Megan adds.

I'm quiet, thinking about some of the changes in my life since I've been part of the book club. Getting my braces on . . . getting my braces off . . . joining the cheerleading squad . . . going to Spring Formal with Zach. And my dad losing his job, of course.

"Enough of this auld lang syne stuff," says Mr. Wong. "Isn't it time for Megan to get her ornament?"

Jess leans over and reaches into her purse. "Megan already knows I was her Secret Santa," she says, handing over a small wrapped package.

Inside is a tiny, old-fashioned sewing machine. "I love it!" says Megan. "Thanks, Jess."

"Read us the card," says her mother.

"'To Miss Mix from Mrs. Ray—I'll be calling on your services often in the year ahead. My girls are growing up, and will soon be off to the Great World. Sincerely, Mrs. Ray.'"

My mother suddenly disappears under the table. "I almost forgot, girls," she says, her voice muffled. "I have something for all of you from my mother." She reappears clutching a bunch of small, peppermint-striped gift bags. "A parting gift as we say farewell to Betsy-Tacy," she adds, passing them out.

Inside are more ornaments, a tiny glass pitcher for each of us with something written on the side in gold script: *The nicest present is the present of a friend.*

"You'll get to see the real pitcher, the one Tacy gave Betsy—I mean Bick gave Maud—when you visit Mankato next spring, Becca," my mother tells me.

"Lucky you," says Stewart under his breath. I hold up my fondue fork, and we fence across the table.

There's a loud knock at the door, and we all jump.

"Who could that be?" asks Gigi, her dark eyes sparkling as she scurries over to answer it.

"Ho-ho-ho," says a deep voice.

"SANTA!" crows Chloe, as a tall figure in a red suit comes striding in. He's got a sack slung over his back, and above the white beard I detect a pair of familiar blue eyes. It's Zach Norton! I look over at Megan, puzzled.

"What's he doing here?" I whisper, but she just smiles.

There's someone else with him too. A tall skinny someone dressed from head to toe in green. Under the peaked elf hat I spot a pair of thick, owlish glasses. It's Kevin Mullins. He waves at Jess.

"This is my helper," says Santa Zach, his beard slipping slightly. Readjusting it, he throws in another "Ho-ho-ho." "We're looking for the Chadwicks. Sorry we're a week late, but my reindeer flew off course, and it took us a while to find our way back here from the South Pole."

My mother raises her hand, gamely playing along. "I'm Mrs. Chadwick."

Santa Zach plunks the sack down in front of her. "This is for you and your family," he tells her. "Merry Christmas!"

"Merry Christmas!" squeaks Kevin, waving at Jess again. Beside her, Darcy is grinning hugely. He gets a kick out of Kevin.

"SANTA!" hollers Chloe again, and Zach pats her on the head.

"Would Santa and his helper like to stay for chocolate fondue?" Gigi asks them.

"Sure," says Zach in his normal voice, plunking himself down beside Cassidy. She whispers something in his ear, and his face splits into a grin. They give each other a high five.

The joy that had bloomed inside of me at the sight of him slowly deflates. She must have told him about California. I take a deep breath and let it out slowly, then tell myself it's time to adjust to the new reality. Zach likes Cassidy. Cassidy probably likes Zach back. Get over it. Move on.

Easier said than done, of course, but I slap a smile on my face and promise myself that things will get better next year. Which starts in exactly eight minutes, according to the countdown clock on the TV.

"What on earth is in here?" says my mother, prodding the lumps and bulges in the Santa sack.

"Why don't you open it and find out?" Mrs. Hawthorne tells her.

My mother reaches inside and pulls out a big envelope. As she begins to read the card it contains, her eyes widen and her face turns red. Not a happy Santa-suit red, though. A much angrier shade.

Uh-oh, I think.

"Who told you?" she snaps, slapping the card down onto the table.

Told her what? I wonder. What's going on?

Mrs. Hawthorne looks taken aback. "Uh, well . . ." Her voice trails off.

My father picks up the card and reads it as my mother scans the room. "You have absolutely no right to interfere in our family's business," she says stiffly.

My eyes slide over to Megan, who's gone a peculiar shade of greenish-white. "You didn't!" I whisper. "You promised not to say anything!"

"I didn't think it would be that big a deal!" she whispers back.

She should know my mother better than that by now.

"Calliope, there's nothing to be embarrassed or ashamed about," Mrs. Sloane-Kinkaid begins.

"I am neither embarrassed nor ashamed, Clementine," my mother replies icily. "I am simply trying to maintain my family's dignity and privacy. I'll thank you all to mind your own business."

An awkward silence falls over the tea shop. Out of the corner of my eye I see the clock on the television ticking away toward midnight.

"We meant well," says Mrs. Hawthorne finally. "Really, we did."

"Does this mean you knew about Pirate Pete, too?" my father asks.

"Uh—" says Mr. Wong.

"Great. Just great. You've all had a good laugh behind our backs, I'm sure." My mother throws her napkin down and pushes back from the table. "Henry? We're going home. I refuse to sit here and be humiliated any longer. We're the laughingstock of Concord."

My father picks up the card and reads it again. Reaching over, he takes my mother's hand. "Perhaps we can give our friends the benefit of the doubt, Calliope," he says gently, tugging her back down into her seat.

"Everyone goes through hard times," says Mrs. Delaney. "We certainly did." She looks at Mr. Delaney and smiles, then turns back to my parents. "Please, just take a look at what's inside the bag."

My mother and father exchange a glance. My father gives my mother an encouraging nod, and she reaches reluctantly into the Santa sack again, pulling out more envelopes and brightly wrapped boxes. She and my father open them one by one. Inside are gift certificates: a six months' supply of fresh fruit, vegetables, eggs, jam, and goat cheese from Half Moon Farm; a VIP "unlimited lunch" pass at Pies & Prejudice; a weekend getaway at the Edelweiss Inn, complete with dog-sitting for Yo-Yo at Half Moon Farm; a request for a landscaping makeover at the Hawthornes'.

"Now that I've sold my second novel," says Emma's father, "Phoebe

Heather Vogel Frederick

and I decided we want to spruce things up at home. The yard was starting to look a little shabby. And who better to consult with than our favorite almost newly minted landscape designer?"

The corner of my mother's mouth quirks up at this. "Thank you."

"And speaking of consulting, there should be a green envelope in there as well," says Mrs. Sloane-Kinkaid.

My father peers into the bag. He pulls it out and hands it to my mother. She reads it, then glances over at Mrs. Sloane-Kinkaid. "You'd do this for me, Clementine? Really?"

"Absolutely. It's what friends are for."

My mother shows the card to my father. There's a real smile on her face now, and the angry reddish color is subsiding. "Clementine recommended me as a gardening consultant for her show."

"Lily's done an outstanding job for us with organic food sourcing, and it occurred to me that I could use some expert help in the garden arena as well. This isn't charity, Calliope—you'll be a wonderful resource."

My father shakes his head. "I don't know what to say."

"A simple thank-you will do," Mr. Wong replies. "You know you'd do the same if it were one of us." He points to the tiny glass pitcher that's sitting in front of Megan. "The nicest present is the present of a friend, remember?"

A hint of a sparkle returns to my father's eye. "Well, I must admit I'm looking forward to retiring Pirate Pete," he says.

My hands, which I hadn't realized I'd been clenching tightly in my lap throughout this whole exchange, start to relax. It's going to be okay. My mother watches with a rueful expression on her face as my father pulls his eye patch from his shirt pocket and pops it on. "Aaaargh!" he says.

"Cool!" says Ryan. Or maybe it's Dylan—I still have trouble telling them apart. "Can I try it on?"

"Aye, matey," my father replies, handing it to him.

I stand up. This is as good a time as any to add my two cents.

"Mom—Dad—I didn't know about the Secret Santa gifts tonight, but I have a surprise for you too." I glance over at Megan's grandmother. "I've been talking to Gigi, and she's offered me a part-time job as a waitress here at Pies & Prejudice."

There's an excited buzz from my friends, but my mother frowns. "What about your cheerleading?"

"I think there's a way I can do both," I tell her. "I'm going to start off assisting one night a week at Gigi's new cooking classes. I've talked to Coach O'Donnell, and she understands that I need to help my family right now. She's willing to cut me some slack on the weekends if Gigi can be flexible with my schedule."

"Way to go, Chadwick," says Cassidy softly. "One more thing I like about you."

I smile at her, almost glad she's not moving.

My mother still doesn't look convinced. "Will this affect your chances of being chosen head cheerleader?" Once my mother heard that there were such things as cheerleading scholarships for college, she was all for me trying out for the squad.

Heather Vogel Frederick

I shrug. "It might. But there's always senior year for that."

"Wait until we tell your grandparents," my father says. "They'll be so proud of you."

"I am too," my brother tells me quietly. "Nice work, Rebecca."

"Thanks," I reply. "But it's just Becca, okay?"

Stewart smiles at me. "Okay."

"Hey!" says Dylan, or maybe Ryan, pointing to the TV. "Look at the clock! They're getting ready to start the countdown!"

Sure enough, it's almost midnight. Mr. Wong rushes over to fiddle with the controls, and suddenly the slide show disappears and we're watching live TV from Times Square. Gigi grabs my arm.

"Come on, new assistant," she says. "It's time to start breaking you in. I could use some help pouring the sparkling cider."

"TEN—NINE—EIGHT!" shout the twins, as we finish filling everyone's glasses. I join in at "THREE—TWO—ONE . . . HAPPY NEW YEAR!"

The tea shop erupts in loud whistles and cheers, and squawks from our noisemakers and party horns.

"KISS, KISS, KISS!" shrieks Chloe, climbing down from Cassidy's lap and running around in excited circles. It's true, everybody's kissing everybody else. Well, except Megan and me, who clink our glasses together instead.

"To best friends?" she says.

"To best friends," I reply.

Across the room, our parents are all kissing each other, and here at our table the twins are pretending to kiss each other too. Darcy really is kissing Jess—while Kevin Mullins patiently waits his turn. I have to avert my eyes at the sight of my brother kissing Emma Hawthorne. Eww! And I try not to watch as Zach Norton grabs Cassidy and plants one on her, too. She doesn't pull away, and I don't see her trying to smack him with anything, the way she did back in seventh grade, so I guess it's official—Cassidy likes Zach.

I suppose I have to get used to the idea.

I look around to say something to Megan, but she's not in her seat. I spot her rummaging in the basket of cell phones by the cash register. She pulls hers out and turns it on. Her face lights up.

"Omigosh, Becca! Look at this!" she cries, running back across the room. She holds up her phone. There's a text message on the screen. It's from Simon. I MISS U. CHAT TOMORROW?

I raise my glass to her again. "Happy New Year!"

As her fingers fly across the keypad, I look around the room. This has been a year of happy endings—for Megan, whose breakup might not really be a breakup. For Emma, who's home in Concord again where she belongs. For Gigi, who's launched her new tea shop successfully. For my mother, who gets to finish school, and for Stewart, who gets to start it. For Jess, who's getting her cast off soon and who's going to nail that audition next month, just like Cassidy says. And last but not least, for Cassidy and her family, who aren't moving to California.

And if my dad hasn't quite found his happy ending yet, thanks to our friends and their New Year's Eve Secret Santa surprise we at

Heather Vogel Frederick

least have enough happiness to tide us over until he does. As for me, soon-to-be waitress here at Pies & Prejudice, well, I'm ready for whatever lies around the bend in the Winding Hall of Fate. One thing's for sure—Rebecca won't be coming with me. If I never see her again it'll be too soon.

Someone grabs me from behind. It's Zach Norton.

"Happy New Year, Becca!" he says, grinning at me. His beard is crooked and his face is flushed. He looks gorgeous. Before I even have time to react, he leans in and gives me a big kiss. Even though I mostly just end up with a mouthful of fake white beard, it's still a kiss. From Zach Norton!

So what if it's not exactly the kiss I'm looking for? And so what if he goes on to make his way around the room, kissing practically everybody else—Megan and Emma and Jess and Chloe and even Gigi, too?

It's still a fantastic way to start the new year.

"Each one of us has to be true to the deepest thing that is in him."

—*Betsy in Spite of Herself*

Mother-Daughter Book Club Questions

This was the first Mother-Daughter Book Club book to include chapters told from Becca's perspective. Did they change your opinion of her at all? In what way?

Do you think you will read the Betsy-Tacy books after reading this book? Do you think you would find the characters in the Betsy-Tacy series as relatable as the girls in the Mother-Daughter Book Club did?

Do you usually spend the holidays with your family or friends? What is your favorite holiday memory?

In the Betsy-Tacy high school books, Betsy is torn between Joe Willard, who's handsome and smart but kind of aloof, and Tony Markham, who's handsome and funny but a little on the wild side. Are you on Team Joe or Team Tony?

Maud Hart Lovelace always knew she wanted to be a writer. Have you ever felt that way about a certain profession? Have you taken any steps toward your goal?

Betsy is based on Maud herself, and Tacy is based on her childhood best friend. Do you like reading novels that were based on real people? Would you like it if one of your friends wrote a book about you?

Do you have a friend whom you would consider your Tacy? Do you have a crowd?

Do you and your friends have secret words and phrases like "Winona eyes" and "snoggestion"? What are some of them? Did you find yourself adopting any of the Betsy-Tacy words?

Megan was devastated when Simon broke up with her. Have you ever been in a relationship that ended before you wanted it to? How did you handle it? Were you able to talk to your mother or friends about it?

Cassidy and her family originally moved from Laguna Beach to Concord; in this book, they consider moving back! Have you and your family ever had to move? After you moved, did you keep your friends from where you used to live?

Have you ever participated in a Secret Santa? Were there any mishaps? Did you or any of your friends try to rig the drawing, the way Megan and Becca tried to?

Have you ever gone on a trip with a friend? Did you get along the whole time?

Has anyone close to you ever lost his or her job? How did that feel? How did you help them deal with it?

Why do you think Mr. and Mrs. Chadwick initially respond to the gifts with anger?

Jess was very upset to see Emma and Felicia become friends. Have you ever felt left out?

Megan manages to put her hurt feelings aside when she realizes that Becca and her family need her help. If you were in Megan's situation, how would you react?

How did I manage to grow up without knowing about the Betsy-Tacy books?

It's a question that still puzzles me. Is it possible my hometown library didn't have them on the shelves that I scoured weekly for new reading material? I can't imagine that was the case. Somehow, though, Maud Hart Lovelace and her wonderful series never made it onto my radar screen when I was younger. It wasn't until a couple of years ago, in fact, when I was in the Midwest on a book tour, that people began ambushing me to tell me about Maud and her books, and how perfect they'd be for my fictional book club.

They were right.

What's not to love about thoroughly modern Betsy Ray and her family and friends? Sure, the setting may be circa 1910, the fashions quaint and the slang unfamiliar, but Deep Valley is a kissing cousin to my fictional Concord. Emma, Jess, Cassidy, and Megan (and Becca too) would feel right at home in Betsy's world of treasured friendships, fun-filled escapades, and cute boys. Lots of cute boys . . .

If, like me, you've never heard of Betsy and her friend Tacy, please go immediately to your bookstore or library and find them. I promise you'll fall in love. Start at the beginning (yes, I know, the girls are five, but trust me on this one) and read them all straight through. You won't want to miss a single word.

Which one is my favorite? Like Becca's grandmother, I have two:

Betsy and Tacy Go Downtown and *Betsy and the Great World*. For this book, though, I focused on *Betsy in Spite of Herself*, which finds our heroine in her sophomore year in high school, exactly the same age as my fictional girls. Plus, it has the added benefit of whisking Betsy to a very German Milwaukee for Christmas, an event I had great fun echoing. My maiden name is Vogel, which means "bird" in German, and I grew up in a family whose German roots were never more evident than during the holiday season, when we ate my grandmother's Springerle cookies, sang *"Stille Nacht"* and *"O Tannenbaum,"* and decorated our tree while listening to other traditional Christmas music on the antique music box that our ancestors brought with them when they came to this country in the 1860s.

Is it any wonder that German was one of my majors in college? After graduation, I lived in Germany for a year, where I spent Christmas with a friend and her family in their tiny Bavarian village. We drank lots of hot chocolate (*mit Schlag*, of course), opened our presents on Christmas Eve, and later that night went to a worship service at a mountainside chapel. I'll never forget the stunning setting—the simple wood-framed building decorated with evergreen boughs and candles—nor the joy my friend Maria and I had providing the music on our recorders. Afterward, when we went outside, it started to snow. Christmas magic doesn't get much better than that.

As always, I have numerous thank you bouquets to hand out. Melissa Posten at Pudd'nhead Books in Webster Groves, Missouri, gets the first one, for literally pressing *Betsy-Tacy* and *Betsy-Tacy and Tib* into my hands as gifts as I was leaving her store. My friends

Vicki and Steve Palmquist heard about this and gave me Winona eyes in Wayzata until I promised to actually read them (which I did, on the flight home). Radhika Breaden pounced on me a few weeks later at a local appearance and mustered her wits enough to invite a total stranger to her home for dinner to meet some Betsy-Tacy fans who happened to be in town. I mustered mine and went, not knowing what I was getting myself into. (A whole lot of fun, that's what.) Now I have a host of delightful new friends, including the inimitable Kathy Baxter, the amazing Colleen O'Neil, and the resourceful Julie Chuba, who went above and beyond the call of duty to cart me all over Minneapolis and Mankato on a research trip. For the record, I would travel with you three anytime, anywhere.

Susan Brown, president of the Betsy-Tacy Society, her husband, Bob, and colleague Pat Nelson took time out of their busy schedules to give us a private tour of the Betsy-Tacy houses that I'll never forget. Bouquets for all three of you, too!

I'd be remiss in not giving one to Alexandra Cooper, my fabulous editor at Simon & Schuster, a Minnesota girl and Maud Hart Lovelace fan herself, for enthusiastically embracing this project and patiently shepherding it to completion.

Betsy-Tacy fans online have showered me not only with love, but also with books and reference materials that were invaluable in writing this book. More bouquets to Kathy and Radhika, and to Julie Schrader, who sent me a copy of her guidebook, *Maud Hart Lovelace's Deep Valley*, as well as Amy Dolnick Rechner for *Between Deep Valley and the Great World: Maud Hart Lovelace in Minneapolis*. And bouquets to all the rest of the Listren for ongoing encouragement and support.

I can't forget my fearless experts—Jami Meyer and her daughters Kylie and McKenna, who clued me in on cheerleading techniques; Barb Odanaka for all things Laguna Beach and surfing; and as always, Lucinda and Helen Quigley, who keep me from wobbling all over the hockey rink. (An extra shout-out to Lucinda, whose U12 team won the USA Hockey National Championship this year!)

And finally, a very special bouquet to my husband. If anyone wants to know if I'm Team Tony or Team Joe, the correct answer is: I'm Team Steve!

Cat Starr's life is no fairy tale.

Get an exclusive preview of
Heather Vogel Frederick's magical novel,
now available!

"Are we there yet?" My little brother pulled his index finger out of his mouth, sounding anxious. Geoffrey's not quite four and doesn't like car trips.

Without taking his eyes off the road, my dad reached over the back of his seat and stuffed the finger back in. It works kind of like a safety plug. Geoffrey's nickname in our family is Barf Bucket.

"Not much longer, buddy. Hang in there."

I was well out of range, sitting in the very back of the minivan next to Olivia. If you can call being braced against opposite car windows sitting "next to" each other. There was practically a force field between us. My stepsister and I are not exactly best friends.

I'd just arrived from Houston, where I live with my mom for most of the year, and was on the way from the airport to my dad's house in Oregon. Usually, I only spend vacations with my father: Thanksgiving or Christmas, take your pick; plus half of spring break and a month every summer.

This time, though, was different. This time I was moving in for three months, smack-dab in the middle of the school year. Well, almost the middle. April 1, to be exact. What choice did I have? It's not like I could stay at home with my mom. She was in outer space. Literally. My mother is an astronaut.

"It's either go to Portland or stay with your great-aunt Abyssinia," she told me when she broke the news that she'd been selected to go to the International Space Station. Obviously, there was no way she could take me with her. Not that I didn't beg her to anyway. Anything would be better than sharing a room with Miss Prissy Pants Olivia Haggerty.

Well, almost anything. The prospect of staying with my great-aunt Abyssinia was marginally worse, I had to admit. Great-Aunt Aby is my mother's only relative. She lives in an RV with her cat, Archibald, and spends her time traveling around to all the national parks. Our refrigerator back in Houston is plastered with her postcards: "Greetings from Yosemite!"; "Having a grand time at the Grand Canyon!"; and my personal favorite, "Chillaxin' at Glacier!" All of them are signed "ABYCNU"—the stupid little jingle she and my mother use when they say good-bye to each other. "Abyssinia!" my mother always hollers as Great-Aunt Abyssinia drives away. "Not if I be seeing you first!" my great-aunt hollers back, and then they both laugh their heads off. They think this is just hilarious, for some reason.

Once, a couple of years ago when I was still in elementary

school, my mother and I flew out to meet my great-aunt at Mount Rushmore for a week. It was kind of cool staying in the RV, but Great-Aunt Aby is weird. She's scatterbrained and disorganized, and she has some strange hobbies (her snow globe collection is about ready to take over the RV) and even stranger ideas about food. I was in my "I don't eat anything but fish sticks and peanut butter" phase back then, and her refrigerator had neither, just pickled eggs, kimchi, and about a hundred bottles of this disgusting green gloop that she drinks for breakfast. Her cupboards weren't any better. Who eats dried seaweed? If it's stinky or looks like it should be thrown in the trash immediately, you can be sure it's on my great-aunt's list of top ten favorite foods. I nearly starved to death on that trip.

Dad was thrilled with the idea, of course. Not me starving to death, but me coming to live with him. Ever since he remarried and became the proud owner of a brand-new family, he's been dying for us all to turn into the Brady Bunch.

Like that's ever going to happen.

It wouldn't be so bad if it weren't for Olivia. My half brother, Geoffrey, is actually really cute, except for the barfing, and my stepmother isn't like one of those fairy-tale stepmothers, the ones who secretly hate their stepdaughters and make them sleep in the scullery or something. Iz—her real name is Isabelle, but everybody calls her Iz—is awesome. The two of us actually have way more in common than she and

Olivia do. For instance, Iz loves the outdoors and she loves classical music, which are my two main passions in life. Sometimes she takes me to the symphony when I visit, just the two of us, and leaves Olivia home to babysit Geoffrey. Olivia hates it when that happens, even though she can't stand classical music and she has all the rest of the year to do stuff with her mother.

No, it definitely wasn't Iz. The real reason we'd never become the Brady Bunch was Olivia. My stepsister is a major pain.

If Olivia went to my school back in Houston, there's no way we would ever be friends. She tap-dances; I'm a tomboy. She's into arts and crafts; I break out in a rash at the sight of a tube of glitter. And I play the bassoon, while she still plays with Barbies. Olivia gets really mad when I say this—"I don't *play* with them, they're *props*," she insists. Yeah, right. Whatever. My stepsister wants to be an interior designer when she grows up, and her room is crammed with boxes she's decorated to look like rooms from magazines. They're wallpapered and painted, and there are curtains made of scraps of fabric from Iz's quilting basket, and carpet samples on the floors. Inside, the Barbies lounge around, reading on their little sofas and cooking in their itty-bitty kitchens and talking on the phones in their miniature offices. It's creepy.

It would be so much better if Olivia and I didn't have to share a room. My dad's house is way different from our super-modern high-rise condo back in Houston. It was built in 1912, for one thing, and for another, it's tiny. I mean *teeny* tiny. It's cute and everything, but it's designed more for Goldilocks or Thumbelina or somebody like that. Not for real people. It's like living in one of Olivia's Barbie dioramas.

My dad and Iz are really proud of their house, though. They call it their Northwest Honeymoon Cottage, and they're always going on about how much character it has, and swooning over the hardwood floors and the tile work around the fireplace and the stained-glass window on the landing of the stairs. Maybe that's where Olivia gets her passion for decorating, I don't know. What I do know is that I'd trade character for a few modern conveniences any day of the week. Another bathroom would be nice, for starters. There's only one for all five of us, which is totally ridiculous. Didn't anybody ever have to use the bathroom back in 1912? I guess nobody had clothes back then either, because the closets are minuscule too. Olivia loathes having to share her closet. She doesn't like having to share anything, especially with me, and especially her room. Stuffing the two of us in there is like throwing a lighted match onto a pile of wood shavings. *Kaboom!*

Dad and Iz have been talking about fixing up the attic into a master bedroom suite and giving me their room, but this trip came up kind of suddenly. There wasn't time for a remodel. Mom was a last-minute replacement for one of the other astronauts, who broke his ankle a week before launch.

She was up and into space so fast we didn't even get a chance to celebrate my birthday. I had to go stay with my friend A.J. and his family instead.

My mother and I had been planning a special trip over spring break, just the two of us. Dad had even agreed to let me skip my usual week in Oregon so that Mom and I could have more time together on our "mystery trip," as she called it. She wouldn't tell me where she was taking me. Not that it mattered now. When she got the news about the space mission, we had to cancel.

I was still brooding about this fact as we pulled off the freeway onto the winding road that led up into Portland's West Hills. We were almost home. Unfortunately, it didn't happen soon enough for Geoffrey.

"Gross!" shrieked Olivia as the car swerved and my dad pulled off onto the road's narrow shoulder. "Couldn't you have held it for five more minutes, you little twerp?"

Geoffrey started to cry. My father frowned at Olivia, then turned to him and said gently, "It's okay, buddy. We'll get you cleaned up in a jiffy. Just a little April Fools' Day joke, right?"

Some joke, I thought, holding my nose and catapulting out of the car. I sprinted past Olivia, waiting until I was safely out of range of eau de barf before taking a deep breath of fresh air. I love the way Oregon smells. Like evergreens and moss and clean earth. It rains here a lot, especially in the winter and spring, which keeps the air crystal-clear, unlike downtown Houston. And unlike downtown Houston, everything in Portland is incredibly green. I've never seen so many shades of the color before in my life.

My dad is a wildlife biologist, and he loves taking me hiking when I visit. I swear he knows every trail in Oregon. And in Portland, too. His house is on the fringes of the city, tucked into the woods up near Forest Park. He loves to brag that he lives on the edge of the biggest city park in the United States, and he loves the fact that the Wildwood Trail passes right by our house. I've always thought it was cool how you could hop on it and be out in the middle of nowhere one minute, then downtown the next.

I glanced back at the car. My father was changing Geoffrey's clothes. Olivia was lounging nearby, fiddling with her cell phone. She'd spent the entire drive home texting madly. She was probably telling her BFF, Piper Philbin, what a loser I was and how I'd completely ruined the rest of the school year for her by coming to Oregon.

Not that I really cared what she said, especially not to Piper Fleabrain.

I think it says a lot about a person, who they pick for their best friend, and the fact that Olivia picked Piper didn't exactly boost my opinion of my stepsister. Piper is one of those empty-headed popular girls that my middle school back in Houston is stuffed full of. Texas, Oregon—it doesn't matter, they're all the same. I swear they're made with cookie cutters in a bakery somewhere. All they care about is clothes and boys and makeup, and they talk in these high, squeaky voices that get higher and squeakier whenever someone male is nearby. It's enough to make a person, well, barf.

My best friend, on the other hand, may be a total nerd, but he's also the nicest guy on the planet. A.J. D'Angelo is the smartest kid in my school, and possibly in the whole state of Texas. He's a computer geek, which isn't surprising because both his parents work for NASA. Not as astronauts, but doing computer stuff. The whole family is scary smart. They live in the same building as my mother and I do, only we're on the seventeenth floor and they're on the fifteenth. I've known A.J. since the day we moved in, when I was six.

"All clear!" called my father.

Olivia and I climbed back into the van, still holding our noses, and a few minutes later we pulled into the driveway. My father tooted the horn to let my stepmother know we'd arrived, and the door flew open and Iz came running down the front steps, her long, curly blond hair bouncing behind her.

"I'm so glad you're here!" she said, throwing her arms around me, and for a brief moment I was glad too. Such was the power of Iz. Then Olivia ungraciously set my suitcase down on my foot, and all of a sudden I would have given anything to be back in Texas.

My stepmother planted a kiss on the top of my head. "You grew again," she said. "At least an inch."

I smiled up at her. Iz knows that my greatest ambition in life—besides playing bassoon for a major symphony orchestra or doing something involving the outdoors—is to be taller. I'm really, really short. Vertically challenged, as A.J. puts it.

"Sorry I couldn't be at the airport to meet you," Iz told me. "I had a shoot up on Mount Hood and I couldn't reschedule."

My stepmother is a nature photographer. Even though deep down I still sometimes wish that my parents would get back together again, I have to admit that Iz and my dad are kind of a match made in heaven. The two of them have a whole lot more in common than my parents ever did.

My mother always tells me that what happened between her and my dad isn't my fault and it isn't my business, either. My business is just to know that they both love me more than anything and always will. I suppose she's got a point, but still, sometimes I wish things could have worked out differently.

"That's okay," I told my stepmother. "I don't mind."

This was true, and Iz knew it. She smiled and gave me another hug. "Wait until you see some of the shots I got. The mountain was out in all its spring glory this morning."

Mount Hood is amazing. There's snow on it all year round, and you can see its white-capped peak from all over the city. It's like Portland's trademark. One of our traditions when I come here during summer vacation is to drive up to Timberline Lodge and take the ski lift to the snow line. Iz takes our picture for the family Christmas card, and then we have a snowball fight. I love telling my friends back in Houston about this. They can't believe there's someplace that has snow in July and August.

Olivia really gets into the snowball fight—big surprise there, especially since I'm always her prime target—but that's about the only outdoor activity she likes. Nature is not Miss Prissy Pants's favorite thing. And Geoffrey's still at the stage where he wants everybody to carry him, so the two of them get left at home a lot when there's an outdoor adventure planned.

"Olivia, why don't you help your sister take her things upstairs?" Iz prompted.

Stepsister, I thought automatically.

"While you girls are getting settled in," she continued, "I'll get dinner on the table."

"Um, someone needs a bath first," said my father.

My stepmother plucked Geoffrey from his arms. "Bathwater's drawn and ready," she said, and gave Geoffrey a kiss too, even though he still smelled faintly of barf. Mothers are amazing that way. "How about I scrub the G-Man while you set the table?"

"Deal," said my dad.

Iz nudged Olivia, who glared at me as she picked up my suitcase again.

I followed her warily into the house.

What are the Mother-Daughter
Book Club girls up to next?

Turn the page for a sneak peek!

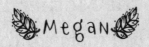

Megan

"If she were a nice, pretty child, one might compassionate her for-
lornness; but one really cannot care for such a little toad as that."
—*Jane Eyre*

"Would you like fries with that?"

I frown at the menu. Since when had my grandmother started serving french fries at the teashop?

I look up to see Becca Chadwick tapping her pen against the notepad she's holding. "Gotcha," she says, grinning at me.

I swat her with the menu. "Dork."

"Hey," she replies, "who's the one with the job, huh? Who's the one earning money right this instant? Speaking of which, you are planning to leave me a big tip, aren't you?"

This is Becca's first day as a full-fledged waitress at Pies & Prejudice, the wildly successful teashop my grandmother opened here in Concord last year. Things got so busy that Gigi decided to hire some extra help. Becca's been her assistant since the beginning of January. She started out working on Thursday evenings at Gigi's new cooking classes, and today is her first shift waiting tables.

"A big tip?" I pretend to think it over. "I guess it depends if you give me extra whipped cream on my hot chocolate."

"You want a little cinnamon sprinkled on that?" Becca's all business as she writes my order down.

"Of course."

"Got it. Back in a flash." She trots off to a neighboring table to take another order, her apron strings fluttering behind her. Like my grandmother, Becca is wearing the Pies & Prejudice uniform: black dress, frilly white apron, frilly white cap. Gigi had me design them, but I hadn't imagined someone my age actually wearing one. Becca looks kind of like a French maid in a bad sitcom. She's being a really good sport about it, though. She wanted this job so badly. Her father's been unemployed for a while, and working here has been a way to help her family out.

My gaze drifts over to the window, and I note gloomily that it's started to snow again. This has got to be some sort of record. Usually this time of year we get New England's famous January thaw, but the month's almost over and so far there's been no sign of it. We've missed more school this winter than any other year I can remember. Not that I'm complaining.

A little while later the bell over the door jangles and Emma Hawthorne and Jess Delaney come in, stomping their snow-covered boots on the mat. They spot me and wave, then cross the room to my table.

"Hey," says Emma, taking a seat. Jess does too.

"Hey back," I reply as Becca reappears with my order.

"I'll take one of those," says Jess, pointing to the hot chocolate that she sets down in front of me.

"Ditto," adds Emma. "But hold the cinnamon."

Jess shrugs off her jacket, giving Becca the onceover. "You look good," she tells her. "Just like a real waitress."

"I am a real waitress," Becca snaps.

"I just meant—"

Becca whooshes out a sigh and smiles. "I know. Sorry. I've just got a lot on my mind here. I was hoping for a quiet afternoon for my first day, but we've been swamped. It seems like everybody in Concord's stopped by for a treat and something hot to drink."

"Can you blame them?" says Emma, and we all look glumly out the window.

"I sure hope they don't have to cancel tonight's hockey game," says Jess.

"Not to mention my birthday party tomorrow night," I add. I've been planning it for ages—you only turn sixteen once, after all—and I've hardly slept a wink the past few nights, I'm so excited. I think my parents have a surprise up their sleeves, too, because there's been a lot of whispering around the house lately, and they keep giving me these goofy smiles. I'm thinking maybe they got me a car.

"I'm coming if I have to snowshoe up Strawberry Hill to get there," Becca tells me.

As she heads for the tea shop's tiny kitchen, Emma and

Jess and I discuss the odds of the hockey game getting canceled. Emma swears that the snow is tapering off, but Jess is less optimistic. I am too—I've been sitting here for nearly an hour, and it looks to me like the snow is still coming down thick and fast. I don't care as much as the two of them do, though—Emma's brother Darcy and boyfriend Stewart Chadwick both play for the team, and Jess is dating Darcy. I'm not dating anybody here in Concord, but I know the guys would really be disappointed if they didn't get to play.

Becca returns with two more hot chocolates, plus a plate of brightly colored round cookies. "On the house," she tells us. "Courtesy of Gigi."

My grandmother blows us a kiss from behind the bakery counter. "*Macarons,*" she calls, pronouncing them the French way. My grandmother loves everything French. "I'm trying out some new recipes in honor of the big birthday."

Somehow my party has turned into a weekend-long celebration. Things kick off tonight after the hockey game, with my friends taking me out to Burger Barn. Then tomorrow night my parents are treating us all to dinner at La Belle Epoque, my grandmother's and my favorite fancy French restaurant. Afterward we'll go back to our house for cake and ice cream, and a dance. My father rented sound equipment and hired a DJ, and he's been busy for days turning our family room into an eighties disco. Becca and Ashley talked me into a retro theme for the evening.

That alone should be enough for anybody, but our next mother-daughter book club meeting is on Sunday afternoon, and that always feels kind of like a party.

I reach for a bright pink cookie and take a bite. It practically melts in my mouth. "Mmm. Raspberry."

"Lemon," says Jess, nibbling on yellow one. "Dreamy."

"Uh, hazelnut maybe?" says Emma. She turns around and waves the pale brown cookie in the air. "These are great, Gigi!"

"*Merci beaucoup,*" my grandmother replies.

"So what's going on with you guys?" I ask my friends. "I've hardly seen you since the New Year's Eve party, Jess."

Jess goes to Colonial Academy, a swanky private school here in town. She's on a full scholarship, thanks to the fact that she's just about the smartest person I know, and thanks also to Becca's mother, who recommended her for it.

"I know," she replies. "Things have been really busy. Let's see." She starts ticking items off on her fingers. "I got my cast off, but you knew that already. I'm riding again. My MadriGals solo audition is coming up next week and I'm freaking out a little over that. Correction, a lot. Oh, and calculus is really, really hard."

"Poor you." It's hard to work up a lot of sympathy for someone who's taking calculus in tenth grade. Math is Jess's favorite subject, and she's incredibly good at it. For me, on the other hand, it's sheer torture.

She makes a face at me. "Having Mr. Crandall for a teacher

again is great, though," she continues. "Hey—did you know that Maggie's getting a little brother any day now?"

I'd totally forgotten that the Crandalls were expecting again. "Have they picked a name?"

"Trevor."

"Cute. Maggie and Trevor. I like it." The Crandalls are really nice. They were Jess's houseparents when she started at Colonial back in eighth grade, and all of us have done some babysitting for their daughter Maggie.

Emma turns to me. "Have you heard anything from Simon?"

I nod, smiling. Simon Berkeley is my back-on-again boyfriend, as of New Year's Eve. He broke up with me for a while last fall, telling me he thought we should be free to date other people, which was really hard. Simon is British, and living three thousand miles away from each other is tricky. It's not like we get to just hang out on the weekends and stuff, you know? We have to rely on e-mails and text messages and videoconferencing to stay close. It seems as if we're over our rough patch, though.

"He sent a package for my birthday," I tell her. "I'm dying to open it, but he made me promise I'd wait until tomorrow. Oh, and his father is guest lecturing up at some university in York this winter. He and his mom and Tristan drive up on the weekends whenever they can to visit him."

"Cool," says Emma, who lived in England our freshman

year. That's how Simon and I met—his family swapped houses with the Hawthornes. "We went to York—it's amazing. There's a medieval wall around the whole city, and it has this gorgeous old cathedral."

Emma's cell phone buzzes, and she pulls it out of her pocket and glances at the screen. "Cassidy's still at practice," she tells us. "She's not going to make it here in time to join us."

Cassidy Sloane is our other friend from book club. She eats, breathes, and sleeps ice hockey.

"She says we should have cranberry almond oat scones on her," Emma continues, smiling. Gigi's signature scones are Cassidy's favorite treat.

"Tempting, but I've already eaten way too many *macarons*," I reply, pushing the plate away. Cassidy may eat like a horse, but I can't. Designing clothes and sewing—my two favorite things in the world—are not cardio activities.

Before Emma can slip her cell phone back in her pocket, it buzzes again. "Oh good!" she exclaims happily, checking the message. "Zach just stopped by the rink and told Cassidy that the game is definitely on for tonight."

Zach is Zach Norton, the most gorgeous guy at Alcott High School. At least I thought so until I met Simon Berkeley. We all used to be in love with Zach back in elementary school. Okay, and middle school, too. In fact, some of us carried the torch into high school. I give Becca a sidelong look. She's wiping down the table next to us, but I noticed her face flush at the mention of his name. She carried the biggest torch of all of us, and she's still trying to come to terms with the fact that Cassidy and Zach are dating. Well, sort of dating. It's not like anybody ever sees them holding hands or anything. But they hang out all the time now.

I glance at the clock. The crowd in the tea shop is thinning out as closing time approaches. My father should be here any minute to get Gigi and me. Pies & Prejudice serves breakfast, lunch, and afternoon tea, so he always swings by to drive my grandmother home in time for dinner. Sure enough, a few minutes later the bell above the door jangles and my father appears, right on the heels of Mrs. Chadwick.

"Yoo-hoo!" Becca's mother calls, waving at Becca likes she's on the far side of the Grand Canyon. Even though we're the only ones still here except for a lone table of two, Becca turns beet red. Her mother has that kind of effect on people. "That's my daughter," Mrs. Chadwick tells the other customers proudly. "This is her first day waitressing. How'd she do?"

Becca makes a beeline for the back of the shop and dives behind the curtain that serves as a door to the kitchen. I don't blame her. I would too.

As Mrs. Chadwick badgers the trapped customers, my father beckons to me. "See you guys tonight," I tell my friends, putting on my jacket and scooping my backpack off the floor. I give my grandmother a kiss on the cheek on the way out.

"Calliope is going to drive me home," she tells me, and I nod.

My father's SUV is parked right outside. As I slide into the front seat, I glance over and notice that he's got that funny smile on his face again. "What?" I ask him suspiciously.

"Nothing," he says, popping one of the *macarons* that Gigi gave him into his mouth. "Oh man, these are good," he mumbles. "How was school?"

"Fine."

"That's it? Fine?"

"It was school."

"Did you have art today?"

I nod.

"And?" Why is it that parents always want to know every detail about your boring day at school? I heave a sigh and relent. "Art was great. We're working on some woodcuts, and when we're done Ms. Malone says we might get to do some soapstone carving." I love art class, actually. It's my favorite thing about school.

My father whistles happily to himself as we head down Lowell Road, passing first the Chadwicks' house and then the Hawthornes', and on over the bridge toward Strawberry Hill. Emma was right about the snow; it's tapered off to flurries. Even though I'm pretty sick of this endlessly bleak winter, I still can't help thinking how pretty the snowflakes look drifting across the headlights of our car.

"I guess we're the first ones here," my father says as we pull into the empty garage a few minutes later. He sounds kind of disappointed.

"I think mom had a Riverkeepers meeting this afternoon," I tell him.

"On a Friday? Don't they usually meet on Tuesdays?"

"It got postponed because of the snow."

"Ah."

Leaving our boots on the rack in the garage—my mother hates wet shoes in the house—we go inside and hang our coats in the front hall closet. Then I head down the hall to my room to change. Mirror Megan—that's what I call my reflection—frowns at me as I pull on my oldest sweats and put my hair up into a sloppy ponytail, but I promise her I'll change before the game tonight. Right now, I just want to be comfortable.

Sliding my feet into my favorite pair of slippers, pink bunnies so ratty they've lost most of their fuzz, I notice that one of the ears on the left one is flopping forward like it's about to fall off. And that's exactly what it does as I reach down to adjust it. I shrug and toss it in the wastebasket next to my desk. With any luck, I'll get a new pair for my birthday. I've been hinting big-time to Becca, because I know that they're cheap and won't break the bank. With her father out of work, she doesn't need to be buying me expensive presents.

Grabbing my laptop off my desk, I settle cross-legged on my bed, throwing the quilt Summer Williams gave me a few years ago over my shoulders. As I tug it around me, one of the corners flaps over revealing an embroidered message. I smile when I see it, even though I've long since memorized the words: *To Megan from her pen pal Summer. Friendship is where the best stories begin.*

She's right about that, I think, flipping open my laptop to check my e-mail and see if there's a new chapter in the Simon Berkeley story.

There is! He sent me an e-card! I click on the link, and it opens to a wintry scene, with snowflakes falling on evergreens and little kids skating on a pond. I smile. Simon has been looking at the Weather Channel again. He likes to do that, so he can see what's happening here in Concord. The snowflakes and skaters onscreen swirl around for a bit while a little tune tinkles in the background, then the snowflakes arrange themselves into the words *Keep warm! Happy almost birthday! XOXO Simon.*

I can't help laughing. It's really cute, and so is he for sending it.

I hop online to check out the weather in Bath, where he and his family live, so I can send him a card back. Not surprisingly, the forecast is for rain. That's what happens in England this time of year. I find a funny card for him with frogs carrying lily pad umbrellas, and add a message: *Keep dry! Miss you! XOXO Megan.*

The garage door rumbles as I press send. My mother must be home. Sure enough, a few moments later the intercom on my wall crackles. Our house is on the large side—Emma calls it sprawling—and my father had this system installed so we didn't have to holler at each other. "Megan!" he says. "Your mother's home. Can you come here for a minute?" He sounds excited.

My pulse quickens as I scuff back down the hall to the living room. Maybe this is it. A car of my own would be so cool!

My mother is hanging up her coat in the hall closet. "Where's Gigi?" she asks my dad. "I thought you were going to wait and bring her home."

"Calliope Chadwick offered to give her a ride," he replies.

My mother spots me and breaks into the same goofy grin my father was wearing on the drive home. "Hi sweetie!" she says.

"Hi," I reply cautiously.

She crosses into the living room, where my father is sitting on the sofa reading the newspaper. Or at least he's holding it. Mostly he's smiling at me. What is up with the two of them?

My mother leans down and gives him a kiss, then straightens, frowning. "Has anyone seen my cell phone?" she asks, patting the pockets of her pants. She starts looking behind the sofa cushions. "I know I had it earlier today."

"You probably left it in your coat," my father tells her. "Megan, why don't you go check for her."

"Sure." I scuff over to the hall closet. My mother's winter coat is on a hanger next to my jacket, and I go right to the inside zip pocket where she usually stashes her phone. "Not here!"

"Are you sure?" she calls back. "Did you check all the pockets?"

The keys! I think. *She probably hid the keys to my birthday present in one of the pockets!* I rifle through the rest of them. Nothing. As I slip my hand into the last one, my fingertips touch something soft. Something soft that's *moving.* I snatch my hand back, startled.

The pocket squeaks. Holding it open gingerly, I peer in.

My heart stops.

I gasp in disbelief.

The pocket is full of white fur. White fur that's attached to a *kitten!* Reaching in again gently, I draw out a mewing ball of fluff.

"Omigosh—you little angel!" I whisper, holding it— him? her?—up to my cheek. It's the softest thing I've ever felt. As I kiss its little nose, I spot something out of the corner of my eye, and look over to see the lens of a video camera peeking around the edge of the closet door. My father is behind it, of course. He's not even trying to hide his broad smile now.

"Surprise!" he and my mother shout.

"Is it really mine?" I exclaim, still stunned. "To keep?"

"It's a she, actually, and yes, she is," my mother replies.

"Happy early birthday, sweetheart," adds my father.

"H-how . . . w-when—" I stammer. I've been asking for a pet—or for a sister or brother—for, well, forever. The answer has always been no. My mother's all into zero population growth, plus both of my parents are neat freaks, especially my dad, and they've always said they don't do pets.

"It's all your grandmother's doing," my mother replies with a rueful sigh. "She and Shannon Delaney have been twisting our arms ever since the party at Half Moon Farm."

The Hawthornes lost their cat Melville last fall, and Jess's family gave them a kitten on New Year's Eve.

My kitten is definitely cuter, though. It yawns and pats at my face with a tiny paw, and I bury my nose in her soft fur again. "This is the best present ever!" I mean it, too. A kitten is way better than a car.

"There's more!" says my father. "Come and see."

"More kittens?" I reply, gaping at him.

He grins. "No, silly. More kitten *stuff.*" He herds me down the hall toward my room, then opens the door to the guest room across from it. "Ta-da!"

It looks like Pet Zone made a house call. There's not one but two baskets with pillows in them for snoozing, a pole covered in carpet and what look like branches sticking out of it—some sort of a combination climbing tree/scratching post, I'm guessing—a feeding station, and another basket full of toys.

"And her box will go in your bathroom," my mother says, grabbing something that looks like a big plastic suitcase by the handle and carrying it back across the hall to my bedroom. "I found ecologically friendly cat litter for it."

Of course she did. That's my mother in a nutshell—saving the world, one litter box at a time.

We stand there, my parents both talking at once as they try to film me, pat the kitten, gauge my reaction, and tell me how they managed to keep it a secret from me all at the same time. They're both so excited that you'd think they were the ones getting a kitten, not me.

"What made you change your mind?" I ask, perching on the edge of my bed and cradling the kitten against my shoulder. I hear the rumbling of a tiny purr as she burrows into my neck, then starts kneading the collar of my sweatshirt.

"I think it was when Shannon sent us the e-mail with her picture, wasn't it, Jerry?" my mother replies, glancing at my father. "She was the last one left in the litter."

He nods. "Shannon said she figured a white kitten couldn't do all that much damage to an all-white house."

I had to smile at this. Trust my parents to pick a cat to match our decor. Our house is really modern, and from the carpets to the furniture almost everything in it is white.

The three of us sit there playing with my new pet until she tires out and curls in a little ball in my lap and goes to sleep. She's so totally adorable I can hardly stand it. I feel like I'm going to burst with happiness. This is shaping up to be the best birthday weekend ever.

My dad is still clutching the camera, of course. I think my entire life is preserved somewhere on DVDs.

"What are you going to call her?" asks my mother.

"How about Snowball?" suggests my father.

I shake my head. "Too boring. I'm thinking Coco, after Coco Chanel."

"Cute," says my father.

"Perfect!" says my mother. "Your grandmother will love it."

Coco Chanel is Gigi's favorite fashion designer. I figure it's a fitting tribute, since my grandmother is the one who talked my parents into getting me a pet.

My mother reaches out a forefinger and strokes the kitten's ears. "Do you remember when Cassidy's little sister Chloe was born, and your grandmother tried to get Clementine and Stanley to name her Coco?"

I nod, grinning. "That's what gave me the idea."

A few minutes later my mother stands up reluctantly. "Well, I guess I'd better get dinner started. Why don't you put Coco in her basket, and come keep me company?"

"Do you think she'll be okay by herself?" my father asks anxiously. "Maybe I should install a video monitor so we can keep an eye on her."

My mother winks at me. "She'll be fine," she says. "Leave your door open, Megan. Cats are smart—if she needs us, she'll come find us."

As the three of us head back down the hall, my father pulls out his cell phone and taps away at the screen, making notes for himself. "We'll need another basket in the kitchen," he mutters. "And I think we could probably use one in the living room, too. And another one of those climbing things."

My mother and I smile at each other. Whenever my father decides to do something, he always does it in a big way.

Just as we reach the living room, I hear the scrape of a key in the lock and the front door flies open.

"*Bon soir!*" trills my grandmother. She trots in, towing a petite dark-haired girl I'm sure I've never seen before, but who still looks vaguely familiar. On the doorstep behind them is a huge pile of luggage.

"Uh, hello," says my mother cautiously.

"This is Sophie," announces my grandmother. "She just arrived from France and she's going to live with us!"

My father blinks. My mother looks from Gigi to the French girl and back again. Then she reaches for my grandmother's arm. "Mother, may I speak to you in the kitchen for a moment?"

The two of them disappear, leaving my father and me standing in the middle of the living room with . . . Sophie? Was that her name?

She regards us unsmilingly. I can't tell if she's unhappy to be here specifically, or just unhappy generally. She doesn't say a word, just looks around the room with her eyebrows raised. Her gaze lingers on our white baby grand piano, and I can tell she's impressed. Then she looks at me, and suddenly I can see that she's not impressed anymore. My hand creeps up to my hair, which I'm deeply regretting scraping back in a ponytail, and I'm very conscious of the fact that my ancient sweats are not just ancient, but also now covered in white cat hair.

Sophie, on the other hand, looks like she's breezed in from a photo shoot. Her curly hair is perfectly tousled, and her outfit is stunning. Simple, understated, but stunning. She's wearing jeans, knee-high black leather boots, a white turtleneck sweater, and a black peacoat, topped with a white cashmere scarf knotted artfully around her neck. Everything about her screams *I am French! I am très chic!*

Which I am most definitely not.

The discussion in the kitchen is getting heated. My mother doesn't like surprises, and she doesn't do houseguests. Add the two things together and it's a surefire recipe for disaster.

"I couldn't just leave her standing there like an orphan!" I hear Gigi protest.

"You could have at least called first!" My mother sounds furious. She's got a point, actually. My grandmother is kind of impulsive sometimes. "This is not your decision to make!"

Sparks are practically flying out from under the kitchen door, and my father gives it a nervous glance. "So Sophie," he asks. "Do you speak English?"

The French girl shrugs. *"Mais bien sur,* but of course."

"Right," he says, and vanishes into the kitchen just as I hear Gigi protest, "She was supposed to stay with Peter and Polly Perkins, but after what happened today, they had to drop out of the exchange program!"

A moment later, the voices subside. Sophie's lips curl up in a hint of a smile. Not a particularly friendly smile, though. A minute ticks awkwardly by. She examines her fingernails. Then the kitchen door opens and my mother and father and Gigi appear. "It's settled then," says my grandmother. "You'll stay with us."

"*Merci*," says Sophie politely.

"I'm sure you're tired after your long trip," my mother says, a little stiffly. "Megan will show you to the guest room. It's Sophie, right?"

The French girl nods. "*Oui*. Sophie Fairfax."

We all stare at her. My heart sinks as I suddenly realize where the resemblance comes from.

"No relation to Annabelle Fairfax, are you?" my mother asks.

Sophie nods. "*Elle est ma cousine.*"

Stinkerbelle has a *cousin*? I stare at Sophie, stunned. No way. Absolutely no way.

There's a small mewing noise behind me, and I look around to see my new kitten hesitating in the living room doorway. I kneel down and stretch out my hand toward her, waggling my fingers. Beside me, Sophie Fairfax does the same.

Coco hesitates for a moment, her tiny tail twitching. Then e scampers straight to the French girl.

 take it all back. This is shaping up to be the worst birth- kend ever.